TO THE RESCUE

The men moved, carrying out their lord's final command by dragging Alison with them.

"No," she gasped. "No," as she tried to fight them, and raised her head to stare at Ralph, in the doorway, a huge blood and smoke and earthstained figure; he had discarded his sword and carried only his revolver. "Ralph!" she cried out with delirious relief.

"Stand aside," Ralph shouted at the samurai.

They hissed, and one released her to draw his sword; neither had ever seen the revolver fired in anger. Ralph dropped the first man with a single bullet through the heart, and then did the same to his companion before the samurai could even release Alison's arm. She stood between them, her ears ringing. Ralph grasped her hand. "Come on," he bawled. "Let's get out of here."

As they tumbled down the stairs, tripping and falling, breathlessly running for the drawbridge, they suddenly came face to face with a solid barrier of gleaming bayonets. . . .

THE
SUN RISES

Great Reading from SIGNET

*Prices slightly higher in Canada

THE
SUN RISES

COLIN MAXWELL

A SIGNET BOOK

NEW AMERICAN LIBRARY

PUBLISHER'S NOTE

This novel is a work of fiction. Names, characters, places, and incidents are either the product of the author's imagination or, if real, used fictitiously.

NAL BOOKS ARE AVAILABLE AT QUANTITY DISCOUNTS WHEN USED TO PROMOTE PRODUCTS OR SERVICES. FOR INFORMATION PLEASE WRITE TO PREMIUM MARKETING DIVISION, NEW AMERICAN LIBRARY, 1633 BROADWAY, NEW YORK, NEW YORK 10019.

SIGNET TRADEMARK REG. U.S. PAT. OFF. AND FOREIGN COUNTRIES
REGISTERED TRADEMARK—MARCA REGISTRADA
HECHO EN CHICAGO, U.S.A.

SIGNET, SIGNET CLASSIC, MENTOR, PLUME, MERIDIAN and NAL BOOKS are published by New American Library, 1633 Broadway, New York, New York 10019

First Printing, May, 1984

1 2 3 4 5 6 7 8 9

PRINTED IN THE UNITED STATES OF AMERICA

CONTENTS

I
THE RENEGADE

—1—

THE FUGITIVE

With a tramping of feet, boots stirring dust into the still air, the company of infantry marched through the center of Golden Gate Park in San Francisco. They wore dark blue jackets and kepis, pale blue trousers, black crossbelts and shoes, and carried long rifles, at the slope, with fixed bayonets. They looked tough and eager, ready to undertake any campaign that might be required of them. On this glorious spring day in 1860, the United States was officially at peace with all the world, but between San Francisco and the eastern seaboard there were sufficient hostile Indians to keep the small regular army in good fighting trim.

As the onlookers well knew. They applauded vigorously as the infantry swung into line and came to a halt in immediate obedience to the commands of their officers, to make room for the squadron of cavalry which trotted behind them. These also wore dark blue jackets above pale blue breeches, but the jackets were tailored to the waist, and the trousers were adorned with a thick yellow stripe, and they carried swords and lances as well as carbines, rode beneath guidons fluttering in the breeze, horses high stepping but maintaining perfect order.

Another ripple of applause, and more so from the group of spectators for whom this military display had been arranged, and who, indeed, were attracting quite as much attention as the soldiers themselves. These special guests occupied a recently constructed dais, sheltering beneath a tarpaulin roof, and were being hosted by several government officials, as well as members of the mayor's staff, all black stovepipe hats and matching suits, incredibly sober-looking gentlemen. The guests of honor, by contrast, wore no suits at all, but the brightest of what, to the rough crowd of ex-miners and shore-leave sailors and ambitious entrepreneurs who had come west to take advantage of San Francisco's phenomenal growth, appeared to be silk undressing robes. The men themselves were small, hardly more than half the size of the big Americans around them, and yellow-skinned, with beardless faces and shaved heads, save for a remarkable topknot growing out of the center of the scalp, and clearly never cut at all, for around it the long strand of hair was tightly wound. The people of San Francisco were becoming quite used to the sight of Chinese coolies, who found their way across the Pacific on American whalers and trading vessels, but these fellows, with their serious mien and absurd hairstyles, not to mention their even more absurd clothing, seemed like refugees from a circus, and had in fact caused some laughter when they had first appeared—but the laughter had soon died as it was observed that each of the strangers carried not one, but two swords thrust through his girdle, and that if the smaller weapon was hardly more than a large dagger, the other was an enormous two-handed broadsword capable of taking off a man's head, no one could doubt, with a single well-aimed swing.

So the crowd watched them with as much interest as *they* watched the military display, which now reached its climax in the entry of the artillery. The American spectators knew what to expect; they had seen Freeman's battery at practice often enough. The strange little men from beyond the seas were not so privileged, and exclaimed in high-pitched alarm as the six cannon galloped across the park, straight at the pavilion, horses straining, gun carriages bouncing, outriders keeping perfect position, the whole obviously under the total control of the young officer who led them, and who now wheeled his horse and brought it to a halt immediately in front of the grandstand. The battery swung into line behind him, and almost before the wheels had stopped rolling, the gunners were down, the cannon were unlimbered and the horses led away, the cartridges were being packed into the muzzles and rammed hard home, the matches had been lit, and the six guns exploded as one, an immense rumble of sound which cascaded across the huge bay and sent sea birds winging skyward from the deserted rock of Alcatraz Island, while the gunners stood rigidly to attention, ignoring the white powder smoke which for the moment enveloped them.

The spectators cheered and clapped their hands. The yellow men had risen together, partly in alarm, at the approach of the artillery and then the enormous sound, but now were starting to smile a trifle uncertainly as they were reassured by their hosts that the shots had all been blank cartridges. While the officer commanding the battery gave another brisk command, the gun carriages were rehitched to their horses, and the entire body trotted off to take its place in the parade between the infantry and the cavalry.

The yellow men left the dais, accompanied by their hosts, and walked along the line of soldiers, staring and pointing, chattering among themselves in the strangest of tongues, those who could speak English turning to their guides for enlightenment on points of detail. That they had been impressed, no one could doubt. The American crowd slowly broke up and began to drift away, also vigorously discussing the afternoon's events.

"Ralph! At ease, man, and get down. These gentlemen wish to shake your hand." The speaker was one of the official American group, a somewhat short and slight man who wore the fashionable goatee beard but who also possessed a pair of burning eyes, indicative of someone to whom all life was a challenge, perpetually to be overcome. As he had overcome most of the challenges presented to him during his forty-seven years of unrelenting energy. His name was John Charles Frémont, and as a young army officer he had spent much of his time exploring the West, earning for himself in the process the nickname of "the Pathfinder"; he was in fact one of the very first Americans ever to have entered California.

Certainly he had been the first to realize that this was the most beautiful, and the most healthy, part of all North America, quite apart from the mineral wealth which had lured so many of his countrymen to the Pacific shores, and with his always ambitious determination he had immediately set about securing it for the Union. As leader in the war against Mexico which had accomplished that aim, he had soon been appointed governor of the new state, only to quarrel with his superiors over questions of jurisdiction and come to a court-martial in Washington. That had led to his resignation from the United States Army, but also to a closer connection not only with California but also with all those who opposed the Washington bureaucrats, and he was now best known as the defeated Republican candidate for the presidency, in the last election, four years ago.

Frémont was a man who inevitably inspired either total devotion or total dislike. But there could be no doubt about the feelings of Captain Ralph Freeman as he dismounted, stepped forward, and again came to attention. Even had his battery not just given a superb display, Ralph Freeman would have been easily the choice of everyone present as the epitome of what a soldier should look like. He was tall and well built without carrying an ounce of surplus flesh, dark-haired and possessing regular if slightly battered features. His blue eyes indicated a glint of perhaps cynical amusement as he gazed at the world—a useful asset for a man who, as a soldier, would have to carry out many a command of which he might personally disapprove. This afternoon his face was unusually serious, even sad, and he seemed to wear his splendid uniform—black hat, dark blue frock coat with gold epaulets and red sash, pale blue breeches with thin red stripe, highly polished black boots—with an almost defiant air, his left hand resting against the hilt of his saber in a caressing gesture. But there was nothing but admiration in his eyes as he gazed at the Pathfinder.

An admiration which was obviously reciprocated. "Here he is, Mr. Ito," Frémont said. "If I may say so, sir, down to this afternoon he was the finest young officer in this man's army. Captain Ralph Freeman, Mr. Ito Shunsuke and Mr. Inouye Bunta."

Ralph reached for the yellow men's hands, was checked

in surprise as they first of all gave him a quick bow, heads bobbing down almost as far as their waists, before straightening again. Then they shook hands in Western fashion.

"Your guns," Ito Shunsuke said. "They are the best we have seen. And the way they were handled, even better."

He spoke English remarkably well, if a trifle carefully.

"Your skill is sublime, Captain," added Inouye Bunta.

"Well, sir, Mr. Bunta," Ralph said, "it just takes practice." He glanced at Frémont, who was smiling broadly.

"The name is Inouye, Ralph. Mr. Inouye. These gentlemen are from Japan, as you know, and they give their names differently from ours. The family name comes first. Is that right, Mr. Inouye?"

The Japanese gave a quick affirmative bow.

"I apologize," Ralph said.

"How were you to know?" asked Ito. "Besides, one soldier need never apologize to another."

Once again Ralph glanced at Frémont. It was difficult to suppose these two men *were* soldiers.

"Oh, indeed they are, Ralph," Frémont said, understanding the unspoken question. "They are here especially to oversee our military strength, our military techniques." He closed one eye. Because of course everyone knew that although the government of Japan, the shogunate, as it was quaintly called, had signed a treaty of peace and friendship with the United States only a few years earlier, that had been entirely because an American fleet, commanded by Commodore Matthew Perry, had forced an entry into Japanese harbors seeking redress for the ill treatment of shipwrecked American sailors. So Washington had decreed that all Japanese missions, of which there had been several over the past couple of years—after two centuries of complete isolation from the world, the Japanese were eager for knowledge of that world—should be left in no doubt just *how* strong was this country with whom the famous samurai had assumed so uneasy a friendship. "No doubt they have artillery in Japan to match yours, eh?"

"Alas, no," Ito said. "We have . . ." He checked himself as Inouye frowned at him and gave a quick shake of the head. "Our methods of soldiering are a trifle different from yours. But we look forward to inspecting your guns more closely, perhaps tomorrow, Captain."

"I'm sure that can be arranged," Ralph said. "But . . ." Another glance at Frémont.

"It'll have to be with a different officer," Frémont said, still smiling. "Captain Freeman won't be here."

"You are leaving San Francisco?" Inouye asked.

"Not exactly. I'm—"

"The captain is leaving the army," Frémont explained. "He has resigned his commission. As of midnight tonight, he's a *free man*. Eh, Ralph?" He clapped his friend on the shoulder.

The two Japanese looked genuinely concerned. "Leaving the army?" Ito asked. "But this is a great misfortune. My dear Captain Freeman, if we can be of any assistance . . ."

Frémont gave a shout of laughter. "He does not require any assistance, I assure you, Mr. Ito."

"But to be forced to abandon one's army," Inouye said. "You have quarreled with your lord, Captain Freeman? Fear not. A soldier such as you can never become merely a ronin. Now, sir—"

"A ronin?" Ralph asked in mystification.

"A lordless man, sir. A wanderer. A renegade, if you like. But you, sir, never! Why, Captain, you have but to say, and we will offer you a command with my lord of Cho-Shu, the great Nariaka."

Ralph looked at Frémont, still mystified.

"I suspect Cho-Shu is the name of their hometown," Frémont said. "And this Nariaka must be the mayor of it. So you would offer Captain Freeman a command, eh? Well, gentlemen, I will tell you this: you would not find a finer officer anywhere in the world. I met this man, gentlemen, as a lad of seventeen, when he came with me to find a new stage route across the Rockies. That was an expedition, eh, Ralph?" He gave his friend another clap on the shoulder. "He was an orphan boy, gentlemen, with just his two fists and his skill with a gun . . . any kind of gun, you name it, cannon or rifle or pistol, and Ralph will hit your target. That was his sole inheritance, gentlemen, but I found him such a *man* that I personally saw him to the West Point Military Academy."

"Which has turned out to be a colossal waste of time and money," Ralph muttered.

"Well, I wouldn't altogether say that," Frémont countered.

"But still," Ito said, "to leave the army, when in possession of such skill and ability . . ."

"I'm told soldiering is the only profession considered worthwhile in Japan," Frémont explained to Ralph. "Over here it's different," he told the Japanese in turn. "Soldiering . . . why, it ain't very well regarded at all. Business, there's the thing."

"Business?" Ito frowned. "You mean . . . being a merchant?"

"That's right. You must have merchants in Japan."

"Of course. Merchants are a necessary part of every community. But in our land they are lower than the hewers of wood and the drawers of water."

"Is that a fact? Is there no profit to be made from business in Japan?"

"Profit, certainly," Inouye agreed. "But what is profit? Merely a matter of money. It has nothing to do with honor."

"Ah," Frémont said, and smiled at Ralph. "Interesting, eh? The fact is, my friends, soldiers are the ones who don't have too much honor in this country. Captain Freeman is leaving the army to go into the shipping business with his future father-in-law. He's going to be a big man in these parts over the next thirty years, you mark my words. A far bigger man than he could ever be as a soldier, even if he made general." For a brief moment the humor died from Frémont's face, to be replaced by a look of bitterness. Then he smiled again. "You'll not tempt him to Japan. He's also going to marry the most beautiful girl in all California."

"The most beautiful woman in all the world is no good reason to abandon one's honor," Inouye commented.

"Now, hold on just one moment," Ralph said, his own good humor starting to fade.

"Easy, boy," Frémont said. "These characters are our guests. And I don't reckon they mean anything rude."

"If we have offended, we are sorry," Ito said. "There are different cultures being discussed here. Captain Freeman, Mr. Frémont, we should be very pleased to continue our conversation at our hotel this evening. Now, in fact," he added, for the sun was fast disappearing into the Pacific Ocean at their backs.

"Well, Mr. Ito, that's right civil of you," Frémont said. "But I'm afraid I have to attend an official function for the bigwigs in your party. Why don't you go along, Ralph? Hell, it's your last night of freedom before the Quentins nail you." Unconsciously—or perhaps all too consciously, Ralph thought—he was contradicting his earlier statement.

He hesitated. But in fact both the Japanese and his friend had touched upon a very sore nerve. The army was the only career he had ever sought, his sole ambition since he could remember. And now . . . Of course Rosalee was right. Rosalee was always right, and in this case her rightness was inarguable. With only Indians to fight, promotion was a matter of a dead men's shoes, no matter how proficient he might be at the military art. It was going to be a long haul up the ladder of command, longer for him than for most because he was widely known as John Frémont's protégé, and that was not a name the powers in Washington really liked to hear too often. Whereas, as James Quentin's vice-president . . . The Quentin shipping line was the biggest sailing out of San Francisco. There was wealth, and prestige . . . and he had always loved ships and the sea, had sailed his own catboat out of Providence, Rhode Island, where he had been born, often enough before his father had decided upon that tragically ill-fated immigration to the Far West.

And there was also Rosalee. As Frémont had said, the most beautiful girl in all California—and none the worse, really, for knowing that fact, just as she could never forget that she was James Quentin's daughter. As such, she had declared that she would *never* be an army wife, doomed to trailing behind her husband from one outpost to another. But, she had said, "I *will* marry you, dear Ralph, if you'll be sensible and come to work with Father."

How could a man not be sensible when such a prize lay within his grasp? But how could a man ever truly reconcile sense with honor, as the Japanese had so brutally suggested?

It *was* to be his last night in the army, and Rosalee had readily accepted that he would not be calling this evening. But to get drunk with his fellow officers promised nothing half so interesting as to get drunk with these strange fellows.

"Why," he said, "I think that's a very kind invitation, Mr. Ito. I'll be along just as soon as I've dismissed my troop."

"A great performance, Captain Freeman. Oh, aye, a great performance." Jonathan Gray spoke with a pronounced Scottish accent, however many years it might be since he had last seen the Firth of Forth. But Ralph, hurrying from his quarters at hearing the Grays were calling, shook his hand with much pleasure. He had, naturally, been drawn more and more into the shipping community during the last six months, ever since his engagement to Rosalee Quentin had been announced and his plans for the future made public by his prospective father-in-law. An amateur seaman himself, Ralph had learned enough about the incalculable forces which make up the sea and the wind to respect any man who took his living from those vast waters—but he had also soon realized that the majority of skippers out of San Francisco were the dregs of humanity, bitter and brutal men who drove their crews to the last limits of their endurance in their determination to turn a profit. Which made the exceptions the more pleasant. Jonathan Gray was one such exception. Actually, the Scot did not trade out of San Francisco at all. His home was in Hong Kong, the recently acquired British colony on the other side of the ocean, where he had settled some ten years before. Thus he flew the Red Ensign rather than the Stars and Stripes. But he traded with the West Coast on a regular basis, and obtained much of his business through James Quentin. He was a man Ralph looked forward to seeing much of in the years to come.

As he also looked forward to seeing much of his daughter? For the girl, as ever, was at his side, smiling in her grave fashion as she too squeezed Ralph's hand, her hero worship evident in her flushed cheeks.

Now, there, he thought with a touch of conscience, was a strange consideration for a man soon to be married to Rosalee Quentin. Alison Gray was as different from that voluptuous beauty as could possibly be imagined, and far more than could be explained by the disparity in their ages. She was no less tall, even at sixteen years old, and possessed the promise of real beauty in the straight nose and wide mouth and pointed chin. But she was as slender as a rake, and whereas Rosalee was seldom seen without a smile or a toss of the head, Alison was utterly serious in demeanor. Her real beauty lay in the splendor of her tumbling auburn hair, which escaped her poke bonnet on either side, making nonsense of the restraining bows, and the depths of her gray eyes. And in the suggestion of calm maturity, for apparently, since her mother's death five years previously, she had never left her father's side, sailed with him to and fro across the Pacific and also up and down the China coast, seas as notorious for their sudden typhoons, which would rip the stoutest ship apart, as for their pirates, who would do the same for the stoutest man—or the loveliest woman. To Alison Gray this was a way of life, and her experienced courage could not help but attract.

Now she gave one of her shy smiles. "To *command* with such confidence, Captain Freeman, must give a wonderful satisfaction."

"A false one, Miss Gray," he said. "From tomorrow I'll command a desk. You'll come to the house for tea in the morning, Captain?"

Gray shook his head. "We're away on the tide, Captain Freeman. I've a full cargo at last. Thanks to the Quentins." He smiled and shook hands again. "But we'll be back in the autumn. Until then . . ."

"I'll look forward to that," Ralph said, and again pressed Alison's hands. "Take care."

As if it mattered. By the fall he would be married. To the most beautiful girl in California.

And tonight he was going to get drunk.

"The Japanese gentlemen?" inquired the proprietor of the Golden View somewhat skeptically. He pulled his mustache. "They've taken the entire second floor. But you want to be careful with those people, Captain Freeman."

"Careful?" Ralph frowned at him.

"Well, sir, it's like this. They're a queer lot, and that's saying something. They come to live in my hotel, but they won't eat my food or drink my wine. They won't sleep in my beds, and they won't be served by my people. Now, what do you think of that? And touchy . . . by God, you have only to look at them too hard and their hands are dropping to those great meat choppers they carry about all the time." He watched Ralph's hand instinctively touch the hilt of his own sword—he had refused to change out of uniform, as he was entitled to wear it, for the last time, until midnight—and gave a sour smile. "And I doubt that pig-sticker would serve against one of them, either."

Ralph found the fellow offensive. He did not like him, anyway. The Golden View was a bayside hotel— presumably the Japanese were not aware that anyone with pretensions lived, or lodged, up the hill—and was widely known as a den from which seamen were shanghaied, kidnapped when full of liquor, to man the hard-sailing vessels which traded out of San Francisco. A place, and a man, with whom he would have to deal soon enough when it would be his responsibility to find the crews for James Quentin's ships. He did not want to be reminded of that fact tonight.

"Then I shall just have to be polite, won't I, Mackenzie?" he remarked, and climbed the stairs, to check in surprise as the door was opened for him by what was obviously a manservant, for although he wore a robe very similar to those of Inouye and Ito that afternoon, his was of coarse cloth rather than silk, and much less brightly decorated, while his head was not shaved and he was unarmed. He also bowed nearly to the floor at the sight of his visitor, and ushered him in, although he did not speak.

Ralph entered the room, and paused again in amazement, for as Mackenzie had said—although Ralph had not taken him at all seriously—the room had been emptied of furniture and even rugs, the bare boards having been covered with mats, all of a uniform size, some six feet long, he estimated, and three feet wide, which, however, laid edge to edge and end to end, and never overlapping, did not quite succeed in covering all the floor—there was an exposed area in the far corner.

"You Americans do not make your rooms symmetrical, you see, Captain." Ito Shunsuke smiled at him from the inner doorway. "In Japan, all rooms are made an exact number of tatami mats."

Again a cause for astonishment; the Japanese wore white socks but no shoes, and he also carried no weapons this evening. Ralph glanced at the servant, who was hovering expectantly.

"Keiko waits for your boots, Captain," Ito said.

"My boots?"

"It is not our custom to wear shoes inside the house. These tatami mats, you see, are not only our floor covering but also our mattresses. Would you be so kind, Captain?"

Ralph hesitated, reflected that his socks had been clean that morning and that it would be discourteous not to agree. Besides, he was intrigued; these fellows were most confoundedly odd. "I shall willingly give up my boots, Mr. Ito," he said, "if you'd show me somewhere to sit."

Ito clapped his hands, and two more male servants appeared, hurrying from the inner chamber of the suite. One immediately dropped to his hands and knees. "Sit on his back, Captain," Ito invited. "He will bear your weight."

Ralph scratched his head; he wondered what one of Mackenzie's bartenders would say were he to suggest *him* acting as a stool. But he sat, and the other two men whipped off his boots. "Well," he said, unbuckling his sword belt and holster, "you'd better have these as well."

The man to whom he offered the weapons gave him a terrified look and shrank away.

"It won't hurt you," Ralph said. "Tell him, Mr. Ito, for heaven's sake; compared with that weapon of yours, mine is a toothpick."

"In Japan, Captain Freeman, a man never gives up his sword, unless he is acknowledging defeat, and no *man* ever does that."

Ralph stood up, the sword still in his hand, feeling distinctly foolish.

"As for that other," Ito said. "That is also a weapon, is it not?"

"A far more deadly weapon than a sword," Ralph said. "This is a Colt .45 revolver."

"Indeed?" Ito asked politely, but clearly unconvinced. "I should like to inspect it at some time, Captain. Not now, please. You must come in and be comfortable."

He stood away from the door, and Ralph, after a brief hesitation, stepped past him, still carrying his sword belt and holster, and entered another almost empty room, save for the tatami mats, as Ito described them, and also for three cushions arranged around a low table. Sitting on one of the cushions on the floor was Inouye Bunta, who now stood up to greet his guest.

"Captain Freeman, this is a great honor you do us."

"It is my pleasure, Mr. Inouye," Ralph assured him, at the same time taking in the rest of the room. Beside Inouye, and also beside one of the two vacant cushions, the great swords had been laid on the tatami mats, their smaller brethren beside them; as Ito had told him, a man kept his weapons at his side at all times. On the table itself were three small china bottles, bowl-shaped but with narrow necks, not more than six inches tall, and each sitting in a larger bowl filled with hot water which still steamed; beside each bowl there was a small china cup. His heart sank; he had come here tonight to drown his regrets at leaving the service, not to drink tea. Equally was he disappointed to discover that he was obviously the only guest—he had looked forward to a truly convivial evening.

But his spirits immediately recovered as he looked to the far corner, where there was a little wood-burning stove under the window, from whence arose the most delightful scent. Far more important, it was being tended by three young Japanese women, each dressed in a brightly colored robe like the men, each with her hair piled on top of her head, not rising from a shaved scalp like the men, but rather an abundance of thick blackness. Each of the women, in the delicacy of her hands and feet—the latter, like the men's, encased in white socks—and especially of her facial features, small and compact and intense, was quite the most exquisite creature he had ever seen.

Once again, absurd thoughts for a man betrothed to San Francisco's greatest beauty. But "exquisite" was never a word that could be applied to Rosalee Quentin. Rosalee was nearly as tall as himself, with long legs and a thrusting bosom to go with her boldly sculptured features and her mass of curling golden hair. Rosalee was the sort of woman a man dreamed of, and then lay awake at night thinking about. He supposed he was just taken by the contrast, as he had been taken by the contrast of Alison Gray. Additionally, he had never seen Rosalee wearing an undressing robe, although he looked forward to achieving that desire after their marriage, but he knew he would *never* see Rosalee kneeling beside a cooking pot, if he lived to be a hundred.

The three girls were no less interested in him, gave him quick, surreptitious glances before turning back to their work with little giggles and whispered comments. No doubt they found him quite as remarkable as he found them.

"Please to sit down," Ito invited, lowering himself to the cushion next to his sword, cross-legged. Ralph managed to accomplish this without overbalancing, but he hit the floor rather heavily. Instantly the girls hurried forward, each to take one of the little bottles from its bowl and fill the three cups. Ito raised his. "Your health, Captain Freeman."

Ralph reflected that he had never had his health drunk in tea before, but he was growing more intrigued by the moment. He sipped the hot, clear liquid, and received a most pleasant surprise. It was not tea, but rather a faintly sweet drink with a very delicate flavor, which he knew instinctively was distinctly alcoholic as it traced its way down his throat.

"You have not had sake before?" Inouye asked.

"Sake?"

"Rice wine, Captain Freeman."

"No, sir, I have not." Ralph drank some more, discovered the cup was empty, instinctively reached for the pot, but was beaten for speed by the girl, who he realized had remained kneeling at his elbow, and now refilled the cup for him. When he looked at her, she gave a quick smile.

"But you like it," Ito commented. "This is good. We find that few people in America understand our customs, or appreciate our food and wine."

"Well, sir," Ralph explained, "your ways are most certainly different from ours. These robes you wear . . ."

"The kimono, Captain. Surely a garment like this, which allows freedom to all the parts of the body, has to be more comfortable than your tight breeches and jackets?"

"But it is the same for both sexes," Ralph pointed out, giving the girl an apologetic glance, although clearly she did not speak English. "In America we like to tell the difference."

"And you cannot do so save by dress?" Inouye asked with a gentle smile.

"Well . . ." Ralph flushed.

"Besides, there *is* a difference between male and female kimono. You see . . ." He gave an order in Japanese, and the girl turned around, still on her knees, to display the back of her gown, on which, from her waist to her shoulder, there was an extra layer of material, a kind of flap, secured at top and bottom but open at the sides. "You see, Aya, being a woman, is equipped for carrying things, from a baby, should she ever have one, to whatever goods may be required of her to transport. Also, she has a smaller sash than a man, because she does not have to wear any swords. So you see, it *is* possible to tell the difference, if one but knows what to look for."

"Yes," Ralph said, feeling that he had made a fool of himself, although the relationship between the sexes in Japan, as exemplified by the utter subservience of these girls, was a subject he would have liked to pursue. "But then, there is also the way you have emptied this suite of furniture. May I ask where you sleep?"

"On the floor."

"The *floor*?"

"The girls will spread mattresses for us when we are ready to retire," Ito explained. "And over there, you see, our pillows wait for us." He indicated two blocks of wood stored in the corner of the room, each hollowed out to receive a man's neck and head. But only two. What, then, of the women? Ralph wondered. "But come, let us eat," Ito said.

Ralph looked at the plate being placed before him, on which there was a whole fish, a sea bream, no doubt caught in the harbor that very afternoon, for it still breathed, its gills opening and closing in a most painful fashion. Ito and Inouye had received a similar dish from their attendants. "That looks superb," Ralph said, and leaned back so that the girl, whose name apparently was Aya, could remove the fish to cook it. But to his consternation, she merely knelt closer to the table, and with a sharp-bladed knife began to carve the still-heaving fish. In a matter of half a dozen expert strokes the fish had been filleted, gasping its last to the final cut, and the layers of meat had been neatly placed upon another plate—even they still seemed to quiver.

Ralph hastily downed another glass of sake, while watching his hosts, who had already commenced to eat, not using knives and forks, but little sticks of carved and exquisitely painted pieces of ivory, which they took from their waist bands. He looked down and saw that Aya was offering him a similar pair.

"You are a stranger to the food stick, Captain," Ito said. "We have been remiss in our duties. But it is very simple. Hold one of the sticks as you would a pen, that is, between thumb and fore and second fingers, and then release the thumb, so that the stick is held only between the fingers. Now, where the thumb joins the hand, place the other stick, and control it with the thumb. There, you see, the two sticks act as thumb and forefinger, and can be used for any purpose you require. Especially eating. Watch Aya."

Ralph saw the girl pick up a piece of fish, as dexterously as if she were using her fingers, and hold it toward his mouth. Without thinking, he accepted it; the still-fresh blood dribbled down his chin, and he had to swallow violently, without chewing, to stop himself from retching. Aya now gave him the sticks; it was the first time they had actually touched each other. He placed them as instructed, trying to forget the taste in his mouth, and found that he could use them, somewhat clumsily, but still with sufficient skill to pick something up—save that he had no desire to eat any more of the raw and to all intents and purposes still-living fish. On the other hand, he had no wish to appear rude or gauche to the Japanese.

"You do not like sashami?" Inouye inquired.

"Why, I am sure it is delicious," Ralph said. "It is just that in America we never sit down to eat without being introduced to our hostesses. Your womenfolk," he added, as Ito was clearly nonplussed.

"Womenfolk?" Ito continued to frown. "Our womenfolk are in Cho-Shu, Captain."

"But . . ." Ralph looked at Aya, who was still kneeling beside him, looking increasingly anxious, as he was not eating.

"Ah." Ito smiled. "These are not our womenfolk, Captain. These are our servants."

"Whom you have brought from Japan?"

"Of course."

"But . . . you will excuse me, Mr. Ito, these girls are clearly young, and certainly of an age to be protected. How can their parents allow them to travel thousands of miles, with just the company of men? Or are those fellows in the other room their brothers and fathers?"

"Those fellows, as you call them, are honin," Ito explained. "As are the girls."

"Honin?"

"The lowest of the low," Inouye told him. "They have no rights, save to work for their betters." He smiled at Ralph. "To serve them in every way, as they may require."

Understanding his implication, Ralph discovered that he had inadvertently taken another piece of fish into his mouth. Hastily he swallowed, and gulped a cup of sake; instantly it was refilled by the attentive Aya. But his mind was occupied by the overall meaning of his host's words. "You mean, she is a slave?" He flushed. "They are all slaves?"

"Of course," Ito agreed. "Warriors must have slaves. You have slaves here in the United States."

"*I* do not," Ralph said, and bit his lip. He could not deny that there *were* slaves in the United States, even if it was an institution of which he personally, and a growing proportion of Americans everywhere, disapproved. But on the other hand, he was about to acquire several; James Quentin certainly had a houseful of Negroes, and Rosalee was used to having them about the place—he could not see her altering her habits after their marriage. But at least, in America, there was a difference in color. . . . He realized that he might be getting himself into very deep water if he pursued the matter, drank some more sake, and sought some means of changing the subject. He picked up Ito's sword, and checked at the sudden tension which became evident. Even the girl Aya, kneeling at his side, seemed to anticipate instant disaster, as he heard her catch her breath, while the male servants, standing in the doorway to the outer room, sprang to attention. Most disturbing of all, Ito and Inouye also appeared to tense their muscles.

He smiled at them, glad to have instigated the surprise for once. "I mean you no harm," he said. "I but wished to inspect the blade."

Ito and Inouye exchanged glances, and then Ito very gently took the sword away from him. "In Japan, Captain Freeman, no man may touch another's sword, unless specifically invited to do so, and even then, never with his bare hands."

"I did not mean to offend," Ralph said. "But truly, you make it sound as if you venerate your weapons as holy things."

"Do you not, Captain?" Inouye asked. "Can there be anything more holy than the guardian of a man's honor, as well as his life, and his family?" Now it was his turn to be embarrassed, as he understood Ralph's bewilderment. "You do not care for raw fish, Captain. Aya, sukiyaki."

Within seconds, thinly sliced meat, freshly cooked at the stove behind him, and served in a stew with bean sprouts and rice balls and bamboo shoots, was placed before him, exquisitely tasty and tender, while the sake flowed, and Ito half drew his blade from its scabbard and showed Ralph the finely wrought designs carved into the steel, and even allowed him to touch the edge, which had the sharpness of a razor, explaining that it came from the forge of the Munamake family, the finest swordsmiths in Japan. Following which the Japanese inspected his own cavalry saber, which had about half the deadliness, he supposed, and then the revolver, but clearly without any understanding of how such an intricate piece of machinery worked, or what execution it could perform—he had to resist their suggestion that he show them by firing it in the room.

While the sake flowed, the floor started to move up and down, and the faces before his eyes to sway, and the plates were cleared away to make room for thin green tea, which was apparently intended to clean the palate, but did nothing to clean the brain.

"Now let us have the girls," Ito cried. "I could take them all. You understand, Captain, that these are not geisha. They have no talents, no art. But they are comely enough to comfort a man. I chose them for that purpose."

For a moment Ralph was uncertain what was being proposed. Then he glanced to his left and saw that his attendant, Aya, had released her girdle and allowed her kimono to open—and that she wore nothing underneath. He caught a glimpse of an entrancingly girllike body, small, button-nippled breasts, flat belly against which the rib cage pressed with each breath, almost hairless groin, and delightfully slender legs, which ended so incongruously in the little white socks.

A glance to his right assured him that the other girls

had also commenced to strip, and that his new friends were equally releasing their girdles, while the male servants had quietly withdrawn from the doorway.

He stood up, swaying slightly, as the floor would not keep still. Aya gazed at him in alarm.

"You do not like Aya?" Ito asked. "Well, then, take this one."

"I like Aya very much," Ralph said. "But . . ."

"You are aware of being unclean," Inouye said sadly. "We are all aware of that, my friend. But in this country of yours we find it impossible to procure sufficient water for adequate bathing, or even tubs of sufficient size. So we are forced to exist in squalor, as you see us. But the girls will not mind. As we have explained, they are but honin."

"You don't understand," Ralph mumbled, realizing that *he* had no idea at all of what the man was speaking. He gazed at the men in fascination, for they had now exposed their own bodies, and they were certainly in a highly aroused state. As he was himself, hidden away by his army breeches. And he had no doubt that to lie with this girl, quite apart from the pleasure of it, would be one of the most intriguing experiences of his entire life—it was impossible not to suppose that a people who did everything else so differently from any way he was familiar with would also perform the act of love entirely differently.

But he had sworn to himself, on the night of his betrothal to Rosalee, that he would never touch another woman, and he was a man who believed in keeping even his private vows. Besides, the idea of making love in public, while others were doing the same, was a bit too orgiastic for his New England morality—especially when he would obviously be the pupil.

Yet he had to explain himself; everyone was gazing at him now, and Aya had lowered her head almost to the floor in apparent supplication. "I must leave," he said. "The time . . . the hour is late. Believe me, I am most grateful for your hospitality . . . and for your . . . offered hospitality." He patted the girl's glossy black head. "And I would stay with you if I had the time." He picked up sword and holster and hurried for the door.

Ito came behind him. "If we have offended you, Captain . . ."

"Good heavens, no." Ralph tucked his boots under his arm. "It is I who am being rude. I beg you to forgive me." He opened the door into the corridor.

Ito's smile was sad. "And we had been hoping to persuade you, later on, to reconsider your decision, and return with us to Japan. We understand you are soon to be married. Believe me that your wife would equally be most welcome in our country."

Ralph allowed himself a brief mental picture of Rosalee sitting on the floor to eat, or tackling a raw fish. "Again, my thanks," he said. "But that is impossible." He hurried down the corridor, pausing at the top of the stairs to put on his boots and belts, and thankfully stumbled into the fresh air, finding himself mounted and walking his horse away before he was absolutely sure what he was doing, listening to a clock striking midnight in the distance.

He was no longer a soldier. The realization came as quite a shock. He had been thirteen when his father, lured by the thought of California gold, had abandoned his Providence dry-goods store and gone west, taking his wife and daughter and young son with him. Harry Freeman had elected to go cross-country rather than take the much quicker sailing route around Cape Horn—in contrast to his son's youthful hobby, he had no liking for the sea. Thus they had joined a wagon train in Missouri, and struck out across the Great Plains. And there both he and his wife, and his daughter, had died, struck down by Indian arrows. From that moment Ralph had known only the art of the gun, first of all for sheer survival in the violent world in which he had found himself, alone and friendless, but always with the dream of carrying the war back to the redskins, in the blue uniform of a soldier. A dream which, thanks to John Frémont, he had made come true, briefly—and unsatisfactorily—and had now abandoned, again at the behest of Frémont, in a search for material prosperity and for that chimera called happiness.

He swayed in the saddle, allowed the horse to find its own way, watched the moon streaming across the hills

on the other side of the bay. Because a soldier could
never be happy? Not in the American culture, he feared.
An American soldier carried too much of a burden of
guilt, since he was required to glory in everything that
a civilized and Christian man should abhor. It was
clearly different in other cultures. In Japan, most
certainly, so far as he could see. He thought that if he
were asked to pick at random two totally happy human
beings, he would have to name Ito and Inouye. Who
were no doubt at this moment being happier than ever,
and equally, no doubt, continuing their conversation as
they enjoyed the girls. Which one would have taken
Aya? And would it matter to her?

But that was a different culture, he reminded himself,
aware that his horse was making its way up the hill
rather than in the direction of the army post, which
was not surprising, as the animal was a recent present
from James Quentin. But he felt no inclination to turn
him in the correct direction, and his narrow, empty
bed, which for the rest of this night was merely on
loan. He did not in fact wish to go to bed at all this
night, save it be with a woman. He shook his head to
rid himself of the thought; if he were not very careful,
he would find himself back at the Golden View, seeking Aya. And betraying Rosalee. Because really, what
could a child like that possibly have to offer, compared
with Rosalee?

His problem was, he told himself, that he had been
too hasty with his promise, too determined to honor it.
It was not as if Rosalee had herself demanded it of
him. He had, in fact, from time to time had the feeling
that she would have welcomed a more vigorous approach to their betrothal than he had ever attempted.
But the fact was that he still felt somewhat in awe of
her, as he was in awe of the wealth and power with
which her family was surrounded. It really was incredible that an orphan from what the Quentins must consider the wrong side of the tracks should be marrying
into such opulence. Once again, he had John Frémont
to thank. It had been at a reception in Frémont's house
that he had first met Rosalee, and it had been Frémont's
praises of him which had first clearly interested her. And

once Rosalee Quentin became interested in something, or someone, life took on an entirely new dimension.

He had resisted her at first. Partly from sheer fright, he knew, a certainty that he would be wasting his time, that she was seeking only a casual flirtation. But equally because he had from the beginning been able to discern her faults. She suffered from an arrogant awareness of her position as well as her beauty, which was no doubt entirely natural. But she also had a boldness, almost a raffishness, in her speech and her manner, a familiarity which he found disturbing when it was applied to himself, and annoying when he saw her bestowing it upon other men, especially when those other men, including his brother officers, were inclined to hint that she was not above bestowing more than verbal familiarity, from time to time. Yet it had been that very resistance which had obviously attracted her to him—she had never experienced such a thing before—and of course, as he had gotten to know her, especially with Frémont ever at his side reminding him that no man could ever have been more fortunate, he had accepted that any disapproval of a girl like Rosalee Quentin was merely his Puritan morality rearing its ugly head. Even the feeling, which he could not escape, that some of the young men who were always hanging around the Quentin household *might* have from time to time stolen a kiss, had become irrelevant—however often he had considered calling one of the louts out—because she was going to be his, not theirs, and stolen kisses were things of the past.

Supposing he could ever become used to the idea. Why *should* a girl like Rosalee Quentin have decided to marry an itinerant army officer, provided he gave up the army? He might flatter himself that she had fallen in love with him, but he could not really believe that, any more than he had been able to believe that James Quentin approved of the match—his wife certainly didn't.

Once again, Frémont had explained, had insisted that the whole idea had been Quentin's—and his own, of course. "James has no son of his own, you see," the Pathfinder had said. "He needs someone to help him with the shipping line, someone he can trust absolutely. It has to be Rosalee's husband. And don't forget that James Quentin raised himself by his bootstraps. He doesn't really go for San Francisco society. So maybe now, with his money behind her, Rosalee could marry into any family on Nob Hill, but Jimmy doesn't want that. They're nearly all his rivals in business, or people who put him down when he first came here. He wants a son-in-law who's going to be entirely his own man, entirely on *his* side. When I had finished talking to him about you, Ralph, my boy, he knew he'd found his man. And Rosalee has always been Daddy's girl."

None of which had made Ralph feel any more sure that the idea was a good one. But Frémont had laughed and given him one of those slaps on the shoulder of which he was so fond. "Don't be a fool, Ralph, and start looking gift horses in the mouth. I set all this up for you. I see you, as Quentin's right-hand man, standing at *my* shoulder in the years to come. So what's eating you? That Rosalee may not be head over heels in love with you? She's going to marry you, boy. And if you don't *make* her fall in love with you the moment you get into her bed, you're not the man I thought you were."

Heady ideas. Which had suddenly become a matter of urgency. The horse had stopped walking, of its own accord, and Ralph realized that they had topped the hill and were in fact standing outside the wrought-iron railing that surrounded the gardens of the Quentin property. The house loomed through the brilliant moonlight, gleaming white, a place of balconies and Grecian pillars, tall chimney stacks and creeping ivy. The center of all his dreams and ambitions, alongside which, he knew, a few minutes of lustful fondling a yellow-skinned girl was utterly irrelevant. But oh, how he wanted to feel his arms around Rosalee this night. And . . . He frowned. He could have sworn he had seen the gleam of a candle at one of the windows. The window, he was equally sure, of Rosalee's bedroom. She was awake, at past midnight, and no doubt thinking of him, as he was thinking of her.

He pulled out his handkerchief to wipe his brow. If ever a man could see the hand of fate . . . Because even if she rejected his advances, she could not help but be delighted that he had come to her, after announcing that he was spending this last military night with his friends. And why should she reject his advances? They were to be married in a fortnight.

Without giving himself time to think further, he dismounted and secured the horse to the railing, then vaulted it and landed in the garden. James Quentin kept dogs as pets, not to guard his property, and they were locked up at night, so there was nothing to stop him stealing across the path and through the flowerbeds, to arrive beneath the balcony. He did not wish to frighten her, of course, and as it was a warm night, her French windows stood open. He thought a single pebble, lobbed onto the floor of the veranda, should bring her outside; that was safer than a whistle. Heart pounding, he stooped, found a stone of the right size, straightened and looked up at the balcony, then saw her silhouetted in the doorway against the candleglow as she stepped onto the balcony. And realized that she was naked.

For a moment he stopped breathing, taken aback at once by the very promise of her, and equally by the sheer magnificence of the woman herself. He had always been sure that she would be like a goddess in the size and perfection of her body, and had yet been afraid to imagine it in all its glory, as it would one day belong to him. But now, clearly delineated in the moonlight, he looked at the flowing golden hair resting on her shoulders before trailing past, some down her back and some strands resting on her breasts, at the breasts themselves, thrusting away from her chest—he could not make out the nipples—at the long gleam of dark-forested groin, at the legs which were flawlessly shaped stems of the most exquisite perfection. He felt a criminal, that he should be staring at such private magnificence without her knowing it. But she had to be warned that he was there. Would she mind? He doubted it. The guilt was entirely in *his* mind.

He took a long breath, and parted the bushes, and stared in total horror at the man who was stepping through the French windows behind Rosalee, still buckling his belt.

The noise of the snapping twigs alerted the couple on the balcony, and Rosalee gave an exclamation of alarm, at the same time stepping back into the doorway. The man picked up his jacket from where he had rested it across the balustrade and drew a derringer pistol from the pocket.

"No," Rosalee gasped, stepping back onto the balcony, and obviously concerned about the likely tumult which would result from a shot. She now advanced to the rail and looked down; clearly she had not yet recognized the intruder. "Be off with you, scoundrel."

Ralph took another step forward. He was aware of a feeling he had not known since that day eleven years ago when he had stood beside the smoking wagon and looked at the dead bodies of his parents and his sister. It was first of all a feeling of sheer disbelief, a desperate private prayer that such a thing could not have happened, could not still be happening. This was immediately overwhelmed by a feeling of total isolation from the world of men, that he had left one life to begin another, and that the new life was not really there to be entered upon. And *that* was immediately overlaid by a burning sensation of outrage and anger, a desire to hurt somebody very badly, to explode into a maniacal rage, to kill.

But this was Rosalee, the girl he loved. The girl who had selected *him* out of all her myriad suitors—because her father and John Frémont had said so. And the girl for whose dream he had eschewed all others, even when they had been presented to him on a plate, as tonight. While she . . .

"Oh, my God!" Rosalee said as the moonlight fell on his face. "Oh, my *God*! He said he was going to get drunk. He said . . ." She made to step back again, had had her arm seized by the man, who was again raising the derringer.

"We have no choice," he said, and Ralph, still unable to see his face clearly, recognized the voice as belonging to one Jefferson Hardy, a fairly regular caller at the Quentin house, and someone with a background of wealth and position somewhat more in tune with the shipping magnate. "We'll have to make it an accident."

"Then you can't use the gun," Rosalee snapped. "And he can't be found here. You'll have to ... Well, he's drunk, isn't he? Look at him?"

Ralph realized that he *was* swaying to and fro. That he was indeed still drunk. And that his fiancée had just given orders that he be killed rather than have herself exposed to scandal.

"Aye," he shouted. "I am drunk, you whore. Drunk," he yelled, and ran at the balustrade, which could easily be gained by the vine-covered trellis reaching up to it from the lower floor.

"Stop him," Rosalee screamed, abandoning her plans. "He'll kill us."

The derringer exploded, but the shot went wide. And Ralph had reached the upper balustrade in almost a single bound. Rosalee ran back into the bedroom, took her own pistol from her drawer, and threw it to Hardy, who had retreated against the wall. He caught it expertly, swung to face Ralph. But Ralph had already drawn his service revolver, and beat him to the shot. The bullet smashed into Hardy's chest, and he arced backward, striking the disordered bed, half-turning on his face, and then subsiding to the floor, clearly dead, leaving the sheets a blood-sodden mess.

"You ... you murderer!" Rosalee screamed.

Ralph turned the gun toward her, his hand already instinctively squeezing again in fuddled outrage. But he had sufficient self-control to pull the muzzle aside, and the bullet smashed into the wall beside the distraught girl.

"Aaagh!" she screamed. "Help me!"

The door burst open, and several people appeared in the hall beyond, Negro butlers and footmen and housemaids, and James Quentin himself, carrying a fowling piece. "What in the name of God ... ?" The moonlight was streaming across the floor and making it quite easy to see that there had been a tragedy.

"He's gone mad," Rosalee screamed. "He's berserk. He's drunk." She pointed. "He and Jeff were going to fight a duel over me, and Ralph made him come here to say good-bye and then shot him down in cold blood."

Ralph, taking long breaths in an attempt to get himself under control, was amazed at once by her quickness of mind and her quite shameless accusation. He could only stare at his fiancée in bewilderment.

"I told you he was no good," another voice snapped, and he realized that Mrs. Quentin had joined the discussion. "I told you. John Frémont's friend! You're a fool, James Quentin, thinking you could take some shavetail soldier and make him into what *you* want. You're a fool, too, Rosalee Quentin, for allowing it. Look at the mess. Think of the scandal."

"Shut up," Ralph shouted, wishing he had so addressed her, so addressed them all, long before. "She is lying. The man was here in bed with her. She is a liar and a whore. She is—"

"Now, boy," James Quentin said, stepping forward, at the same time jerking his head so that the Negroes also entered the room, moving to left and right. "Sounding off ain't going to help. You've killed a man."

"He tried to kill me, too," Rosalee gasped. "There's his bullet in the wall."

"Boy, you shouldn't have tried to kill my daughter," Quentin said. "Now I'm placing you under arrest." He held up his hand as Ralph would have spoken. "You can make a statement to the sheriff. But first things first. Give me the gun now, slow and easy. Give me the gun."

Ralph stared at him, and at the same time assessed the position of the slowly advancing black men. He was well aware of James Quentin's reputation for ruthlessness, as well as the manner in which he protected and indeed idolized his daughter. There was the making of an almighty scandal here, but only he could tell of it—Rosalee was unlikely ever to. If he were to meet with an accident on his way to jail, the only version of what had happened here would be the Quentins'.

"Come on, boy," James Quentin said. "Give me the gun."

"I'll take *myself* to jail, thank you," Ralph said, and leaped backward through the door and onto the balcony.

—2—
THE VOYAGE

James Quentin promptly threw up the fowling piece and fired, proving that he had already decided a dead prospective son-in-law was preferable to a live ex-son-in-law blurting the truth about his daughter's morals to the entire community. But Ralph was already over the balustrade, somewhat before he had intended to be, turning a complete somersault and landing on his hands and knees, fortunately in the softness of a flowerbed, and still grasping his revolver.

"Did you get him, Pa?" Rosalee cried, her voice shrill. "Oh, say you got the bastard."

One day, Ralph thought. Oh, one day . . . He got up and ran across the lawn.

"He's up, by God," Quentin snarled. "Give me a fresh charge, God damn you."

Ralph paused and looked back, gasping for breath, saw them all gathered on the balcony while Quentin stuffed a new cartridge into his piece. Rosalee was there too; she had not even bothered to put on a robe, despite the presence of the slaves. By God, he thought, I'll tickle them up. He fired twice more, not at them, but aiming immediately above their heads. He was, as Frémont had described him to the Japanese, a naturally accurate marksman, and he sent his bullets into the girl's bedroom, smashing into the paneling to terrify everyone inside; he watched them drop to their knees in their fear. Then he was vaulting the railing onto the street, releasing Royal, the horse, and galloping down the hill, hooves striking sparks from the cobbles. Horse and rider skidded down the slope before he could draw rein, panting and gasping, holstering his revolver, looking from right to left as if he expected sheriff's deputies to be emerging from every doorway, and realizing he was almost sober, with that deadening feeling of catastrophe which invariably accompanies a thumping hangover.

But the catastrophe was real, not merely drink-induced. He had indeed killed a man, and a fellow American rather than a Comanche brave. Perhaps he had shot in self-defense, but he doubted, after everything that had happened, his plea would stand much chance in court—supposing he ever got there alive. Even more than that, he had entirely wrecked his prospects. He had resigned from the army, and now he had shot himself out of a wife and every dream he had ever had. And regretted not a moment of the past ten minutes. When he thought that he might very well have married her . . . Clearly part of her bargain with her father had been that, in return for marrying his choice of a son-in-law, she would continue to live the sort of life she had always led, as he had been warned often enough by his friends—without ever doing more than taking offense.

But satisfaction at having escaped *that* fate was no substitute for the mess he was now in. His breathing under control, he listened, and heard nothing save the odd shouted inquiry from aroused Quentin neighbors. But no citizen of San Francisco was going to venture into the street in the dark to investigate gunshots, and the Quentins themselves had apparently decided pursuit was useless, and instead would be making their plans. Plans which would involve his murder, he did not doubt; certainly the sheriff was a personal friend of the shipowner. Plans to which he had no answer . . . save for John Frémont. Frémont had created this situation, in his anxiety to manipulate people, his principal hobby; helping his friend and protégé had been merely coincidental. Frémont would have to know what to do, would have to be able to provide some antidote to the situation.

Ralph wheeled his horse, walked it to Frémont's house. This was an altogether grander affair than even Quentin's mansion, and was guarded by several of the California roughnecks who had followed the famous gen-

eral against the Mexicans. But they all knew Captain
Ralph Freeman, and readily allowed him entry, even at
three o'clock in the morning. Butlers were summoned,
and these in turn aroused the Pathfinder himself,
wrapped in a maroon-and-gold dressing gown, peering
through the candlelight at the young officer. "Ralph?
By God, but you look as if you've seen a ghost. What in
the name of God can be amiss?"

Ralph looked at the servants, and Frémont waved
them from the study. "Close the doors. Now, boy."

Ralph told him what had happened, and Frémont
gazed at him with a consternation to equal his own at
the Quentin mansion. "You shot Jefferson Hardy? Jesus Christ!"

"You don't seem to understand," Ralph said. "He
was with Rosalee. And she was . . ." He couldn't bring
himself to say it. He could hardly believe it himself,
now that more than an hour had passed.

"So she likes her oats," Frémont remarked. "You mean
you haven't been ramming her yourself?"

"Ramming her? She's my fiancée?"

"And that's a reason for not touching her? Oh, Ralph,
Ralph, what am I to do with you?" He raised his head.
"What *am* I to do with you? They'll have you for murder.
You know that?"

"That's why I'm here. With your help . . ."

"*My* help? I can't testify. I wasn't there. As for taking
on Quentin . . . he's supposed to be on my side. That
means I'm supposed to be on his. And there's big
political matters coming up. You must have forgotten
there's a presidential election this year."

Ralph frowned at him. "Is that important?"

"Is that important," Frémont remarked. "Jesus Christ!
I'm the choice of the Republican party, boy. At least, I
was last time around, and no talk about some country
lawyer from Illinois is going to push me to one side.
There's big things going to happen this year, Ralph,
and I need all the support I can get. Sure as hell I can't
afford to split the party here in California. I'm sorry,
boy, but you're on a hiding to nothing."

"So you're telling me just to go back up to the Quentins and let them lynch me," Ralph said.

"Hell, boy, there must be someplace you can go. . . .
The *English Rose!*"

"Eh?"

"Your friend Gray. He leaves on the morning tide.
In only a couple of hours' time."

"For Hong Kong."

"Well, you could hardly be farther away from Quentin than Hong Kong."

"But . . ." Surely he had to be dreaming. "What am I
to do in Hong Kong?"

Frémont shrugged. "You'll find something. Here . . ."
He unlocked the desk, pulled open a deep drawer, and
took out a bag of coins. "Silver dollars. A hundred of
them. They'll tide you over until you can find some
work. Hell, boy, it'll be experience for you. And it
needn't be for very long. When I'm elected President—
and I will be this time, you know, because this slavery
business is coming to a head, and we'll have the whole
Northern vote solid behind us—well, when that happens,
I won't need Quentin anymore, and I'll be able to think
of my friends. Give it a year. A year in Hong Kong.
Hell, you'll enjoy that."

Ralph gazed at him for a moment, then picked up
the bag of coins and left the room.

His friend, he thought bitterly as he walked his horse
once more down the hill. Who wanted only to be rid of
the nuisance of him, whose only advice was to become a
self-exile on the other side of the world.

But if Frémont was not truly his friend, he realized,
then he did not possess such a thing anywhere on *this*
side of the world. He was absolutely alone, to face all
the angry might that James Quentin would be marshaling against him. He might as well cut his own throat
here and now.

Save for Jonathan Gray. There *was* a friend. And
Alison. . . . If he would ever trust a woman again, Alison would have to be the one.

But he was never going to trust a woman again.

The *English Rose* was alongside, but was already abustle,
waiting for the boatmen who would tow her away from
the quay as the tide turned and set her on her way.

The watchman on the gangway recognized him and summoned the captain.

"Mr. Freeman?" Gray peered at him. "You've trouble?"

"Aye. Can we have a word in private, Captain?"

"Surely." Gray ushered him across the deck and down the companion ladder. Alison waited at the foot, fully dressed, staring at Ralph with wide eyes. Now, there was innocence, he thought, and real beauty, because it was untarnished. And certainly trustworthiness.

"My apologies for this intrusion," he said. "When I know how busy you are. But . . . well, sir, Captain Gray, I seek a passage."

Gray frowned at him. "To Hong Kong? I do not stop before."

"To Hong Kong, sir. I can pay for it."

"You wish to go to Hong Kong." Gray sat down. "Are you not due to be married within the month? To Miss Quentin?"

"No, sir." Ralph glanced at Alison and flushed. "That marriage will not now take place."

"And you must flee your native land," Gray mused. "There is a mystery here. I am sorry, Mr. Freeman, but I must know the truth of it."

Ralph sighed, and sat down in turn. "Perhaps Miss Alison would prefer to withdraw."

"I would prefer to stay," she said quietly. "If you will permit me."

Ralph hesitated, and then shrugged. Certainly she would know of it in time. "Simply, sir, I discovered that my fiancée was playing me false with another. We both drew, and I shot him down."

"Holy Christ!" Gray muttered. "He's dead?"

"Yes, sir." Ralph gazed at the girl. She had bitten her lip but made no comment.

"And his name?"

"Jefferson Hardy."

"Oh, my God," Gray said. "And Quentin?"

"Regards me as a murderer, and will have my scalp. If he can find it."

Gray stared at him.

"Then he shall not," Alison said. "Of course you are

welcome on board my father's ship, Mr. Freeman. I think that man deserved to die."

"Are you gone crazy?" Gray shouted.

They both turned to look at him.

"The man is a self-confessed murderer," Gray said. "And Quentin knows it. I have to return to San Francisco, sir, time and again, and I have to deal with Mr. Quentin. Oh, aye, and Mr. Hardy senior as well. I have liked you, sir, and I consider you unfortunate. But I can assist no criminal to escape justice. Because of our friendship, I will not arrest you myself. But I must ask you to leave my ship. And if you have any sense, you will turn yourself in to the sheriff this very night."

Ralph stared at him. "And do you suppose they will let me come to trial?" he asked, speaking quietly, for all the bitter rage which was surging at his mind. "To give evidence of what I saw and heard this night?"

"The law, sir," Gray said. "You must trust in the law."

Ralph continued to stare at him for a moment longer, and then turned for the door.

"No," Alison cried. "Father, you cannot turn him away. Mr. Freeman—"

"Be quiet, miss," Gray snapped. "You know nothing of the matter. Be quiet."

Ralph had hesitated in the companionway. Now he looked back at her, watched a tear trickle out of her eye and down her cheek. Alison Gray, he thought. She at least was a friend. But helpless to assist him now. "I thank you, Miss Gray," he said. "But I shall not trouble your father again."

"Take care, Mr. Freeman," she said. "Oh, take care."

His horse stood patiently on the dock, and he mounted and walked it up the street. The night was nearly over; already the first streaks of dawn were appearing in the eastern sky. How he wanted to go east. To ride back onto the great prairies and challenge the world with his revolver in his hand. But there, too, he knew, Quentin would reach behind him. So, would it not be a pleasure to die, still with gun in hand, if he could take Quentin with him? And perhaps Rosalee as well?

Save that that never *would* be possible. So he would die for no purpose at all. Whereas, were he to live, even after playing the coward's part for a while, it was conceivable that *one* day . . . He could at least dream of it. Supposing he *could* manage to live. But if he could find no one to help him . . .

He found himself gazing at the Golden View Hotel. It too was in darkness, the night's roistering done. But in there, asleep with their beautiful handmaidens, were men with ideas different from those of Jonathan Gray, or John Frémont, or James Quentin. Men who believed only in the sword, and the preservation of honor. Men who recognized and wished to employ his talents. And Japan was at least as far away as Hong Kong, and even more inaccessible to an American warrant.

So it went against the grain to beg succor from such strangers. But the decision had already been taken. He would survive, no matter what he had to do. To face all of his detractors and betrayers, one day.

There was no one to prevent his entering the side door of the hotel and climbing the stairs; Mackenzie's lodgers were supposed to take care of themselves. And the outer door to the Japanese suite was also unlocked. But when he pushed it, he encountered resistance, and realized that there was a body lying across the inside in the same instant that the man woke up, to pull the door inward and yank the intruder into the room, where he could be instantly surrounded by the three angry manservants, each one armed with a knife, while the three girls huddled naked in the far corner in terror, all black hair and gleaming limbs, and the inner door opened to reveal Ito and Inouye, also naked, but both grasping their huge swords, scabbards now discarded.

But now it was light enough to see. "Captain Freeman?" Ito cried. And spoke sharply in Japanese. Instantly Ralph was released. "Welcome, Captain," Ito said again, and shook his hand, at the same time escorting him into the inner room.

"You cannot have changed your mind about the girl?" Inouye asked a trifle slyly. Neither man appeared the least embarrassed at receiving him in the nude.

"Well, not about the girl," Ralph said, wondering if

he meant what he was saying, and trying to appear as nonchalant as possible. "But I have been considering the matter of your offer most of the night, and I realize I may have been hasty in not accepting." He watched the girls, who were hurrying into the room to wrap their masters in kimonos and prepare tea. How graceful they were. And how innocent and unaffected their movements, however long forgotten their virginity. He could not stop himself imagining Alison Gray kneeling naked on the floor to assist him, and hastily put the thought from his mind. And wondered why. Alison, whatever her private sympathy for him, was by her circumstances ranked with his enemies. He could surely imagine her as he chose.

Ito had followed his glance, and now sat down cross-legged on the end of the mattress which had been spread across the tatami mats—Ralph realized that *he* was still wearing his boots. "My boots," he said. "I apologize."

Ito waved his hand. "It is a habit you will become used to, Captain. But this is splendid news. Splendid. If you will return with us, Lord Nariaka will be delighted with what we have accomplished. As for the others . . ." He looked at Inouye.

Who spoke in Japanese. Ito nodded thoughtfully. And Ralph realized that he was not going to be able to sustain the lie any more than he had considered lying to Jonathan Gray; it was not in his nature. "You understand that I have not told you the entire situation," he said.

Ito raised his eyebrows. "You are *not* coming to Japan?"

"I would like to do that, Mr. Ito, if you will have me. But I am being forced to it." He spoke quickly and concisely, outlining what had happened. Ito and Inouye listened to him in silence, while Aya knelt beside him with a cup of tea; he could almost feel her.

"And you say they will hang you for killing your betrothed's lover?" Ito asked. "In Japan you would be honored. But you should have slain the woman as well."

"Aye, well, the thought did cross my mind. But there

you have it, gentlemen. I come to you as a fugitive, begging aid."

"Never begging, Captain. It is we who are the gainers by this episode. You *belong* in Japan, Captain. You will do great things there. But I think the situation calls for a change of plan, would you not agree, Bunta San? Our instructions were not to differ with the Americans on any subject, merely to look, and learn, and profit. We have done all of these things, and now in a greater measure than our lord can have anticipated or even hoped. But to remain here a moment longer may well bring us into conflict with the authorities and ruin all we have accomplished."

"You say no one knows you have come to us, Captain?" Inouye asked. "Well, then, if we conceal you on our ship . . ."

"Even there the captain may be found," Ito objected. "And as long as our ship remains in this harbor, all on board are subject to American law. I say we have no reason to remain further in this place. We have completed every purpose behind our mission. Why stay?"

"No one else is ready to sail at this moment," Inouye objected.

Ito gave a quick smile. "So let them remain. We are ready to sail, by happy chance. The water tanks were filled but yesterday, and a supply of fresh food was taken on board. And do you not suppose, in our circumstances, that it would be best to return by ourselves, and privily?"

Ralph glanced from one to the other, aware that they were talking above his head, and aware too that in referring to their circumstances, Ito had not been thinking specifically of him.

But whatever was concerning them, or they were intending, he had no alternative but to go along with them in every way.

Inouye hesitated only a moment longer, then nodded. "You are right, of course. We shall leave within the hour. Do you take Captain Freeman to the ship, and I will see to matters here."

Ito stood up. "Come."

"I did not really mean you to have to terminate your

visit so suddenly," Ralph protested. "I am sure I can remain on board your ship in perfect safety until you are ready to sail."

"The decision has been taken," Ito told him. "Now we must cease discussion and act." He thrust his swords through his girdle, put on his sandals, summoned the man Keiko, who had first admitted Ralph the previous night, and the three of them stole out of the hotel. Ralph's horse, Royal, was still tied to the rail, and him they released, Ralph giving him a smart slap on the rump; he would undoubtedly make his way back to the Quentin stable, and hopefully further confuse his pursuers. Then they made their way through the still-deserted streets, and while there were people on the waterfront, no one paid the yellow men and their military companion much attention; the *English Rose* had already cast off and was in mid-channel, setting her sails. Within half an hour after leaving the hotel, Ralph was being rowed out to where the Japanese junks lay moored some two hundred yards from the shore.

Both to his surprise and his relief, he discovered that they were somewhat larger vessels than he had expected, having previously only glanced at them from the shore without much interest. But he felt no more reassured as to their seaworthiness, for they had low bows and high sterns, and if three-masted, the sails were enormous square pieces of canvas—rather than the carefully shaped rectangles used by the Quentin barques, for example—across which strips of wood had been stitched at intervals of perhaps two feet; there were no booms to be seen, and the only sheets led back from the clew of each sail to a belaying point immediately in front of the next mast. They were also, he reckoned, grossly overloaded with men and arms, cannon as well as personal weapons. It occurred to him that he might well be committing suicide in any event—but then he reflected that this strange fleet *had* succeeded in crossing the Pacific once, and therefore was no doubt capable of doing so again.

Now he was all but forgotten in the hustle and bustle as Ito gave the necessary orders. He was not the captain of the ship—that was obvious; but equally

obviously, he was superior *to* the captain. Ralph stood
on a corner of the huge poop deck, which seemed to
stretch almost a third of the length of the hull, and
watched the preparations even as he watched the sun
begin to swing above the hills to the east, and felt the
land breeze playing on his cheeks. And watched, too,
the boats bringing Inouye and the girls out from the
shore—and wondered if Alison Gray, on the poop of
the *English Rose*, was interested in the Japanese goings-on
and would trouble to look at them through a glass. But
she and all the others were best forgotten until he
could return in triumph.

If such a day would ever dawn.

Ito stood behind him. "The rising sun," he said. "Is
that not a splendid sight?"

"Why, I guess dawn is a good time to sail," Ralph
agreed.

Ito gave one of his quick smiles. "I meant, Captain
San, that the rising sun is the emblem of Japan." He
pointed, and Ralph for the first time noticed the huge
ensign, representing a red sun rising from a yellow sky
and sending its beam darting in every direction, flying
from the stern of the junk.

"That is your flag now, Captain San," Ito said. "As it
is mine. Together we will make it great, eh?"

Ito's words and the sight of the flag brought home to
Ralph for the first time just what he was doing. The
entire night seemed like a vast nightmare, contained an
unreality which could not be faced. But if he were not
still dreaming, then he *was* standing here in the chill
dawn breeze listening to the clank of the anchor as it
was brought up, to the chanting of the sailors as they
pulled on the ropes to raise the sails, to the gentle swish
of water away from the hull as the wind filled the
canvas and the ship started to gather way, conned by
her captain, all frowns and mustache, gazing fiercely
ahead at the magnificent sweep of the Golden Gate,
beyond which lay the trackless ocean—and the dimin-
ishing shape of the *English Rose*, by now almost hull-
down.

And after the ocean? Ralph looked up at the flag

again, and had the strongest urge to throw himself over the taffrail and swim to shore, no matter what awaited him. But there at the least would be the Stars and Stripes, and the men of his battery, to whom he had not even yet said good-bye; they had been going to have a little ceremony this morning, at which time he would no doubt have been presented with some keepsake to remind him of their days together. Instead of which they would be awakened to hear that their captain had committed murder and was a wanted outlaw fleeing for his life to a land of which he knew nothing, where an utterly incomprehensible language was spoken, and where, he suspected, every moral tenet was as different as possible from everything he had been brought up to. And entering that world, all he possessed were the clothes he stood in—and which he no longer had any right to wear—and the ambitions of two men he had known hardly twelve hours.

One of whom was now approaching him as the ship began to gather speed and they raced through the narrows, tide rips boiling away from their bows, to meet the enormous swell of the great sea. "You did not sleep last night," Inouye observed.

Ralph attempted a grin. "I didn't really have the time. But I am not tired, truly."

"You mean, you are *too* tired to sleep. And you are dispirited, and aghast at what you have done."

Ralph gazed at him in surprise. "You understand that?"

"Of course. I felt the same way when we left Japan, how many months ago. And *I* was certain of returning, if I lived."

"Do you doubt I shall return to America?" Ralph demanded.

"I do not doubt that any man can do anything he desires, if fortune favors him," Inouye observed. "And if he is always true to himself." He smiled. "Which is but another way of describing fortune, is it not? But no man should spend his time in looking over his shoulder, in regretting what has happened to him, in perhaps wishing that things might have been different. Whatever happens to a man, provided only he is not a coward and at some stage has turned away from his destiny in fear, is ordained by fate, and will happen, whether he would have it or not. To consider otherwise is to make yourself ill, and we cannot have that. There are only two ways to overcome your mood of despondency. Come."

Ralph followed him to the companion ladder leading down to the after cabin.

"A man can either get drunk," Inouye observed, "and remain so, until his mood passes. Or he can seek the comfort of a woman." He gave one of his sly smiles. "Some men find it necessary to do both." He descended the ladder in front of Ralph. "But there is a yet surer way than either of those. Be certain that you will not sleep soundly and regain full control of yourself until you have relieved your spirit." He opened a door leading off the main cabin into one of the small single-berthed sleeping quarters. "This is Kioya. He will be of great comfort to you."

Ralph stared at the boy in consternation. He was young, certainly not more than fifteen, and handsome— and naked, and aroused.

"Believe me," Inouye said. "He is flattered to have been chosen to honor an American."

"A *boy*?"

"Can there be greater comfort?" Inouye replied. "I know, we were warned not to indulge our instincts while in America, because boys are not well regarded there. It has been hard, I can tell you. We have had to come out to our ships from time to time to relieve our tortured minds."

"But . . . the girls last night?"

Inouye shrugged. "What is a woman? Oh, they are necessary to bear our children, to cook for us and do our laundry. And occasionally, like last night, when a man has had sufficient wine, they are sweet to fondle and even to enter. But they are not like us. They do not truly understand our needs. And do not pretend to me, Freeman San. You felt no desire for a girl last night. Perhaps you were afraid to admit what you really wished. But here there is no cause for fear."

"I refused the girl . . . because of many things, Mr.

Inouye. Things which have brought me here, perhaps. But a boy . . ." He shook his head.

"Have you never been with a man?" Inouye was obviously amazed.

"Of course I have not. The idea repels me."

"You are a strange people," Inouye observed. "I cannot believe you do not wish to. It is not good for a man to repress his natural instincts, Freeman San. But if you wish a girl, then you shall have one. It is but important that you give your tortured spirit rest." He spoke to the boy in Japanese, and Kioya, after a moment's hesitation and a quick, contemptuous glance at Ralph, picked up his kimono and hurried from the cabin.

Ralph found his handkerchief and dried his brow. The youth had been beautiful; no doubt about that. And *had* aroused all manner of obscene thoughts. Thoughts which would have to be got rid of as rapidly as possible. And for all his exhaustion, he did want a woman. Aya, that little slip of girlish beauty. If he had remained last night with Aya, he would not be here now.

But this catastrophe would still have happened, one day, perhaps when he was even more alone and vulnerable.

"Aya," he said. "I would like Aya."

"And she is here," Inouye said. "She is yours. I give her to you. Use her as you wish. I will leave you now. Remember, relieve your spirit of all you desire. *All* desire, Freeman San. Then will you sleep soundly and awaken a new man." He gave his sly smile. "A Japanese man."

He stepped past the girl and left the cabin, while Ralph gazed at her, suddenly embarrassed. As a soldier, he had naturally been with prostitutes—they were in fact his only experience of women. But this was not a prostitute, however often she might have *been* prostituted. She had been given to him carelessly. She was *his*. And he was afraid to touch her.

Aya released her girdle, and the kimono swung open. She did not speak, as she knew he would understand nothing of what she would say. But she knew her art, remained facing him for several seconds, allowing the roll of the ship to sway both kimono and hair shroud, slowly to and fro, now revealing, now concealing. Then with a quick movement she shrugged the kimono from her shoulders and came toward him.

She was more entrancing than he remembered from the very quick glimpse of her he had gained the previous night. She seemed to glow, and while she was so slight he felt he could pick her up in one hand, there was no suggestion of emaciation; every bone, save for the trembling rib cage, was neatly and adequately covered with flesh. Flesh he desperately wished to touch, to hold in his arms, and dared not. Because he did not know the Japanese custom. What they *did*. Oh, if only he had stayed last night.

She stood in front of him, waiting, and he took off his uniform jacket, only then realizing that as this was a Japanese ship, there were no bunks, not even a chair—only the tatami mats on the deck. He dropped the jacket, while she expertly released his belt, remained for a moment puzzled by his suspenders, and then gave a little smile and slid them from his shoulders before unbuttoning his shirt. She wanted, he realized, to see his chest, and she gave a little shiver when she did uncover the mass of curling black hair. He wondered if she had ever seen an Occidental chest before, or had merely heard her masters talk of them.

He sat down on the mats, and she knelt to remove his boots. Now he could restrain himself no longer, and stroked the glossy crown of her head. Her eyes came up watchfully, and he suddenly knew that she was as uncertain as himself, for all her experience—because she did not know *his* ways. He felt enormously relieved; they were strangers together, entering paradise hand in hand.

He knelt to remove his breeches and drawers, and once again she gave a little shiver at the amount of hair. Certainly not at his size. The events of the night were after all proving too much for him, at least physically. He sat down, and to his consternation and delight she touched him, held him between her hands. Such a thing had never happened to him before; he could not imagine any white woman doing that, and the thought that Rosalee *might* have so loved Jefferson Hardy, and even himself in the course of time, made him sweat—but he was never going to think of Rosalee Quentin again.

Yet had the damage been done. Aya gave a little frown and released him. Then she clearly considered the situation for a moment before turning away from him, on her knees, and when she saw that he did not understand her meaning, she picked up his hand and dropped it onto her small buttocks.

"No, no, girl," he said. "I am not going to beat you for the sake of an erection. I am tired, that is all. Perhaps . . ." If you lie in my arms, he thought. But perhaps Japanese women did not lie in their lovers' arms.

Her frown deepened as her perplexity grew. Then she had an idea, crawled to her kimono, and from the pocket took a most remarkable object, two little ivory balls, pierced in the center and thus secured together by a short length of silken cord; they clicked as she took them in her hand. Now she smiled at him, and lay down on the mats on her back, with her legs pointing toward him, so that he could see what she was doing, and to his increasing stupefaction, inserted the two balls into herself, and then moved them by manipulating both the cord and her thighs. She was inviting him to watch her masturbate, in the hopes of arousing him. He did not even know that women indulged such a habit, and again could not believe it of any white woman he had ever known.

Yet already she was sweating and gasping, and the sight of her was having an equal effect upon him. He crawled toward her, lay beside her while she watched him with wide eyes, and lowered his face toward hers. She turned her head away as his mouth opened, anticipating a bite, so he held her chin with his hand and kissed her lips, and found her tongue, and felt the manhood glowing through his body. "This is how we do it in America," he whispered as he covered her, and felt her hands on his back, slowly tightening.

* * *

The piece of wood, about the size of a man's hand, thrown from the deck, bobbed in the water as the junk drifted lazily through the calm sea. Ralph took a quick but careful aim and squeezed the trigger of the revolver; the bullet sent the wood spinning out of the waves.

"But that is remarkable," Ito cried. "May I use it?"

Ralph gave him the gun. "Use the sight," he told the little man. "And do not *pull* the trigger. The whole hand must be squeezed, if you would hit the target."

But Ito's shot went wide and aroused a chorus of scornful laughter from the seamen as well as the girls gathered at the forward end of the poop to watch the white man's tricks. Aya was among them, observing his skill, Ralph thought, and swelled with pride. And with guilt. Because, hull-down on their port bow, there was a sail. It had been there ever since they had left San Francisco, and he could not doubt that it was the *English Rose;* whatever faults he could find in the design of the *Asa Maru,* as the junk was named—"maru" being the Japanese word for "ship"—there could be no argument that off the wind, and the wind had been easterly since leaving America, she was as fast as any vessel ever built. But there, always in sight, was a memory at once of his betrayal and of what he had abandoned. For Aya. Because equally she epitomized all that he had fled to. And so far, succeeded in conquering; in the fortnight they had been at sea, she had obviously come to admire him and to need him, in every way. As he needed her. He had learned more about the art of lovemaking in the past two weeks than in his whole previous life. So, then, did he love her? The question could be avoided by asking himself if she loved him. If she could possibly love any man to whom she had been carelessly given and to whom, she had to accept, she had the importance of a domestic pet.

Besides, love was not a word he felt the Japanese truly understood—certainly not as an emotion to be shared by man and woman. When in their cups, which was nearly every night, Ito and Inouye boasted of the various beatings they had administered to their women, which seemed to include their wives. "Women need to be beaten," Ito would say. "They are more responsive when they are sore."

Apparently they did not need to beat their young men to obtain a response. Truly had he stepped into an existence he had never imagined possible; and the fact of the British vessel only a few miles away, on the deck of which he could not doubt Alison Gray was standing and gazing at her distant companion, only made his own position the more confounding. Sometimes he almost supposed he might actually have been hit by one of Quentin's bullets, and have died, and been transported into the next world. But it was impossible to consider the Japanese world, so dedicated to the pleasure and comfort of the male of the species, as heaven; if it was, a good many very reverent and self-confident ladies were going to receive a very rude shock one day. On the other hand, for a man it could hardly be considered as hell, where there was Aya to come to his cabin every night. Unless this was but purgatory, and there was far worse to follow.

And however strange, and perhaps repulsive, some of the Japanese habits, there would be no gainsaying the seriousness of their approach to what they considered to be the important things in life, among which weapons and skill in handling them was the most important of all. Ito had now come on deck carrying a suit of what Ralph at first supposed to be fancy dress and then realized was intended to be armor. But here were no layers of chain mail, rather an enormous breastplate of lacquered leather, brilliant red in color, and secured by straps to a backplate of similar material. He touched it, at his new friend's invitation, and found it to be remarkably tough. There was a skirt of similar material, to protect the thighs and groin, greaves for the shins, and a matching helmet, broad and flat, with a low, rounded crown from which hung a red-dyed horsehair plume and from the front of which there was suspended a grotesque mask with huge nose and hanging mustaches surrounding a gaping mouth.

"Such things are intended to terrify the more faint-hearted of one's enemies," Ito explained a trifle shamefacedly. "But it is good armor, is it not?"

"I would say so," Ralph agreed.

"You are skeptical. Watch." He summoned one of the samurai who formed their party, and the man came aft, carrying his bow. This was a formidable instrument, made, Ralph discovered to his surprise when he was invited to examine this also, not from a single length of wood, but from several pieces carefully jointed together to form an enormously strong but flexible weapon. To this the soldier now fixed an arrow, while the suit of armor was suspended against the mainmast, a good sixty feet away. The wind had dropped over the last couple of days and would hardly interfere with the shot. And now the marksman released his bolt, and it hummed through the air, striking the exact center of the breastplate, hanging there for a moment and then falling to the deck. The spectators applauded, and Ito and Ralph went forward to examine the effects of the blow. The plate had been penetrated, but only for a fraction of an inch; its wearer would have been bruised but not incapacitated in any way. "Will your bullets do better than that?" Ito asked.

Ralph took the revolver and returned to where the samurai still stood. Again he took careful aim and squeezed the trigger, listened to the cries of dismay and amazement. He did not have to go forward again to see what had happened; the flying lead had ripped the entire breastplate open and embedded itself on the inside of the backplate beyond. "That is why, you see, our soldiers no longer wear armor," he explained to the astonished Japanese. "Only concealment is effective against a modern firearm, and a rifle will do twice that much damage at several times the range."

"But that is marvelous," Inouye cried. "You have a large store of these bullets?"

"Unfortunately . . ." Ralph checked his cartridge pouch. "No. I have eight left. But if your lord has gunpowder and lead, I can make as many as you wish."

"Be sure that gunpowder and lead will be provided," Ito promised. "But can you also make the guns themselves?"

"Probably," Ralph agreed. "But not very well. It would

be better for you to purchase them from the United States."

"Yes," Ito said thoughtfully, not looking altogether convinced.

"You will have to do this," Ralph insisted, "if I am to be of any value to you. As you will have to purchase new cannon. These . . ." He indicated the ancient pieces forming the junk's armament. "How old *are* they?"

"They have been in our lord Nariaka's possession for many years," Ito said. "And before him, they belonged to his father and grandfather."

"That's obvious," Ralph said. "I doubt they'd even fire now. I can see your entire army needs overhauling, Mr. Ito."

Ito smiled. "That is what we intend that you shall do, Freeman San."

"Oh, for a breeze," growled Jonathan Gray, closing his telescope with a snap. "Those confounded pirates drift too close. That comes from being flat-bottomed."

For during the calm the *Asa Maru* and the *English Rose* had drifted to within two miles of each other.

"Now, Papa," Alison said. "You know they are not pirates. That is one of the junks out of San Francisco."

"All Japanese are pirates, given the chance," Gray reminded her. "I shall have the guns loaded, in case they wish to assault us by night."

"Oh, Papa . . . Anyway"—she continued to level her own glass—"do you know, I can swear . . ."

"Aye," Gray said. "I saw him clinging to the rigging for a look at us. They don't seem to have telescopes of their own. Now, doesn't *that* prove they're pirates? The man is a self-confessed murderer."

"You wronged him," Alison said. "And forced him to seek aid where he could."

"And so he turned to creatures of like disposition," Gray remarked crushingly. "And you admire the man. Beware I do not take a rope's end to you, miss. Such thoughts are not even proper for women, much less girls."

Alison sighed, but had the sense not to reply.

"Anyway," Gray said, "the moment there is a breeze,

I intend to alter course to the southwest and leave those fellows. And your Mr. Freeman. And trust that they will go to the bottom in the first storm." He gazed at the sky. "There is weather about, to be sure."

Alison bit her lip, but again did not reply, and her father stumped forward, leaving her alone, again to level her telescope. How desperate must a man be, she thought, to have taken refuge with such heathen and abominable people. Because she knew her father was right; if there was one mishap the sailors who traded the China Seas feared even more than a typhoon, it was to be shipwrecked on the shores of Japan, where, by repute, immediate and unpleasant murder was their only fate. As for women . . . But she did not know what might happen to a white woman so cast away. There had never been any to say, and the men by whom she was surrounded would never discuss it in her presence.

She knew so little. For five years she had lived in an entirely male world. She knew all about men, men working and men playing, men fighting and men getting drunk. But they were men always fully dressed when in her presence. And she knew nothing of men making love, or enjoying lust. Her father had always seen to that.

It was not a lack that had bothered her until that morning in San Francisco. Ralph Freeman had always been a man to admire, for his looks and his courage, for the very aura of him—but again, as a fully clothed and sexless man. But now, because of his relations with a woman, he had been turned into a fleeing renegade, forced to turn away even from the religion to which he had been educated. And become a pirate, as Father had said. What tremendous emotion must have been aroused to make a man kill and then flee so far. Would *she* ever know such an emotion? Or any man have such an emotion for her?

And now he clung to the rigging of his strange ship and stared across the water at them. At her, perhaps, even without a glass. She took off her hat and allowed her hair to flow in the light breeze. Perhaps he could see that. She hoped he could. She felt that if he could, he would know that there was at least one person in the world who cared and hoped he survived. And perhaps one day he could find his way to Hong Kong? That was something which did not even bear thinking about, except in the privacy of her narrow bunk.

And not even then, if she would avoid the sin of self-pollution. Because for Ralph Freeman, she thought, she might be able to feel such emotion, as to wish to kill, and then flee, no matter where.

Her hair suddenly covered her face, and her father was hurrying aft. "A breeze!" he shouted. "A breeze! Now we'll show those Japs the color of our wake." He put his arm around Alison's shoulders and hugged her. "Say good-bye to your murdering pirate friend, girl. You'll not look on *his* face again."

The disappearance of the *English Rose* to the southwest—and by the following dawn she was out of sight—left Ralph feeling more lonely and discouraged than at any time since the morning they had sailed out of the Golden Gate. As the days passed and the junk pressed steadily west before the wind, which sometimes blew quite fiercely and at others was hardly more than a zephyr, but which always remained fair, he came to realize that his new friends regarded him very much as a freak. Certainly they admired his skill with the revolver, but attributed at least part of that skill to the marvelous properties of the weapon itself. His sword they regarded with contempt, and Ito promised him that as soon as they reached Japan he would teach him the proper use of a blade.

"I have studied swordplay," Ralph assured him. "Including the old Italian style."

"Italian style?" Ito asked politely.

"It is similar to yours, I would say," Ralph said. "In that they also used a dagger to be held in the left hand, to act at once as a second line of defense and as a means of delivering the coup de grace, should you get close enough to your assailant."

"Dagger?"

"Your short sword. It is larger than the ones the Italians used, certainly, but will serve the same purpose."

Ito gazed at him for several seconds. "We do not

fight with our short swords," he said. But did not
explain further. Nothing, in fact, was explained, except
when it became absolutely necessary, and Ralph realized that if he was ever going to become one of these
people, as he knew he must if he was going to live with
them, even for a year, for his own comfort and safety
he would have to learn the language, and preferably
before reaching their homeland. He set to work with
Aya, much to her amusement and that of the men, but
he slowly began to make progress.

But for Aya, he thought he might well have lost his
reason. He had always been a thoughtful, even studi-
ous man, had taken his profession seriously, studied
long and hard at the theory and practice of ballistics
and weight and strain ratios; he had also studied history and geography, and even a smattering of eco-
nomic theory, preparing himself, he had hoped, for
ultimate command, just as, over the past few months,
he had been studying navigation and the theory of
seamanship, to add to his practical experience of the
art and make himself, hopefully, as much of an expert
in his new profession as in his old.

On board the *Asa Maru* there were no books at all,
that he could discover, even had he been able to read
them. His friends did not appear to need books, for
everything in their lives was rigidly controlled by custom and tradition, and this they had been taught from
the day of their birth. "A man is what he was born to
be," Inouye explained to him. "And the only crime he
can ever commit is to act beneath his station." He gave
a grim smile. "There are those who would hold that it
is also a crime to attempt to act *above* one's station, but
not all would agree with that. However, it is certainly
very dangerous." He continued, observing Ralph's
interest, "The emperor, for example, is born to be
emperor, and succeeds the moment his father abdicates,
which is generally while he is still quite young. Our
emperors stretch back in an unbroken line for thousands of years, to our first great ancestors."

"And they are called shoguns?" Ralph asked.

"No, no," Inouye said. "The emperor is the mikado,
the son of the gods, their representative upon this

earth. As such he is of course the front of all authority, but he does not wield such authority himself. That is done, as you say, by the shoguns. Or *should* be done," he added darkly. "The shogun is 'the general who repels the barbarians.' That is the meaning of his title, Sei-i-Shogun. He is responsible for the defense of the realm, as well as the good order of the country. For two hundred and fifty years now, the shogunate has been in the hands of the Tokugawa family. Once they were great men, mighty warriors and administrators. Now . . ." He gave another significant pause and then hurried on, perhaps, Ralph thought, before he said too much. "All men in Japan live and work and prosper, and own, by gracious permission of the mikado. The mikado grants the shogun his power, and the shogun in turn has divided the country into great fiefs, over which he has placed the daimyo, the lords."

"Of whom your lord, Nariaka of Cho-Shu, is one," Ralph commented.

"Lord Nariaka is the greatest of the daimyo," Inouye said reverently. "And he is now your lord as well, Freeman San."

"I understand that," Ralph said. "But tell me, Inouye San, does this shogun, who clearly commands all the temporal power in your country, never seek to make *himself* mikado?"

"How could he do that?" Inouye asked, genuinely surprised. "Only the sons of the gods may be mikado."

"Ah," Ralph said. "Well, then, these daimyo, these great lords, like the lord of Cho-Shu, do they never dream of becoming shogun?"

"Now, that is possible," Inouye agreed. "When a shogun has proved himself incompetent, it is almost the duty of the daimyo to replace him. But as I have said, to aspire to the shogunate itself is a dangerous business, whatever the provocation. It is . . ." He checked himself again, seemed to realize that he might be about to say too much, if he had not already done so. "We were speaking of a man's place," he said. "A daimyo, and in this context the shogun, is no more than the greatest of the lords, draws his strength from his samurai."

"His fighting men," Ralph suggested.

"Not exactly, if you are thinking of your private soldiers, Freeman San," Inouye objected. "We have observed that you recruit your soldiers from all walks of life. In Japan, while it is true that only a samurai may be a soldier and carry weapons, it is also true that only a gentleman can be a samurai."

"Now, there's a philosophy that would not appeal to our prosperous Yankees at all." Ralph smiled. "They like others to do their fighting for them, where possible. But then, do all samurai have the same rank?"

"Indeed not," Inouye said. "I am a hatamoto. That is, a commander of a hundred samurai. Ito is also a hatamoto," he added somewhat disparagingly. "But of inferior rank to myself. Yet are we all still samurai, and must be samurai, at all times. Our code of honor was laid down many centuries ago, when Japan was still in a state of internecine conflict, and woe to any member of our class who breaks his vows or denies his responsibilities. You will become a samurai in Japan, Freeman San, as you were undoubtedly a gentleman in your own country. And if you prove worthy, of course. But I have no doubt of that."

"That's very kind of you," Ralph said dryly. He was not sure he really wanted to take on some rigid honor code in support of a morality of which he did not actually approve. "And you say that merchants and the like are lower in rank?"

"Merchants are almost the lowest of the low," Inouye told him. "Below the samurai, we have the producers, the farmers and the artisans, and the seamen, like the sturdy fellows who crew this ship. The merchants, the sellers and transporters of goods, the makers of money," he said contemptuously, "are ranked below even these. They are merely above the honin, the landless ones, like these girls we have with us. They have no rights at all. Were you to decide to cut off Aya's head, she would have no cause to complain. She is entirely yours."

"I'm sure I like her head right where it is," Ralph said. "So the honin are the lowest of the low."

"But for the eta," Inouye said. "They are the dregs of society, the gravediggers and the slaughterers of animals. The unclean. Which is why sea travel like this makes us all so miserable. On board a vessel far from land we are all unclean all of the time."

As Ralph had no idea of what he was speaking, he continued his investigations. "But even a hatamoto like you must have an income, some source of livelihood."

"Of course, but I cannot earn it. It is provided by my lord, in proportion to my position."

"Ah." He began to realize that not only was he now living entirely in a man's world, but also that it was a samurai's or a daimyo's world. One he would *have* to join, to prosper. "And having been born into one class"—he thought of his own father's dry-goods store in Rhode Island—"you may never change it for another."

"Only in the most exceptional circumstances," Inouye said.

"Upward. But what about downward? What happens if a samurai disgraces himself?"

"A samurai who disgraces himself commits seppuku," Inouye said. "That is, suicide."

"By God! Then you consider I should have killed myself?"

"No, no, Freeman San. You have not disgraced yourself. Quite the contrary. A samurai only disgraces himself by playing the coward. Had you *not* shot your fiancée's lover, then ... But in your case, you are a samurai who has quarreled with his lord, so to speak. You are a ronin, a landless man. Or you *were* a ronin. No longer. Now you march beneath the banner of the great Nariaka, and there can be no finer situation than that."

Ralph refrained from commenting that no American would consider taking his own life because of some failure to measure up to an ideal, unless he were mentally deranged, or equally, that no American would accept that to be born poor meant that one had to remain poor all of one's life; that was indeed the exact antithesis of the American dream. But it was nearly impossible to argue with the Japanese, not only because he did not yet know enough about their land and its customs, but because they were so utterly complacent, so completely certain that their way, their customs, their traditions, had to be right. Ito and Inouye had just completed a considerable tour of the United States, but yet had apparently seen nothing to suggest that anything American was better than what they possessed in Japan—save for American guns. And these they were determined to have, and to master. Even in their attitudes to the sea, they adopted an air of total superiority, although clearly they understood nothing of it. For two hundred years, apparently, the Tokugawa shogunate had closed the island empire, forbidding any Japanese to go abroad, executing all strangers save for a handful of permitted Dutch traders who landed on Japanese shores. Thus the art of seamanship in deep waters had been lost. Now the Tokugawas had been forced to open the country again by the guns of Perry's fleet—could this be the reason for Inouye's thinly veiled hostility to the shogunate?—and the Japanese were taking every advantage of their newfound freedom to travel. Yet they sailed in these junks rather than European-type vessels, and they had learned no more navigation than the art of taking a sun sight every noon. Doing this, Ito explained, they could maintain a course along the thirty-sixth parallel of latitude, or due west from San Francisco, and this latitude, they knew, would eventually bring them to the coast of Japan. They possessed no knowledge of longitude, or even the ability to calculate a dead-reckoning position, simply because they had no clocks and therefore no means of estimating their speed. How far they traveled every day was of no interest to them; Japan was there, and they would reach it eventually. Nor were they concerned with adjusting the sails to get the best out of the wind, or with possible changes in the weather.

Which certainly concerned Ralph as he studied the gathering high clouds being whipped into mare's tails by a wind which had not yet reached them. Ito laughed at his apprehensions. "Why, Freeman San," he said, "we had contrary winds the whole way across. It took us three months to come from Edo to San Francisco. I doubt it will be as long this time, with the wind behind us." He looked at the calm sea. "Even when the wind drops away like this, we are doubtless still drifting in the right direction. We will get there, Freeman San. If the gods will it so."

And he apparently had complete faith in the gods. Ralph could not be so sure. For although the wind indeed had dropped, the swell remained, and it seemed to him larger than before, rolling up astern, raising the ship to the top of its crest for several moments and then gently lowering it down into the following trough, so deeply that the horizon was entirely lost to view. The crests were several hundred feet apart, and the surface of the sea was an oily calm; far from being uncomfortable, it was an almost soporific motion. But it did not take much imagination to think of those huge crests topped by even larger breaking waves, and of troughs from which a ship might never be able to emerge. An imagination which the Japanese, never having experienced a storm at sea, did not seem to possess.

That night, not even Aya could properly soothe Ralph to sleep, and he was up before dawn, easing himself past her sleeping body, dragging on his now sorely tattered breeches, and tiptoeing through the cabin to climb the companion ladder to the deck. Here all was peace, for the wind had now dropped to a flat calm, and the junk merely rose and fell on the swell, rolling now as well, her dead sails occasionally striking the masts with dull thuds. The helmsman leaned against the wheel, half-asleep, and the mate leaned on the rail farther aft, looking at the phosphorescence in the water. He glanced at the big American and made a remark. Ralph's Japanese was not yet good enough to enable him to catch more than a word or two, but he gathered that the sailor was commenting on the beauty of the night.

"It is beautiful," he agreed, and gave a little shudder of increased apprehension. He studied the sky, already beginning to lighten, although the stars remained overhead. But the sky was clear. Or was it? He looked aft, at the ocean out of which the sun would soon be rising, and saw nothing but darkness there, except, well above the horizon, little streaks of light. And realized he was gazing at an immense bank of cloud, obliterating the entire eastern sky, behind which the sun could make no impact upon the gloom. And even as he watched, it seemed to him that the cloud bank was growing, overtaking the stationary ship.

He touched the mate on the arm and pointed. "Cloud," he said in Japanese.

The mate shrugged. "Rain," he replied. And smiled. "Water."

Because their casks could certainly do with refilling.

"And wind," Ralph reminded him.

The mate shrugged again.

"We should shorten sail," Ralph said. "Sails down."

The mate merely looked puzzled.

Ralph chewed his lip, took a turn up and down the poop deck, and gave a sigh of relief as Ito appeared from the companionway, yawning and stretching. Ralph seized him by the arm, hurried him to the taffrail to show him the cloud. "Ito San," he said, urgently, "there is going to be a storm."

Ito followed the direction of his pointing finger; now it was broad daylight, although still gloomy, as the sun had not yet broken through the cloud bank, which was now stretching up to some sixty degrees from the horizon itself.

"That is an awful lot of wind, I would say," Ralph told him. "What do you call a great deal of wind in Japan? A big storm? What we would call a hurricane."

"A big storm is called a typhoon in Japan," Ito said.

"And it causes much damage?"

"Much damage," Ito agreed.

"Well, we are going to be hit by one, and pretty soon, I think. I think we should get all the sails off the ship, and quickly."

"Take down the sails?" Ito was astonished. "But why? Will not the wind make us go faster?"

"The wind is going to make us go *too* fast," Ralph explained. "And the waves are going to become very big. If we are not careful, they may well roll us over and sink us."

Ito frowned at him in disbelief. "You have been in such a storm at sea?"

Ralph hesitated; he could not lie in a society where

only honor counted. But then he reflected that to be caught out in half a gale in his twenty-foot catboat—which he had most certainly experienced—was probably the equivalent of being out in a typhoon in a two-hundred-foot-long junk. "Yes," he said. "At least, a very bad storm."

"But your ship did not sink?"

"No, because I took down the sail. Believe me, Ito San, a typhoon can sink a ship very easily."

"In Japan," Ito said, "typhoons tear the roofs from our houses, and sometimes knock down the walls as well. But our houses are not built of strong wood, like a ship. And typhoons create big waves which they throw onto our shores, and sometimes these waves pick up boats, and even ships, and throw them onto the shore as well. But these were anchored, you understand. Out here in the ocean, Freeman San, there is no shore. The wind and the waves will merely hurry us onward. And should they indeed overwhelm us, then that is surely the will of the gods. But we are men, and samurai. We should not be afraid to meet this challenge, as we are not afraid to meet any challenge. Let the wind come, Freeman San. And let us face it like men."

Ralph felt very inclined to tear his hair out by the roots. Confidence and honor were admirable qualities, but it was possible to carry them to absurd lengths. He wondered if he should appeal over Ito's head, to Inouye, but decided against it. Inouye would certainly have the same point of view, and he did not wish to cause a rift with the Japanese. He could only hope that the storm would develop slowly and give them the opportunity to change their minds. But he knew in his heart that there was no hope of that, as the immense black cloud spread across the entire sky, while the wind remained nothing more than fitful puffs.

"At least let us close all the hatches," he begged. "And double-lash the cannon."

"Now, there is a sensible suggestion," Ito agreed. "There is certainly going to be some rain." He went off to give the necessary instructions.

Aya came on deck. "My lord will not come below to eat?" she asked.

"Not this morning," he said.

Immediately she looked anxious. "My lord is not well?"

"I have things on my mind. But, Aya . . . do you go below and stay there until I come for you."

She gave him an even more concerned look, but obeyed him as usual, while he resumed leaning on the taffrail and staring aft, watched with amusement by the crew, among whom the rumor had quickly spread that the American was afraid of the weather.

He did not have very long to wait. He first heard the wind about ten o'clock. Before then there had been several peals of thunder followed closely by vivid flashes of forked lightning, striking the sea a mile or so behind them, bringing the sailors clustering to the gunwales to watch the display—in wonderment, to be sure, but not apparently in alarm—and then driving them to shelter as the rain began, an almost solid downpour which surrounded the ship in a wet cloud and cut visibility to a few hundred feet. Ralph remained on deck, beside the helmsman, but now there was a noise such as he had never heard before, a tremendous screaming wail. He stared aft and could see the surface of the ocean suddenly whipped into whitecaps. "For God's sake," he shouted at the captain, "let go your sheets."

But even had the Japanese been disposed to obey him, it was too late. The wind came from dead astern, which he supposed was in one way a blessing; they were picked up by a giant hand and hurled forward, down the slope of the next trough, gathering speed every moment, burying their short bowsprit in the back of the water wall in front of them. The junk seemed to check, while the roaring noise came up astern. Ralph had only the time to wrap both arms around the balustraded rail before a huge gush of water broke over him. For several seconds he could not see, and when the last of the wave did move forward, leaving him drenched and dripping, it seemed to him that the entire ship was submerged, and doomed to go straight to the bottom. Yet, amazingly, even as he watched, the bows came up again, and she seemed to slide up the back of the trough to the next crest; the closed hatches had prevented too much of the water from getting below, and had undoubtedly saved them—for the moment.

He looked left and right, and was aghast at what he saw. The entire surface of the ocean was torn into white foam, and the morning was filled with the screaming anger of the wind, while even as he drew breath, another huge wave came up astern.

This one proved too much for the masts. The sheets had already been torn free, and the sails were merely flogging and ripping themselves to shreds. Ralph supposed this might be a good thing, as some of the pressure driving the junk onward was thereby relieved. But the mast stays had also been whipped away, and as the ship plunged into the next foaming maelstrom, the mizzen suddenly gave a loud crack and fell forward, splitting some twelve feet above the deck. The immense falling spar struck the remaining shrouds for the mainmast, and that too snapped, followed immediately by the foremast; in a matter of a few seconds the junk was reduced to a helpless wreck.

Now the Japanese sailors *were* afraid. Several of them indeed had already been lost overboard. The others were clinging to every handhold they could find while they shouted at each other and prayed to their gods; the helmsman had already abandoned the helplessly spinning wheel. Bereft of any fore and aft stability— like all junks, the *Asa Maru* was virtually flat-bottomed— the vessel fell broadside to the seas, and was driven in that precarious state sideways by the next wave, lee scuppers under water, while tons of foaming green swept the decks.

Ralph saw Ito crawling toward him. "We are lost," the Japanese shouted.

"We're still floating," Ralph shouted back, remembering the occasion his catboat had been almost filled by a big wave, but had yet survived. "We'll have—"

"Lost," Ito shouted again. "Inouye San wishes your presence in the cabin."

"The cabin?" Ralph cried. "But he should be on deck."

"He is the commander of our expedition," Ito explained. "And now he has been defeated by the gods and by the seas and the skies. He knows this, and prepares seppuku. But he asks for you as a witness, Freeman San, as he brought you to this fate."

—3—

THE LORD OF
CHO-SHU

Mind tumbling, Ralph followed Ito below, into the main cabin, where, despite the chaos on deck, everything had been arranged for some kind of ceremony; the other samurai, as well as the captain of the ship, were gathered at one end of the room, desperately trying to keep their balance as the ship lurched and rolled, and creaked and groaned—there was water running down the bulkheads and trickling to and fro across the deck. The girls had apparently been placed in one of the sleeping cabins, for they were not to be seen. And Inouye stood by himself, amazingly stripped to the waist, although he still wore his girdle and both of his swords.

Now he beckoned Ralph forward. "Freeman San," he said, having to shout above the roaring of the storm, "I wish to say good-bye. But you will see me depart this life with honor, as a samurai. Now I must make haste. Shunsuke San . . ."

Ito nodded, and Inouye shook hands with each of the waiting samurai, then walked away from them, turned around, and sat facing them cross-legged on the damp tatami mats. Once seated, he carefully drew his long sword from its girdle and placed it on the deck in front of him. Then he drew the short sword instead, but this one he took from its sheath, and tested the blade.

"I must go to him," Ito said to Ralph. "Do you remain here. And do not move until the ceremony is over."

"But . . ." Ralph's brain seemed unable to grasp what was going on.

69

"The moment he cuts his belly," Ito explained, "and is sure to die, I must strike off his head. That is the duty of a friend." He drew his own great sword, and went forward, standing just behind Inouye, the sword raised, desperately pawing with his bare feet to maintain his footing, while Ralph finally realized that Inouye actually intended to stab himself with his short sword—was that the only reason a short sword was carried?—and that Ito would then behead him.

All because they had been dismasted?

"My God!" he shouted, and sprang forward. "No!"

His arms were seized by two of the samurai, while Inouye raised his head, his expression sad.

"That was ill done, Freeman San," Ito snapped. "It takes much resolution to perform seppuku. To interrupt a man who is so composing himself is a disgraceful act."

"But *why* must he kill himself?" Ralph shouted, attempting to shrug himself free.

This time Inouye himself replied. "I am the commander of this expedition, Freeman San," he explained. "And I have brought us all to a dishonorable death, struck down by the wind and the sea. It is my duty to lead you to honor. Fear not, if you choose, you may follow my way, when I am gone."

"But we're not defeated yet," Ralph bawled at him.

Inouye regarded him with polite interest.

"We can ride this storm," Ralph insisted. "If we just *try*. For God's sake, Inouye San, kill yourself when there *is* no hope. Not now."

"You can save this ship?" Ito demanded.

"I can try," Ralph said. "If you will but help me."

Ito looked at Inouye, who regarded the short sword for a moment longer. "You take my honor into your keeping, Freeman San," Inouye said at last. "If you fail me, I am damned through all eternity."

"Then let's get at it," Ralph shouted, and led the men on deck. Here there was even more chaos than before, with the guns starting to break loose, with huge waves coming on board every minute, with the ship being rolled through a ninety-degree arc, bulkheads smashing, unsecured ropes and halliards flailing—yet, amazingly, the ship was still afloat, so sound had been her construction. It was almost tempting to do nothing and let her wallow like a log until the storm had blown itself out. Except that he doubted any ship could stand up to such buffeting for more than a few hours without opening a seam and going down.

"Get those cannon overboard," he shouted.

They stared at him in dismay.

"They are useless anyway," he insisted. "Cut them loose and let them go."

"Do as he says," Ito commanded.

The ropes holding the guns were severed, and with the next roll they plunged toward the lee gunwale, increasing the list so that Ralph's heart seemed to come into his throat as he thought the ship might go right over; then the bulkhead gave way beneath the huge weight and the guns disappeared into the foaming seas; instantly the *Asa Maru* came upright again, twice as buoyant as before.

"Now, break out some canvas," Ralph said. "And raise it on the foremast."

Once again they gaped at him, and then at the stump of the mast, rising only fifteen feet above the deck.

"That will be sufficient," Ralph said. "And more will be too much."

He made his way aft, followed by Ito and the captain, splashing through water sometimes to their waists, having to hold on all the way, scrambling up the ladder to the poop, and tested the helm. There was still resistance down there; the rudder had not yet been carried away. He gazed at the morning. There was no break in the clouds, which seemed to form a solid mass only a few feet above his head; the lightning continued to flash and the thunder exploded in immediate succession; the rain teemed down, striking the sea with enormous sizzling splashes—and the wind continued to howl as the great waves picked up the helpless ship and hurled her onward. It would take only a couple of those waves to drop on the deck itself to drive them to the bottom, he knew. But so far this had not happened, and now the men forward had at last found a spar and bent on one of their spare sails, a mere postage stamp of a square of canvas, but sufficient, when hoisted by an improvised halliard to the top of the foremast stump, to drag the bows around and downwind.

"Now," he shouted. "The wheel."

The three of them wrestled the helm around as well, and then brought it straight again, and the *Asa Maru* seemed to shake herself and career forward, water streaming from her scuppers. Immediately she smashed into another wave and disappeared into foaming water, but up she came again, held by the storm foresail, and running onward, to the west.

The fore hatch opened, and the watch below came streaming on deck, wailing and shouting.

"Now what's the matter?" Ralph demanded.

"They say there is water below," Ito told him. "We are sinking."

For a moment Ralph's heart almost stopped. But the ship was still buoyant. It could not be that severe a leak. "Tell them to pump," he said. "And keep pumping. We're not going to lose this ship, Ito San." A fierce exultation seized his mind, seemed to redouble his physical strength. "We're going to take her home to Japan."

"You are a man among men," Inouye Bunta said. "There will be a song written about you, Freeman San, and whenever our people go to sea, they will sing it, that they may gain courage to fight the seas and the winds and defeat them."

Ralph found it difficult to believe, himself, that they had come through so violent a storm. He was not even sure how long it had lasted, how long he had clung to the helm, how long the waves had soaked him in company with the rain, how long he had shivered, and how long he had felt his muscles turning into rivers of pain. Nor how long he had slept, when the storm had finally abated.

It was all long ago. Several weeks ago. When he had awakened, it had been a matter first of all of patching the leak—the ship was dangerously low in the water, as the crew had also taken the opportunity to rest rather than man the pumps. Ralph had had to drive them back to work, reaching into the memory of the books he had read for the necessary inspiration, and showing them how to carry another of their spare sails, well coated with tar, over the bows, secured by long warps to either side, to be dragged down the underside of the hull until it covered the split timbers, there to be lashed into place from the deck. Water still seeped in, but it was nothing regular pumping could not cope with.

Then it was a business of creating new spars; they had even torn up lengths of decking itself to erect at least a jury foremast, on which they had been able to set a single sail to draw them onward; had there then come another typhoon, Ralph suspected they would have sunk like a stone. But the weather had once again been fine, with a steady easterly breeze. Now their enemy was time, as they only barely made way, and their food dwindled, and their water supply as well, even if the casks had been replenished to overflowing by the rain. Food, water, and uncertainty of the future were their problems. He found this strange in a people who so trusted to fate and the will of the gods—but yet could understand it. On the voyage to America, they had been in company with several other junks, from the crews of which they had been able to draw mutual strength. Besides, nothing quite so devastating as the typhoon had happened to them. When the wind had blown and the masts had fallen, they had assumed themselves to be lost, and had been prepared to accept this, again as the will of the gods. It was he who had made them fight for life, successfully. Thus it was he who had now taken charge of the ship. It was to him, rather than Ito or Inouye, that the captain came for orders. A state of affairs which appealed to his rather cynical sense of humor; he actually knew less about the sea than any of them, for they had at least made this voyage once before, whereas he had never taken his catboat out of sight of land.

As they would soon discover, he did not doubt. For over the last couple of days the wind had dropped almost to a calm again. At first he had suspected this might mean another storm, but the sky, instead of clouding over, had merely become opaque as they had sailed into the midst of a sea mist which had soon thickened into fog. Now they drifted onward through a gray cloud, unable to see more than a hundred feet in front of the bows, unaware of what might lie within a mile of them to either side. As if anything would lie there. No one had the least idea where they were, save that, when the captain had last seen the sun at noon and taken a sight, he had placed them still on the vital thirty-sixth meridian. But the meridian was some six thousand miles long, measured from San Francisco to the coast of Japan. Where on that immense arc they actually were, no man could say.

But everyone supposed he *knew*. "When will we see our land, Freeman San?" Aya asked. She had even more faith in him than everyone else.

He lacked the courage to confess that he did not know. Over the three months the voyage had so far lasted, she had become almost a wife to him. It was impossible to consider life without Aya ever at his side, bringing him food and drink, attending to his laundry— his shirt and breeches had long since disintegrated, and in their place she had supplied him with a kimono, distinctly too small for his shoulders but sufficient to cover his nakedness—and more than anything else, attending to his every desire, the Japanese way, which meant that she took at least as active a part in lovemaking as he did, and that, while she would accept his every demand, she would make love as *she* preferred as often as possible, sitting in his lap or mounting him when he lay on his back. And did he not prefer such ways as well?

She had quite driven the memory of Rosalee Quentin from his mind. And Alison Gray? But what did he have to remember of the little Scots girl, save that he thought she had waved to him that afternoon before her father had taken the more southerly course—and that he wondered if the *English Rose* had also encountered the typhoon and survived it. But he did not doubt that. To Jonathan Gray a typhoon was all in a day's work.

But Alison, like Rosalee, was a symbol of that past upon which he had so completely turned his back. Aya had to be his future. And like everyone else on board the *Asa Maru*, he knew, she would turn against him when they really began to starve—such was their confidence in his skill as a navigator, a combatant of the elements, they had not even considered rationing themselves, and there was only a week's supply of food left. Because he had come to realize that the Japanese were essentially an impatiently practical people. They worshiped success, not endeavor. And they abhorred failure, regarded it as worthy only of death, no matter how hard the effort to avoid it. Thus he would soon be worthy of death himself.

He leaned on the rail and peered into the fog—always thicker at dawn than any other time, save dusk—and wondered if there *could* be a fate. It did not seem logical that he should have avoided Quentin's bullets, not to mention Comanche arrows, and then the storm, to die of starvation after three months at sea. That was to suppose there was no order in the universe at all, no scheme of things, merely chaos and uncertainty. But what else was he to believe? What else . . . ? He stared down from the poop as the light grew into pale green water. *Green*, where for so many days it had been a deep impenetrable blue.

He ran forward. "Have you a line to sound with?" he demanded; his Japanese was by now quite fluent.

They had no idea what he meant. So he made his own, tied an iron belaying pin to the end, and heaved it over the side. And found bottom. Where the line had cut the water was marked, and then it was brought in and laid out on the deck, and he measured it in spans of his arms, each of which was near enough to a fathom. The Japanese watched with reverent interest.

"Forty feet," he said. "We are in only forty feet of water."

"And yet there is no land," Ito commented, peering into the gloom.

Think, Ralph told himself. Think. The bottom had clearly started to shoal during the night. It could not possibly have risen in only a few hours from the immeasurable depths of the Pacific. Unless they were about to encounter some reef-encircled coral atoll. In which case ... "I wish absolute quiet," he said. "Everyone listen."

"For what, Freeman San?" Inouye inquired.

"For the sound of surf," Ralph told him. Although why should there be surf? The sea was calm. Even the swell had died over the past couple of days. Even the swell.

"I hear noise," Ito said.

Heads turned.

"It is a bell," Ito said. "I hear a bell ringing."

"Then we must anchor," Ralph snapped, and led the men to cut the ropes catting the anchor, and allowed it to plunge into the still green water. "And get down that sail." Not that the sail was making much difference.

The *Asa Maru* slowly glided forward, snubbed the anchor warp, and came to rest, absolutely still. After three months. And as the sun rose, in front of them the mist began to lift, and they saw, looming through the murk, a beach, and then what appeared to be a large gate, two uprights surmounted by an elaborately carved crosspiece, all painted a brilliant vermilion; the crosspiece, Ralph estimated, was a good fifteen feet from the ground.

The sailors gave a great shout and fell to their knees, while Ralph scratched his head. "What does it mean?" he asked Ito, who was also kneeling.

"That is a torii, Freeman San," Ito said. "The gateway to a holy shrine. We are in Japan, Freeman San. You have brought us home, as you said you would."

Japan! They had, after all, arrived. And in a country which continued to amaze. Because, Ralph realized, he had formed no expectation of what it would be like. Perhaps he had never truly expected to get here.

But this was a land which might almost fulfill the biblical concept of flowing milk and honey. The moment the mist arose, they were seen from the shore, and within minutes were surrounded by small boats filled with eager yellow-skinned fishermen and their women, chattering at them, welcoming them, and gazing in wonder at the American who had brought them through the typhoon to safety—as the crew were quick

to relate. Ashore was nothing but green, closely culti-
vated fields of rice, little villages with charming houses
huddled around a pagoda, busy draft animals, and
again, eager, neat, and above all clean and friendly
people. In the interior, to be sure, he could make out
mountains, but they seemed far away from this delightful coastal strip—because it was no more than a strip.
Only a few miles west, the water began again. But this,
Ito told him, was the Inland Sea, a vast saltwater lake
which stretched for some hundred miles and more to
the north, and was central Japan's busiest thoroughfare,
a sea on which they knew how to sail, as they had done
it all of their lives, and a sea upon which the waves
never amounted to more than a few feet, and the
bottom as well as the shore was always close to hand.

They had, apparently—and this redounded even more
to Ralph's credit than their actual arrival—come to
land not in the vicinity of Edo, the Tokugawa capital,
many miles to the north and indeed where the thirty-
sixth parallel crossed the Japanese coastline, and which
might, he gathered, have proved tricky and even
dangerous, as there was no love lost between the men
of Cho-Shu and the men of Edo, and their single-
handed return when the rest of the fleet remained in
America would have been viewed with suspicion. Instead they were in a district known as Bungo, belonging to the Satsuma clan, the dominant lords of the
southernmost of the three islands that composed the
main body of the country, called Kyushu. And the
Satsuma were friends of the lord of Cho-Shu, the great
Nariaka, and therefore prepared to welcome his ship,
with its strange passenger. Indeed, before he would
provide them with a vessel to continue on their journey
toward Shimonoseki, the chief city of the Cho-Shu, the
local hatamoto wished them to travel even farther south,
to the huge inlet known as Kagoshima Wan, or the Bay
of Kagoshima, so that the Lord Shimadzu, leader of
the Satsumas, could himself interview the outsize barbarian who could tame the winds and the sea. Inouye
had to explain that they were in great haste, and that
Lord Nariaka would be angry were they delayed an
instant. The hatamoto hesitated, and then clearly de-

cided it was not his business to cause trouble between the Satsuma and the Cho-Shu. "You have but to tell me your requirements, Inouye San."

"A ship, of course," Inouye said. "As ours lacks masts. But first, a bath."

An odd request to come head of the list, Ralph thought, although in fact the idea of a warm tub was certainly attractive, and he had gathered that the Japanese took personal cleanliness far more seriously than the average American. But he was quite unprepared for the experience he now underwent.

As he was regarded as being of the same rank as Ito and Inouye, he was invited to accompany them to the bathhouse, which he discovered was a large enclosed room, the floor of which was slatted wood, each slat set an inch from the other to make a grating. Beneath the floor, to either side, fires had been lighted to create a steamy effect; at the far end there was a huge deep well of obviously very hot water. It looked so good, and he felt so filthy, that he immediately went toward it, stripping off his kimono, only to be checked by exclamations from his friends. "Truly, you Americans are strange people," Ito commented. "You would enter the water dirty, and contaminate it?"

Ralph scratched his head, as he had assumed the idea *was* to become clean. But now the doors opened again and they were joined by three naked young women, earnestly serious about what they had to do. They undressed the men and poured buckets of cold water over them, and then soaped them very carefully and tenderly—Ito and Inouye immediately began soaping the girls in turn, with the inevitable result, and Ralph decided that he might as well follow the local custom. Decorum and seriousness very rapidly disappeared as they romped and laughed and the girls squealed their pleasure; clearly, Ralph decided, his friends were a trifle hysterical at having come to safety after so long a trial of their strength and resolution, but it was only after they had again been douched in cold water that they were allowed to enter the well, by which time he was in fact cleaner than he supposed he had ever been in his life.

The water in the well was every bit as hot as it had appeared, one of the fires being situated immediately underneath. It seemed to boil him, and yet sent utter relaxation seeping through his system as well, making him realize just how exhausted he was after the long, dangerous weeks at sea. There was a ledge stretching right around the well, midway between the floor and the surface of the water, and on this he and the two Japanese sat, so that they were immersed to their necks, while Ralph discovered that the water was constantly being changed, bubbling up through an inlet in the floor, and then overflowing from the edge of the well across the slats to disappear between them into a gutter below. It was incredibly wasteful of heat and water, and he could well understand why his friends had been unable to obtain anything approaching this in America, but it induced the most delightful feeling he had ever known, an awareness of being alive which approached any man's ideal of heaven when the girls, having washed themselves free of soap, came to join them, sitting on their laps and with gentle fingers and smooth sliding bottoms completing their relaxation.

"I agree," he said. "You must have found us a barbarous people in America."

"There is too much haste and bustle," Inouye said dreamily. "And your women do not know their place. Here there is time for a man to enjoy the more subtle pleasures of life. In America, people always seem so *concerned*."

Well, Ralph thought, what American matron would not be concerned at the thought that her husband was being attended by such delicious houris—who apparently found nothing sinful or even lascivious in their duties, but were intent only on pleasing—whenever he took a bath? Did Japanese wives have no jealousy? Certainly Aya did not, when he finally reached the room he had been allotted in the local inn, and sent for her—to discover that she was also more clean and sweet-smelling than he had ever known her. "And have you, also, been bathed?" he asked.

"I have bathed myself, my lord, to please you," she told him.

"But no others?" he demanded, himself suddenly jealous.

"How could I, my lord?" she asked. "I am but a low creature. I should not be here now, certainly not to sleep beside you. The people are speaking of it."

He pulled her down beside him, suddenly contrite for the way he had spent the afternoon, knowing that it was impossible for him to generate any more passion for several hours. "Let them talk," he said. "You are here because I wish you to be here. I wish you to be here, always."

Her eyes were wide. "My lord is too kind," she said. "But soon, now we are in Japan, my lord will take a wife, and I will be sent to sleep in the yard, with the other honin, where I belong."

"Never," he said. "Take a wife? Why, Aya, have I not already got a wife in you?"

The next morning they commenced the final stage of their journey. The captain and crew of the *Asa Maru* remained with the ship, as the Satsuma men were prepared to supply them with materials and assistance in repairing the battered vessel. The Cho-Shu samurai, with their women and boys, boarded one of the local craft, a half-decked ship which was very suggestive of a Mediterranean galley, although the oars were hardly necessary, as an east wind had sprung up to send them on their way. And a most delightful way it was, too, for the Inland Sea was studded with islands, many of them, so far as Ralph could make out, uninhabited, but all beautifully verdant. The inhabited islands and the coastal areas of Kyushu that they passed were marked by the myriad roofed pagodas, each roof on top of the other, and thus smaller than the one below, to create a pyramid effect, despite the strangely upturned eaves, and all painted the brilliant red which seemed to be a favorite color in this country, while every so often they also saw the looming height of a torii, equally spectacular.

And everywhere was an atmosphere of peace and tranquillity and busy cultivation; women and children came down to the shores to wave at them, and then hurried back to their work in the fields. The sound of their laughter drifted on the breeze. "Truly," Ralph remarked to Inouye, "this land is very much of a paradise."

"Paradise?"

"Well, that is our name for the place men go after they die, supposing they have lived worthwhile lives, where they spend all eternity in peace and contentment."

"Here in the south, the people are happy, and the country is in good order, because of the rule of the Satsuma," Inouye told him. "Happiness depends on the strength and the generosity of one's lord. We are not less happy in the west, in Cho-Shu, because we too have a great and noble lord to rule over us. It is not always so in the north. And if the Tokugawa have their way, it will not be so anywhere in Japan."

"You will have to explain something of Japanese politics to me, Inouye San," Ralph said, "if I am to live with you and work with you. This is not the first time that you have suggested you are unhappy with the Tokugawa shogunate."

Inouye considered for a few seconds, then obviously decided Ralph might as well understand the situation, as they had actually arrived. "Why, Freeman San, as I have told you, the Tokugawa have been shoguns now for more than two centuries, and once they were great and strong. Now they are timid and weak. They have surrendered to the fleet of your Commodore Perry, virtually without a shot being fired, and now would command the entire country to open its ports and accept foreign traders, and foreign goods, and even foreign missionaries. The first of the Tokugawa expelled all foreign missionaries. Those of them," he added darkly, "that they did not execute."

"And you would revert to such barbarity?" Ralph asked in consternation.

"No," Inouye said. "There can be no doubt that in closing our ports and forbidding our people to travel and observe the ways of the world, we also allowed Japan to fall dangerously behind other nations in such things as weapons and industry. Ito and I have seen this with our own eyes, and it is our duty to convince Lord Nariaka that it is so. It is possible that by contact with the barbarians Japan may again grow great. But by refusing to oppose the white men, by meekly surrendering to their demands, Tokugawa Iyemochi has disgraced all samurai everywhere."

"But . . . does this mean you will resist the American traders when they come? Because I must tell you frankly, Inouye San, that I will not create a force of artillery for use against my own countrymen."

Inouye regarded him for several moments, but refrained from pointing out that he might find it very difficult to refuse such an assignment, as he was now in Japan. "We will not oppose the foreigners," he said at last. And smiled. "Principally because we cannot. Ito and I have seen that, too. We must submit until we too have secured the necessary strength to fight with the barbarians, successfully."

"Well, then . . ."

"But that does not absolve the Tokugawa from the charge of having failed in their duty and having brought disgrace upon the honor of Japan."

Ralph scratched his head. "You don't suppose he also knows that he cannot oppose American sea power?" he asked.

"I am sure he does," Inouye agreed. "But you must understand, Freeman San, that it is the duty of a leader not to survive his surrender, however inevitable that surrender may have been."

"By God," Ralph said. "As you would not have survived our defeat by the sea."

"I had a duty," Inouye said. "And this you must learn, Freeman San, if you would be one of us, for it may well come about that *you* will be given a command. Indeed, such is your undoubted prowess, I would say that is certain."

And you'll expect me to kill myself if I lose a battle, Ralph thought grimly. But, he recollected, whom was he supposed to command against? Unless . . . "Are you trying to tell me, Inouye San, that if the shogun does not commit this seppuku, the daimyo may attempt to depose him?"

"Many would consider it their duty," Inouye said enigmatically.

"But . . . would that not mean a civil war?"

"There have been civil wars in Japan before, where it has been considered to the country's benefit." He smiled. "This is why your skill may be of great value to the lord of Cho-Shu."

Well, well, well, Ralph thought. So here I am about to embark upon a civil war, in a totally foreign country. In fact he was not the least disturbed at the prospect. He had spent all his adult life in the pursuit of arms, and indeed had found the duties of a garrison officer in San Francisco extremely tedious, while he was only slowly realizing what a sense of relief he was feeling at having avoided not only Rosalee Quentin's nymphomania but also the deadly burden of spending the rest of his years in the offices of Quentin Incorporated. And although he knew very little of the rights and wrongs of the situation in Japan as outlined by Inouye, and could not help but feel that the daimyo were being a little hard on their prime minister—who had merely accepted a situation which they themselves did not know how to combat—it certainly made no difference to him which side he fought on. He had learned enough about his new friends and employers to understand that only physical success could bring advancement, and he had no doubt that only advancement would ever enable him to return to the United States sufficiently set up to counter any charges the Quentins might bring against him; after the reception he had received from Frémont on his last night in San Francisco, he was not disposed to trust the Pathfinder too far in the future.

The physical success, he thought, would be most easily achieved by force of arms. Nor was he particularly concerned about the prospects of defeat; he certainly had no intention of committing suicide should he lose a battle, no matter whom it might have been against. And if his new friends considered that he had dishonored himself, that was their problem. It only seemed a shame that there might be a possibility this clean and lovely and so prosperous land might suffer the ravages of a war at some time soon. Or would only the samurai take part in the conflict? The common people seemed far too contented to indulge in any such foolishness.

But it was the samurai who ruled the land, and the
common people who did as they were told, and suffered for any disobedience. By noon on the second day
since leaving Bungo they had beached the galleys, and
horses were waiting to take them over the road to
Shimonoseki—but mounts were provided only for the
samurai; the rest of their party, including the girls and
Aya, had to walk. Ralph would have remonstrated, and
offered her a seat behind him, but she begged him not
to insist upon it. "You have your own way to make, my
lord," she said. "And remember, you go to meet *your*
lord, the mighty Nariaka. All of your future depends
upon the next twenty-four hours; it would be foolish to
lessen your chances of success by flouting Japanese
customs."

She was a girl considerably older than her years or
her station suggested possible, and as such was clearly
capable of maintaining a station in life much higher
than any yet offered to her. Or ever could be offered
to her? That at the least he was determined to change,
whether this Nariaka liked it or not. But for the moment,
he could understand that the first essential for both
their sakes was to create a good impression on the lord.
So he mounted and rode off with Ito and Inouye, who
had waited with patient resignation for him to cease
acting the American.

They crossed a low range of hills, and again looked
down on the sea, to the west, indeed, what appeared to
be a new ocean, while to the south, and dominated by
the castle which stood on the very edge of the shore,
was a narrow strait from which the Inland Sea de-
bouched into the greater body of water. "Why did we
not sail into the harbor down there, if that is our
destination?" Ralph asked. "Instead of landing on the
other side of the peninsula?"

"No ship not flying the flag of Cho-Shu may enter
the harbor of Shimonoseki, or indeed pass through the
strait that bears our name, without paying tribute," Ito
explained. "We would not inflict such a charge upon
those good fellows from Bungo."

"But . . . as they were bringing you home, would
they not have been exempt?"

"No one is exempt," Inouye told him. "That is the law of our lord Nariaka. Control of the Strait of Shimonoseki is the source of his power and his wealth."

Ralph studied the strait again; it would take careful navigation, he decided—the water raced through at considerable speed. And certainly it was completely dominated by the fort which lay on the seaward side of the city beneath them—because it was a city, he could tell at a glance, a teeming metropolis of busy streets and close-crowded houses and shops and towering pagodas. But his interest was entirely taken by the fort, for he had no doubt that that was his destination. From a distance it was impossible to make out any cannon, but obviously there would be cannon. Yet it was the architecture which for the moment concerned him more; the walls, some of which rose sheer from the sea, were composed of huge blocks of stone; he could not make out any facing or even mortar which might have been used to cement the blocks together, and yet there could be no doubt of their solidity. Rising above the battlements was what appeared to be a palace rather than a barracks or a keep, a huge wooden building, dominated by the pagoda roofs, mounting some eight stories to a small watchtower which must have a horizon, he estimated, of some fifty miles on a clear day, and from which a mass of multicolored flags fluttered in the breeze.

Inouye was observing his interest with pleasure. "That is the citadel of Lord Nariaka," he said. "And will be your home from now on, Freeman San."

Ralph pointed at the land on the other side of the strait, hardly two miles away. "What country is that?"

"That is also Kyushu, which we left yesterday," Ito explained. "We have sailed along its northern coast."

"And that sea beyond the strait?"

"To the north is the Sea of Japan, but you are actually looking at the Strait of Tsushima, which separates our country from Korea. The Chinese call it the Strait of Korea, but they are wrong. It is the Strait of Tsushima, from the island of Tsushima in the middle of it. Sometimes you can see the island from the fort."

"And this island of Tsushima which gives the strait

its name, it belongs to Japan, of course," Ralph suggested somewhat sarcastically; it was difficult not to be amused by the jingoist nationalism of these people.

"Of course," Inouye agreed, without taking offense. "South of the strait, to the west there, is the Yellow Sea."

"And then China?"

"That is so." Some of the complacency left Inouye's face, and Ralph recalled from his history books that the Chinese and the Japanese had always been hereditary enemies.

"Do the Chinese, then, trade with you?" he asked.

"No foreign vessel is permitted to pass the Strait of Shimonoseki," Ito told him. "No foreign vessel is permitted to sail upon the Inland Sea."

"But if no foreign vessel ever passes through the strait, then . . . do you mean that your lord collects his tribute entirely from other Japanese?"

"If they would pass into the western seas, or from the western seas into the Inland Sea," Inouye said, "then they must pay tribute to the lord of Cho-Shu. This is the law of the land, and has been the law of the land since time began. Now, come, Freeman San, let us go to the castle."

They walked their horses down the slope and into the streets of the city. Now, to Ralph's surprise, two of the samurai dismounted and proceeded in front of them on foot. They did not draw their swords, but still paraded, taking great strides, to left and right as well as immediately in front, so that they constantly moved from side to side of the street, glaring at everyone they encountered, and at the same time making hissing noises through their nostrils. They actually presented a ludicrous sight, to Ralph's American eyes, but there could be no doubt about the terrifying effect they were having on the Japanese. Ito and Inouye were obviously well known to the local inhabitants, as well as the fact that they had departed across the great ocean to the east, and had therefore returned from faraway lands. People hurried from their houses and shops to line the street, making an attractive picture with their many-colored kimonos and the equally bright parasols which

the women used to repel the rays of the afternoon sun—
but no one ventured too close, afraid to risk an encounter with the two warriors.

"Would your people actually harm someone who
crowded you?" Ralph asked.

"They would cut him down, or her, without hesitation,"
Inouye said.

"But . . . these are your own people," Ralph protested.
"You live in their midst."

"Yet they are not samurai. In Japan, as I have told
you, Freeman San, it is necessary to know one's place at
all times."

They approached the entrance to the castle, a mas-
sive wooden gateway set into the stone walls and reached
by a wooden drawbridge across a wide moat of stag-
nant salt water, used, Ralph decided, as a sewer. But
inside the castle the air was clean, although again he
was astonished by the size of the garrison, for he estimated not less than five hundred soldiers were assembled to greet them, wearing the quaint armor he had
been shown on board the *Asa Maru,* and to be sure
armed only with bows and arrows, spears and swords,
but obviously highly disciplined troops. In this outer
courtyard they dismounted, to walk across another drawbridge into an inner courtyard, in which the palace
itself was erected. Here they were gravely greeted by
several older samurai, men who cast interested glances
at Ralph, and then Inouye was hurried away, while Ito
indicated that they should wait in the shade of the
veranda on the lowest level, squatting on the floor, as
usual, and surrounded by warriors who asked a great
number of questions, none of which Ito was disposed
to answer until he and Ralph had had an audience with
the lord. But most of their interest continued to be
centered on Ralph himself, presumably on account of
his size, he thought; he doubted any of them understood the significance of the holstered revolver which
hung from his belt, so incongruous when worn over
the kimono. He also presumed it was safest for him to
pretend to no knowledge of Japanese until he was sure
of a welcome here.

"How long must we wait?" he asked Ito, speaking English.

"Until Lord Nariaka sends for us," Ito said. "It is the hour of the day when he transacts business and punishes transgressors. But it will not be long once Inouye San has told him of our adventures, and of you. Perhaps this is the messenger now."

He stood up, as did Ralph, for there was a crowd of people approaching, making a great deal of noise. But it was not a happy crowd. One of the men, indeed, was being driven by the others, who rained blows on his head and shoulders, while shouting curses at him, wishing him and his family eternal damnation, and as the men were followed by several women and children, all wailing most piteously, Ralph was forced to suppose that they were the family in question.

Now the crowd reached the steps close by where Ito and Ralph were standing, and the man was again pushed, to go stumbling forward, miss his footing, and roll down the steps to land on the earth below. The samurai followed, laughing and jeering now, and one placed his foot upon the fallen man's back, at the same time drawing his long sword with his right hand, and with his left seizing the topknot of the helpless man. Ralph supposed he was about to witness an execution, and instinctively started forward. But the huge blade was already slicing the air, and the topknot too, close to the scalp but not even bruising the skin.

The women gave an even louder shriek of misery as the severed hair was thrown into the dust, while another samurai broke both the prisoner's swords across his knee. Then their victim was dragged by his ankles through the dust to where a long pole lay on the ground. To this pole the samurai tied the unfortunate man's wrists and feet, from behind, so that he hung, belly downward, and when the pole was lifted, his stomach and face were constantly being dragged over the earth, to his obvious discomfort. Yet he made no sound as he was carried toward the drawbridge—unlike his family, who followed behind, setting up an even louder din.

"What in the name of God can be his crime?" Ralph asked.

"That matters nothing, now," Ito said. "He is being punished for not committing seppuku when commanded to do so by Lord Nariaka."

"You mean your lord has the power to command his people to kill themselves?" Ralph cried.

"Of course, if they have disgraced themselves."

"And that fellow has refused? What will happen to him now?"

"He is being cast out, and his family with him. They are the true sufferers. By committing seppuku when it is necessary, you see, Freeman San, a man assumes the entire burden of his guilt or his failure upon his own shoulders; his family, his property, is left inviolate. But once he has refused to die with honor, why, his family is also dishonored, and all their goods are taken away from them. A samurai without honor is lower even than the eta, who bury the dead. But come. Do not waste your sentiments upon such as he. Here is the messenger from Inouye San. Lord Nariaka awaits you."

—4—
THE GIRL

Feeling vaguely sick, Ralph climbed the steps, Ito at his side, four samurai walking behind them. On the next level they entered the palace itself, finding themselves in a lofty hallway paneled with dark-stained wood, where there were several more samurai waiting. Another flight of stairs led up into a smaller antechamber, and here they found Inouye waiting for them.

"Lord Nariaka commands your presence," Inouye told Ralph. "Now, Freeman San, it is very important that you do exactly as I do, that you do not speak unless spoken to, and that you do not differ with Lord Nariaka on any point. I have explained all about you; he but seeks confirmation of what I have told him. Do you understand me?"

"I think so," Ralph agreed, the sickness now overlaid with apprehension; sycophancy and humility were not arts he had ever practiced, even with commanding generals.

"Then let us go in," Inouye said, and nodded to the two armed samurai who stood in front of the doorway. This was immediately thrown open, and Inouye entered a similar dark chamber, devoid of all furniture, as usual, at least as far as Ralph could see from a very quick glance, because he was given no time for a closer inspection, because Inouye, once within the door, dropped to his knees and then placed his hands on the floor in front of him, slowly inclining his body forward until his forehead touched the mat. "Do it," he whispered urgently in English, as Ralph hesitated.

It seemed an absurd humiliation, but he reflected that he was really here as a supplicant, and so he followed his friend's example, performing the kowtow, still attempting to see just whom he was bowing to, for the room was absolutely empty in front of him; behind him, to be sure, there were several elderly men seated cross-legged on the tatami mats, neither moving nor speaking. But the lord of Cho-Shu would hardly be among those. Ito had remained outside.

"Let the barbarian come forward, Inouye Bunta," said a quiet voice in Japanese. "Do you accompany him."

Inouye immediately drew his long sword and placed it on the floor beside him, gesturing Ralph to do the same with his saber. The Japanese retained his short sword, and Ralph understood that he was not to discard his revolver. But now, to his dismay, Inouye advanced, still on his hands and knees, crawling over the mats. Once again Ralph's pride rebelled against such an absurd performance, especially when watched by the men seated behind him. But it was equally absurd not to act the part now, having come so far. So he crawled behind Inouye, and discovered that the room was actually a vast L in shape and that Lord Nariaka was seated around the corner, where he could hear what was going on in the rest of the room, but could not be seen except by those he had summoned forward.

Now once again Inouye performed the kowtow, and again Ralph copied him. He could see, despite the gloom, that the tatami mats ended a few feet away and that the center of this floor was bare dark-stained wood surrounding a dais reached by two steps. On this dais, sitting cross-legged on presumably a cushion or a mat— there were no chairs in the room—was a man. He wore a richly embroidered kimono and carried both swords in his girdle, and of course wore also the topknot of the samurai class to which he belonged. And undoubtedly he was complete lord of this castle and all who lived in it, as well as the city and the surrounding countryside. Yet Ralph was conscious of disappointment. Again, he was not sure *what* he had expected, or if he had consciously expected anything at all, but he had supposed he would be aware of majesty, of an aura of command and omnipotence, and of a man who would reveal these assets in his features.

Lord Nariaka of Cho-Shu was thin-faced and surprisingly long-nosed for a Japanese. He was also quite old, Ralph estimated; he wore a beard and mustache, both long and straggling, and streaked with gray. He sniffed constantly, as if he had a cold, and his mouth turned down, accentuated by the mustache, to suggest the pessimist.

The best thing about him was his voice, which was quiet and composed and certainly did not lack the confidence which went with his position. "Let the barbarian stand," he said.

Ralph pushed himself to his knees and thence his feet, and stood to attention, while Nariaka gazed at him. At last he asked, "Are all barbarians of a size with this man?"

"A goodly number, Lord Nariaka," Ralph replied, before realizing that the question had actually been addressed to Inouye. Nariaka's head turned sharply, and Inouye began to tremble.

"And as ill-mannered?" Nariaka inquired softly.

"We are a direct people, my lord," Ralph said, reckoning the only way he was going to extricate himself from this mess was by boldness.

"You are barbarians," Nariaka said, "who seek to impose your will upon the empire of the mikado with your guns and your ships. You know of this?"

"I have heard of it, my lord," Ralph said cautiously.

"And have you also heard how others have tried to impose their will upon the empire of the mikado? Have you heard of Kublai Khan?"

"I have, my lord."

"He tried to invade us," Nariaka said. "And failed."

"His fleet was destroyed by a great storm," Ralph agreed. "But that was many years ago, my lord. Many centuries. And he did not possess guns such as are now used by the men in the ships."

Now Inouye was positively shaking, while Nariaka continued to study Ralph. "And you will give us guns to match those of your countrymen?" he asked after a brief interval.

"I cannot *give* you guns, Lord Nariaka. I can tell you which are the best guns for you to purchase, and I can teach your people how to use them. But I will not do so for use against my own people."

Inouye sighed, and his head bowed. But Nariaka almost smiled. "I think you are a man who speaks the truth," he said. "No man who speaks the truth can altogether be a barbarian. Inouye San also tells me you know of ships."

"A little, my lord," Ralph said.

"False modesty," Nariaka pointed out, "is just as great a lie as boasting. Show me this marvelous weapon of yours."

Ralph unclipped his holster, drew the revolver, and offered it, holding it by the barrel. But Nariaka merely stared at him, so he went forward, stepped onto the dais, and placed it on the floor beside the lord, who picked it up and looked at it.

"I am told it makes a great deal of noise. Is this so?"

"A great deal, my lord."

Nariaka put down the revolver again. "Then you must show it to my generals. Outside." Once again he almost smiled. "I would know of these barbarians of your nation. I would talk with you again. But I also wish you to teach my army of these guns. Ask, and you shall receive. You will commence these duties immediately. But it is necessary that you have the commensurate rank to command my samurai. Inouye San, you will attend to this matter. The barbarian will also need a wife. . . ."

"I beg your pardon, Lord Nariaka," Ralph said. "But I am well satisfied with the woman I possess. I would take *her* to wife."

Nariaka glanced at Inouye, whose teeth were chattering at this latest interruption. It took him several seconds before he could speak. "It is the honin Aya, of whom I spoke to you, my lord," he said.

Nariaka gazed at Ralph. "You have much to learn about our ways, barbarian. It becomes you to do so as rapidly as possible. You must learn to be a samurai, and you must prove yourself worthy of that honor. When that is done, come and speak with me again. By then you will have learned to do so as a Japanese instead of as a barbarian, and you may please me."

* * *

"Yet I meant what I said," Ralph told Inouye when they had left the audience chamber. "I will not fire upon my own people, and I will take Aya to wife."

"You are a remarkably wayward fellow," Inouye pointed out. "And I may add that you have been a most remarkably fortunate fellow, in that Lord Nariaka did not have you beheaded there and then for your insolence. You must remember at all times that Lord Nariaka is a blood relative of the mikado, as are all daimyo, and is as far above you as is the sun above the earth. To argue with him is sacrilege."

"Yet I still think he is a man," Ralph said.

"A man with power of life and death over all who serve him. I repeat, you have been fortunate. It may well be that you will continue to be fortunate. No American vessel has ever been seen off Shimonoseki, and perhaps such a sight will *never* be seen. As I told you, Lord Nariaka's quarrel is with the shogun rather than the barbarians themselves. As for the girl, enjoy her as you choose. But seek no final answers until you have learned more of us and our ways. Is that too much to ask?" He smiled, and rested his hand on Ralph's arm. "It is my life also at stake, Freeman San. As I introduced you to Lord Nariaka, so will I certainly die beside you should he grow weary of your insolence. And I can at least claim to have saved your life in America, as you saved mine in the storm."

"Inouye," Ralph cried, seizing both his hands, "you are right, and I am a wayward fellow. I would not harm you for all the world."

"Then I am greatly relieved, as will be Ito. Now, come, I would have you meet my family."

A samurai, especially a hatamoto, was apparently allowed to maintain a house in the city itself, and to this Inouye now took Ralph, once again to introduce him into surroundings more beautiful than any he had known in America. Here was a spacious and extraordinarily lush garden, a place of rushing streams and curving bamboo bridges and damp arbors, in the center of which was the house, a tiny cottage, with walls hardly thicker than paper, screens instead of doors, and as

usual a complete absence of furniture, save for the
tatami mats which covered the floor and for exquisitely
arranged vases of flowers in every corner. Clearly, Ralph
understood, where people lived as simply as did the
Japanese, and one chamber served for both day living
as well as sleeping, a great number of rooms—as in a
European or American house—was unnecessary. But
he could not help but ask Inouye about the flimsy
construction.

"Why build more strongly," Inouye asked, "when at
any moment there may come an earthquake to knock it
down? In Japan, at any rate, when the earth shakes,
people are not killed by falling masonry."

"But that fortress," Ralph said. "I should think that
would withstand an earthquake."

"It is built to do so, Freeman San. It is the ancestral
home of Lord Nariaka. But we humble folk must make
do with what we can, and believe me, Freeman San, it is
far better to build again when the earthquake or the
typhoon has passed by than to attempt to resist the
angry gods. Only princes may do that."

"I am sure you are right," Ralph agreed, determined
to suppress his own feelings on the matter in the interests of politeness. "But I have to tell you that if your
lord ever has to contend with warships from the great
powers, that castle of his will be destroyed."

"How can the castle of Cho-Shu be destroyed? It has
stood a thousand years."

"Don't remind me, it was here when Kublai Khan's
Mongols tried to invade. But they didn't possess explosive shells or incendiaries. Those stone walls may just
withstand a modern bombardment, but that wooden
palace will be a death trap."

"That cannot be so," Inouye declared flatly. "And it
would be best for you not to make such rash statements
to your superiors. Now, come and meet my family."
Which turned out to consist of a charming lady, of an
age with her husband—which Ralph estimated to be in
their middle thirties—and three children: a boy who
was already a samurai, although still a teenager, with at
once the shaved skull, the topknot, and the hissing
nostrils, who clearly did not approve of the lavish praise

his father heaped upon the barbarian; and two younger girls, all dimpled smiles and neat little bows, and the snowiest white of both kimonos and socks. Their flawless bone structure suggested that their mother might be equally pretty, but to his disappointment Mrs. Inouye had covered her face with such a thick coat of white paint, and delineated her lips with such a wide and bright gash of red, that it was impossible to decide what she actually looked like, while when she smiled, he was equally disgusted to see that her teeth had been painted black. He made no comment, of course, but could not help but reflect on Aya's unadorned beauty and simplicity. Was this what Nariaka, and Inouye himself, would have him change for?

Clearly it was going to be a long and hard struggle to maintain his own point of view, the more so as he discovered, on his return to the palace, that Aya would have to sleep in the yard with the other honin. "It is unthinkable that such a low creature should sleep in Lord Nariaka's house," Ito said. "That is reserved only for the lord's family and his unmarried samurai."

"Then I shall sleep in the yard with her," Ralph declared. "I am not yet a samurai. In fact, after what I saw this afternoon, I'm not sure I have any desire to *become* a samurai."

"I beg of you, Freeman San, do nothing so foolish. You will bring disgrace upon yourself, and upon Inouye and myself as well, and you will not help the girl in any way. In attempting to change her station, which *she* knows is unchangeable, you merely confuse her, and cost her the friendship of those who share her lot. Enjoy her during the day, as you wish. If you require a woman for the night, let me take you to a geisha." He gave one of his sly smiles. "Or perhaps, as you are now in Japan, you would prefer to sample a boy? They are truly far better company than any woman."

Ralph knew that his friend was right in the substance of his advice. Certainly he could do nothing for Aya until he had firmly established himself here in Shimonoseki. "I'll use the nights for sleeping, if you don't mind, Ito San," he said. "I am impatient to get to work."

* * *

The next morning he was introduced to the commander of Nariaka's army, Katsura Tadatune, a little man with a grizzled countenance and a skeptical eye, like Inouye's son and most of the samurai, Ralph suspected, prepared to dislike on sight the man from across the seas who was supposed to teach him a fresh aspect of an art he had practiced all his life. He wore full armor, and surveyed Ralph with gloomy concern. "I will set our armorers to work," he said. "They have never made a breastplate that big."

"Then do not trouble them," Ralph said. "A helmet will be sufficient."

"A helmet? A helmet will not keep out a sword thrust, barbarian."

"Sword thrusts are things of the past, Lord Katsura," Ralph pointed out.

Katsura looked more skeptical than ever, although from his smile when he inspected Ralph's saber he was apparently prepared to believe that of Americans—but he was certainly impressed at once with the Colt revolver and with Ralph's accuracy. He was deeply thoughtful as he took his guest first of all to inspect the garrison, which, as Ralph had gathered the previous day, were a fine-looking body of men. "But they have no firearms at all?" he asked.

"Not the garrison," Katsura told him. "Lord Nariaka forbids their use within the palace. He dislikes the noise. We have firearms in the army itself."

"I should like to inspect these," Ralph said.

Katsura was happy to oblige, and took Ralph down to the main barracks in the town. Here there were another two thousand samurai readily available as a fighting force. They formed, in fact, a militia, as they did not live in the barracks, except as they chose, but were always on call should their lord require them. And they were undoubtedly far more highly disciplined and cohesive a fighting force than any Western militia. But again they were principally armed with the bow and the sword; such firearms as they possessed were only smooth-bore muskets. There was not a rifled barrel to be seen.

Nor were the cannon which lined the castle wall of

any more modern vintage, being in the main nine-pounders such as might have been used by the British at Waterloo, with a maximum elevated range of just over a mile and an accurate range of a quarter that distance. Ralph supposed they were sufficient to make any attempt to force the Strait of Shimonoseki itself a fairly hazardous business, but they would be quite useless were it ever to come to a conflict with an enemy fleet prepared to sit out at sea and bombard the fortress. "These will not do at all," he told Katsura. "We must have a battery of larger and more modern guns."

"These guns have commanded this strait for fifty years," Katsura declared.

"That, I can tell," Ralph agreed. "It is the next fifty years we are concerned with."

At the same time, he was aware of very mixed feelings regarding what he should recommend. On the one hand, he certainly wished to be on the winning side should the civil war for which everyone was preparing actually start; these nine-pounders, presuming proper carriages could be made for them, and with properly trained gunners—what would he not give for his San Francisco battery?—were sufficient to blast their way through any army which was equipped in a similarly antiquated fashion. All that was really needed to support them was sufficient modern rifles to arm a regiment of foot soldiers—supposing he could ever persuade the samurai to regard their swords as only a second line of defense. He also felt he owed these people a considerable debt of gratitude for having taken him in so generously—whatever their actual feelings toward him—and certainly he would be failing in his duty did he not make some attempt to improve the defenses of the castle. If, as seemed certain, Nariaka had no intention of changing his palace or his political allegiance, then the only defense would have to be guns powerful enough to keep an attacking fleet at maximum range. The trouble was, he couldn't be sure that such an enemy fleet might not one day be flying the Stars and Stripes.

But there was even more to be considered. When Aya left him that evening—and as Ito had prophesied, she seemed perfectly happy with the arrangement, by which she came to his quarters in the palace at dawn to see to his requirements, and remained there throughout the day, washing and cooking, before departing at dusk—he lay on his back on the floor bed and did some serious thinking. Because he was realizing that the problem was not merely how to discharge his debt to Ito and Inouye, and thus to the lord of Cho-Shu himself, without at the same time risking acting the traitor to a possible American fleet in the future, it was also how to come to terms with his new surroundings. For it had taken him just twenty-four hours to understand that there was as much that was repulsive about the Japanese way of life as there was attractive. He had had thoughts like that on board ship, and had not taken them seriously. He had reflected that he was dealing with a different culture, and he had no doubt that the Japanese found many aspects of American life equally repulsive. He had assumed then that because he was not one of them, and was going to be in their country for a limited period, he could remain on the sidelines, so to speak, playing the part of a mentor, enjoying those things which appealed to him and rejecting those which did not.

He was now finding out that this was not possible. If he was going to remain in Japan, it was apparently necessary for him to become a samurai, otherwise he had hardly any rights to existence. Even that had appeared as vaguely attractive on board the ship; the samurai had merely seemed to be the extreme examples of the rulers of a man's world. But now he knew that he could not become a samurai and remain on the sidelines. He had scornfully reflected that no one was ever going to make *him* commit suicide. But was not the alternative, to be expelled with ignominy, far worse? It was in fact far worse even than being drummed out of the United States Army as a coward or a traitor, for then at least one's ability to earn a living was not taken away, and the United States was a vast country where it was always possible to make a fresh start somewhere. But as samurai could only *be* soldiers and retainers of their lords . . . And that ultimate degradation was not

the half of it. As a samurai he would be expected to act
the bully at all times, when with anyone of inferior
rank, while at the same time kowtowing with humiliating subservience to any superiors. How they reconciled
such double standards with their absurd pride was a
mystery to him. But then, it was a mystery to him why
the rest of Japanese society—so delighting in neatness
and beauty and manners—put up with such an archaic
and unjust system, and even appeared to prosper and
be happy beneath its yoke, and how men like Inouye
and Ito, intelligent and broad-minded in non-Japanese
matters, good-humored and even jolly on occasion, and
certainly highly civilized, could allow themselves to be
so dominated by the will of one man that they would
even kill themselves at his command—and all because
of his hereditary position rather than any talent or
personality of his own.

Certainly he could never be happy here. He doubted
he could even remain here a year without offending
someone mortally—as he had already so nearly done,
apparently. In which case he had made the most ghastly
mistake in coming here at all.

But a mistake, he thought, which could be rectified,
and in such a way as to salve his conscience—and provide him with a means of escape, and reacceptance into
that American society from which he had so rashly
fled. He would leave the decision as to whether or not
to sell guns to Nariaka up to Washington. And at the
same time he would report to the State Department on
just what was happening in Japan—for Nariaka could
not be unique—how the daimyo were all arming themselves as feverishly as possible, ostensibly to overthrow
the shogunate, but obviously, as their quarrel with the
Tokugawa was over the opening of Japan to foreign
infiltration, with the ultimate intention of opposing the
foreigners themselves. He thought that might be sufficient to have him reinstated in the army he had been
such a fool to abandon, especially when the true facts
of the fracas in San Francisco were known.

His decision taken, he could hardly wait again to be
summoned to Nariaka's presence, which in fact occurred before he had been a week in Shimonoseki.

*   *   *

This time he was accompanied by Katsura as well as by Inouye; to his surprise, even the commanding general was required to perform the kowtow.

"You have decided what it is we require to give us superiority over all other forces in Japan?" inquired Nariaka.

"I have, my lord," Ralph said in Japanese.

"Well?" demanded the lord of Cho-Shu.

"You need to raise a regiment of riflemen, my lord," Ralph said. "That is, samurai armed not with muskets, smooth-bored and with a range of a hundred yards, but with rifled weapons which will strike an enemy down at half a mile distance and more."

Katsura snorted in disbelief.

"How may a man see what he is aiming at, at half a mile?" Nariaka asked.

"It is possible, my lord, with training and practice," Ralph told him. "And a rifle has the added advantage that a man may fire from a concealed position, and thus stand a better chance of surviving any return of shot."

"Great Lord Nariaka," Katsura said. "Even if such weapons exist, which I doubt, is that an honorable way of warfare? Shooting men with muskets is bad enough, but there at least a warrior looks upon the face of the man he kills, as samurai have always done. To shoot a man down from half a mile distance, and from under cover, that surely cannot be pleasing to the gods."

"I have observed, Katsura Tadatune," Nariaka remarked, "that the gods have a habit of favoring the side with the most deadly weapons. Do these weapons of which you speak truly exist, barbarian?"

"The army from which I came to you, Lord Nariaka, is armed with them," Ralph said.

"I see. And what of cannon? Have you cannon to match such rifles?"

"Indeed, my lord. There is a man called Captain Dahlgren, of the United States Navy, who has invented a cannon which will throw a nine-inch shell, that is, a missile nine inches in diameter, packed with explosive, and shaped into a point, so that it will penetrate thick wood and even iron, and then burst, raining iron splinters all around it. It has a range of two and a half miles; there is no greater weapon in the world today; such guns, mounted on your walls, would restrain any fleet from approaching close enough even to hit your fortress."

"Bah," Katsura said. "If they cannot hit us, how can we hit them?"

"And these guns are also available in America?" Nariaka asked.

"The rifles may be freely purchased, my lord," Ralph told him. "The Dahlgren guns are being made only for the United States Navy. It will be necessary for you to send an embassy to Washington to inquire if it would be possible to purchase them."

"Washington?"

"It is the Edo of the Americans, my lord," Inouye explained. "A great distance away."

"What is distance?" Nariaka inquired. "You will prepare to leave immediately."

"Me?" Inouye cried, quite forgetting his respect.

"You do not wish to go?" Nariaka asked quietly.

"My only wish is to serve you, my lord," Inouye said, hastily regaining control of himself. "But I have only just returned after a year's absence. And Washington is farther away than San Francisco. Nevertheless, if this is your command . . ."

"This is my command," Nariaka said. "You may take Ito Shunsuke with you again, as your last joint venture was so successful."

Ralph's heart was pounding fit to burst. He was dreadfully sorry that Inouye was again being separated from his family after such a brief reunion, but he could have asked for no better companions to accompany him. "I am also ready to undertake such a journey for you, Lord Nariaka," he said. "I am known in Washington, and even more important, I know exactly what guns we require."

Nariaka gazed at him for several seconds. Then he said, "I think not, barbarian."

"But, my lord, without my knowledge to guide him, Inouye San might make a mistake."

Nariaka gave a thin smile. "My emissaries do not make mistakes, barbarian, if they wish to keep their heads. You will write down what it is Inouye Bunta must seek, and he will obtain it. But you have too much to do here, training my soldiers to use these weapons. And learning to become one of us, Freeman San. This is your task now."

Ralph realized that Nariaka was probably somewhat more intelligent than he looked, an understanding which was accompanied by a mood of black despair as he realized that he was virtually being made a prisoner in Shimonoseki, followed by an urge to stow away when his friends left. But a brief reflection convinced him of the folly of that. Ito and Inouye might like him, but they feared and respected Nariaka more; they would certainly put back rather than risk offending their lord. And in any event, stowing away, he would be unable to take Aya, and he could not contemplate leaving her behind—he had seen enough of Nariaka to know that the lord would avenge himself on anyone even re- motely connected with his fled barbarian. No, he told himself, that plan must be discarded; it was a little too transparent. He must simply lay his plans more care- fully in the future.

But now he was faced with the sad task of saying good-bye to his friends. "Believe me, Inouye San," he said, "I had no idea the lord would send you away so soon. I but sought to do my best for Cho-Shu."

Inouye embraced him. "Then you have nothing with which to reproach yourself, Freeman San," he said. "Always endeavor to do your best for Cho-Shu, and for Lord Nariaka, and your future prosperity is assured. Be certain that we will return, and with the guns you need. Until then, you must make the best of what you find here. But we know you will do that."

A homily which left Ralph feeling thoroughly ashamed of his attempted deceit. Whatever the mental blocks which lay across their brains, and which they seemed content to endure, there *was* something noble in their complete dedication to honor, to truthfulness, to their fellow samurai, and to their lord. Which but made him

miss them the more; none of the other samurai seemed
as willing to regard him as anything more than an
upstart barbarian. He endeavored to throw himself heart
and soul into the reconstruction of the army along
Western lines, and encountered nothing but brick walls
wherever he turned. The samurai were willing enough
to carry their muskets, but had no intention either of
drilling and accepting the discipline of volley fire or of
using them at the beginning of a battle. Firearms were
apparently only to be used for destroying those enemies who had already lost their courage and therefore
their honor and were running away; the concept of a
body of men trained to use musketry to *induce* such a
disaster in the enemy ranks, and then to follow the
advantage thus gained with a sword charge, was regarded as dishonorable. Nor were they inclined to waste
their time even in practicing to achieve such limited
accuracy as was possible with their smooth-bore weapons.
One fired a musket, and if the ball struck home, then
clearly the gods were punishing a coward. If the ball
missed, then no doubt the man did not deserve to die
in so dishonorable a fashion.

An even bigger problem was presented by the cannon.
Here the samurai were quite willing to learn; even they
could understand that they could not fight ships with
their swords. But Lord Nariaka would not permit the
guns to be fired in practice; the noise of the explosions
apparently upset his delicately balanced health. On the
other hand, he would not permit any of the cannon to
be removed from the walls and mounted on carriages
for transportation to a distance from whence he could
not hear them, or for composing a force of field artillery.
"The guns are to defend the castle," he insisted. "When
the new guns come, if they are as good as you say,
Freeman San, *then* you may have some of these."

Ralph had to resort to practicing loading with empty
cartridge cases. He flattered himself that within a very
short space of time he had trained his gunners to be
very fast—but there was absolutely no way he could
train them to be accurate, since he was not allowed to
use a single live charge.

These frustrations were accompanied by the equally

galling experience of his own training as a samurai. His schooling was entrusted to a warrior named Munetake, chosen by Katsura obviously because he was larger than the average Japanese, was in fact only an inch or two shorter than Ralph himself, and was also regarded as a master swordsman among even the sword-worshiping samurai. Munetake regarded Ralph as skeptically as did everyone else in Shimonoseki, and seemed less interested in teaching him how to handle a sword than in constantly displaying to him his ineptitude. Certainly there was a great deal that was strange to be learned about Japanese swordplay. In a sense it was easier for Ralph than it might have been for an infantry officer, in that the long sword was essentially a cutting weapon, somewhat like a cavalry saber; there was no question of thrust and riposte. But there the resemblance ended. The long hilt of the Japanese sword called for both hands, and the art consisted of delivering blows of tremendous power combined with a quite startling physical dexterity. Ralph was amazed at the way Munetake, advancing with his blade held directly in front of him, the haft immediately before his belly, would suddenly be galvanized into action, perform not one but two gigantic sweeps to describe a perfect figure eight, each sweep certainly powerful enough to cut through any flesh or bone that might be opposed to it, but yet treating the double delivery as merely a part of his maneuver, which involved leaping through the air to arrive at a position a good eight feet from where he was standing, turning and presenting his weapon, as perfectly balanced as before the whole play began, and scarcely breathing the harder for his exertions. To smile, as Ralph attempted to follow his example, with a total lack of success. He could perform the figure eight, but considerably slower than the Japanese. Nor could he leap as far or as quickly, and when he turned, it took him too long to regain his balance.

"You are a dead man, Freeman San," Munetake commented. "Now, let us do it again."

And again, and again, and again, with progress, if there was any, painfully slow.

Munetake also delighted in teaching him the exact

performance of seppuku. "For this," he explained, "is just as important an art as the handling of the long sword. When a samurai decides to die with honor, he strips to the waist and sits cross-legged on the ground. It is normal to have one's male relatives and friends to witness the event, but this is not always possible, as, for example, after defeat in battle. Yet must he always have a close friend to assist him. Where this is not possible, then someone must be found, even a servant if there is no one else. The reason is that no one expects a samurai to die in slow agony. It is sufficient that he make the decision to take his own life. The decision is the difficult part for the fainthearted. Now, listen carefully, and watch. The short sword is taken in both hands, so, with the blade pointed inward. You will see that unlike the long sword, the short sword has a sharp point as well as a sharp edge. Held in both hands, like this, it is driven into the left side of the belly, so." He made the movement, but of course stopped short of his flesh. "Then the blade is turned, and pulled to the right, thus opening the entire abdomen. This is done because, while it is possible to survive a single thrust, once the whole gut has been exposed, death is inevitable. When this has been done, and *only* then, Freeman San, the dying man must release the haft of his sword with his right hand and throw the arm away from his body in a horizontal movement, like this. At that signal, his friend will strike his head from his body. I may say that the friend who fails to obey that signal instantly, or who fails to strike off the head with a single blow, is as dishonored as if he had refused seppuku himself. And the second is never blamed for any transgression of law by the dying man. I mention this because it is said that on occasion a samurai in the past has thrown out his right arm the moment the point of his short sword entered his body. This is dishonorable. But the second must yet act upon the signal, instantly. It is the dead man who has committed the dishonorable act."

Ralph found it incredible that they should be sitting on the grass in the warm sunlight discussing such a ghastly subject. "And suppose it is a matter of his strength failing him?" he asked.

Munetake gave a scornful smile. "It is no physical strength that can fail, Freeman San," he said. "This is well known, that the pain of a sword thrust does not come for perhaps a second, or even longer, which is sufficient time to complete the side cut. Only the mind can fail in strength, and a samurai whose mind fails in strength is dishonored. Now, let us turn to happier things."

"Yes," Ralph agreed. "Let's."

"Let us suppose that you become a mighty warrior, Freeman San . . ." His smile widened, indicating that he was but letting his fancy roam free to the impossible. "And thus meet with nothing but victory in battle. And thus it falls to your lot to slay some great lord or commander in single combat. This is a feat which will surely entitle you to much reward. But you must prove the deed, and this can only be done by producing the head of your victim. The head must be presented to your lord in the proper fashion, by taking the dead man's food sticks, so, and thrusting them through his topknot." He showed Ralph on his own head. "Then your servants can each grasp a stick and carry the head. It is for this reason that a samurai must never be separated from his food sticks, but must carry them in his girdle at all times. He must also carry a small knife, like this." He drew the tiny blade, hardly larger than a penknife, but with no hinge for folding. "You will see that this one has my personal design upon it, so that no one finding it can have any doubts that it is mine. When you are accepted as a samurai, you will be given one of these knives. Now, you see, it has but one purpose. If you quarrel with another samurai, and wish to settle the matter, you will first of all take one of your enemy's servants prisoner and cut off *his* head. That done, you will stick your knife into his ear, and have your servants deliver the head to the house of your enemy. This constitutes a challenge which he may not refuse, for fear of dishonor."

"I really am quite puzzled how any of you gentlemen have managed to survive at all," Ralph remarked in English.

"What is that you say?" Munetake inquired.

"I was wondering when we got onto those happier things you mentioned."

"We will now practice the bow," Munetake decided.

"The bow, my friend, is a thing of the past," Ralph pointed out. "As I am trying to convince your people."

"The samurai who cannot handle the bow is not a samurai," Munetake declared. "How can the bow ever be replaced with gunpowder? Bah. We will now practice the bow."

Strangely, the only sympathy Ralph received was from Katsura himself. "You have a difficult road to travel," the old warrior agreed. "Most samurai, you see, are trained from birth. From their earliest memory they are taught the importance of honor and of obedience to the code of bushido. From the moment they can walk, they are taught the use of the sword and the bow. But you . . . you must master all of these arts within the space of a few months."

"You think that's possible?" Ralph asked him. "A few years, maybe."

Katsura smiled. "You will learn, Freeman San. And you will make a good samurai, when the time comes."

Ralph supposed he could look for no greater compliment. From a Japanese.

And in fact, as the weeks became months, Ralph slowly began to feel at least familiar with Japanese weapons, even if he doubted he would ever approach Munetake's mastery. More important, he began to feel that he was earning some respect from the samurai themselves, as they came to appreciate his determination as well as his real skill in his own fields, and to understand that he was in Shimonoseki to help them prepare for whatever conflicts might lie ahead. Because the oddest thing about this strange new country, he rapidly discovered, was that although the samurai's entire being, from birth until death, was dedicated to the martial arts, because of the iron grip exercised by the Tokugawa shogunate for so long, it was two centuries since there had been a war of *any* kind in which a Japanese army had been involved. There had been blood feuds often enough, and clashes between armed bands of samurai representing rival daimyos, and apparently the art of political assassination had been raised to a high level in Japan, nor was it regarded with the abhorrence it attracted in the United States or Europe, but there was no living man who had experienced, there was no man who had even heard his grandfather talk of, an actual campaign. The samurai existed on necessarily glorified and distorted legends of the heroes of the past. The greatest moment in their military history had been the Battle of Sekigahara, a place well to the north, where in 1603 nearly two hundred thousand men had taken the field as the Tokugawa and their allies had defeated the heirs of the kwampaku, Toyotomi Hideyoshi, the Napoleon of Japan, to seize all power for themselves.

It was intensely reassuring to consider that in this respect he had forgotten more about warfare—even if only against Indians and Mexican irregulars—than they would ever learn.

And in fact life in Shimonoseki was pleasant enough, provided one obeyed the rules, and for him, both as a foreigner and as a not-yet-samurai, the rules were elastic enough. There *was* much to admire in the extreme cleanliness of the average Japanese, and in their true love of beauty, as represented by the care with which their women arranged flowers or their artists executed the most exquisite designs upon silken screens. There was much to respect in their acceptance of parental authority, and in its natural concomitant, their extreme devoutness toward their dead ancestors, a worship which was combined with the forms of Buddhism—but none of the renunciation of the flesh and ambition of that religion, for in Japan even the monks carried swords and were happy to use them—to make up Shintoism, which was the national religion. And there was so much to enjoy in the loveliness of the country, especially, he gathered, down here in the south, where he was situated, and where weather extremes could be avoided. Certainly the winter, which set in not long after the departure of Inouye and Ito—he hoped they had gained San Francisco before the gales started—was hardly more severe than one in Southern California, while his new comrades told him that Edo and the north would be covered in snow. He would have loved to be able to travel to Edo, the seat of the Tokugawa bushido—or military government—and even more to Kyoto, the home of the mikado himself, a place of exquisite beauty, he was promised. But travel outside of the lands of the Cho-Shu was forbidden except by the express permission of Nariaka. Ralph duly applied for such permission. "I can prepare your soldiers better for the tasks which may lie ahead, my lord," he explained, "by studying such armies as you may one day have to face."

Nariaka smiled his thin smile. "Time enough for that, Freeman San, when you have completed your task here."

He obviously had no doubt that to lose sight of his American adviser would be to lose him altogether.

Meanwhile there was the contentment of having nothing to do but practice being a soldier. For as Inouye had indicated on board the *Asa Maru*, a samurai—and Ralph was so treated in anticipation of his becoming one—was entirely cared for by his lord. Income, or wealth, in Japan was divided up into portions of rice, called koku, each koku representing the amount of rice required to keep one man for one year. Ralph found himself in possession of six koku as an embryo samurai. This meant that he had five spare, which could be used either for the purchasing and upkeep of servants or for exchanging with merchants for goods. As he had only the one servant, Aya, and did not wish for more, Ralph therefore possessed a considerable surplus, but the system had the desirable social aspect of preventing either hoarding or saving; the koku had to be consumed, which kept the economy in a very healthy state. It also meant that a samurai could leave to his son only his ability as a warrior, his honor, and the favor of his lord; only a daimyo could bequeath real property. In fact, the sons of samurai, being made samurai themselves in most cases before their fathers' deaths, never suffered want, and were invariably permitted to continue enjoying the same house and property as their ancestors—provided they always obeyed their lord and never dishonored their caste. Ralph was informed that he could expect his wealth to grow to ten koku once he was accepted as a samurai, although this was still a long way from the eighty koku that was Katsura's lot, or even the forty that went to hatamotos like Ito or Inouye, and which made them, Ralph realized, very wealthy indeed.

But all things were relative. Lord Nariaka was apparently worth six hundred and ten *thousand* koku, and if even he ever got above his station, there was the salutary reminder that the shogun commanded nothing less than two million, five hundred and fifty seven thousand. Obviously, as koku in real terms represented the amount of support a leader could summon, Nariaka could not possibly consider opposing the Tokugawa in the field without finding considerable allies—even if he were able to arm his troops with modern weapons.

Ralph decided to be content with his own modest portion, which left him able to purchase in the city anything he might desire, and at the same time to enjoy the contentment of being bathed by Aya, of eating the delicately prepared slices of pork or beef, sukiyaki, or skewered chicken, or fried fish, tempura—she knew better than to offer him the raw variety—of drinking vast quantities of the heady rice wine, sake—drunkenness was certainly not regarded as dishonorable, or even as ill-mannered, among the samurai—and most of all, of enjoying the girl herself. As he had already observed, Japanese lovemaking was shared in a way he had never considered might be possible in an American woman. Aya expected to touch him as freely as he might wish to touch her, and to lead him, as well, whenever he appeared overtired or distracted, constantly varying her positions so that sometimes she would lie on him, or kneel before him, or sit in his lap, which was apparently the most usual Japanese manner of performing the sexual act—a testimony, he decided, to the strength of the back and belly muscles of the average male. The missionary position she regarded as absurd and even dangerous, as it involved her slender body bearing all of his weight, but she humored him in this as in all things, when he demanded it.

At the same time, to his immense regret, he began to

realize, as the weeks went by, that charming and delightful and sexually stimulating as she was, their relationship was entirely physical, and for that reason, entirely unsatisfactory. Nor could it be changed, in their present circumstances. But he doubted it could be changed at all. It was more than a matter of perhaps teaching her to read, of achieving some mental rapport, some intellectual pursuit which they could mutually share. Those things might have been possible. But he simply could make no impression upon her almost cowlike acceptance of life as she found it, with herself at the very bottom of the pyramid. Even to consider altering that state of affairs she regarded as sacrilege, and if her lord did not punish her for it, the gods certainly would.

So, was he now going to accept that Inouye and Ito, and even Nariaka himself, were right, and if he would find happiness with a woman it must be a woman of the samurai class? He did not doubt that Inouye and his wife were happy, on the scant evidence he had seen. But he also doubted whether Mrs. Inouye provided any true companionship to her husband—or whether Inouye would have wished it even if she could. Women, even from the best class, were there to bear children and manage households. Men found their pleasure with men. And if he refused to accept so homosexual a point of view, then it was he condemning himself to a life of at least mental loneliness.

Thus the return of Ito and Inouye daily loomed more important. Because surely, once Nariaka's army was reequipped with Dahlgren guns and modern rifles, and taught how to use them, he would be free to leave. In any event, he was watching and listening, and he was prepared to make his own salvation if he could achieve it no other way. For word had come down the coast that the Americans had actually been permitted to establish two embassies in Japan, one in Nagasaki at the very southernmost end of Kyushu, and the other in Edo itself. This sacrilegious intrusion upon Japanese soil had the samurai growling more than ever about the weakness of the shogunate, but to Ralph it was the best news he had heard in a long while. If he was not permitted to return to San Francisco when he had completed his task here, he had no doubt that if he could reach either embassy, with the information he would be able to provide about Japanese intentions, he would at least be given a fair hearing regarding the death of Jefferson Hardy.

Thus the plan of escape hardened in his mind, and he began to wonder if he should even wait for the return of his friends. That might be to embarrass and even endanger them. Far better to have left before they came home. And as for completing his mission, he had recommended the guns, and he was doing his best to teach the samurai some concept of modern military tactics; he could do no more even after the new weapons arrived—presumably Nariaka would no more permit him to fire the Dahlgrens than the nine-pounders.

Thus it became a matter only of waiting for the winter to end. He intended to take Aya with him, of course, although he really had no idea what he was going to do with her, even supposing he managed to get her back to the States; he could not imagine any American girl he might ever marry welcoming Aya in the pantry. But he could not contemplate leaving her, any more than he could contemplate turning a faithful dog out to starve. And even if she was not executed by Nariaka for being the chattel of a man who had betrayed his lord—which was certainly how the lord of Cho-Shu would look on the matter—but was instead given to some other samurai, he could not contemplate that either, after she had shared his bed and board for so long; he had seen enough of the way the samurai treated their honin, the beatings and kicks, as well as the insults, which were daily handed out, to know that Aya, coming as she would from his bed, would be doubly ill-treated and would indeed be better off dead following his departure without her. But he dared not tell her of his plans until the actual moment arrived. Aya could not conceive of abandoning her lord without instant retribution. He had to convince her that he was her lord more than Nariaka. When the time came.

So he taught the samurai gunners how to load and fire their imaginary shells, and he practiced his sword-

play and his archery, and he worked at making bullets
for his revolver . . . and he paced the battlements and
watched the clouds rushing by, sheltered when it poured
with rain, frowned at the whitecaps which often enough
tore up the waters of the Strait of Tsushima as the
breeze freshened to a gale, and stared at the ship,
which, on a wintry March afternoon, could be seen
vainly trying to beat against the northwesterly gale to
prevent herself being driven on to the rocks of Kyushu.

The ship had obviously been in difficulty for some
time; she had lost her foretopmast and her bowsprit,
and was therefore incapable of flying any jibs, which
made the task of beating next to impossible; it would in
fact have made more sense for her to run off before
the wind and attempt to reach the safety of the open
sea that way. But now even that option was lost to her,
as the combination of wind and sea had sucked her too
close to the shore, and she was barely holding her own
as she clawed forward, plunging and rolling, her sails
flogging in between filling again to give her some steerage way—but all the while drifting closer and closer to
the rocks.

Her progress had been overseen by the sentries, for
now the battlements were filled with samurai, and with
their women as well, while from above their heads in
the palace Ralph could hear the excited shouts of the
other onlookers.

"She fights the sea well," Munetake observed at Ralph's
elbow. "With fortune, she will not strike until she passes
the strait."

"Either way, she is going to be wrecked," Ralph pointed
out.

"Of course," Munetake observed. "But if she strikes
on the southern side, it will be the men of Kyushu who
will gain the prize. You may be sure they are watching
just as closely as ourselves."

Ralph gave him an astonished glance, and then reflected that it was not so astonishing, after all, that the
Japanese should be more interested in what the vessel
might be carrying than in saving the lives of the crew.

Because she was definitely not a Japanese ship, or even a Chinese one; her lines were European or American.

"She will pass the strait," Katsura said with grim satisfaction. "But only just. We must get down there. These barbarians are good seamen. They might still bring her to safety." He struck Ralph on the shoulder. "She may have guns, Freeman San. What do you think of that?"

"That it is unlikely," Ralph said, for she did not look like a warship. "And in that sea, I do not think you will salvage much from the wreck. It is the people we must think of. We must take ropes to throw to them, to bring them ashore."

Katsura gave a grim smile. "They will come ashore," he said. "Enough of them for sport. Eh, my samurai?"

The warriors gathered around them gave a hiss of impatient excitement through their nostrils as they stamped their feet and stared at their victims. Because, Ralph realized with a sudden dreadful understanding, that was exactly how they viewed anyone who might come ashore from the wreck. He opened his mouth to protest, but the Japanese were already hurrying behind Katsura and Munetake for the drawbridge. He turned back to gaze at the ship again, peering into the gathering gloom, and wishing he had the use of a telescope to make out her colors—but there was no such thing in Shimonoseki.

On the other hand . . . He stared at her, his throat growing dry. He had looked at that ship often enough, almost every day for a fortnight, hardly a year ago. And the last time he had looked at her, he had thought he had seen the wave of a scarf before she had vanished to the south.

Because he could no longer doubt that the doomed vessel was the *English Rose* and that somewhere on board, expecting the worst, would be Alison Gray.

He ran behind the samurai to the beach.

—5—
THE FLIGHT

The crack of the parting foremast had seemed like the snapping of her own heartstrings to Alison Gray. She had been below, aware that there was a gale blowing, and in somewhat narrow waters, but as ever totally confident both in her father's seamanship and in the strength of this ship; why, had they not ridden the tail end of that typhoon last year, the very storm which must certainly have sent the Japanese junk—and poor, poor Mr. Freeman—to the bottom, without sustaining even the slightest damage. As they had ridden several gales since.

But that noise . . . She had gathered her shawl around her shoulders and hurried up the companionway, to gaze forward in stark horror at the welter of cordage and fallen sail, at the severed bowsprit, all lying trapped against the hull, at once bumping and grinding and robbing the vessel of steerage way. Vital steerage way, she had immediately understood, as she had looked to starboard and seen the craggy peaks of the land. Japan! And they were in danger of shipwreck.

"Get to it, God damn you!" Jonathan Gray was shouting, sending his crew forward with axes to cut away the fallen spars. "And you, keep her up. Keep her up!" he bawled at the two men on the helm.

Alison stared into the afternoon. The clouds were low and heavy, and the wind was out of the northwest, and gusting up to forty knots, she estimated; already it had plucked her shawl away, and was now whipping her hair into snarled strands. And the land was only a few miles away.

She held on to the rail and pulled herself around to

116

stand beside her father. "Run her off, Father," she
cried. " Run her off."

He looked down at her and shook his head. "She'll
not do it, Ali. By the time we wear ship, she'll be in the
grip of the shore current. We'd have to turn away, and
she'd be on the beach. She'll clear, if those louts would
hasten."

Alison peered forward once more. They were on the
edge of a bay, and if they could hold their present
course they should certainly clear the next headland.
But the bay ... She looked inland, saw the castle and
the houses, and then the strait. Everything would depend on how far offshore the current extended. Yet
she knew her father was right; without headsails they
could not come about by turning into the wind, tacking;
they could only do so by turning *away*, jibing, and
before that could be accomplished they would most
definitely be embayed, with no hope of struggling clear.
They could only keep her as close to the wind as possible,
and pray they cleared the promontory.

But suddenly she knew they were not going to do it.
Because now they were in shallower water, and the seas
were becoming steeper; every time the *English Rose*
came off a crest and plunged her battered bows into
the following trough, she lost way, and the helmsmen
had to let the bows fall away to fill the sails again. And
every time *that* happened, the shore inched closer.

Her fingers were tight on the rail. Yet she was not
aware of being afraid. She was the daughter of a seaman,
and virtually one of his crew; no one who took his
living from the sea could doubt that one day the sea
would seek to claim him as its own. Or her. Nor did she
feel any great resentment or sadness that her life might
soon be ended before it had properly begun; she had
recently found it difficult to imagine her life ever properly beginning, as another woman's might. It was not
merely that she was hardly ever in one place long
enough to be wooed and won—she had in fact managed to create a very comfortable home in the little
Hong Kong house in which her mother had died. Nor
was it even the obvious and growing dependence of her
father on her for every detail of his domestic life. It

was more the streak of romanticism which plagued her
soul and which caused her to look on most men, and all
acquaintances of her father's, with dissatisfaction. She
read too much, he would say, and she would not argue
with that. Only in the novels of Jane Austen could she
discover even the suggestion of a life that might truly
be worth living.

And in occasional men, like Ralph Freeman, who
had appeared to her the epitome of a gentleman, at
once hard and yet gentle, a man who had fought, and
killed, and yet was obviously kindhearted and generous
by nature. A truly romantic man, in that he had committed a crime any man might be excused, and yet had
been rejected by society for that crime, to find a watery
grave in the company of only heathen pirates.

Heathen pirates who would even now be watching
them, she realized, her head jerking as she again stared
at the shore, now come perceptibly closer. She looked
forward and saw the promontory, and then the line of
rocks, peeping from the welter of foam which surrounded them. Now they were definitely in the grip of
the ground swell, and in addition to rising and falling,
were rolling scuppers under; the sails were no longer
filling at all. While only half a mile away huge waves
were pounding on the beach, tearing at the great boul-
ders which formed the edge of the land, sending spray
flying high into the sky.

And there were people there, beyond the spray. Japanese pirates! She turned to her father, but as she did
so, the ship struck.

The force of the impact wrenched Alison's hands
from the rail and tumbled her to the deck. Her head
swung with the noise, composed of so many things: the
grinding crunch of the timbers biting into the rocks,
the report of the remaining masts snapping as they
were torn from their steps, the wail of terror from the
crew—and rising above even that, she realized, a tremendous paean of sound from the beach.

She regained her feet, having to hold on now as the
ship commenced to list, all the while grinding and
tearing herself apart on the rocks; where before Alison

had been quite dry, now a cloud of spray came over the stern to soak her to the skin. "Father!" she screamed. "Father!"

Jonathan Gray continued to stare forward at the hulk of his ship, at the crewmen who were hurling themselves over the side, as if they had any hope of surviving the giant seas. Alison dared not imagine what he must be thinking. The ship was more than his sole possession and the source of all his income. It was also the only thing he had ever truly loved. She knew that, also without resentment; it was an emotion she could understand. Between a skipper and his ship there can grow a relationship as intense as any shared between man and woman. Perhaps he had felt that way for his wife, once. Since her death his devotion had centered on the *Rose*, and now she too was gone.

But he had not entirely forgotten his daughter. Now he turned his head, and frowned at her, then threw his arm around her shoulders. "That life belt," he said. "Come on, now, Ali."

"To go where?" she asked him.

He stared at her, and then at the shore. "While there's life, there's hope, Ali," he said. "And remember, do not be afraid. There is nothing worse than death; therefore, you can endure anything you may suffer until the moment of death. Remember."

She wanted to fight him as he tied her to the life belt, wanted to resist him as he carried her to the rail. "Father," she screamed, "you—"

"I will be right behind you," he promised. "Now, remember, the current will carry you to the beach. If God wills it, you will not strike a rock before then. Keep faith!"

He threw her into the sea.

"Come," Munetake shouted to Ralph. "You can practice your swordplay."

He led the rush of samurai into the surf, drawing his sword, as the first sailor was washed into the shallows. Katsura remained beside Ralph on the beach while the spray clouded around them. "Fine sport," the general cried. "Oh, fine sport. But you should join them, Freeman San."

"For God's sake," Ralph shouted. "Those men are not your enemies. They are not invading you. They are but seeking rescue and shelter."

Katsura looked surprised and hurt. "This is how our ancestors dealt with the Mongols," he pointed out. "When they sought to land in Japan, their ships were wrecked in a great storm, and as they came ashore, we hit them on the head. Many thousands were killed that day, along this very beach. It was a great victory, the greatest in our history over foreign enemies, and it saved our country. This is how we have always dealt with those who land on our shores uninvited."

"And this is what the shogun would stop," Ralph shrieked at him, looking at the teeming surf again, his heart seeming to constrict as he saw the first sailor reach the supposed safety of the beach, stumbling through the boiling foam, reaching out with both hands to the men he saw waiting for him, his mouth sagging open in uncomprehending horror as he watched the flailing blades carving the air toward him.

"My God!" Ralph shouted, and dashed forward, breasting the first wave he encountered and nearly losing his footing, having water break over his head and realizing to his disgust that it was tinged with blood. Because now the massacre had become general, as the crew of the ship came into the shallows, unable to stop themselves as they were picked up in the surf, unable to believe that such a catastrophe could be overtaking them after they had actually survived the wreck. He ran toward the nearest sailor, checked as he saw that the white man had already been beheaded, shoulder-charged a samurai away from another victim, but failed to save the seaman, who was immediately cut down by yet another swinging blade. Ralph lost his balance and fell to his knees, head ducking beneath the waves, struggled up again, gasping and spluttering, and heard a scream of "Help me!" in English.

He turned, and watched a cork life belt being thrown at him by the next towering wave. Clinging to the belt was a slender figure, wet hair still streaming in the wind, eyes staring in horror as she realized the enormity of what was taking place around her. As the belt came into the shallows, Ralph reached for the woman and brought the gasping body against him, and knew that he had found Alison Gray.

A wave broke over Ralph and sent him staggering, still clutching his precious burden. He hastily retreated into shallower water, and could free her of the belt and set her on her feet, panting for breath, her body swelling through her sodden gown as she leaned against him. Then she turned her head left and right, looking at the dreadful sights and listening to the dreadful sounds around her, and then gazing straight into his face, clearly unable to comprehend. "Mr. Freeman?" she whispered.

"I will save you," he said in English. "I will—" A hand came through the gloom to seize the auburn hair. The girl's head jerked and she gave a little whimper. Ralph gazed at Munetake, the grinning teeth, and bloodstained sword.

"This head," the samurai said, "I will mount."

Ralph bunched his fist and drove it straight from the shoulder, getting all of his weight into the blow and landing in on Munetake's jaw. Munetake had never suffered such an assault before in his life, and went down as if poleaxed, arms and legs scattering in the shallow water, even releasing his long sword as he momentarily lost consciousness. Instantly they were surrounded by samurai, hastily raising their hero into a sitting position, excitedly showing him where the sword was, as of course none of them dared touch it.

"Oh, God," Alison whispered in English, still held in the crook of Ralph's left arm. "Oh, God, Mr. Freeman."

Ralph sucked at the gash in his knuckles. "You are safe now," he promised. "But, Miss Gray . . . your father . . ."

"Father!" Her head swung as she looked back at the wreck, now already breaking up as the seas continued to rise. "Father . . ." Tears welled out of the enormous eyes and rolled down her cheeks.

"Aye," he agreed. "Maybe he was fortunate. But you'll not be harmed. You have my word. Come ashore."

He half-pushed her onto dry land, and then turned again to face Munetake, who had regained his feet, and his sword, and was advancing toward him, still surrounded by his friends, water streaming from his clothing and even his topknot, face contorted with anger. "Draw your sword, white man," Munetake snarled. "Draw your weapon and die with it in your hand."

"I'm damned if I will," Ralph said, allowing his hand to drop to the holster which never left his waist. "But by God, if you come a step closer I'll blow you apart."

Munetake hesitated. He was well aware of the deadly properties of the little firearm. "Then would you be dishonored," he growled.

"You would be dishonored," shouted his companions.

"Can anyone be dishonored in your company?" Ralph demanded. "Famous warriors," he said, loading his voice with all the contempt he could manage, "whose greatest victory is murdering shipwrecked sailors."

Certainly he had succeeded in offending them all, from the hissing and stamping with which he was surrounded.

"You cannot fight so many," Alison whispered.

"They may make a lot of noise," Ralph told her, "but they actually have a healthy respect for their own skins."

"Freeman San," Katsura said, hurrying down the beach. "This nonsense must stop."

"Aye," Ralph said. "Let them withdraw. I will not say, here, what I think of your murderers, Katsura San. But this girl is mine. I plucked her from the sea. I claim her."

"If she is not to be killed, then she belongs to whomsoever Lord Nariaka decides," Katsura said. "That is the law of the land." He looked more closely at the girl. "He may even choose her for his own bed."

Alison shivered; she could not understand Japanese, but she could tell from the way they were looking at her that more than her life was now at stake. Ralph's arm tightened on her shoulders. "No one is going to touch you," he promised. It was indeed difficult to imagine a cold fish like Nariaka sharing a bed with anyone.

"He struck me," Munetake said. "He is dishonored. As am I, unless I take his head."

"This is true," Katsura said. "This is a grave matter, Freeman San."

"Balderdash," Ralph told him. "It is how we settle our differences in America."

"Now, that is also true," Katsura said thoughtfully. "Inouye San has told me of this. It is a matter for Lord Nariaka to decide. Do you give me the woman, Freeman San, and we will attend Lord Nariaka in the morning, and learn his decision."

"We'll attend his decision now," Ralph said. "And the girl stays with me until we have done so."

"You would hope to be received by Lord Nariaka when you have been fighting and your clothes and your person are stained with blood?" Katsura was horrified.

"Yes," Ralph said. "Munetake can come too."

"Mr. Freeman," Alison said as he carried her up the cobbled street of the town, gazed at by the excited townspeople, who knew that some crisis had entered their lives, "we thought you were lost in the storm. But . . . you *live* with these creatures?"

"Your father didn't leave me much choice," he said. "And now I'm trying to teach them how to defend themselves, believe it or not."

"But . . . what is going to happen, Mr. Freeman? They have murdered my father's crew, and he is dead . . ." Her voice was trembling, and rising.

"I know," he said, squeezing her hand. "And unfortunately I can't promise you any redress for that. Not here, at any rate. But nothing will happen to you, I swear it."

"But . . ." She bit her lip. She dared not ask what *could* become of her in such a savage community. Yet her tears had dried; she did not lack courage, although he knew she was still suffering from shock. The true extent of her loss, the true horror of her fate, had not yet surfaced in her consciousness.

They waited, surrounded by staring and hissing samurai, while Katsura went ahead to see if an audience could be arranged. He was soon back. "In view of the seriousness of the situation," he said, "Lord Nariaka will see you now, Freeman San. But I must warn you that he is very angry. The girl will remain here until the lord has decided the truth of the matter."

Ralph hesitated, looking at the waiting samurai, then released Alison's hand. "She is not to be harmed," he said. "Or even touched." He stared from face to face."

"No one will lay a finger on her until Lord Nariaka has made his decision," Katsura promised.

Ralph held both Alison's hands and squeezed them. "Have courage, and faith in me," he said. "I shall not be long."

He followed Katsura and Munetake into the reception chamber without waiting for her response, knowing only the utter despair she must be feeling—and equally that only he could now overcome that despair. But how, in such a community, without taking her for his own?—as if he did not wish to do that.

He performed the kowtow with the two Japanese, water squelching from their clothes, and then crawled around the corner.

"So," Nariaka said. "Now you seek to brawl like some eta. Do you know the penalty for striking a samurai, barbarian? It is instant decapitation."

"I fought as an American would, my lord," Ralph said, keeping his temper under very careful control.

"This I understand," Nariaka said. "And am prepared to take into consideration. Yet as you are here in Japan, and not in America, it behooves you to fight like a Japanese. Munetake has reason to claim compensation for the injury you have done him."

"Let me face him, Lord Nariaka," Munetake begged. "Sword in hand. Let me face him."

"That would certainly be the proper thing to do," Nariaka agreed.

"It would also mean the death of the American, my lord," Katsura pointed out. "And there is no one to replace him. When Inouye Bunta and Ito Shunsuke return with the cannon and the rifled muskets, they will not be bringing another American soldier with them, because they will expect Freeman San to be here."

"You expect me to condone his crime?" Nariaka demanded.

"When one is climbing to the top of a mountain, great lord, it is sometimes necessary to forgive the slip of a foot, where that foot is necessary to the success of the climb."

"Ha," Nariaka commented, staring at Ralph.

"I have committed no crime, my lord," Ralph said. "Rather is it your samurai who are guilty of murder, in their treatment of the shipwrecked sailors. There is no nation in the world, with the least pretense to civilization, which would condone these acts."

"Is there no end to your insolence?" Nariaka demanded.

"I seek to warn you against the consequences of your deeds, my lord," Ralph insisted. "When the British government learns of what happened here this evening . . . Lord Nariaka, the British command the greatest battle fleet in the history of the world, a fleet which could reduce this castle and this palace of yours to rubble in fifteen minutes."

"Now he speaks treason," Munetake cried. "How can the castle of Lord Nariaka *ever* be destroyed? Did it not withstand the might of the Mongols? And that *was* the greatest fleet in the world."

"Do you believe what the barbarian says, Katsura San?" Nariaka asked.

"He has said it often enough, my lord," Katsura replied. "So *he* must believe it. But it is of no matter. The British can never discover what happened to their ship and their people, because there have been no survivors of the wreck."

"Except for the woman," Munetake said.

"The woman," Nariaka remarked. "Let me see the cause of so much anger."

Katsura returned to the door, and Alison was brought in, pushed to her knees to perform the kowtow, obviously completely bewildered by these increasingly strange surroundings.

"Come closer, woman," Nariaka commanded, and

when Alison made no response, he added, "Tell her to advance, Freeman San."

"Approach the lord, Miss Gray," Ralph said in English. "I'm afraid you have to do so on your hands and knees. It's the custom here."

She hesitated, her wish to survive obviously conflicting with her sense of dignity and propriety; she could move only with difficulty in her still-wet skirts. Slowly she crawled forward.

"Now tell her to kneel erect and look at me," Nariaka said.

Ralph translated, and Alison obeyed.

"By all the gods," Nariaka remarked. "But I have never seen a woman like this. Are all barbarian women this large, Freeman San?"

"A fair number, my lord," Ralph said.

"She has the height of a man," Nariaka mused. "And the chest, too. Tell her to show me her chest, Freeman San."

"My lord," Ralph protested, "it is not the custom among barbarian women to reveal themselves to any men but their husbands."

"Am I concerned with barbarian customs, Freeman San? This is Cho-Shu. Command her."

The girl could tell there had been a difference of opinion. She looked anxiously at Ralph.

"The lord wishes to look upon you," Ralph said.

She frowned at him, and then gave a quick look down at herself.

"Only the top half," Ralph said. And hoped that indeed would be so.

Her cheeks flamed. "Must I do this, Mr. Freeman?"

"It would be best to obey without question, Miss Gray," he said. "These people do not regard nudity in the same way as ourselves. And this man has the power of life and death over us all, here in Cho-Shu."

She hesitated for a moment, and then turned away from them, on her knees, so that she directly faced Nariaka and only he could see when she unfastened her bodice.

Nariaka gazed at her, his face as ever expressionless. "Truly," he remarked, "she must bring forth healthy sons. And it was for possession of this that you fought with my samurai, Freeman San?"

"I do not wish to possess her, my lord," Ralph said, and realized that he might have made a mistake. "That is, my lord, I regard her as being in my care, not only because she is of my race, and because I pulled her from the sea, but because I have known her for several years and . . ." He bit his lip, but any lie was worth it, if it would save her from Nariaka's lust. "I have loved her for that time, too. Yes, I would have her as a woman." He wondered just how much of a lie that was.

Once again Alison looked from face to face, aware that her fate was being decided. Slowly she refastened her bodice.

"There is some justice in your claim, Freeman San," Nariaka said. "And yet, on this occasion, not enough. You may have acted hastily, and indeed out of lust. That is no crime. But you struck a samurai, and before his fellows. That is a *great* crime, where circumstances do not permit Munetake to avenge his honor. You must be punished, and be seen to be punished. As Munetake must receive compensation, and be seen to do so. Munetake shall have the girl."

Ralph reared back on his heels, unable to believe his ears. "That is impossible, my lord."

"It is my command, Freeman San. She will bear strong sons for Munetake. This will be good. And besides, as Katsura San has reminded us, she alone can carry the tale of this day's work back to these British barbarians of whom you spoke. If she remains with Munetake, this can never happen. This is my command."

"No!" Ralph leaped to his feet. "You cannot do this, my lord. This girl knows nothing of your ways, your customs. In England and America women are treated entirely differently from here in Japan. You will be condemning her to a fate worse than death."

They stared at him, principally because he was daring to stand in the presence of his lord.

"Do you then wish her executed?" Nariaka asked.

"My lord," Ralph said, "I beg of you—"

"I understand. You would have her for yourself," Nariaka said. "I have been told how none of our people appeal to you, barbarian, save for some honin woman. Now your insolence has gone too far. Katsura San, summon guards to remove this wretch. Put him in the pit, that he may reflect upon the anger of Lord Nariaka. Munetake San, you may take this girl. For this night she may remain with you in the palace, that you may avenge the wrong that has been done you. From tomorrow she will be placed with the honin." He gave one of his thin smiles. "Enjoy her, Munetake San."

"No!" Ralph shouted again, and discovered that he was surrounded by samurai. He did not doubt that he could deal with several of them—the revolver still hung from his belt—but they would kill him in the end. And perhaps the girl as well.

She certainly realized *his* danger. "Please do not destroy yourself on my behalf, Mr. Freeman," she shouted. "Enough men have died this day."

"I shall help you," he gasped as his arms were seized. "I swear it, Miss Gray. Believe me, I shall help you." Then he was dragged from the lord's chamber, his weapons pulled from his girdle and his belt, his kimono stripped from his back, and he was thrust down the stairs, and down more stairs in the interior of the palace, where he had never been taken before, until he found himself on the edge of a pit, somewhere in the very bowels of the building, in a damp chamber lighted only by guttering torches.

And realized that Katsura had accompanied him. "You have acted the fool this night," the general said. "To be reduced to such a level, and over a woman. Shame on you, Freeman San. And pray that your lord is forgiving, before you drown."

The hands grasping his arms thrust him forward and then released him. He stood on the edge of the pit, turned to face them, and was pushed in the chest with a pole, which tumbled him backward into darkness.

Alison had scrambled to her feet as Ralph was dragged from the room. Now she turned to Munetake, who had also risen. "What are you doing to him?" she shouted. "You cannot kill him!"

But obviously the Japanese had no idea what she was

saying. Instead he looked for instruction to the seated man who apparently ruled this terrible land. The lord spoke, and Munetake bowed. Then without warning he drove his fingers into Alison's hair and dragged her to the door.

The suddenness of the assault, together with the quite tremendous pain, drove the breath from her lungs even as tears started from her eyes. Before she could recollect herself, she was kneeling in the antechamber, surrounded by the same men who had leered and hissed at her a few moments before while she had waited for her summons. She gazed at them, blinking the tears back and trying to catch her breath, and also to prepare herself for the instant death which she supposed was about to be her lot. Instead the big man, whose name, she had gathered, was Munetake, seized her arm and pulled her to her feet, and then, grinning and chattering to his friends, himself tore open her bodice and the shift beneath to expose her breasts. She gave a gasp of outrage and anger, and swung her free hand, but it was caught by another of the samurai, and thus held, she had to submit to their inspection, and to being touched and pinched and squeezed as well. She wanted to kick at them, but dared not, for fear of interesting them in that part of her body, and reflected that this could last only a few minutes before blessed oblivion.

Again she was surprised. The other samurai were obviously congratulating Munetake upon the size of his victim, and now he made another of his sudden movements, caught her by the waist, and laid her across his shoulders, her head bumping on his thighs behind, her hair trailing on the floor. Again the breath was driven from her lungs, with such force she thought she would suffocate, and was only dimly aware that she was being carried down several flights of stairs and then out into the night air, always passing groups of samurai, and even, sometimes, she thought, women, who would peer at her and chatter in their high-pitched voices. Then a door opened and Munetake entered another chamber, at the same time unceremoniously dumping her on the floor.

It was a slatted floor. When she sat up, her fingers slipped through the grating, even as she was immediately clouded with steam rising from the well at the far end. She looked left and right, discovered that there were already three young women in the room, each naked, and then, to her horror, that Munetake was also disrobing.

She rose to her knees, and the girls clustered around her. "No," she gasped, and tried to push them away, listening to the sound of ripping material as they completed the destruction of her blouse and then turned their attention to her skirt. Now she did try to kick, and was thrown down again while they completed the stripping of her. Then they stood away, and she gazed up at Munetake, huge and naked and aroused, standing above her.

She thought she would faint; she had never seen a naked man before, and there could be no doubt what he intended to do to her. But apparently not yet. He spoke to her, and then, as she obviously did not understand him, jerked his head to indicate that she should stand up. This at least seemed to offer more protection than lying down, so she obeyed, gazing into his eyes as she did so, trying to understand something about him, some indication of what he would do next, and how much he would wish to hurt her.

But his eyes were fathomless as he gazed at her, looking in delighted wonder at the freckles which dotted her pale skin, bending to stare at her pubic hair, and then seizing a handful of her head hair to hold it close, and frown at the difference in color, and then sliding his hand over the firm-muscled flesh of her thigh, and around to feel the buttock, which instinctively tensed to suggest even more muscle. The uncertainty and the tension of it became unbearable, and she thought she would cry out, when yet again the breath was forced from her body, this time not by a blow but by a bucket of what seemed icy water being emptied right over her head, instantly followed by several others. She gasped, and tried to turn, and had her arms seized by the girls to hold her still while Munetake himself now soaped her, beginning with her neck and sliding down her body, remarkably gently, smiling at her as he tickled her nipples into erection, caressing her buttocks, and then suddenly slipping between, actually to enter her body with soapy ease.

"No!" she gasped. "You wretch! You . . ." She attempted to kick, but his hands had already moved down to her feet, and he held the ankle as it left the floor, sliding between her toes and inducing a most peculiar feeling of being possessed.

Then she was released, and again douched in cold water to leave her gasping, before being abandoned, while the girls soaped Munetake and then rinsed him in turn. It was the first opportunity she had had for considering her surroundings, and she looked left and right to determine her best course of action. She did not suppose there was any escape; outside there would only be more Japanese. Nor did she particularly wish to escape. Her father was dead, and with him his crew, as his ship was lost. Nor could she doubt that Mr. Freeman was also by now dead, executed in trying to defend her honor. Therefore only death was now an acceptable fate. And suddenly she saw the means. Munetake, in disrobing himself, had laid his swords beside his kimono on the one solid and dry patch of floor by the door. Alison did not suppose she would even be able to lift the long sword, but the short sword was little more than a dagger. It would require only the resolution to plunge that point into her own breast, and her misery would be over.

She drew a long breath, waited for the girls, giggling and chattering, to commence emptying their buckets over Munetake, and then ran for the corner. But they were faster than she, saw immediately what she was after, and threw themselves behind her. Her fingers closed on the short sword's scabbard, but before she could reach the haft to draw it, they were dragging her back over the grating by her ankles, to lie on her face before Munetake, gasping and weeping in sheer frustration.

Her head jerked as a searing pain tore through her buttocks, and she realized that she had been hit by . . . She tried to turn, and saw the doubled kimono sash coming down again, to drive her flat with the agonizing force of the blow. Before she could move, Munetake had come around to her head and was standing on her hair while he struck her again and again. She screamed her anger as well as her pain, and tried to rise to her knees, but in doing so only presented a better target. She tried to grasp his ankles, and had her own seized by the attentive girls to stretch her flat again, while the blows continued to thud down on her, driving all thought from her mind, leaving her aware only of sobbing and twisting in an effort to gain some relief.

The blows stopped, and the feet left her hair; it was impossible to decide which hurt the most, her scalp or her bottom, or her breasts from being pressed into the slatted wood, or her lungs and stomach from the screams torn from them. She panted, and sobbed, and attempted to roll, but fell forward again at the pain of touching the wood with her tortured flesh. Dimly she became aware that Munetake had entered the well at the end of the room and was immersed in the water there up to his neck. And that the girls were still standing around her, waiting for her to move. But as she did not, Munetake gave a command, and they seized her arms and shoulders to drag her to her feet.

She moaned with pain, but she was past resistance now. They had to half-carry her to the lip of the well and then slide her in. She shrieked her pain, both from touching the wood and from the enormous heat of the water, which seemed to be tearing the skin from her flesh. She sank to her knees, and her head disappeared, and she thought that at last she had succeeded in ending it, but immediately she was raised by Munetake himself, and taken toward him. He turned her so that she faced him, and then sat her on his lap, pushing his own legs between hers. When she would have fallen back, he gave another command, and the girls also entered the bath, holding her upright and against him, whimpering with pain, and then crying out in total desolation as she felt him enter her.

For a moment Ralph hung in the air above only blackness, not knowing what was awaiting him below, and then he struck the water with a huge splash, sank into it, and touched mud, came back up again, and found that he could stand, up to his waist in salt water, on a muddy bottom on which there was a liberal selection of crabs, to keep his feet stamping as they attempted to nibble his toes. He stared upward at the ring of light marking the lip of the hole, at the samurai standing there some fifteen feet above him—and then the torches were taken away, and he was plunged into absolute darkness.

To seethe in discomfort, and with a mixture of anger and the most utter despair, as he imagined Alison, all of that clearly well-bred beauty and dignity, being subjected to the horrors—as they would certainly appear to her—of a Japanese bed, with the death of her father and her friends just beginning to penetrate her consciousness—and all at the behest of a brutal monster like Munetake. And he had promised to save her. Would it not have been better to allow the samurai to cut off her head there on the beach?

Munetake, he thought, his anger crystallizing in the one direction. One day, he promised himself, I shall look at you down the barrel of my revolver. One day soon. But now he had the simple matter of survival to consider, as the tide rose—for the pit was undoubtedly open to the sea moat surrounding the castle. Soon he was standing on tiptoe, and then swimming, as he could no longer stand, realizing that he must be very careful to keep control of his emotions if he would not drown, treading water, slowly feeling the pain in his muscles turning to leaden exhaustion, and then, just as he thought he had reached the limit of his endurance, being able to touch with his toes again. The pit had been cleverly constructed, so only the last hour of tide actually went above six feet—but that meant in most cases it had to be an execution cell for all but the strongest of the much shorter Japanese. But he had survived, and there was twelve hours before he need face the ordeal again—when he would be that much weaker, he knew. But twelve hours . . . It was impossible, in the Stygian darkness, to know when it became dawn outside. He knew only that he was slowly beginning to feel the cold, to suffer numbness in his toes. He had to keep moving to maintain his circulation, and this was itself exhausting, and he knew that all the time the twelve hours were passing. The tide went out and out, until he was exposed to his knees, and for a blessed hour he could sit in the water—having by now completely discouraged the crabs by stamping several of them to death—however cold and unpleasant it had become. But then he found himself kneeling, and soon standing again as the sea once more crept remorselessly toward his chest.

And there, above him, was the ring of light. "Well, Freeman San?" Katsura demanded. "Have you repented of your rashness? Or have you drowned?"

"I have not drowned," Ralph said.

"Then be grateful to the goodness of your lord," Katsura recommended, and a rope struck the water beside Ralph. He knew he lacked the strength to climb it, with his cold- and water-softened hands, but they had made a bowline in the end, and this he was able to pass under his armpits, and allow himself to be drawn to the surface.

"I did not think you would drown," Katsura said.

"Where is the woman?" Ralph asked.

Katsura sighed. "With Munetake, where she was sent. Do not ask after her again, Freeman San. Do not even think of her. She belongs to another, and your portion can only be death, if you attempt to interfere, because you would be inexorably in the wrong. Lord Nariaka's patience will not last forever, and he remains very angry with you. Now you must seek your way back into his favor by your deeds. Remember this."

A rather typical Japanese reaction to the situation, Ralph thought with bitter contempt. Katsura could conceive of no attitude better than to please the lord. As if *he* would ever work for such an ignorant, callous monster again—or for any of his barbaric samurai. In fact, his sole ambition at the moment was to reach the British Navy and tell them what had happened here, and if possible guide them back, and stand on the deck of one of their ships as they pounded the castle of Shimonoseki into rubble.

But first, it was a matter of escaping. And of rescuing Alison Gray.

"I had supposed my lord to be dead," Aya remarked as she bathed him—the hot water felt like the most magnificent of tortures as it slowly penetrated his frozen muscles. She would, of course, know exactly what had happened; there was no one in all Shimonoseki who would not know exactly what had happened. He wondered if she was jealous. He was sure she had no reason; he would have attempted to rescue the Englishwoman had she been as ugly as sin and if he had never seen her before in his life. He was sure of that. And Aya had to be trusted, because without her he could accomplish very little. Besides, more than ever, if he intended to escape with Alison, the Japanese girl could not be left behind to suffer Nariaka's wrath—whatever complications he could foresee in taking both the women.

"I quarreled with Lord Nariaka," he agreed. "And was thrown into the pit."

She frowned. "No man may quarrel with his lord, Freeman San. And few men survive the pit," she added as an afterthought.

"No Japanese man, Aya. But I am not Japanese. I have quarreled with Nariaka, as I said. He did not execute me because I am still useful to him. But I shall work for him no longer, except to facilitate our departure from this place."

She stared at him, her mouth open; she could not comprehend what he was saying.

"But when we leave," Ralph said, "we must also take the English girl, Miss Gray."

"The white woman belongs to Munetake," Aya said, her eyes watchful.

"That is another difference between you Japanese and us white people," Ralph told her. "In our society, women do not belong to men. They go to them freely, if they choose. Miss Gray is not a slave, and I will not have her treated as one. And Munetake and his friends murdered her father and her friends. I will take her to safety with us when we go."

"Go, Freeman San? How may we leave Shimonoseki without Lord Nariaka's permission?"

"By walking out of here one night."

"My lord," she said, "no man who deserts Lord Nariaka may escape his vengeance."

"*We* are going to, Aya. Now, listen. Can you get to speak with the white woman?"

Aya hesitated. "She has not yet left Munetake's chamber, my lord."

"You know of this?"

"I have heard."

"Tell me."

She was not reluctant to do so. "I have heard that the white woman attempted to take her own life in the bathhouse, and had to be beaten. And then I have heard that when Munetake took her to his chamber, and would mount her, she opened the door and ran out, naked, and attempted to throw herself from the battlements."

"My God," Ralph said.

"But she was prevented, and taken back to Munetake's bed, and beaten again," Aya said with some satisfaction. "Since then she has remained with him."

Ralph discovered that his nails were eating into his flesh, so tightly were his fists clenched. But losing his temper was self-defeating. "Will she be sent into the yard?"

"When Munetake is finished with her," Aya said.

"Thank God for that. Now, she does not speak Japanese. So I will give you a written message for her. You must give her this message secretly."

"My lord Freeman," she said, "Lord Nariaka will have us all executed."

"Only if he finds out what we are doing, Aya. And he cannot do that unless you make a mistake. So do not make a mistake."

She remained very doubtful, but after they had made love she seemed more reassured; he realized that at least part of her hesitation was caused by fear of being replaced in his bed. He kept the message very brief: "For God's sake, be patient. Trust this girl. Do whatever she indicates. We will escape together. Courage. Freeman." At least there was no risk of anyone understanding it, even if Aya did make a mistake; no one else in Shimonoseki could read English.

Then for the rest of the day it was simply a matter of performing his duties, although when it came to practicing his sword play, he discovered that he had a new instructor; Katsura obviously felt that Munetake might be unable to restrain his hatred for the man who had knocked him down. In fact, he did not see Munetake all day, and when he inquired, he was told, with a contemptuous grin, that "Munetake San has been given the day to rest and play with his new toy."

A thought which but increased the bubbling anger in his veins, his determination to get them out of Shimonoseki just as soon as was possible.

The Japanese girl placed the still-breathing fish in the bowl and held it toward Alison, who sucked air into her lungs and hated the way her hands trembled as she reached for it. She had been shown what to do, but she was not at all sure she could do it properly. And failure might result in another beating. She did not think she could stand that; she thought she might go mad.

Carefully she stood up, every muscle trembling now, as they all could see, because she was naked. They were all naked, as this was their lord's pleasure. As was Munetake himself, reclining in the corner, watching them. And his nakedness was the most frightening thing of all, because she could see that he was regaining his vigor yet again, and would then no doubt wish her, yet again. She had no idea how many times he had already entered her; the last twenty-four hours were a terrible blur. She did remember several occasions on which he fondled himself with one hand while fondling her with the other, to restore his erection.

But it was the beatings she feared more than the rape now. The beatings precluded thought, any chance to consider the future, what her future might be—she realized the pain might actually have *saved* her reason.

She knelt beside him, placed the dish on the floor, drew another long breath, and cut down as the girl had shown her—and instead of a clean slice, at right angles across the fish's back, her stroke was diagonal, ensuring that the entire job would be a botch. She checked, staring at it in horror, waiting to be thrown to the floor and held there . . . and instead Munetake merely smiled, and took the knife from her hand, and finished slicing the fish himself, with total expertise, even managing to eliminate the evidence of her mistake. Then he held out a piece for her to take. She swallowed without thinking, although she was not in fact hungry; all day as they had cooked, the girls had fed themselves, and her, with nibbles from the pot. She did not understand them at all. They had been there from the beginning, and were clearly Munetake's more usual bed companions as well as his servants; she was an alien creature who had replaced them, at least temporarily—and yet they showed no dislike for her. They had been there from the beginning, had watched her stripped and beaten and raped, time and again—and yet they showed no contempt for her. They obeyed their master absolutely, would, she knew, do *anything* to her that he might command—and yet treated her almost as one of themselves, in the matter of food, or drink, or even quick smiles.

And now . . . She gazed at Munetake as he offered her another piece of fish, still smiling, and chewing himself. He was a total monster, who had treated her as she had not supposed it possible to treat any woman. And now he smiled and offered her food, like the most perfect gentleman. And then, equally surprisingly, dismissed them, speaking to the girls as he did so. When Alison did not immediately respond, as she did not know what he was saying, they took her hands and raised her to her feet, draped her in a kimono considerably too small for her—it came only to her ankles—and loaded her with pots and bowls to be removed from the room; Munetake's bed did not need to be made up, as he had not left it all day.

To step outside at all required an immense act of courage. To her the Japanese girls were all but indistinguishable, one from the other. But she, with her height and the paleness of her skin, and above all, her auburn hair, stood out among them like a beacon—and there could not be a samurai or a slave in Shimonoseki who did not know what had happened to her last night and all today—for it was again nearly dusk. Yet no one paid any attention to her at all as she hurried with the girls down the stairs and into the yard and across the inner drawbridge ... to what appeared to be a large pigsty. She recoiled in horror from the huge barracks, in which men and women, children, and dogs were indiscriminately situated, sleeping on an earthen floor, surrounded by almost a miasma of odors, few of them pleasant, and all *too* interested in the new arrival, surrounding her to feel her hair and her skin, peer into her eyes, chattering among themselves. She thought that to be raped by these filthy creatures, after a day such as she had had, *would* drive her mad, but the girls protected her, chattering as loudly as anyone else, and she heard the name "Munetake" several times. They were obviously reminding their menfolk that she was Munetake's, and to interfere with her would bring down on their heads the wrath of the samurai.

But the idea of sleeping in this place was repulsive. The idea of sleep at all was repulsive, because sleep might bring dreams. It was also necessary to think, and plan ... but she was exhausted, and could hardly keep her eyes open.

The girls lay down together in a vacant corner, giggling and chattering now, scouring the pots with their fingers to seek the last morsels of food, draining the half-empty china bottles of cold sake, offering her some as usual. When she shook her head, they ignored her. She stood up cautiously, went toward the door, and they still ignored her. A moment later she was in the blessed gloom of the evening, and the even more blessed fresh air, and could approach the battlements and look down at the sea, some sixty feet below her.

So what was there to think about? She could end it, here and now. Certainly there was no reason for waiting. Mr. Freeman was dead, and she possessed no friend in all the world. Tomorrow there would only be Munetake, and then tomorrow and tomorrow and tomorrow, until he tired of her, and then ... She did not need to speak Japanese to understand that the bent old crones who cleaned the castle yard must once have been pretty young girls like her three companions.

She sighed, and rested her elbows on the battlements, and heard a soft sound behind her. She turned in terror, and gazed at a young woman, clearly, from her dress and her lack of makeup or hairstyling, one of the servants, but yet a girl who seemed to stand straighter than the others, and whose face was less dull. And who was holding out her hand toward her.

Alison hesitated, frowning, and the girl said, "Freeman San."

Alison's heart gave a leap, and began to pound; she took the girl's hand and felt a piece of paper pressed into her palm. "Freeman San," the girl said again, and disappeared into the gloom.

He was alive, and, as she saw the next day, clearly restored to his rank and privileges. He was a friend. And he was a man. Who had lived here in Shimonoseki for a year. The girl who had brought her the message was clearly his slave. Did he ever stand on her hair to beat her? She could not suppose that of Ralph Freeman. But she could not doubt that the girl sat on his lap to be entered, or knelt before him, or did all the other things Japanese men apparently required of their women . . . and more important, she could not doubt that *he* knew this was what Munetake would have done to her.

And yet he was apparently contemplating risking his life to save her. An impossible thought, for what could he do with her, even supposing he could succeed. She was Munetake's.

But yet, it was hope. Life without hope was not supportable, and she had not, after all, jumped from the battlements. She had to wait, she told herself, at least until they had a chance to speak, and she could tell him not to be a fool. As if she would ever dare speak to him, could ever dare even look him in the eye. But she hoped—for what, she dared not consider—and thus lived, and worked with the honin women, bathing with them first thing in the morning, so that she was sweet-smelling when she attended her lord, cooking and washing with them, and attending Munetake's couch whenever he summoned her. She even avoided being beaten, by keeping her wits always about her and obeying his every gesture or command. She was concentrating on survival, because of Ralph Freeman, because she felt that she could happily die if, for one instant before that happened, she could be held in his arms, and be made a woman again.

However great his impatience, Ralph knew that it was necessary to proceed with the utmost caution; despite his confidence to Aya, he was under no illusions as to their likely fates, should they fail to make good their escape. He had first of all to set up a pattern, over the next few days, of leaving the fortress with Aya every evening shortly before dusk. The samurai on guard duty at the drawbridge made ribald remarks, but after the first couple of occasions took no great interest in them; that the American was a man of very peculiar habits, which no doubt included wishing to beat his servant, or mount her, in the privacy of the woods outside the city, was well known to all. Besides, they returned about an hour later, just before dark. In this, as, Ralph hoped, in the whole plan, he was of course aided by the utter inability of any of the Japanese to suppose that he, or anyone, might actually be considering deserting his lord. Thus equally, no one commented as they each day left the castle a little later, until they were actually departing in the dark—they always returned.

There was no way in which he could secure horses, but he felt confident that with a night's start he could get them to the shores of the Inland Sea, where he had landed with Inouye and Ito, and there steal a boat. He was a little bit disconcerted by the loss of his revolver; his sword had been returned to him, but not the Colt. "Lord Nariaka commands me to hold it in safekeeping for you, Freeman San," Katsura said. "So as to remove any temptation you may have to use it in anger. Fear not, should we ever go into battle, the weapon will be restored to you." But presumably, Ralph reflected, if any pursuers got so close that he had to fight them, they would be lost in any event.

His principal concern was the girl herself. Like all

the other honin women, she spent most of each day inside her master's apartment, performing her chores, and again like them, she was sent into the yard at dusk. By carefully studying the times he managed to find himself in the right place at the right moment a week after her arrival, so that she walked right past him. "Have courage," he whispered.

She checked, and her head turned to look at him. She wore a kimono, but as a honin her hair had not been dressed and her face not been painted. And in its tragic misery it was a more beautiful face that he remembered. "Do not be a fool, Mr. Freeman," she said. "Why risk your life for what I have become?"

Then she was gone again. It was necessary to send her another written message, by an increasingly unhappy Aya. But at least she had not again attempted suicide. However great her misery and despair, she had read his first message, and she was prepared to trust him. "Do not give up, Miss Gray," he wrote. "I do intend to rescue you, and myself. Do as Aya indicates, and trust me. Freeman."

"Did she take the message?" he asked Aya the next day.

"I gave it to her," Aya said. "Freeman San, this woman will be the death of us all."

"That is not true," he insisted. "If you play your part. We will leave tomorrow."

"Tomorrow?" Her head came up.

"It will be the easiest thing in the world," he told her.

As it was. Aya carried out the instructions he had given her to the letter, managed to pass one of her kimonos to Alison, and then left the fortress during the day, ostensibly on an errand for her master; there was so much coming and going during the daylight hours, it was an acceptable chance that her non-return would not be noticed by any of the guards, nor did anyone investigate the contents of her basket, which contained several days' supply of rice. Then it was just a matter of waiting for Alison to play *her* part, which could not begin until she was released from Munetake's requirements. But this was to the good, as Ralph did not wish to attempt to pass the drawbridge until after dark. His only fear was that Alison might not be able to bring herself to act positively if she was still in a mood of despair. But he remembered that she had already proved herself a young woman of considerable courage, and considerable determination, too, or she would not have survived this far.

Munetake laid down his food sticks and leaned back on his mattress, yawning and belching as he did so. The girls knelt around him, gathering up the remains of the meal, waiting for their dismissal—the sun was drooping toward the horizon as it prepared to plunge into the Strait of Tsushima.

That sun was the signal. Alison knelt closest, as he liked her to do, and like them all, she was naked, as he liked them to be. Munetake's interest in her had not abated in the slightest during the ten days she had been in Shimonoseki; even now his fingers toyed with her hair, slid around to finger her arms or slip into the armpit to gently tug the down; in this, as in so many other physical aspects, she was totally unlike the almost hairless Japanese girls. Surprisingly, the only part of her body which did not seem to interest him was her face. For which she was truly grateful. Here at least was something she had retained; he had never even kissed her.

But the rest never ceased to fascinate, as now; he was as usual huge and impatient, and now pulled her forward to lie on his chest. The other girls sighed their impatience and lit the lamps while she moved against him, because if she ceased moving he would certainly slap her behind with his open hand, while he assisted her by seizing a buttock in each hand and himself pulling her to and fro. While he stared into her eyes. Because he did not wish her to lie on him; she had to keep herself above him with her arms extended so that he could look at her face, or play with her breasts if he chose, and so that her hair would stroke back and forth across his face, which apparently he enjoyed.

But tonight was taking longer than usual. Tonight, of all nights. He had eaten too well. She wanted to scream with impatience. But he would climax eventually and dismiss her, and within a few hours she would either be free or she would be dead. She was determined of that. And death was the easier to contemplate. To be free, with Ralph Freeman . . . Could she ever *be* free, after Munetake? After . . .

Great shudders tore through Munetake's body, and he held her hair to pull her head back and look into her eyes. Then he threw her off him.

As the sun settled into the Strait of Tsushima, Ralph equipped himself with a stick and sauntered across the inner drawbridge into the yard, past the noisome barracks which were the honin sleeping accommodation, and found her waiting for him. She wore Aya's kimono, and in the darkness it was impossible to tell that her hair was not as black as any Japanese'; it hung straight past her shoulders as Aya's did.

He could not see her face properly, but her voice sounded different from how he remembered it; it trembled. "I am too tall, Mr. Freeman," she said. "Can this possibly succeed?"

"It'll succeed," he promised her. "I am going to beat you through the gate, Miss Gray. Remember not to scream in English. And trust me." He led her toward the first drawbridge, then took a long breath and bellowed in Japanese, "Foul slut, I shall take the skin from your back." He twined his hand in her hair and slashed his stick across her buttocks, pulling the blow as much as he dared, but yet bringing a whimper of real pain from her startled lips. "Slut," he bawled again, and pushed her past the guards and onto the bridge, hitting her again and again. "Whore!"

"Beat the bitch," said one of the guards. "Beat her till she bleeds."

They were not interested in what she might have done, only amused at the spectacle.

"Tie her to a dog," recommended another.

"That is sport," said a third.

"I shall beat her," Ralph growled, and hit Alison again. She gave a scream and tried to get loose, then they were across the field and into the gloom of the empty exercise field, beyond which were the lights of the town. "Run," Ralph whispered, and released her hair. Alison sprang away from him and ran over the grass, gathering the skirt of her kimono around her knees. Ralph ran behind her. "Bitch!" he bawled, waving his stick. "Whore!"

They were outside of the fortress, and free.

After a few steps Alison stumbled and fell to her knees. Ralph scooped her from the ground and into his arms, and set off again, bearing to the right to skirt the town itself and follow the shore, as he had instructed Aya to do.

"Mr. Freeman," she gasped, and he realized she was weeping. "Oh, Mr. Freeman . . ."

He hugged her against him. "I am sorry about the spanking," he said. "But it was necessary to distract them."

"And I did not feel a thing," she lied. "You do not hit as hard as . . ." She bit her lip, and nestled her head on his shoulder. "But, Mr. Freeman, to risk so much. Surely . . ."

"Let's say I wasn't going to leave you behind, Miss Gray," he said. "I only wish I had been able to help you before. And in fact I have been planning to leave these rascals since a long time ago."

How matter-of-fact their conversation. As if neither of them had anything to remember, to fear. To hate. But she must match his mood. "Where can we go?" she asked.

"We'll take a boat and go up the Inland Sea to Osaka. Then to Edo. There is an American consulate in Edo. It is actually because of the way the Japanese have been mistreating shipwrecked sailors for so many years that my country forced concessions from the shogunate. Once we reach the consulate, we'll be safe, I promise you." He stopped walking and set her on her feet again. "Aya should be around here somewhere."

"The Japanese girl? She seems very faithful. Is she . . . your wife?"

He shook his head. "She is my slave. I'm afraid I have had to adopt *some* Japanese habits."

She turned away from him, and he realized his error.

"Miss Gray," he said, and bit his lip in turn. He wanted to tell her that there was nothing obscene in what had happened to her, except in the fact of its happening at all. He wanted to reassure her that she was as lovely as she had ever been, and as untarnished, at least in his eyes. But he didn't know how to say these things without at the same time conveying a suggestion that he would take her for himself, if she would have him. Which already contained more than a little truth. Because one of his most regular midnight dreams was of being able to make love to a white woman the way he made love to Aya.

"I am sorry, Mr. Freeman," she said. "I . . . I shall not burden you with my misery or my memories, I promise you." She turned back again, forcing a smile. "You have risked your life to save mine. I owe you everything I possess. I'll not let you down now. You have my word. Just tell me what you wish me to do."

He realized, with rather a shock, that he had apparently made no impact whatsoever on her as a man. "I guess we'd best find Aya," he said, and turned, to find her standing beside him.

"There is hardly much time for talk, Freeman San," she pointed out.

"Right as usual. Let's go."

He would not let them run, although both girls wished to hurry as fast as possible. But they had a long way to travel, and he did not want them to be exhausted when they reached the fishing village. This was done about an hour before dawn. A few dogs barked, but no one interfered with them as they selected a suitable boat, about twenty feet long, with a mast and sails as well as oars, and pushed it down to the beach and into the sea. The girls scrambled over the side, and Ralph followed, stepping the mast and setting the single junk-type sail before he unshipped the steering oar and settled down aft. There was a light breeze from the south, which was ideal, at least until dawn came and he could actually see what they were doing. But for the moment it was sufficient that their escape had proved so simple and that they were on their way.

"My God," Alison said. "To be at sea again, and free of that monster . . ."

"Where were you coming from?" Ralph asked her. "When you struck the rocks?"

"We were from Hong Kong," she explained. "And bound for Vladivostock." She sighed,

He squeezed her hand. "Have you no other relatives to whom you can go?"

"Oh, I have aunts and uncles and cousins in England," she said. "But . . . will they want me, Mr. Freeman? Will anyone want me? *Can* anyone want me now?"

"Well . . ." he said, and was grateful for the interruption as Aya brought them some of the food she had secreted from the castle.

Alison was clearly grateful too. "How far is it to this island of Honshu?" she asked.

"Why, we have only just left Honshu," he explained. "Shimonoseki is the southernmost end of it. And this lake runs most of its length. As to how far that is, I have no idea." He switched to Japanese. "How long is the Inland Sea, Aya?"

"I do not know, Freeman San," she replied. "But it is very long. There is no lake like it in the world."

"The Japanese have a tendency to exaggerate when it comes to anything they possess," he told Alison. "But I suspect we have a journey of several days ahead of us."

"Several days? But . . ."

"We'll manage. Aya will catch fish, and there are innumerable little islets where we can put in for the night, all deserted, and all perfectly beautiful." He looked at the flapping sail. "Provided we get a breeze."

It was the dawn calm, and a few minutes later they were bathed in a delightful warm sunlight, while Ralph was pleased to discover that they seemed to have the lake to themselves and were a good mile from the nearest shore, drifting quietly along. Aya promptly removed her kimono and dived over the side; she swam like a fish. Ralph looked at Alison.

"I think I am all right for the time being," she said, and wondered why, and how easily she reverted to type. She had spent most of the past ten days naked in the company of a man, and being abused by him, too. But this was an American, not a Japanese. Yet, did she not want him to look on her, and love her, more than anything else in the world? But simply to remove her clothing and go swimming . . . Or was she afraid of suffering by comparison with the girl who was already his woman?

"Do you mind if I do?" he asked.

"Of course not, Mr. Freeman," she said, and went forward, to sit in the bow, while he went over the stern with Aya.

And again wondered why she did it.

"If you want the white woman," Aya remarked, "why do you not take her? She is yours now. You are going to die for her in any event. You should enjoy her while you may." Her face twisted. "Then you might enjoy me as well."

"Nobody is going to die for anybody," he said. "And I intend to enjoy you many times when we get to the American consulate. That could be a breeze."

They scrambled back into the boat, resumed their kimonos so as not to embarrass Alison, and looked astern—to see a ship just appearing over the horizon.

"That is a Cho-Shu ship," Aya said with gloomy satisfaction. "Now we all will die."

Ralph held on to the mast to steady himself while he peered aft, shading his eyes. It was impossible at this distance to make out the golden sunflower of the Cho-Shu clan, if indeed the craft were flying such an ensign. But she was definitely traveling faster than was possible with the very light breeze under sail alone; there were rowers at work back there.

"They cannot possibly have missed us yet," he said.

"Do you not know that you were overlooked at all times, Freeman San?" she asked. "They may not keep you under constant surveillance, but your chamber is inspected secretly at least once in every night. As soon as it was discovered that you had not returned to the castle at all . . . Lord Nariaka is a very wise man. He has greater wisdom than any man in Cho-Shu. He knows all things, understands the minds of men. He would have known immediately what you had done. And when the barbarian woman could not be found either, then he would even know where you had gone. And as he knows you could not hope to escape on foot, he would know you must have stolen a boat."

"How come you didn't tell me all of this before?" Ralph asked.

"Would it have changed your mind, Freeman San?"

He gazed at her for several seconds, then shrugged. "I guess not."

"Are those people after us?" Alison asked.

"I'm afraid so." His brain seemed to have gone dull. It had all seemed so easy. But now . . .

"Have we any hope at all?" Alison asked, still speaking in a very quiet, matter-of-fact voice.

Ralph sighed. How he wanted to say yes. How he wanted to be able to conjure up all the images of the boys' adventure stories he had read in his youth. Then, often enough, the hero was in exactly such a situation as this—save that his pursuers would be redskins and his lake somewhere in North America—and had always escaped. A storm should now spring up, turning the surface of the lake into a maelstrom, into which the pursuing vessel would sink, while he, with superb seamanship, would bring the two women to safety. Or they should be able to reach an island, where they would be able to hide. . . . But their pursuers could see them as clearly as they could see the Cho-Shu ship, and they were closing every minute. "None," he said.

"Well, then," she said, "I would ask a great favor of you, Mr. Freeman. You wear a sword. I would ask to borrow it, but I doubt I possess so much courage. Yet be sure that you will be accused of no crime in heaven if you plunge your blade into my heart. Please, Mr. Freeman. You cannot let that creature take me again."

Ralph chewed his lip.

"You must kill us all, Freeman San," Aya said. She had not understood what Alison had said, but her thoughts were moving along the same lines. "Believe me, my lord, after what we have done, we will be granted no easy death. Not even you, my lord, as you are not yet a samurai. It will be slow and painful, and

they will laugh at your screams. It would be best, Freeman San."

Ralph gazed at her and then at Alison. His left hand
rested on the hilt of his saber. It could be done in two
quick sweeps, and he could then presumably fall on the
point himself.

But it could *not* be done, on a beautiful sunlit morning,
to two lovely women, with all of their lives before them.
Aya was as usual taking an apocalyptically Japanese
view of the situation. Nariaka would undoubtedly be
very angry, but he still had no one to replace his American gunner. No doubt they would be beaten, he thought.
And no doubt Alison would be returned to Munetake's
bed. But whatever she suffered, she would survive it, as
he would survive his punishment. And one day they
would escape, and live, and laugh, and be happy—if
only they were sufficiently determined to do so.

"Please, Mr. Freeman," Alison said; the following
vessel was now very close.

"No," Ralph said. "I do not think we will be executed.
I think we have but to determine to survive, and conquer,
eventually, and we shall. I think it would be the coward's
way to kill ourselves while there is no certainty of our
fate. Remember, Alison. No matter what happens, we
will escape, one day. We will." He kissed her on the
forehead. "Now, let us show these Japanese we have as
much guts as they." He ran down the sail and stood up
to face Munetake.

II
THE
SAMURAI

—6—
THE MASTER GUNNER

Munetake stood in the bow of the galley as it nosed up to the little sailing boat. Ralph was relieved to see Katsura beside the big samurai. But the general looked gravely angry.

"Throw down your sword, barbarian," Munetake commanded. "Or use it."

Ralph drew his sword and presented the hilt to the Japanese; the men in the galley gave a great shout.

"He has surrendered," Munetake said.

Katsura shrugged. "It makes no difference."

"Yet will I use him as a dog," Munetake said. "Seize him. Seize them all. Strip them and bind them."

"They are to be returned alive," Katsura warned. "With their skins unmarked. This is Lord Nariaka's command."

Munetake grinned as the samurai ripped Ralph's kimono from his shoulders, pulled his hands behind his back and bound them, and dragged him into the galley. "They will be returned alive and unmarked," he said.

Ralph heard gasps of pain from behind him, and turned to look at the two women, who were being similarly treated. He wanted to close his eyes, but could not, as the long whiteness of Alison Gray was exposed, the thrusting breasts, the flat girl belly, the dusting of darkness at her groin—even the faint marks on her buttocks where he had hit her. All Munetake's now. No one looked at Aya, perhaps not less beautiful, but more familiar, as she was thrown into the bottom of the galley. She made no sound.

Neither did Alison, now that she had clearly composed her mind. But she stared at him, into his eyes. He had caused this humiliating agony to overtake her yet again.

"Give way," Katsura commanded. "Return us to Shimonoseki as quickly as possible."

"Tie the barbarian to the mast," Munetake commanded. "Let him look upon the woman. The woman he wants." He sneered.

Ralph was dragged to the mast. As they were now rowing directly into the gentle breeze, the sail had been furled, and he was tied with his back to the timber, a rope passed around his neck to keep him upright. He gazed at Alison, and she gazed back at him, her eyes great orbs of gray misery.

"The woman he wants," Munetake said again. "Let us show him what he is never going to have."

Alison looked at Ralph again, and he could only stare back at her. He could not even speak, tell her to have courage. Because he also knew they were going to die now, despite his earlier promise.

She could imagine how sick and despairing he must feel, and was suddenly angry, that a man who so desperately sought to live life according to all the rules of his obviously Christian upbringing could have been so bedeviled by fate and ill fortune as to come to this.

He could only understand that he had made a ghastly mistake, that the women had been right in asking him to kill them quickly and mercifully.

Now he could only try to make amends.

"Munetake," he shouted. "You challenged me once, and your challenge was refused. Agree to spare the women, and I will meet you now, sword in hand, the Japanese way."

Munetake grinned at him. "I do not fight with dishonored cowards, barbarian," he said. "I merely watch them die, and spit on their carcasses."

Ralph looked at Katsura, but the general shook his head. "I can do nothing for you, Freeman San," he said. "You have brought this calamity upon yourself." He looked at Alison and Aya. "And upon your women."

"At least tell us what to expect," Ralph said.

Again Katsura shook his head. "It were better you do not know," he said. "Until the moment arrives."

When, after the longest four hours Ralph had ever known, they reached the water gate of the castle, they found Nariaka waiting for them in the courtyard, surrounded by his lords and his samurai, and his ladies, eager to comment behind their fans on the size and attributes of the big American, and of the Englishwoman. What their giggles and pointed fans indicated was obvious, and Alison hung her head in desperate shame. If only the world could come to an end this instant. She told herself that no humiliation could possibly matter now, when she was about to die. But these silk-clad women were not the slaves she had known; they were ladies, such as she had once aspired to be. And they were laughing at her.

And she could not doubt that even now their ordeal was only beginning. It was past noon by the time they reached the castle, and their throats were parched as their bellies rumbled, but they were given nothing to eat or drink as they were dragged across the dusty yard and pushed to their knees before the lord, who sat on a raised portable dais, his women kneeling about him, shaded by a huge yellow parasol. Here their faces were ground in the dust as their guards made them perform the kowtow, and here too they could look at their fate, something that closely resembled a Western gallows which had been erected at the far side of the yard.

She was going to be hanged. Somehow she had not considered that possibility. But she was going to be suspended, naked, before all of these people, her legs kicking feebly—while they laughed and jeered. Because they would laugh and jeer. It appeared to be a national pastime to enjoy those in torment.

She could no longer look at them, or at anything. Her stomach seemed to have collapsed, and her mind as well, and she was content to wait, her face in the dust, until she felt the rope at her neck.

"Thus low has your barbarian disregard for the law of Nariaka brought you," said the lord of Cho-Shu.

Ralph forced himself upward to face his tormentor.

He could at last be done with temporizing, with thinking in terms of survival. If they were to die, then the sooner it happened, the better. "The law of Nariaka!" He sneered. "The law which commands the murder of helpless men, the abuse of helpless women? This is a law? *Great* Nariaka," he said, loading his voice with all the contempt he could, "you have the honor of a dog, and your samurai are lower than the crawling things in the field."

Nariaka's head jerked as if he had been slapped in the face, while the samurai around him stamped on the ground and hissed their disapproval. Ralph did not suppose the lord of Cho-Shu had ever been so addressed in his life before.

Nariaka pointed. "I had considered a merciful death for you, barbarian," he said. "Because you are a stranger to our ways, and because your people do not seem to have any concept of duty or honor. But now I decree that you shall die the death. You and your women," he said, raising his voice. "The death of a thousand cuts."

The crowd gave a great shout of approbation, and for the first time Aya uttered a sound, a little moan of terror. Tears rolled down her cheeks, and Ralph realized that he had never seen her weep before. The sound even aroused Alison, who half-turned her head in dismayed surprise.

"Commence with the honin woman," Nariaka said. "She will die this afternoon. The white woman will die tomorrow, and the barbarian the next day. Let us give him time to enjoy the sport. Commence."

The samurai descended upon the three prisoners, seizing their arms and dragging them toward the gallows. Here two stout stakes had been driven into the ground, and to these Ralph and Alison were secured loosely by their bound wrists, so that they could slide up and down, stand or kneel as they wished, but could not lie, and could not escape.

Alison understood that they were to be executed in turn, and that Aya was to die first. And that they were going to have to watch. And be watched. She turned her head to look at Ralph, and was concerned to see that all the resolution seemed to have left his countenance.

Now *he* needed to borrow courage from her, as the moment approached. "Courage, Mr. Freeman," she said. "It is but the matter of a single breath."

He stared at her and then looked away. My God, he thought, she still does not understand. But then, he did not understand himself. The death of a thousand cuts? He did not know what that meant, what it *could* mean. It was too horrible to contemplate logically.

"Aya!" he shouted. "Aya, forgive me."

He thought perhaps she heard him, even above the din with which they were surrounded, a cheering and a stamping of the feet which was shared even by the honin and the eta, permitted to gather in a vast crowd on the far side of the second drawbridge. The inner court was reserved for the samurai and their families. Ralph wondered if Mrs. Inouye and her children were also here, to report on his execution to his friends when they returned from their mission, but he found it difficult to see clearly because of the red mist swimming before his eyes. Except when he looked at Aya, because then he could see as clearly as ever in his life.

The girl was dragged beneath the arm of the gallows, and her hands were untied from behind her back, and tied again in front of her, before being raised above her head so that she could be suspended from a hook let down from the gallows. Thus secured, her arms were pulled tight, and then raised a little more, so that she swung perhaps two inches from the ground, her naked body slowly turning in the breeze, her long black hair fluttering; her eyes were closed and she hardly seemed to be breathing.

For several seconds she was left swinging, to be jeered at by the crowd, while one of the honin men slowly crossed the drawbridge to perform the kowtow before his lord. The executioner, Ralph realized with a shudder. For the man was now presented with a knife, something like a Western butcher's tool, clearly as sharp as a razor, which he tucked into his girdle, and then, to Ralph's surprise, with something that resembled pictures he had seen in books of a surcoat of chain mail as worn by armored knights a few centuries before, save that in this garment the links were very widely spaced, allowing perhaps as much as an inch between each metal square—far too loose to keep out a flying arrow.

Again the executioner performed the kowtow; then he took the mail shirt and approached Aya. At the sound of his footfall her eyes opened, and at the sight of the shirt she gave a little shiver and her mouth opened; it was impossible to hear above the din, but Ralph thought she had cried out.

Gently, almost tenderly, the executioner wrapped her in the shirt, inserting it into her armpits and then carrying it around her body; it reached to just above her knees. With the same loving care he then commenced to draw the four leather straps with which it was provided, securing them first of all so that the shirt fitted snugly, and then beginning to tighten them again and again. Aya's eyes opened once more, in discomfort and then pain, as the links ate into her flesh—and as, between the links, her flesh began to protrude beyond the iron. Her softest flesh first, obviously, Ralph realized with horror—her breasts and belly and buttocks.

Tighter and tighter the executioner drew the straps, until Aya's eyes were almost starting from her head, and she breathed in huge gasps, while her flesh became mottled as the blood was driven from the protruding segments. Now the executioner looked at Nariaka, who nodded. His eyes were gleaming with anticipated pleasure, as were those of his court.

The executioner stood back to survey his handiwork, giving Aya a little push so that her mail-clad body again rotated, and the watchers could also appreciate his skill. He was clearly a practiced actor, pinched his lower lip and pulled his ear in apparent indecision while the crowd shrieked advice and instructions at him. They were recommending which pieces of flesh they wished removed first. Ralph's stomach rolled and his entire body seemed to swell as the executioner at last seemed to make up his mind, drew the knife from his girdle, raised it above his head so that everyone might see it, and then stepped forward and with the utmost delicacy took hold of a nipple between thumb and forefinger and sliced it away.

Aya screamed, a shriek of the most terrible pain and

terror and humiliation which rose above even the hubbub, while the executioner turned to Nariaka with a bow, was given a signal with a nod of the head, and threw the little piece of severed flesh at Ralph's feet. Then the honin turned back to make another slice and bring another scream of animal agony from the woman's lips.

Alison felt a sudden rush of bile into her mouth. She had not believed what she was seeing. That any human being could be made to suffer so ... and for a simple act of fidelity to her master. That *she* would have to undergo the same torment, from which there was no escape, no hope of escape. ... She did indeed want to vomit from sheer despair, but there was not sufficient food in her stomach.

Ralph's brain suddenly seemed to snap. He had always prided himself on preserving a cool and dispassionate judgment toward all the events of life, good and bad, sublime and terrible, but he was now aware of a maniacal anger far transcending the rage he had felt beneath Rosalee Quentin's window. He gave a scream of outrage and fury which drowned even Aya's, inhaled until his lungs seemed about to burst, and tensed his muscles until they too seemed about to burst. But the cords holding him to the stake burst first, and with a gigantic bound he was free and in the middle of the courtyard.

The crowd's shouts changed to a wail of concern; the executioner, attending to a quivering buttock, turned to face him, his expression registering sheer terror; Nariaka leaped to his feet and hastily retreated behind his dais, accompanied by his shrieking women. The samurai shrank back in a body, totally confused by what had happened. Then one, bolder than the rest, drew his long sword and ran forward. Ralph gave a roar of mingled anger and pleasure, that someone should be challenging him, leaped backward out of the way of the two sweeps he knew were coming, and then forward again, swinging his fists, catching the samurai, in the act of assuming his second position, on the side of the head and stretching him unconscious on the ground. A moment later Ralph faced the mob, sword in hand.

"Freeman San," Aya screamed. "Please, Freeman San. Please!"

His every instinct was to rush into the crowd of samurai, and there die gloriously, taking as many of them as possible with him—and certainly Munetake and Nariaka. But that would still leave the two women to be tortured. He had a duty to them first, to save them from any more torment, as he should have done this morning.

He leaped toward the hanging girl, swinging the blade. The honin made to step in front of him and was struck a tremendous blow which carved from his shoulder into the middle of his chest, left him dead before he hit the ground. Another sweep cut the rope holding Aya's hands; she dropped to her knees and then to her face, leaving bloody imprints wherever she rolled; she could not now be saved except as a helpless, mutilated half-woman, as she knew. She herself stretched her neck away from her shoulders. "Please, Freeman San," she screamed.

Ralph took an immense breath and swung the blade again.

Ralph gazed in self-horror at what he had done, at the severed head rolling away in the dust; for a moment he was unable to move.

It was a moment too long. He heard the stealthy footstep behind him, started to turn, and was struck a savage blow on the back of the head, which stretched him unconscious on the earth beside his victim.

His last thought was that he had been killed. But a moment later he knew better, as a bucketful of water was thrown on his face to revive him. Now he was again being dragged to the stake, held by a dozen pairs of hands to stop him from breaking free, while he could hear Nariaka's voice in the background, shrieking, "Fools! Did you not know of his strength? Bind him with iron. Bind him with iron."

Iron mooring chain was brought, and Ralph was secured again; he knew he would not burst this in a hurry. His body and his mind sagged with despair as the samurai stood away from him.

"Mr. Freeman," Alison said, "that was magnificent. I have never seen anything like it." And indeed her heart swelled with pride, that the man who had tried to save her could behave so grandly. Almost it restored her own courage.

"You know I would have killed you next," he said. "But I had to help her first."

"I know that, Mr. Freeman," she said. "And I am proud of it. I only wish you had been able to reach me. But, Mr. Freeman—"

Nariaka stood above them. "We have been robbed of our sport," he said. "Fetch another honin who understands the use of the knife. Let us resume on the barbarian woman. She will be sport. And let us see if you can break *iron* chains, barbarian."

Alison needed only a glance at Ralph's face to understand what the lord of Cho-Shu must have said. "No," she whispered, even as she knew what it had to be. "Oh, God," she said, and felt the tears rolling down her cheek.

Her hands were released and she was pulled to her feet. Her knees gave way, and she was dragged across the dirt, while the crowd once again chattered into a hubbub. Clearly everyone could expect more pleasure from seeing the white woman cut into pieces than one of their own.

Two men held her, sagging between them, while two others stripped the chain shirt from Aya's headless body. Alison tried to breathe, and found she could only pant. She tried to blink the tears from her eyes, and saw Ralph desperately straining every muscle against the chain. But not even Ralph could help her now.

She was dragged forward to stand beneath the gallows, and a moment later was dangling. Here was discomfort, as all her weight was taken on her wrists. But here was nothing.

She opened her mouth to cry out, because if she did not scream, and scream, and scream, she knew she would go mad. But the scream died as she felt the metal, sticky with Aya's blood, being wrapped around her and drawn tight. She gasped for breath, and stared at this new executioner, a small-faced man who grinned and winked while he fingered her private parts in adjusting the straps. He spoke as well, but mercifully she could not understand what he was saying; instead she stared at Ralph. Just now he had given her courage. Now she wanted courage again, desperately, if only the courage to die with dignity. But now he had none to offer, and she saw that he was weeping himself, from sheer despair at being unable to help her.

The executioner left her side to perform the kowtow for Nariaka. For a blessed moment she was left to swing free, while the afternoon breeze freshened and even cooled the sun sweat which had gathered on her skin. But it was fear sweat too. It was terror sweat. She was not going to die with dignity. She could feel the hysteria gathering just behind her eyes, and knew that at the first cut she would explode into screaming mania.

Nariaka had given the signal, and the executioner returned to her side. Once again he smiled at her and said something. He was even more of an actor than his predecessor, and walked round her several times, pinching nipple and buttock where they seeped through the iron mesh, pulling her nose and her hair, tickling her armpits, while the crowd roared its pleasure, and she discovered that she had been holding her breath in anticipation of the cut, and was almost suffocating. But immediately she inhaled, and her body swelled some more, and she could feel more of it pressing into the iron, and therefore going through.

And now . . . the executioner daintily stooped, and pulled on her pubic hair. Her body jerked, and he held the hair tighter, and cut it away, scattering it into the breeze while the crowd cheered and Nariaka shouted something. Alison closed her eyes, because she was aware of a tremendous drumming in her ears. The onset of madness, she knew. The merciful oblivion of not feeling or caring, she hoped and prayed.

"What is that disturbance?" Nariaka shouted, turning his head this way and that to discover where the hooves were coming from. "Who dares to gallop at the castle of Shimonoseki?"

The executioner released Alison and waited, while Ralph could scarcely breathe—his emotions had been stretched so tight as he had waited for the first cut that he had wanted to scream himself. Alison hung absolutely still, as if she might have fainted.

"A messenger is here from the lord of Satsuma, my lord," Katsura said, having gone to investigate.

"A messenger?" Nariaka stood up. "What can my lord of Satsuma have to tell me, of such importance?"

The samurai, wearing the Satsuma emblem of the cross enclosed in a ring—so suggestive of Christianity as to confuse the early Portuguese priests—performed the kowtow. He gave no more than a glance to the dangling woman or the corpses. "My Lord Shimadzu of Satsuma sends greetings, Lord Nariaka," he said. "But also important information. For your ears alone." He raised his head to look directly at the lord of Cho-Shu. "Information of vital importance, my lord."

Nariaka gazed at him for a moment, then made an almost girlish flounce of annoyance as he turned away. "Very well," he said. "Come to the audience chamber." He looked at Alison. "Let the woman hang there for the night. We will recommence in the morning."

The samurai grumbled their discontent at having their evening's sport so abruptly ended, and the honin and the eta made even more noise as they were dismissed. Munetake stood in front of Ralph and grinned at him. "You have the night to anticipate your death, barbarian," he said. "Be sure that I shall spit upon your corpse. And as your woman is stripped of her flesh, I shall feed it to the dogs before your face."

Ralph gazed into his eyes. "As the dogs will undoubtedly feed upon *your* worthless carcass, Munetake," he replied, "supposing I can find dogs to eat rotting flesh."

Munetake's smile faded into a glare, and he hissed and then turned and walked away. By now it was quite dark, and Ralph could barely make out the swinging body of the girl twelve feet away.

"Miss Gray?" he asked.

He heard her sigh.

"I am sorry, Miss Gray," he said. "I should have done as you asked on board the boat. I am sorry."

"You did what you thought was best," she said. There was a short silence, and then she spoke again. "I will not be able to keep quiet tomorrow, Mr. Freeman. You must forgive me for that."

He didn't know what to reply.

"Will they give us anything to drink, do you think?" she asked. "I am so very thirsty."

Again, nothing to say. To the Japanese, they were already dead. They could only now provide sport for the living. He closed his eyes and tried to think where he had gone wrong. But the mistake had surely been in leaving America at all. Far better to have taken his chances on the Great Plains with the Indians. At least he had known what was the worst he could expect from them. But here . . . He did not suppose he could blame the Japanese. Theirs was a totally alien culture, turned inward and made rigid by their centuries of isolation, and one which contained none of the Christian ethics of mercy and charity. One lived, and one fought to maintain one's place. And if one lost, one had no rights and no expectations. It was, he realized, a culture very like that of the Plains Indians, after all.

And besides, had he not come here, he would never have encountered Alison Gray again. She would still have been shipwrecked, but she would have been beheaded there on the beach. He would never have known where the slip of a girl he had last seen waving farewell in the middle of the Pacific had disappeared to. She would have been spared all of this torment . . . and he would never have fallen in love.

Because he knew now that he did love. Without ever having done more than touch her hand and strike her back. Hers was a courage and a dignity quite equal to that of the Japanese, and a beauty, too. A beauty he was going to have to watch destroyed slowly and with remorseless cruelty. Once again his blood seemed to boil, and he strained against the iron chain ineffectually, closing his eyes with the effort. Dust scuffed against him, and he opened them again, but for a moment could not identify the man who stood above him. Then he saw it was Katsura.

"Have you, too, come to gloat?" he asked.

"I would save your life, barbarian," the general said.

"Not because you do not deserve to die, but because we have need of you."

"You have need of *me?*" Ralph asked.

"That messenger from the lord of Satsuma," Katsura said. "He has brought word from his lord that a fleet of Western ships has been seen sailing northward along the coast of Kyushu. They are warships, Freeman San."

Ralph's heart gave a great leap. "British warships?"

"That I do not know. They certainly cannot know of the English ship which was wrecked a fortnight ago. But there was also a French ship wrecked on our shores last year. Before you came to us."

"And the crew was murdered, as usual."

"The trespassers upon the sacred soil of Cho-Shu were put to death," Katsura said carefully. "It is possible that the news of that event has leaked out. But the nationality of the ships is unimportant. Suffice that there is a fleet headed for us, armed with modern weapons. Our brothers of Satsuma are hastening to our aid with all the force they can muster, but they cannot reach Shimonoseki before noon tomorrow. It is estimated that the ships will be here by dawn. Lord Nariaka is very concerned."

"I hope he'll stay alive long enough to watch his palace burn," Ralph said. "And him in it."

Katsura came closer. "Would you rather *not* die, Freeman San? And instead become a famous warrior?"

Ralph gazed through the darkness at the old man's features. But already the insidious thought had been planted. He did not want to die. No sane man could wish that. And perhaps he could save Alison as well. It would have to be Alison as well.

"With these guns we possess," Katsura said, "could you repel a fleet of war, armed with those great cannon of which you spoke?"

Still Ralph hesitated, because he had to be very sure what he was doing. It would be easy to say yes, and perhaps die fighting the French. He had no wish to do that either; he had no quarrel with any Frenchman. Or any Englishman. At this moment, because of Alison, he was very inclined to welcome the British, at least, as brothers. But it would still be better to die in battle than to be sliced to pieces before his own eyes. And even if he did die, Alison could still be saved.

"No, Katsura San," he said. "I cannot fight those ships, and beat them, if they are armed with Dahlgren guns. But I do not think they will be, as such guns are not in general use as yet. With these cannon you have here, I can certainly give them a fight. And perhaps even drive them off."

"That will be sufficient. I will speak with Lord Nariaka."

"You will hear me first, Katsura San."

The general looked back at him. "You think you can bargain?"

"When a man has been condemned to the most terrible death there is, Katsura San, he has nothing left to lose. You will know by now that I care nothing for your concept of honor. I have my own concept of honor."

Katsura's turn to hesitate. Then he said, "Speak."

"No matter what happens in the battle, no matter what happens to me, Katsura San, the Englishwoman must not be harmed, nor must she be returned to Munetake. Instead she must be sent to the American consul in Edo. I must have Lord Nariaka's sworn word on that."

Katsura studied him. "Lord Nariaka will never agree to such terms, Freeman San," he said. "Nor would I expect him to. Because we are not as simple-minded as you suppose. We have understood that at least part of your concept of honor has to do with the protection of your women. A Japanese would have died, this afternoon, fighting his enemies, regarding the women as the legitimate spoil of his conquerors. But you threw away all your advantage to put the honin out of her misery. Should we agree to your terms, you might well contrive to die in the battle, without attempting to win it, sure that this woman would be sent to safety. My lord will agree to this: that the woman will belong to you, if you fight and triumph, and that once the battle has been won, he will permit the two of you to leave Cho-Shu and go wherever you wish. If you lose or die, then she will die also. But if you have fought to the best of your ability, and die with honor, then she will die quickly, from a single stroke of the sword, and she will be buried beside you, that you may face your ancestors together."

They gazed at each other while Alison hung silently, able to hear what was being said, understanding that here was a glimmer of hope, even if she could not tell which direction it might come from. Suddenly her shoulders became excruciatingly painful, whereas before she had hardly noticed the fact that they were slowly being dislocated by her weight. Because suddenly she was again prepared to live.

Ralph knew he would not secure better terms than those just offered. And it was at least a fair chance. As for Munetake, at the very worst he would not again get his hands on her, and if they survived, then he could be dealt with. He *would* be dealt with.

"I will agree to those terms, Katsura San," he said. "Do you tell Lord Nariaka that I will command his guns for him, if he will give his sworn word in agreement on what we have said together. There is but one thing more. The white woman must be taken down from that gallow immediately, and bathed and clothed, and fed and given water to drink, until the battle is over."

Katsura smiled at him. "It shall be so." He snapped his fingers, and men Ralph had not previously observed came out of the darkness, to take Alison down, and release Ralph himself, while honin women waited with gourds of water for them to drink.

"You are a sly one, Katsura San," Ralph commented. "You had already proposed this matter to Lord Nariaka."

Katsura bowed. "I study to serve my lord in all things, Freeman San," he said. "It would be well were you to do the same."

The conch shells were sounded, to send their wailing cry through the night, and Shimonoseki once again came to life, despite the lateness of the hour. Samurai hurried to and fro, and in the city behind the castle there was no less hubbub as the women and children prepared to evacuate their homes for the interior, supposing the barbarians managed to land, and the fishing boats were dragged up the beach until they were clear of the water. Lights flared in the castle, too, and here the ordered confusion was even greater. Alison was taken inside, and Ralph had nothing to concentrate on but his guns, once he had been bathed and fed and given his helmet and his sword. He refused body armor, which the samuari were hastily strapping on.

Then he watched as the powder and balls, some of them as old as the guns themselves, were brought up from the storerooms and stacked where he indicated, while the gun crews took their places, chattering happily among themselves. These were the men who only hours ago had hissed their enmity to him, had laughed and jeered as he had been humiliated, had looked forward to seeing him cut to pieces in a most horrible and degrading fashion. Now they were perfectly happy to take his instructions as they prepared for battle. Nor, despite their bravado, were they the least afraid of the coming conflict. But perhaps they did not know enough of what it would be like.

And no matter how good they proved themselves in battle, he reminded himself, they were still his enemies, and the enemies of all *his* people; certainly he did not mean ever to be taken captive again by any Japanese— his revolver had also been restored to him, and was fully loaded. He had every intention of using it should he lose the coming battle.

But yet he could not stop himself considering the possibilities should he drive off the enemy fleet. Because not for the first time he was being amazed by the pragmatism of the Japanese. They knew his opinion of them, even his hatred of them. But when it came to fighting, they wanted the best available—and he had more than a suspicion that he had already redeemed himself in their eyes by the way he had burst his bonds that afternoon, even if they could not understand his decision to attend to the women first. Victory would bring him freedom—and Alison. It was hardly possible to allow himself to imagine that. But it *could* be done, even with these old cannon, if he were allowed to fight as he wished. So he peered into the darkness as eagerly as any of the samurai, straining his eyes for a first sight

of the enemy, suddenly afraid that the ships might not
be coming here after all, and joining instinctively in the
great shout of excitement and approval when lights
were seen out at sea, first one, and then another, and
then several more.

"How many, do you suppose?" Katsura asked, coming to stand beside him.

"Difficult to estimate. Perhaps half a dozen," Ralph
said.

"If we can see their lights, they can surely see ours."
Katsura looked up at the palace, which was ablaze with
multicolored lanterns. "Should we not open fire?"

"That would be to waste our ammunition," Ralph
told him. "They are still well out of range."

"But the noise . . . I have heard these cannon fired,
Freeman San. The entire castle trembles, and the noise
can be heard ten miles away. Will not the noise, the
knowledge that we possess such weapons, frighten them
away?"

Ralph smiled grimly. "Those men out there have also
heard cannon before, Katsura San. They will not be
frightened by the noise, I can promise you that. The
battle will not commence before daybreak."

Honin women brought him and his gunners food to
eat and sake to drink. If only the Satsuma messenger
had come a little sooner, Ralph thought, even half an
hour, Aya might have been among them, alive and
well. But *he* had murdered her, in every possible way,
and from the beginning she had known the fate she
was risking. Yet she had made nothing more than a
token protest, because he was her master. He sighed,
for a moment overwhelmed by the guilt and disgust
and misery lurking just beneath his consciousness, and
raised his head as a dull explosion rumbled over the
morning. It was first light, cool and gray, and the lead
ship had fired, the ball plunging into the sea some
yards short of the beach.

The samurai gave a great shout of contempt and
looked at Ralph. But he had taught them to wait for his
command, and the ships were still far distant. The only
mistake he could make would be to give the approaching commanders an opportunity to calculate the size

and age, and therefore the weakness, of his armament.
Besides, he wished to be able to identify the flags.

More guns spoke, and now the warships had the
range. Balls screamed over their heads to plunge into
the city beyond; even from the battlements Ralph could
hear the screams of terror and dismay from down
there as the cardboard houses were no doubt scattered
like the paper they were. But the broadsides were en-
abling him to make some calculations of his own. There
were no really heavy pieces in the fleet, just as there
had been no attempt to parley, to seek financial or
human redress for whatever crimes the men of Cho-
Shu were suspected of. This fleet intended to adminis-
ter a punitive bombardment of Shimonoseki. They had
not come either to destroy or to take possession. But
undoubtedly, if they found the task easy enough, they
would land marines to spike the defenders' guns, and
probably burn Nariaka's palace as well. It was on that
premise, on the fact that to do so they would have to
close the shore and anchor, that he was basing his
tactics.

Katsura came hurrying up once more, ducking and
tumbling to his knees in a most undignified fashion as
a ball smashed into the battlements, scattering stone
splinters, one of which struck down a samurai gunner,
leaving him dead and bleeding on the ground. "Why
are you not returning fire, Freeman San?" the general
shouted. "Lord Nariaka is angry, and demands your
head. He says the noise will bring down his palace."

"He's terrified, you mean," Ralph remarked in English,
with some pleasure, before using Japanese. "Not the
noise, Katsura San. But he may have to accept one or
two knocks. At this range our cannon would do very
little damage to those ships. Our weapons are too old. I
warned Lord Nariaka of this. We must make them
come closer, lure them into thinking there will be no
resistance. Only then can we hope to damage them
sufficiently to make them withdraw."

Katsura hesitated, his face a picture of indecision. "I
do not know that Lord Nariaka will understand such
strategy," he complained.

"Tell him I will win this battle for him, if he will but

have faith in me," Ralph said. "And then tell him I am not winning it for *him*, but for the Englishwoman."

Katsura hurried off, shaking his head at the barbarian's insolence. Ralph fell to studying the approaching fleet again, as usual desperately wishing he possessed a telescope. Yet they were now within three miles; he counted six frigates under shortened sail, the better to permit the aiming of their guns, and flying the tricolor of France. And then, some distance behind, a seventh ship, also a frigate, he estimated . . . and flying the Stars and Stripes of the United States.

He stood upright, ignoring the balls which were now flying in every direction, thudding into the walls beneath him, scattering stone, and now striking the lower levels of the palace itself, to send brightly lacquered tiles and splinters of wood cartwheeling in every direction. To a man the samurai were cowering behind the battlements, afraid to look out, although by now several had been hit by the flying splinters; their courage had at last been collectively shocked by the impersonal violence of this form of warfare, of which they had no previous experience. And there was an American warship. . . . But what could he do? He glanced at the upper veranda of the palace and saw Nariaka waving his arms and shouting at Katsura. He dared not attempt to change his tactics now, because should the French decide it was too risky to continue, and merely sail away, content with the damage they had inflicted and without suffering any themselves, he could not doubt that his life and Alison's would be immediately forfeit.

Katsura was back at his side. "Have you identified their nationality?" he shouted.

Ralph nodded. "They are French." And waited for the inevitable question as to the ship flying the different flag. But Katsura had clearly never seen Old Glory before in his life, assumed it was some sort of a signaling pennant.

He was more concerned with the cannonballs screaming around them. "Are they not yet close enough to hit?" he demanded. "Lord Nariaka—"

"Lord Nariaka knows nothing of warfare," Ralph

snapped. "Go back to him and tell him to count his blessings, that his enemies have not thought to use red-hot shot, or his palace would have been burned to a cinder by now. And leave me to fight my battle my way. I have said I will gain the day. Be content with that."

Katsura hesitated, biting his lip, and then turned and hurried off. Certainly the moment was approaching, because his strategy had worked, Ralph could tell. The French warships had been pounding the town and the castle for some half-hour, and not a shot had been fired in reply. They must have assumed the Japanese were not capable of sustaining an artillery duel, and even as he watched, the ships began to swing into the wind, still in perfect line, and to hand their sails as they prepared to anchor, scarcely more than a mile from the beach, in a position where they could continue to bombard the fortress at their leisure, and also most conveniently put ashore landing parties; he was sure he could make out the gleam of bayonets gathering in the waists of the warships as the sun rose out of the eastern sky to bathe the scene in brilliant light.

He crawled from gun to gun, laying each one himself, while the samurai hissed and stamped their feet with impatience. The American vessel was the last in the line, and could conveniently be ignored; he suspected that her captain, whatever his orders, was more than a little reluctant to join his European allies in what was, after all, as much an act of careless barbarism—in view of the shot which had been poured into the town—as any committed by the Japanese.

"Light your matches," he commanded the gunners. "But do not fire until I give the signal."

The nine-pounders were elevated to their highest possible range, and he knew that accuracy was out of the question, even had the gunners been sufficiently practiced. But they *had* been trained to speed in reloading and firing. He squinted through the nearest embrasure. The warships had ceased firing as their anchors were let go; they considered they had all the time in the world. He even thought he could hear the notes of a bugle call drifting on the wind as the boats were swung out. At this moment the fleet was at its most vulnerable.

"Now," he shouted. "Fire!"

The eighteen guns exploded almost together. An immense hot wind and a cloud of white smoke enveloped the gunners and then rose into the air, leaving them choking and coughing.

"Reload," Ralph shouted. "Haste, now, reload." He ran from gun to gun, chivying the men to their fastest. The balls were rammed home against the cartridges, the samurai hissed their excitement. "Fire!" Ralph shouted again. "Reload!"

Once more the guns were loaded and fired, three times in the splendid time of five minutes, he calculated. Now at last he paused to gaze at the French fleet, while all around him there broke out tremendous shouts of "Banzai!" the Japanese paean of victory. Actually, he did not suppose very much damage had been done; he could make out only one topmast lying at an odd angle, and the sails had been sufficiently furled to escape much cutting. But several of the balls had struck the decks; there were dead and wounded men out there. Even more important had been the moral effect, for the water all around the French ships was still dotted with slowly settling plumes of spray, and so rapid had been the succession of salvos that the French commanders could have formed no idea either that there were only eighteen guns on the battlements or that they were all at maximum range.

Yet now was not the time for relaxation. Again he hurried up and down, from gun to gun. "Load," he commanded. "Fire! Load, fire! Load, fire!"

The rumble of the guns became continuous. Men slipped in their own sweat, but kept on working, imbibing some of the tireless energy of the big American, reeling from exhaustion, gasping and panting, but never ceasing their labors, until the shouts of "Banzai!" rose again, and they could peer through the smoke and see the warships raising their anchors and making sail, to hurry back over the horizon.

*   *   *

The noise was tremendous, the shouts of "Banzai!" mingling with the clashing of cymbals and the blowing of the trumpets and conch shells as the people of Shimonoseki celebrated. And mingled with the cries of victory was the shouted name of "Freeman San!" Everyone knew who had commanded the guns so well.

Ralph was aware only of utter exhaustion. The battle had lasted only a short while, but he had had a wearying and emotionally terrifying day before it, and no sleep. He sat beside one of the guns, while the samurai stamped about him, no longer hissing, but singing his praise. The fact of his triumph was almost impossible to take in, to appreciate. Even the fact of his survival was impossible to appreciate at this moment. He was suffering the inevitable reaction which follows any battle, an almost physical sickness. He had nothing to be proud of, he knew. He might have avoided the actual treachery of firing into an American ship, but those other men had equally been on *his* side. They would have rescued him, could they have found him alive—and no one could deny that the vipers' nest that was Shimonoseki deserved to be destroyed.

He had preserved it, to save his own life. And that of Alison. Therefore he knew there was still much to be done. There was his reward to be claimed, and quickly. But for the moment he could just sit beside the gun and sip a cup of hot sake, and feel, despite himself, the joy of victory.

He listened to hooves, and more cheering, looked up as Katsura approached. "That was well done, Freeman San," the general said. "And here is Lord Shimadzu of Satsuma to offer you his congratulations."

Ralph pushed himself to his feet, faced the greatest of the provincial daimyos. They were not a class his relationship with Nariaka had encouraged him to appreciate. He looked only for cruelty and deceit. But this man, considerably older than Nariaka, and somewhat smaller and plumper, as he dismounted from his horse, had an expression of calm dignity which was certainly noble; even the drooping mustaches which were apparently a requirement of his rank could not hide that.

Katsura dropped to his knees. "Kneel, Freeman San," he hissed. "Kneel."

"Why should so great a warrior kneel to me?" Lord Shimadzu inquired. "We came with all haste, American, yet expecting to see nothing but the burned-out rubble of a city, for we know the power of the barbarian guns, and instead we discover a victory. You are a man among men."

Ralph could think of nothing to say. Except from Inouye after the storm, it was the first time he had ever been praised by any Japanese.

Shimadzu observed his confusion, and smiled at him. "Be sure your name will go down in history." He held out both his arms, and Ralph, in utter surprise, stepped forward and was embraced. "I must offer my congratulations to Lord Nariaka, in turn," Shimadzu said softly. Was there contempt in his tone? Ralph was sure of it. "But my general, Lord Saigo, would speak with you. Listen to his words, Freeman San. At this moment, the world lies at your feet."

He released him and walked away, Katsura hastily scurrying behind him, while the samurai gazed at Ralph in total reverence, and he in turn gazed at the fully armored man who now approached him. Because he had already heard of Saigo Takamori, from Katsura as well as from Inouye and Ito, and even from Munetake. Still a young man, and of no more than average height, with an almost gentle expression and soft black eyes, the Satsuma general was by repute the most famous soldier in all Japan. Now, to Ralph's continued surprise, he did not attempt to embrace him, but after a quick bow held out his hand as an American might have done; his grip was firm and dry.

"I count this moment the most valuable of my life until now, Freeman San," he said. "Show me these guns of yours."

"I must tell you that our success was mainly bluff," Ralph confessed as they walked together away from the crowd to the battlements. "These are old cannon."

"But skillfully handled," Saigo observed. "I know their age, Freeman San, which is why I had anticipated a catastrophe for the men of Cho-Shu. I had heard, of course, how Lord Nariaka had secured for himself a foreign warrior of great repute, but I still did not suppose that one man could save him from the consequences of his own folly." He looked into Ralph's eyes. "Lord Nariaka does not have the gift of eliciting a man's best service."

"I won't argue with that," Ralph agreed.

They were now out of earshot of the samurai, which Ralph guessed was Saigo's intention in wishing to look at the guns at all—he had obviously seen them all before.

"Yet you fight for him," the general observed. "And have lived here a year. Have you not observed?"

Ralph frowned at him, unable to believe what he was hearing. "Do you mean, Lord Saigo, that all Japanese are not as Lord Nariaka?"

Saigo continued to gaze at him for some moments and then smiled. "No, Freeman San," he said. "All Japanese are not as Lord Nariaka. In his cruelty and his deceit he betrays us all. His can be no honorable way, Freeman San. But especially, no honorable way for you."

"You must speak plainly with me, Lord Saigo," Ralph said. "I am but a simple soldier."

Saigo patted the gun barrel beside which he stood. "Not so simple, American. What I have to say is this. You are not yet a samurai, I understand. You have taken no oath of allegiance to Cho-Shu. I have even heard of quarrels and condemnations. Were you to seek another lord, no man could reproach you."

"You would have me march with the Satsuma?"

"I speak with the full knowledge of my lord and master," Saigo agreed. And again smiled. "I would not have you return to America and judge all Japanese by the standards of Lord Nariaka."

"I am honored and flattered by your invitation, Lord Saigo," Ralph said. "And you may believe that I will take with me many pleasant memories of Japan, not least this conversation. However, I may also have to take some unpleasant memories as well. But Lord Nariaka has sworn that should I triumph here today I may return home immediately with an English lady to whose care I am determined to devote my life. This I must do."

Again Saigo studied him for several seconds. Then he said, "And who am I to turn a man from his duty? But should things perhaps not turn out as you wish and hope, Freeman San, my offer stands."

The Satsuma men had gone. They had ridden hard and long to be with the men of Cho-Shu in the hour of battle; they had remained for nothing more than a meal and to rest their horses before returning to their own lands beyond the Strait of Shimonoseki. Another indication that there was no love lost between Shimadzu and Nariaka. The pair were allies, not only because between them they controlled the southern extremity of the Japanese empire, and thus could hardly afford to quarrel, but also because their fathers and grandfathers before them had always been allies, sworn to assist each other in time of need.

Besides, Ralph had gathered from the snatches of conversation that he had overheard, the lord of Satsuma was as one with the lord of Cho-Shu in opposing the decision of the shogun to sign a treaty with the United States, and even more with the other barbarian nations, the British and the French, who had hurried to take advantage of Matthew Perry's boldness. Not that the Satsuma made a practice of murdering castaway sailors. On the other hand, they did not welcome them, either, but sent them to the Chinese mainland as rapidly as possible. The Satsuma wished to maintain the traditions of the old Japan, but in the noblest fashion.

And they had offered him employment. There was heady praise. He might even have been tempted, but for the certainty that Alison could never again look on any Japanese without shuddering—he could hardly bring himself to do so. And for the equal certainty that he could never find happiness in this strange land. And for his great ambition to take Alison home to the States, and in particular to Rhode Island, and show her all the wonders of that wonderful land. Here was thought, desire, leaping ahead of achievement. She had never shown the slightest spark of feeling for him save gratitude and admiration. But it was inconceivable that two people should have shared so much and not learned either to love or to hate each other. He was sure they did not hate.

He was desperate to see her again, to reassure her that now all would be well, but first he had to share in the celebrations, which went on far into the night following the victory. Katsura promised him that Alison too was celebrating, with the women, that she knew all about the victory, and had indeed watched most of the battle from the upper windows of the palace, and that she also knew all about his fame. "She will be waiting for you, Freeman San," the general said. "After you have spoken with Lord Nariaka."

"And when do you suppose that will be?" Ralph inquired.

Katsura smiled. "When Lord Nariaka is ready to receive you."

In fact it was not until dawn on the following day that he was at last summoned to the audience chamber, his brain still fuzzy with the sake he had consumed, his ears still ringing with the wail of the conch shells and the rattle of the cymbals; there were still celebrations going on in the city.

As on all of his visits since the first, he was accompanied by Katsura, but to his surprise, Munetake was also present. He had almost forgotten Munetake in the excitement of the battle and the euphoria of his triumph. And certainly the big samurai was not pleased with the way things had turned out, refused to meet his gaze, and knelt some distance away from his rival.

"This is a great day, Freeman San," Nariaka said. "A great day for the men of Cho-Shu, and especially for you. We have taught the world a lesson, you and I. The mighty shogun has stated that he signed the peace treaties with the barbarians for fear their fleets would lay our cities in ashes if he refused. Well, we have opposed a barbarian fleet, and gained the victory. Perhaps this will teach the shogun the error of his ways."

Ralph decided against reminding the lord that this had been a squadron, not a fleet, that they had repelled. And that the French had not really come to destroy;

had they used red-hot shot, Shimonoseki would very rapidly have been laid in ashes; in any event, the French had inflicted far greater damage than they had received themselves. But he did not suppose it would be to his advantage to diminish the apparent victory in any way.

"In consideration therefore of your great services to the men of Cho-Shu," Nariaka went on, "I have decided to eradicate all memories of any of your past errors, and to make due allowance for your foreign ways in our future dealings. As of this moment, I appoint you hatamoto of the guns of Cho-Shu, with an income of eighty koku of rice. Your induction into the order of samurai will follow as soon as it can be arranged."

Munetake hissed his disapproval, while Ralph knelt straight. "I am indeed grateful to my lord for his kindness," he said. "But I wish only the safe conduct to the American consulate in Edo that was promised me, and for the woman."

Another hiss from Munetake.

"I have said that it is my wish you remain here, Freeman San," Nariaka pointed out.

"And I have your promise that I may leave, my lord," Ralph said.

"I am not yet ready to carry out that promise," Nariaka said. "How can you leave, until the new guns are received and installed, and my samurai trained to use them? Do you not suppose the French may come back? Or even the British? You will remain in Shimonoseki, barbarian."

"If you break your promise to me," Ralph said, "then you are dishonored, Lord Nariaka."

Katsura drew a quick breath, and Munetake gave another hiss. "Let me fight with him, great lord," he said. "Let me strike his insolent head from his shoulders."

"Anytime," Ralph snapped. "The sooner the better."

"You will not fight with each other," Nariaka said. "Listen to me, all of you. Freeman San is now the hatamoto of my guns. There will be no fighting, except against the enemies of Cho-Shu. This is the word of Nariaka."

Ralph was so angry he could hardly speak. Once again he had been utterly deceived and betrayed. But the fault was his for having trusted this man at all. He made himself control his temper. "And do you suppose you can make a prisoner fight for you, Lord Nariaka?"

Nariaka smiled. "You will fight for me, Freeman San, and you will be happy here. Because I am not only going to give you eighty koku of rice, I am also going to give you the white woman once a week, provided you do not attempt to escape."

"No," Munetake shouted. "That cannot be."

"Hold your tongue, insolent dog," Nariaka said, without raising his voice. "How dare you address me in such terms?" He turned back to Ralph. "Once a week," he said. "You may visit her chamber. Fear not. From this moment she will be cared for, and fed and bathed and clad in silk, and she will await only you, Freeman San. But should you ever attempt to play me false, then I will have her tied to a dog before I cut off her head."

Ralph stared at him, his hand instinctively dropping to his belt. But in his sake-induced state of euphoria he had trustingly allowed himself to be divested of revolver as well as sword before entering the audience chamber.

Besides, would killing Nariaka save Alison? He did not even know where she was. Once again he had been utterly outwitted.

Munetake now gave an almost animal shriek of anguish. "This cannot be," he shouted. "The woman is mine. She was given to me by your own decree, Lord Nariaka. Either she is mine unto death, or she is a criminal, and must be executed here and now. That is the law of Cho-Shu."

Nariaka turned his cold gaze on the stricken man. "*I* am the law of Cho-Shu, Munetake San. Any samurai who does not accept my law is dismissed from my service." He smiled. "Except you, Freeman San. You will remain in Shimonoseki. And be happy with your woman."

—7—

THE BRITISH

The three men found themselves outside the audience chamber, surrounded by the waiting samurai. "Let it be known," Ralph said, "that your master has no honor. How can a man who does not keep his word have honor?"

The Japanese hissed their disapproval, but Katsura waved them down. "My master, and yours, Freeman San, has decided to overlook your intemperate barbarian ways. As for his honor, you will discover that he *is* a man of his word. You will be set free, and your woman with you, when you have completed your task here. All my Lord Nariaka desires is that you await the return of Inouye San and Ito San. They are your friends. They brought you here. Can you consider leaving Shimonoseki without saying farewell to them?"

Ralph glared at him, but the old man knew he had won at least a partial victory.

"And thanks to your triumph yesterday," Katsura went on, "and to Lord Nariaka's gracious acceptance of your different ways, your residence here promises nothing but happiness from now on. Your woman awaits you. Why do you not go to her?"

"The woman is mine," Munetake hissed. "In that, too, Lord Nariaka is dishonored."

The samurai stared at him in amazement. For a barbarian to make such statements was barely acceptable. But for a samurai . . .

"You had best withdraw your words, Munetake San," Katsura said.

"Never," Munetake declared. "Until the woman is returned to me."

"Your brain is addled," Katsura told him. "What

does she, or any woman, possess, but legs and a belly, breasts and a mouth? You are a fool, Munetake. But because you were once also a great warrior, I shall not degrade you or report your words to Lord Nariaka. They will reach him soon enough. You had best leave Shimonoseki, the lands of the Cho-Shu, while you may."

Munetake's brows drew together. "Leave?"

"In one hour I shall declare you an outlaw," Katsura said. "And degrade you from the rank of samurai. I shall break your swords and cut away your hair. One hour, Munetake San."

Munetake glared at him, looked left and right at the samurai, and found no support. He turned and went down the stairs.

"You should have let us fight," Ralph said. "I have too much to settle with him."

"And would be avenged? Munetake is perhaps the greatest swordsman in Japan, Freeman San. Not even your strength and courage could stand against him. As for revenge, be sure that now you are far more avenged than if you had struck him down. Now you must learn to live again, and be happy. Freeman San, your woman is waiting for you. Why do you not go to her?"

It all seemed a dream. If only, Alison thought, she could be sure which was the dream, and which reality . . . and which the darkest nightmare.

Life had provided the most certain security until the snapping of the foremast—could that have been only a fortnight ago? Then she had been plunged into the deepest of hells, but except for those dreadful hours when she had supposed him dead, and those equally dreadful more recent hours when she had tried to compose her mind to meet her own fate, it had been a hell with a gleam of hope seeping through it. Ralph Freeman!

The night before last, she had watched him command the guns. She would have wanted to do so anyway, even if it had not been made clear to her, by the gestures of the men around her, by the way her hair had more than once been seized by impatient samurai, and the swords held to her throat, as the French balls had smashed into the palace, that upon his success depended her own life. He had been magnificent in the confident patience of his courage. When the French had sailed away, she had even shouted "Banzai!" with the men around her.

She had supposed he would immediately come to her, and been terrified at the thought. To have any man touch her sexually at that moment, after what she had endured, would, she was sure, snap the still very slender thread of sanity to which she was clinging like a drowning woman. And yet she so wanted to be held in his arms, and be reassured that the nightmare was finally over.

Instead she had been left to the women. But no honin these. She had been bathed and perfumed by the ladies of the court, giggling and chattering, and in fact as eager as any of their menfolk to investigate her, to them, outsize attributes as a woman. Then they had feasted her, on sake and sukiyaki, tempura and ginger. She had been afraid to look at anyone, save Ralph, when she had been exposed in the courtyard. So she recognized none of their faces. But she could not doubt these were the same women who had watched with eager anticipation as she had been suspended from the gallows, waiting for the first cut. Now that was behind them, and they were happy to welcome her into their community.

So she had slept, having deliberately taken too much sake, as much drugged as weary. Only to be awakened this dawn, and again bathed and perfumed, before they had dressed her hair as they dressed their own, scooping it into a huge pompadour secured by several large pins. Then they had clad her in a green-and-white silk kimono, pulling little white stockings over her feet before inserting these in turn into exquisitely made sandals.

While this had been going on, the chamber in which she had slept, alone, had been aired and perfumed, and the mattress bed remade on the floor. To this she was now escorted, and made to sit, while a glass of plum wine was given her to drink—to give her courage as she awaited her lord and master. Then again she had been left alone.

She did not know what to think. She did not know what she *dared* think. She had not seen him since the moment of triumph, and even then only at a distance. She did not really know if he had survived unhurt—or indeed if he had survived. That was a heart-constricting thought. Because she understood enough of the Japanese mentality by now to be sure that, having promised her elevation to the ranks of lady should he win his battle, they would honor that promise even if he had been killed—but equally, they would expect her to belong to a man. If Munetake were to come through that door . . .

But of course it would be Ralph. Wanting . . . He had fought a battle, and gained a victory. She knew enough, by repute, of what men wanted when they had fought and won. And she . . . She drew a long breath, because the door was being opened by one of the ladies who had helped dress her, and another was also bowing as she relieved him of his sword and pistol, to lay them reverently in a corner of the room before hurrying away, closing the door behind her.

Alison rose to her knees. He wore a white kimono, and had obviously been recently as carefully washed and groomed as herself. Had he also been given a cup of plum wine for courage?

She held her breath as he came across the room and knelt before her. They gazed at each other.

"I was not sure you were even alive," she said. "What is going to happen to us now, Mr. Freeman?"

He sighed and told her what had been agreed between Katsura and himself, what had happened in the battle, and how Nariaka had betrayed his promise. "So you see," he finished, "I have made another mistake, and landed you once again in prison."

She gazed at him for some seconds, still unsure of his mood. Then she looked around the room. "The cell is not uncomfortable," she said quietly.

"But I'm damned if I'm going to let that scoundrel hoodwink us for too long," he went on, as if she had not spoken. "I know how to do it this time. And I know where to go. Of course I was foolish to suppose we could escape virtually the length of Japan, with every man's hand against us. But now, after my talk with Saigo Takamori ... If we can just cross the strait out there, not more than two miles of water, we are in Satsuma territory. There we will be welcomed and protected."

She frowned at him. The thought of attempting to escape, of again risking such humiliation and torture, was impossible. Besides ... "Do you really suppose you can trust any Japanese, Mr. Freeman? After Nariaka?"

"I believe I can trust Saigo Takamori," he said. "And Lord Shimadzu. They knew Nariaka would not honor his promise. They virtually told me so. And like a fool, I ignored them."

"And if you are wrong, we will again suffer the mail shirt and the knife." She gave a little shiver, and hated herself. But suddenly she had arrived at a state of equilibrium, a moment in time when she saw no future, and when her past was irrelevant. Here she wanted, she needed, to remain, for just a while, to regain the mental stability she had to have. Because facing a world of white ladies, with their prim and proper outlook on life, and their so superior pity for those of their sex who had fallen upon hard times, was nearly as terrifying a prospect for someone who *had* fallen upon hard times as facing the knife. Nor was she yet sure that even Ralph Freeman would be able to sustain her in those circumstances. "Forgive me, Mr. Freeman, but I am not really very brave. I am just happy to be alive. When I think of what those men were going to do to me ... of what that girl Aya must have suffered ..." She hugged herself.

"What would you have me do?" he asked.

"Is it so very long, to wait for your friends to return? They must have been gone something like a year ..."

"Nine months," he said.

"Well, they must be on their way back by now. And then ... if Nariaka does not keep his word, then perhaps ..."

"You are talking about at least another year," Ralph

said. "And for all of that time you will be kept here, a prisoner."

A cue, at the least. "I will not have to suffer Munetake," she said.

"No," he said. "No. Not Munetake." And bit his lip.

She gazed at him as steadily as she could. She had forgotten that Munetake had only ever been an idea to him. And yet she also knew that he wanted her more than he had ever wanted anything in his life before.

As she wanted him, if only to make her sane again. "I know you can only look on me with abhorrence," she said. "I sometimes feel that I cannot look upon myself with anything but abhorrence. But I promise that, as we share this burden together, I will do my best to be a . . . a woman to you, Mr. Freeman."

"Abhorrence?" he asked. "Miss Gray . . . Alison . . . you are the most wonderful thing that has ever happened to me. If I thought you could ever look on me with the slightest desire, or even without shuddering . . ."

"Mr. Freeman," she said, "I have never loved before. I was a virgin when I was taken by Munetake. I know naught of men save him, and him I hated more than I thought it was possible to hate. Mr. Freeman, I do not know if I can *ever* love, after what that man did to me. But, Mr. Freeman, I know *this*: that if I ever can love, it will be you."

She drew a long breath and loosed the girdle of her kimono.

She had been a dream for so very long. To make love to a white woman, any white woman, the Japanese way, had been a dream almost from the first time he had lain with Aya, but he had seen no white woman between then and the reappearance of Alison Gray. In her the dream had crystallized.

And she was a woman, in any event, of whom a man might dream. He had looked at her constantly during their ordeal in the courtyard. But then had not been a time to see, to appreciate, to imagine what she must be like to hold. Therefore those glimpses of her beauty

need never have been. Now she was real, and close at
hand. He could stroke the wealth of red-brown hair.
Her flesh was like velvet. Her breasts overflowed from
his hand, as did her buttocks. Yet her crowning glory
was her legs, long and slender, but muscular, legs to
feel against his own, while the whole was dominated
and commanded by that serious, thoughtful face. She
wanted to please him, to take away some of *his* anxiety,
as he wanted to make her smile. And failed dismally.
Even lying on her, feeling her from shoulder to toe,
breathing against him, able to kiss her, to worship at
her opened mouth, he remained incapable of doing
more than sighing, and at last rolled from her to lie on
his back and stare at the ceiling.

"You must be patient with me," he said. "I am more
tired than I supposed."

But that was only half of the truth. There was
too much catastrophe jumbled together in his mind.
Thoughts of Aya, who would never smile again, and
even more, thoughts of Munetake, who had possessed
all of this, had sent his fingers and his tongue and his
penis questing where *he* dared not even consider, knowing all the joys of ownership.

She lay beside him, her head on his shoulder. "Perhaps
you are too used to the Japanese way," she said.

"And would that not disgust you?"

She appeared to consider. Then she said, "I would
have you possess me, Mr. Freeman. The way . . . the
way Munetake possessed me. Only that way can I know
that I am truly yours, and not still his." She gave a
half-smile. "You may have become *used* to the Japanese
way; I have known no other. I thought I would go
mad, I thought I would burst with shame, when he
touched me, when he . . ." She gave another little shiver.
"I wanted to die."

"I know of that," he said. "But you did not. I am glad
you did not."

"Does it anger you, to speak of him?"

"No," he said, and realized it was the truth. To speak
of Munetake was necessary for both of them. "Not if
you wish it."

Her eyes were closed. "He touched me where I have

never touched myself, Mr. Freeman. He seemed able to feel, with his hands and his fingertips, and he knew no shame. Even when he beat me, he would keep his left hand ... between my legs, to feel me move against him. Mr. Freeman ..." She sighed. "When I did not die, when I was dragged into his chamber from the veranda, or when I was laid before him in the bathhouse, and was beaten until I cried, and when I realized that I could not escape him, oh, Mr. Freeman, I ..." A tear rolled down her cheeks, escaping the closed eyelid.

"My dear Alison," he said. "Oh, my darling Alison." He held her close, and kissed away the dampness. "Do not say it."

"But I must, Mr. Freeman," she said fiercely. "You must know. Because only that way ... I surrendered, Mr. Freeman. Because I did not really want to die, and I did not want to be beaten. I surrendered, even as I hated him and loathed and despised him. Mr. Freeman, you *must* take me, as he did, but more and more and more than he ever could. You must, Mr. Freeman, or I can never ... I must be yours, Mr. Freeman. I want to be yours, now and always."

While she spoke, her hand slid down to his belly to hold him. Because now he could do as she wished.

Could ever a man have been so blessed? Because when she was so content, then he could hardly be otherwise. And as the summer drew on, many of the events of the previous winter became nothing more than bad dreams. If the thought of Aya could still haunt him, Munetake was gone, vanished into the hills; either he had committed seppuku in despair at losing his lord, or he had become a ronin, a landless samurai, an outlaw, with every man's hand against him. Truly, for a Japanese, that was a worse fate, as Katsura had promised, than if they *had* faced each other, swords in their hands, and he had managed to cut the warrior down.

In the strangest of fashions, he had triumphed. Or perhaps, he would think in moments of pride, it was not so strange after all. He had been brought here to command the guns, and he had carried out his task successfully. That he had hated what he had had to do, still longed to see this pirate fortress leveled to the ground, no longer mattered; no other ship had been wrecked, and no other fleet of war had come seeking revenge. He had no doubt that the French admiral had reported that he had successfully carried out his mission, bombarded the port and knocked down a few houses, been fired upon in reply and suffered a few casualties, and then sailed away in triumph—and that the American captain, so clearly an unwilling participant in the events, had been happy to concur rather than suggest that the fleet return again to inflict more damage upon the Japanese people, and, far more important, the Japanese pride. Time for the outside world to forget the troublesome nuisances of Cho-Shu and get on with the business of opening Japan to foreign trade—until again the men of Shimonoseki intruded upon the peaceful affairs of the barbarians.

A day which would certainly come, although hopefully after his departure, for all that he commanded the teams of honin which worked to repair the walls where the cannonballs had pounded. He could repair them as much as he wished, he knew; they still would not withstand a proper bombardment when the day came.

Lack of knowledge of what was happening in the outside world was the gravest curse he had to bear. As the year came to an end, even his memories began to fade. It would soon be 1862, and he would have been away from home for two years come March. By now the new President would be nearly halfway through his term of office. Would it be John Frémont? It seemed unlikely. Just as it seemed unlikely that after two years the name of Ralph Freeman would be remembered, by either President, or courts, or army. No doubt he was still remembered by the Quentin family. But if he returned quietly with his bride, the Quentins might not be aware he was home at all.

These things would happen, he could at last feel sure—because it was no longer essential for them to happen. Because, whether he returned or not, his bride was here with him. Not yet his bride, of course, in any

Christian fashion, or even any Japanese fashion. He fretted for six days, to be with her on the seventh, just as they mutually wished they could share more than the single room, could picnic on the hills overlooking the Inland Sea, or even take a boat ride to one of the beautiful islands that dotted that placid waterway. But perhaps the very limitations imposed on their meetings served a useful purpose, reminded them both at all times that they *were* prisoners. Had Nariaka the sense to give them more freedom, there was the real fear they might become too comfortable here. Certainly any memory of what had so nearly happened to them had, as Nariaka had commanded, been eradicated from memory. Ralph was treated with the greatest respect, and his refusal to complete the necessary ritual training to become a samurai was greeted merely with shrugs. It was accepted that he was eccentric, but as the man who had gained the great victory of Shimonoseki, he was permitted all the eccentricity he wished. Nariaka's only desire was for him to remain until the next time he was needed. The restrictions on his seeing Alison were entirely to prevent them from having the time to hatch another escape plot together.

So there was nothing to do but eat, and drink, and sleep, and work, and look forward again to holding her in his arms. They no longer felt any embarrassment when with each other; that had disappeared the first day. Neither did they discuss such things as love or the future. They loved. It was not a matter for discussion. And seeing each other once a week, there was never time for passion to diminish or grow cold. He bought her the most elaborate presents he could discover; it was quite impossible for him to spend eighty koku of rice on anything essential, as he had no desire, like most hatamotos, to surround himself with a retinue of lesser samurai, sworn to do his bidding, to march in front of him when he went abroad—but also sworn to obey Lord Nariaka over and above anything Ralph might command. Thus he exchanged his surplus rice with the merchants of Shimonoseki, and loaded Alison with silks for kimonos, with brightly colored parasols, with jade jewelry, regarded as more valuable than pre-

cious stones by the ladies of Nariaka's court, and with
every knickknack he could think of, just as he bought
her several honin women to attend her every need, and
then would strain to catch a glimpse of her as she
walked with the lord's ladies, either on the verandas of
the palace, or in the rose gardens, or on her way into
Shimonoseki itself, for she was permitted considerable
freedom, provided she enjoyed it in the company of
the ladies, and not himself.

She often felt she was a doll or a pampered and
petted lapdog on whose physical form her master heaped
every conceivable luxury. Because he was her master,
however much and however often he might deny such
a charge. And for the moment she was content that it
be so, even if she increasingly yearned for more than
he could apparently give her—at least in their present
circumstances.

She was prepared to blame those circumstances for
everything. They saw each other only once a week, and
he was determined never to touch another Japanese
woman, apparently, so they spent at least half of their
precious time together making love. Because he needed,
because she was still new to him, because she was so
young and healthy and willing—and beautiful. These
things she believed, as he told her so often. They lived
in a perpetual state of illicit courtship. And it would
have been idly false of her to pretend that she did not
herself hunger for the touch of him, the feel of his
arms, did not look forward to being stroked and cuddled,
and most of all, to being entered, to being sent into
dizzy ecstasy—not every time, but sufficiently often to
make every time a threshold of experience. She supposed,
in real terms, she had become an utter wanton, too
much of her concept of life arising from between her
legs. But here again, circumstances. The circumstances
of her imprisonment had made her so; the circumstances of her relationship with Ralph kept her so.

But she knew there was more, without knowing what
to seek, or how to seek, or if she *dared* seek. She knew
they did not *love*. They merely loved each other's bodies.
Or certainly, he never asked for more. And she . . . she

was too aware that to him their present existence was but a purgatory, that life would only really begin when they succeeded in leaving this place—when, at the same moment, their love would soar from the profane to the sacred. It was a heady dream, but one she mistrusted. She mistrusted it because she was not sure she wanted to escape Shimonoseki. The old nightmares kept coming back. Other people would know, or discover, that the beautiful Alison Gray had been stretched naked on the floor and beaten until she wept, had spent ten days impaled upon Munetake, had been raped continuously for four hours, and had been suspended naked before an entire community. There was no hope of comfort in any community where there existed the possibility of a single one of those things ever being known.

But she also mistrusted it because she mistrusted Nariaka and knew it would never happen. No doubt Ralph also mistrusted Nariaka, but Ralph, being the man he was, simply determined that should Nariaka again betray him, he would simply leave at the first opportunity. As he had done before. She could not imagine what she would say, or worse, do, if he arrived in her chamber one day and announced they were stealing from the castle that night.

And most of all she mistrusted his dreams of the future because, incredibly, she was discovering that she could be happy here. Like him, she would have preferred to live in a house and to have been not quite so obviously a prisoner. But she even enjoyed nesting in her single room, which was in any event very nearly as large as the average Japanese house. She would cheerfully have done all the work involved, from cleaning to cooking, if only to keep herself occupied. Ralph had insisted she have the honin women as her servants, and this she had not found difficult to accept—she had employed Chinese women in her father's house in Hong Kong and knew how to keep them busy; she still wondered at times if the house stood empty and shuttered and if the *English Rose* had finally been written off, lost at sea.

But her happiness even extended beyond the walls of her chamber. She had an ear for languages, and very rapidly picked up sufficient Japanese to carry on a conversation, and certainly to understand what was being said around her. Spending all of her time, as she was forced to, in the company of the court ladies—except when actually with Ralph—she discovered them to be lively and even delightful companions, utterly obsessed with the beautiful in life. They found beauty in their menfolk and each other, and in the sexual act, and were not afraid to discuss these things with complete frankness; they also found beauty in a single flower, or an arrangement of flowers, in a sunset or a sunrise, in the very delicate artwork which they all practiced, having apparently been trained from birth. Even the sheer physical art of preparing and then pouring a cup of tea had to be performed in an exact and beautiful fashion. Was it possible that they also found beauty in brutality and death? Alison could not accept that. Rather, she concluded, they found beauty in enjoying what their menfolk enjoyed—which was a sufficiently Japanese explanation. But Japanese men also appreciated the beauty of nature and movement, or of words and thoughts. Sometimes she felt they were too double-natured ever to be understood. And sometimes she wondered if the people of Europe and America were not the double-natured ones, in that from birth they were taught to suppress any emotion or pleasure anyone else might find unpleasant. Not the Japanese.

There were, of course, aspects of what they considered to be beautiful which were totally incomprehensible to her. She was fascinated by the way the married woman blacked their teeth and caked their faces with white makeup before filling in outsized red lips. Assured that men did find this irresistible, she tried it herself once; the look of horrified disapproval on Ralph's face quite ended that experiment—to her relief.

As the weeks became months, she could no longer pretend to herself that she was not happy, happier in Shimonoseki than she could conceive of being anywhere else. Then why did they not turn their backs entirely upon the lives and mores they had left behind, and strive even more to fit into the circumstances in which they found themselves? Only because they both

knew they could never truly belong here, either; for all
the pleasures and contentment with which they were
surrounded, they *had* been allowed a sufficient glimpse
into the streak of savagery which ran so close beneath
the surface of Japanese life, just as they had also been
allowed a glimpse into the world of ruthless selfishness
and immature self-esteem that was Lord Nariaka's mind,
and knew that if he chose to smile upon them now, he
could just as easily order their execution the next
moment, should Ralph ever fail him.

So after all, life came down to a matter of living for
the present, of refusing to contemplate the future, the
possibility of achieving greater love or greater happiness,
until the return of Inouye and Ito. If that were ever
going to happen. It was not until the spring of 1862
that an excited messenger brought news that the
embassy, after an absence of eighteen months, had in
fact returned and was even now on its way across the
Inland Sea.

Ralph stood with the other samurai to watch the
arriving procession, listened to the shouted questions,
which he knew would not be answered until the ambassadors had first reported to Nariaka. Yet the failure of
their mission was easy enough to decide. They did not
smile, as they had done when they had returned with
Ralph himself, and if behind them were carried several
boxes of what were obviously rifles and ammunition,
there were no cannon to be seen, and these would
surely have had pride of place.

Remarkably, Ralph had not actually considered the
situation which might arise should his friends return
empty-handed. He had expected them to, in the
beginning, had intended to use their failure as a tool to
gain his own freedom. But that had been before Alison,
and their catastrophic snatch at escape. Since then, the
success of the embassy had become so important to his
own future that he had ceased to consider the possibility of failure. Now he could only wait—but not for very
long—until he was summoned to the audience chamber.

Ito and Inouye knelt before the dais with Katsura,

and Ralph joined them in the kowtow. Yet, strangely, Nariaka looked less angry than amused.

"My ambassadors bring strange tidings, Freeman San," he said. "And as you will have observed, no cannon."

"I have seen, my lord," Ralph said. "But these tidings . . . ?"

"You may speak, Inouye San," Nariaka said.

"Your country is at war, Freeman San," Inouye said.

"At war? But . . . with whom?"

Nariaka gave a short laugh. "With itself, Freeman San. The barbarians have split into two nations, and fight to the death."

"This is true, Freeman San," Ito said. "Never have we seen such conflict and such preparation for conflict."

A civil war? Ralph found it difficult to credit. If the wrangling between the slaveholding Southern aristocracy and the Northern industrialists had been simmering for years, and in Kansas and Missouri had even erupted into violence, very few people in California had envisaged the possibility of a war. Nor could he see John Frémont allowing things to reach that stage. "You will have to explain it to me," he said.

"Why, very simply, they fight over possession of the American honin, the black people," Inouye told him. "This new President, Lincoln San—"

"Lincoln? Not Frémont?"

"His name is Lincoln, as we understand it," Inouye said. "He would make all these honin free. And so the southern half of your country, where most of these honin are situated, has broken away and declared itself an independent nation. But this Lincoln San has refused to accept, and invades the South with great armies."

"But without great success," Ito added.

"How can he have success?" Nariaka asked contemptuously. "Free the honin? Could any man accept such nonsense? But you see, Freeman San, that is why my ambassadors have obtained no guns. Your barbarians are using them all, against each other." He smiled.

"I see that, my lord," Ralph said. "My lord, if my country is at war, even against itself, I must return. I am a soldier, my lord. I must play my part."

Nariaka shook his head. "Our agreement was that

you remain here until these new guns are purchased and installed and my people have been trained in their use. That has now been put back until the end of this war. That is not your fault, Freeman San. Neither is it mine. It is the fault of your own people, and the will of the gods. Besides, Inouye San and Ito San *were* able to purchase some of these rifles of which you have spoken. You will have much to do, training my samurai to use them."

"My Lord Nariaka," Ralph said, "once again you are playing me false. I do not believe you ever mean to let me go."

Nariaka continued to smile. "One would suppose that you are not happy here, Freeman San. Are you not rich, and respected? Do you not have the woman for whom you were prepared to die? Has not your archenemy been sent away into miserable exile? And are you not the most famous warrior in the land? Be sure that I have sent an account of your exploits to the shogun in Edo, and even to the mikado in Kyoto. You complain because it is in your nature to do so. This war among your people will end eventually, and then we will get the guns, and you will go home. Until that time comes, your place is here. And your honor as well."

"Our master is undoubtedly right, Freeman San," Inouye said. "When I look at you, a hatamoto, and see what you have accomplished, when I hear the tales of your fame, of how you defeated the French Navy, I am bound to say that you are the most talented of men. But also, I understand, the most fortunate."

"Do you know anything of that fortune?" Ralph asked.

"Indeed I have learned of it. And I repeat, any man who has been condemned to death and has lived to achieve greatness must be fortunate above his fellows."

"And do you really suppose I can spend the rest of my life fighting for a man who murders shipwrecked sailors?"

Inouye sighed. "I understand, my friend. It is difficult for a man like Lord Nariaka, who has not seen the outside world, the progress and the interrelation of peoples, to understand that any man not of Cho-Shu is not naturally an enemy such as a wild beast or a poisonous snake, to be slaughtered at sight. But he will understand, as time goes by and Japan becomes used to foreigners. Even more will his sons understand."

"And will Japan ever become used to foreigners?"

"It is happening, Freeman San," Ito said. "Edo is now full of them. Their embassies are protected by their own soldiers. The shogun accepts this."

"But you do not," Ralph pointed out. "Even you, my friends."

Inouye and Ito exchanged glances. "Perhaps we fear that the change is too hasty. But it is happening. And we know enough about the strength of the foreigners to understand that it is irresistible."

"Then you will also know that mine is a spurious fame," Ralph said. "I cannot defend Shimonoseki against any determined attack. Not with these cannon. But I could not do so even with Dahlgren guns. Nor can I turn your samurai into a force capable of withstanding any disciplined modern army, even when armed with rifles. I am wasting my time, and your lord's, and my duty calls me elsewhere. Could *you* remain in the United States, knowing that Japan was in the grip of a civil war?"

"I could more readily do so for a civil war than an external one, Freeman San. Civil wars are terrible things, and they leave unpleasant scars behind them. My advice to you would be to remain here, enjoying this great success you have achieved, enjoying the favor of Lord Nariaka. And when you return to the United States, this war will be over, and you will be above the passions it will have generated."

"And when another, more powerful Western fleet appears on that sea out there?"

Inouye smiled and clapped him on the shoulder. "Why, Freeman San, for all your doubts, you will defeat that as well. But as we are sensible men, we will pray that such an event will never occur."

Advice which was echoed by Alison, when he told her what had happened. "I am sure your friend is right, Ralph," she said. "The French came against

Shimonoseki and got their fingers burned. They will not come again without a fresh cause."

"And the British will not come at all," he remarked, "because they know nothing of the crime committed against them. And you are content to continue living amid your father's murderers."

She met his gaze. "I am alive, and content, when I had not expected to be. I am even happy, from time to time. You make me happy, Ralph. Forgive me for doubting if I shall find such contentment, such happiness, so easily in other circumstances."

She was being at once honest and sensible, he knew. Because of course he could not take her back to a nation torn in two by its own passions, just as he could not take her back and immediately abandon her to go off and fight. Like her, he had no family in whose care he could leave her, and he doubted he retained any friends; in the present circumstances, he and Alison might find themselves more isolated in America than they were here in Cho-Shu.

But war! All his adult life he had been trained to fight with his artillery batteries as part of the United States Army. And despaired of ever being able to do so, save against the Indians. Now that army, and his battery, was at last fulfilling its proper function—and he was six thousand miles away. Never had he felt so lonely. In an explosion of militaristic energy he threw himself into the training of his samurai riflemen, drilling them most of every day until they were exhausted— but of course they could never reveal such weakness to a barbarian, and so continued their marching and countermarching, and their practice at the butts outside of the castle. Some of them even showed signs of becoming excellent shots. Disciplined volley firing was a different matter, but, he thought savagely, there is time. He had nothing but time.

He longed for news of the American conflict, but with the return of Ito and Inouye, Shimonoseki settled once again into summer somnolence, with life continuing as it had done for hundreds of years, the tea ceremonies and the garden walks, the picnics which he was now sometimes allowed to join, provided there were sufficient other people around to prevent his having any heady thoughts of escape—he was never allowed from the castle after dark nowadays—and the nights with Alison, where alone his angry spirit could be soothed. The outside world might not exist, even the outside world of Japan, much less that of the barbarians across the sea. Yet it was there, as they discovered when a messenger arrived one day from Lord Shimadzu, and was closeted with Lord Nariaka for nearly an hour.

It was Katsura who told the samurai what had happened. "These intolerable barbarians," he said. "They dare to flout every Japanese law and custom. Thus it was that as Lord Shimadzu and his people marched through the streets of Yokohama, this white man rode his horse across their path. Across the path of a daimyo. And what a daimyo!"

"He was arrested?" Ralph asked.

"Arrested? He was cut down, on the instant, by Lord Shimadzu's guards."

"Cut down?" Ralph cried. "You mean killed?"

"When a samurai cuts a man down, Freeman San, the man dies."

Ralph scratched his head. "This man, was he an American?"

"No, no. He belonged to an even more stiff-necked race, the British. A man called Richardson."

"The deed was well done," growled one of the samurai. "It should be done to all who defy the laws of Japan."

"Of course I agree with you," Katsura said. "But these British are making much trouble about it, and demanding great indemnities and goods and the punishment of the men who defended their lord. These things Lord Shimadzu has refused to concede, and thus he has cut short his visit to the north, and returned to Kagoshima, there to await the outcome of the negotiations between the shogun and the British. But he has sent to Lord Nariaka to inform him of the situation, and to have him prepare himself to march to the aid of the men of Satsuma, if it becomes necessary. We shall teach these insolent barbarians, as we taught the French, that they cannot provoke Japanese samurai. Death to the British!"

"Death to the British!" shouted the samurai.

And death to us all, Ralph thought as he gazed at the ocean and remembered everything he had ever read of the British fleet, the greatest in the history of the world.

And then thought, as he listened to Nariaka and Katsura deciding their dispositions, that the situation could well turn out to his advantage. Nariaka was obliged by treaty, as well as by tradition and honor, to send all his available strength south to Kagoshima to the aid of the Satsuma, if called upon to do so, leaving only sufficient strength to defend his own citadel. This at first seemed a promising development to Ralph, as he would actually be sent into the lands of the Satsuma to fight under Saigo, who had offered him friendship; but then he realized that of course he would not be allowed to take Alison with him and that it would be to fight against *her* people. In any event, Nariaka now decided that whatever force was sent into Kyushu, his master gunner would not accompany it. Ralph's task was to defend Shimonoseki—Nariaka had no intention of removing any of his guns for use in the field.

"Thus we are as much prisoners as ever," Alison observed without regret.

"Save that I shall be in a position of command here, once the main Cho-Shu army marches away," he said. "I'll be damned if I cannot turn that to our advantage. I'll confess I'm quite impatient for those countrymen of yours to lose their tempers."

"I doubt that will be allowed to happen," she said. "Nariaka and Shimadzu may huff and puff, but the shogun will bring pressure to bear on them, and they'll pay the indemnity."

"I wonder," Ralph said. The daimyo had clearly obtained a wholly incorrect but immensely stimulating estimate of their powers since the Battle of Shimonoseki, as they called the skirmish with the French, and they were well aware that ultimately the wrath of the foreigners would fall on the shogunate itself, were the indemnity to be refused—and the humiliation of the shogunate was what they wanted more than anything else. On the other hand, he by now understood that Alison had very mixed feelings, perhaps did not *want* to escape at all.

Here they were happy, and incredibly, they appeared to be safe. He was wealthy by most Japanese standards, she was pampered and had not a care in the world. And that world, outside Shimonoseki, suddenly looked a harsh and frightening place. A place in which there would have to be explanations, and even apologies.

Alison would have to be prepared for the great adventure, carefully and soothingly. But escape they must. He could not see himself dying of old age parading these battlements—there was really no hope of the United States government ever allowing a brigand like Nariaka to purchase modern artillery to be used against American vessels in the future—and thus he was determined to seize every opportunity which might present itself, when the British finally decided to take action against the Satsuma on their own account.

Ralph's growing impatience was very obvious to Alison. It was a crisis she now knew she could not avoid for very much longer. Because, knowing her own countrymen, she equally knew they would avenge the murder of a British national, and with all the force at their command—however many times the matter might be debated in Parliament before the decision was taken. So every day she walked the battlements and scanned both the sea and the land south of the strait, dreading the moment when this existence, the happiest she had yet known, would be torn apart.

And then, one day in the summer of 1863, one of the honin women indicated to her that she was most certainly pregnant.

It was not an event which had ever occurred to her as possible, with Ralph coming to her only once a week. But now . . . She had undoubtedly missed two periods; she even waited a third, to be absolutely sure, before she told him. "How I have prayed for this to happen," she said, because she had, in her dreams. "Now I feel I really belong to you." She flushed. "I need never think of Munetake again, even in a nightmare."

He was obviously delighted in her joy. But she could see the other thoughts racing through his mind. Any attempt to escape, with all the attendant risk and hardship, was out of the question while she was carrying a child—but it would also be out of the question for many months afterward as well.

"I am sorry," she said, "that the prospect of becoming a father does not please you."

"Oh, my darling girl," he said. "My darling, darling girl." And he held her close.

But she wept, because his disappointment was plain to see.

To be a father, by Alison Gray, was surely all that any man could ever desire. But in these circumstances ... It seemed to him that his feet were being increasingly caught in the quagmire that was Japan, and that eventual escape was receding further and further into the distance. Presumably the war in America was over by now—he had had no word of it.

Inouye and Ito were as pleased as Alison. "The boy will be a Japanese," they said. "Now, Freeman San, you *must* become a samurai, that your son may be one as well."

"What makes you so sure it's going to be a son?" Ralph asked, but he could not help but smile at their enthusiasm. As if he would ever let a son of his be educated into so stiff-necked an order, bound to serve one master throughout his life—or become an outlaw— and bound too by the hideous requirements of seppuku.

"How could such a warrior have anything less?" Ito asked, still smiling. "But you may rest assured, Freeman San, that should the child be a daughter, then will she be the most beautiful girl in Japan."

"And a son will soon follow," Inouye promised him.

So now it was a case of praying that the indemnity *would* be paid, and that the quarrel would be settled, and a further season of peace be secured. All the while knowing that the indemnity would never be agreed and that in fact it was a case of awakening every morning and peering from the battlements to see if a messenger from the Satsuma was galloping toward Shimonoseki, summoning aid, and of standing there one morning in August 1863 and looking past the strait at the open sea and at the fleet of war which lay there.

*   *   *

Katsura was hurrying toward him. "Lord Nariaka demands your presence," he cried. "What are those ships? We have never seen ships so great."

"That is a British battle fleet," Ralph told him. He could not yet identify the flags, but he had no doubt. His stomach seemed to have filled with lead. And as he looked more closely, he thought he could make out the differing tricolors of France and Holland as well, flying from some of the smaller ships. This time the European nations meant to settle their account with the men of Cho-Shu once and for all. He could only be grateful that there were no American vessels to be seen—presumably the United States Navy had other things on its mind.

"The French were not so many or so big," Katsura complained.

"The French, Katsura San, as I have told you more than once, merely sent a squadron of frigates against us. They came to punish, not to conquer or destroy. The British do not deal in such half-measures. And I can tell you this," he added. "Those great ships are but a fraction of the force that the British can dispose. Theirs is the greatest fleet in all history."

Katsura did not seem convinced. "Lord Nariaka wishes to speak with you," he said again.

Nariaka was on the upper floor of the palace, surrounded not only by his lords, but even by his ladies, this day. Such was the excitement that Alison herself was present, watching Ralph with anxious eyes; she had of course not yet begun to show her condition.

He could do nothing more than repeat to Nariaka what he had said to Katsura.

"And what are they doing here?" Nariaka demanded, staring at the huge spreads of canvas slowly driving the yellow-and-black hulls closer and closer; the gun ports were presently shut, and indeed there was little activity to be seen on the decks of the warships; but the men, and the powder and balls, were there, Ralph knew.

"Well, my lord," he said, "they have either mistaken you for my Lord Shimadzu or they have learned of the ship which came ashore on your beach two years ago."

"Bah," Nariaka said. "How can they have heard of that?" He turned his head to look at Alison, as if suspecting her of possessing some secret means of communicating with the outside world. "Still, they are only ships, like those others you defeated."

"My lord," Ralph said, "believe me when I say—"

"Look there," Katsura interrupted, pointing. Out at sea a single gun had exploded, certainly loaded with a blank cartridge, and intended only as a signal; the watchers could neither hear the noise nor see the plunge of a ball into the sea—only the puff of white smoke denoted what had happened. Immediately all the ships swung up into the wind, not anchoring but heaving to in perfect symmetry, while from the largest of the battleships a boat was immediately lowered, and commenced to pull for the shore, the Union Jack flying from her stern, an equally large white flag in her bow. "They are invading us."

"Not so, Katsura San," Ralph said. "That white flag is known as a flag of truce. They are sending a message to Lord Nariaka."

"A message?" Nariaka gripped the balustrade to stare at the boat. "What message can a barbarian send to me, save an insult? Freeman San, sink that boat before it reaches the shore."

"My lord," Ralph cried, "a flag of truce is an internationally recognized device. Anyone who fires upon such a flag brings himself universal condemnation."

"Bah," Nariaka said again. "What care I for this universal condemnation of which you speak? I am Nariaka of Cho-Shu, lord of the Western Sea. I have commanded you, Freeman San, to fire into that boat and sink it, and then drive away that fleet as you did the French."

"My lord . . ." Ralph drew a long breath. "I cannot do it."

"Cannot?"

"That fleet will destroy you, Lord Nariaka. It will destroy this castle, and it will destroy all Shimonoseki, if you cause it to open fire. My lord, those ships are bigger by far than anything the French brought against you. Their guns will be more powerful, and will be better served. My lord, I beg of you, accept the flag and the message; it can do no harm to learn what they have to say."

"I will deal with no barbarians," Nariaka shouted. "They will be destroyed. You say they are powerful? Then we shall call upon our allies. Inouye San!"

"I am here, Lord Nariaka." Inouye performed the kowtow.

"Take horse, and ride north to Edo. Haste, Inouye San, and stop for no man. Tell the shogun that we are being attacked by the British and that we need aid. Tell him that the sacred soil of Japan is in danger from these barbarians and that if he ever wishes to look his ancestors in the face, he must march to my assistance with every possible man."

"Yes, Lord Nariaka," Inouye said. But he looked at Ralph with sad eyes as he hurried for the stairs; he well understood the hopelessness of their situation.

"And you, Ito San," Nariaka shouted. "You will cross the strait and ride for Kagoshima, and summon Lord Shimadzu and Saigo Takamori and their men. Tell them that the British have come against me, and not them. Tell them that the men of Cho-Shu welcome this, and will destroy the barbarians, but that they should march to our assistance with all possible haste. Now, go."

Ito followed his friend down the stairs.

"My lord," Ralph said, "this is madness. There is no way in which the shogun can reach you in time to help."

Nariaka smiled. "I know that, Freeman San. And I do not really wish his help. But that I have summoned him is all that matters. If he does not at least march, he will be disgraced in the eyes of all men of honor."

"But even the Satsuma cannot get here," Ralph shouted desperately. "And if they could, there is no effective help they could give you. There is no force in all Japan capable of withstanding those ships. You *must* parley."

Nariaka's arm came up, the forefinger pointing. "I know you, Freeman San, for a traitor who would see us collapse into ruin. This will not happen. Bring me the woman."

Two of the samurai leaped forward to seize Alison and drag her to the front of the crowd. She was so taken by surprise she could only stare at Ralph in total consternation. She had allowed herself, in her happiness, to forget that she was a hostage whose life hung by the slender thread of Nariaka's mood and requirements.

"Now, listen well, Freeman San," Nariaka said, as Alison was forced to her knees before him. "You will sink that boat before it reaches the shore. And then you will destroy or drive away that fleet. Because if you fail me, this woman's throat will be cut, and then her belly, and she and your unborn child will together be hurled from this battlement into the sea, where you will join them. Mark me well, Freeman San. Go down and sink that boat."

Ralph hesitated, gazing at Alison, who gazed back, her eyes wide with mingled discomfort and fear. Once again they had been overtaken by utter catastrophe. And there was nothing he could do, save obey. They might at least survive the coming bombardment; there was no hope at all if he refused to fight the guns.

"Haste, Freeman San," Katsura said gently.

Ralph ran down the stairs, followed by the excited samurai. The powder and balls had already been brought up, the guns were waiting. And the longboat was half-way to the shore, dancing gently over the waves; he could even make out the two blue-coated officers seated in the stern.

"Load," he commanded, himself laying the gun. The boat was well within range. He had no wish to commit murder, aimed to put the shot immediately in front of the Britishers, rather than into them. "Fire!"

The cannon exploded, and a plume of water leaped into the air some thirty feet from the longboat. Immediately the oars were checked, and then backed, as the two officers conferred, and looked over their shoulders at the ships of the fleet, seeking instruction.

"Fire!" Ralph commanded the second gun. Another roar, and another plume of water scattered across the seamen. Now a signal gun was fired from the flagship, and the boat turned and began rowing back as fast as it could. The shouts of "Banzai!" rang out, and the samurai waved their swords and spears in triumph.

"Fire into the fleet," Katsura cried, having joined Ralph on the battlements. "Do not wait."

"They are still out of effective range," Ralph told him.

"Will they not come closer? They must, if they are to join battle."

"Yes," Ralph agreed. "I think they will come closer." He looked up at the verandas, at the excited people gathered there, and wondered if they realized that most of them were living their last few minutes on earth? Then he looked back at the fleet, as the longboat was taken up, the sails were shaken out, and the gun ports slowly lowered. He had had no chance to speak with Alison, but she was at once English and a seaman's daughter and would certainly understand what was coming; she must also know that it was her business to survive the approaching holocaust, because it was her own people out there.

The fleet began to move through the water, wearing ship, bringing each mighty war machine about, so that together they could run down before the wind.

"Bah," Katsura said. "They are fleeing, like the French."

"No," Ralph said. "No, I do not think they are fleeing, Katsura San."

He looked at white smoke. The entire fleet, eight battleships and twelve frigates, disappeared, save for their mastheads, as some two hundred and fifty cannon, he estimated, their combined starboard broadsides, exploded together. He never actually heard the noise of the explosions at all. He was picked up by a gigantic hot wind and thrown against the battlements; but these battlements had disappeared, and he found himself hanging over a sheer precipice, with the sea fifty feet beneath him. Desperately he scrambled back over the lip, lay on the ground panting, gazing at a cannon which had been thrown on its side, the unfired ball rolling away from its muzzle, at the samurai scattered about it, arms and legs and armor a smother of blood, at Katsura, almost cut in two, lying in a tumbled heap. He smelled smoke, and looked at the palace, hearing now the shrieks of fear, watched flames leaping from the upper pagodas.

The morning was filled with sound, but it only reached him from a great distance. His ears were ringing with a mighty resonance, and beyond that there were only faint human cries of terror and misery. The sound he anticipated and feared, the boom of a second broadside, was for the moment absent. But only momentarily. He got to his feet and stared out to sea at the warships, and saw that they were again wearing ship, to bring their port broadsides to bear. As he watched, they completed the maneuver. Desperately he threw himself flat, trying to merge with the ground itself, and was once again enveloped in the wind from hell.

He tried to think, to make himself do something. He got to his feet again, gazed at the horror which had been the battlements. Those samurai who had survived the two broadsides were sitting or standing in bewildered incomprehension of what was happening; of the eighteen cannon, twelve had been dismounted, and lay, useless lumps of iron, under or over the scattered bodies of their gunners. He ran to the rear of the gun platform, gazed at the sheet of smoke and flame that was Shimonoseki. That had been Shimonoseki. This was destruction on a scale of which not even he had any experience.

This was also a battle lost, as it could never have been won. It was time to save himself, if he could. And Alison.

Alison had not really known what to expect when she saw the smoke. Her senses were in any event still reeling from what had just happened. Because she *had* allowed herself to be lulled into a sense of well-being. She had even felt happy here, had even contemplated spending the rest of her life here, with her lover, and now, her children.

She had almost felt she belonged.

Now there was only fear, and revulsion, and bewilderment . . . and before any of those could be resolved, a searing wind which bowled her over and left her scattered on the floor gasping for breath. Someone trod on her, and she sat up to see men and women running to and fro in their astonished horror. But not all. One of the flying balls had actually smashed into the palace, tearing the thin wood as if it had been paper, leaving a trail of smoldering splinters, and leaving too a beheaded woman, and worse, another whose legs had been blown off and who lay screaming in a high-pitched voice, while unable to utter any words.

But they were all, again, strangers to her, after Nariaka's pronouncement. Out *there* were her people, even if they were firing at her. She drew her feet away from the seeping blood, tried to make herself think what to do next, and was overtaken by the second blast, which tumbled her across the floor as the entire castle seemed to be shaking on its foundations. Now she smelled nothing but flame, and realized that she must get down the stairs if she would avoid being burned to death. She regained her knees, and had her arms seized by two men, while a third held her hair.

"No," she gasped. "No, please . . . it is not Ralph's fault. They are too strong for him. Please!"

But they were actually dragging her *to* the stairs. For a moment she almost hoped, supposing that some sort of humanitarian common sense had finally prevailed—and knew better as on the next level she was dragged into the audience chamber.

Nariaka sat on his dais, but today his women were kneeling around him, huddled close, staring at the barbarian woman with wide eyes, as if they had never taken tea or picked roses together, shrieking their fear as another immense rumble filled the morning, and the palace shook again; now she could hear the crash of falling timbers, and the smell of burning wood grew stronger.

Nariaka pointed. "Your master has betrayed me," he shouted.

Alison drew a long breath. "That is not so, my lord," she answered. "He has told you many times that your fortress could not withstand a battle fleet, and you have not believed him."

Nariaka gazed at her for several seconds. Then he said, "He has been defeated." He looked at the guards. "Does he live?"

Alison's heart constricted; somehow the thought that Ralph could have been killed in one of those broadsides had never entered her head. Life without Ralph was not conceivable.

"It is unlikely, great lord," said one of the samurai. "There are few living on the battlements."

"Fetch him here," Nariaka said. "His body, if he is dead. Fetch him here, that I can cut off his head. And that of the woman."

Alison's heart was pounding and her brain seemed to be spinning. But she had to think. She refused to believe that Ralph could be dead. Therefore he could still be saved. As could she and the unborn child in her belly. Who *must* be saved.

"My lord," she said. "Yes, Freeman San has been defeated. But that does not mean all is lost. Those men out there are Christian gentlemen. They will treat with you the more readily, having won their battle. But you must surrender now, or they will reduce this fortress and this palace to a hole in the ground."

Another samurai hatamoto stood in the doorway, ignoring ceremony. "My lord," he cried, "the barbarians have landed, and we cannot stop them. They will be here any moment. My lord—"

"I cannot wait," Nariaka said. He stared at Alison. "Lord Nariaka does not surrender," he declared. "He will die now, as he has lived, with honor. I will show the way. But when I have gone, the moment I have gone, do you cast that woman into the sea, before her barbarian friends. And Freeman behind her, if he can be found."

He shrugged his kimono from his shoulders, while the fingers tightened on Alison's arm. She gazed in horror as the women stopped their wailing and knelt in orderly rows to either side—because every woman was also clutching a dagger. But Alison's concern was Ralph. The samurai had not returned with either him or his body. And she knew he would never flee without her.

Therefore he had to be lying out there, perhaps seriously wounded. . . .

The appointed samurai took his place behind Nariaka, long sword drawn and resting on his shoulder, firmly held in both hands. Everyone in the room was staring at the lord, rapt in attentive concern, as the lord of Cho-Shu raised his short sword, gazed at it for a few seconds, and then plunged it into his stomach. The movement was so sudden and decisive it took Alison entirely by surprise; she had not really supposed he would do it. She watched the first seep of red, the sideways drag of the dagger which split the taut brown flesh as it might have cut paper, the terrible spurt of blood and gut which tumbled from the ghastly wound, the outward movement of Nariaka's arm, a convulsive jerk even as the lord's eyes glazed as the last breath hissed from his nostrils, and the sweep of the long sword which sent the head bumping down the steps of the dais to roll across the floor.

Yet what followed was far more horrible, as the women, with a combined shriek, immediately stabbed their own bellies with their knives—and there were no friends standing by to end *their* agonies with a single cut of a sword.

The men were moving, dragging her with them, to carry out their lord's final command. "No," she gasped. "No," as she tried to fight them, and raised her head to stare at Ralph, in the doorway, a huge blood- and smoke- and earth-stained figure; he had discarded his sword and carried only his revolver. "Ralph!" she screamed with delirious relief.

"Stand aside," Ralph shouted at the samurai.

They hissed, and one released her to draw his sword; neither had ever seen the revolver fired in anger. Ralph dropped the first man with a single bullet through the heart, and then did the same to his companion before the samurai could even release Alison's arm; they seemed to strike the floor together. She stood between them, her ears ringing, and had her hand grasped. "Come on," he bawled. "Let's get the hell out of here."

She realized that the noise of his revolver had sounded so loud because the cannon had at last ceased, and she was sure that in the distance she could hear voices shouting in English, even as she most certainly could hear the notes of an English bugle call.

But they were not yet safe. Even as Ralph half-carried, half-pushed her down the stairs, the flames crackled to either side, and gusts of smoke clouded around their heads to threaten their lungs. No one attempted to stop their progress now. The samurai had either committed seppuku, or fled the burning building, or were too afraid to face the deadly revolver—they did not know there was only one loaded chamber left. Together Ralph and Alison tumbled down the stairs, tripping and falling, scrambling to their feet again and reaching the yard, looking back at the flames issuing from the pagoda roofs above them. They smelled the sizzle of the burning lacquer, ran for the drawbridge, and faced the myriad red jackets and tall shakos and gleaming bayonets of the British marines who flooded at them across the inner courtyard, led by an officer with huge mustaches and a drawn sword.

Ralph holstered his revolver, raised his hands, Alison doing the same. "We are English," he shouted. "Well, she is."

"I am Alison Gray," Alison shouted. "Alison Gray."

The officer held up his hand, and the men panted to a stop, not ten feet away. "By God," the officer said, "you must be Captain Freeman."

"Why, yes," Ralph said in surprise. "That is my name. Have you heard of me?"

"Heard of you?" The officer gave a brief laugh. "Oh, yes, Mr. Freeman, I have heard of you." He beckoned his sergeant. "Place this renegade under arrest," he commanded. "I believe Admiral Kuper means personally to attend to his hanging."

—8—
THE TRIAL

For a moment Ralph could think of nothing to say. Alison uttered a scream and tried to pull the marines away from him. "There must be some mistake," she shouted.

The officer touched the brim of his shako. "You are safe now, Miss Gray, I do promise you that. There is nothing to be afraid of any longer."

"But Captain Freeman has done nothing wrong," she cried.

"He is the biggest villain on earth, by all reports," the officer said. "But he will trouble you no more. There is nothing for you to be afraid of now. We'll take care of him. Take him away," he told his sergeant. "The admiral will be ashore by now. Show him the scoundrel."

Ralph was jerked forward, and the marines had the sense to relieve him of his pistol as well as his sword. "Murdering bastard," the sergeant remarked. "Wearing this heathen outfit and all."

"Does that make me a murderer?" Ralph asked.

"We'll watch it flap when we hoist you," the sergeant said. "Oh, aye, that'll be a sight for sore eyes."

Ralph realized that he had to start thinking, try to understand the situation. But thought was intensely difficult. Behind him, he could still hear Alison's voice begging and shouting, and even as she faded into the general din raised by the marines as they charged into the remains of the palace, whooping and yelling, clearly destroying everything and everyone they encountered, he found himself staring at the harbor, where the fishing boats and the trading junks lay in sinking confusion, many on fire, and then at the burning houses of Shimonoseki itself, listening to the moaning wails of the women and children, huddling together, momentarily expecting to be raped and murdered themselves. At present the marine officers seemed to have their men in hand, and the women were merely being herded away from the houses and on to the open space of the exercise ground, where they were safe from the flames, but the morning was still young, and the marines had not yet got at the sake.

He was thrust down the roadway toward the beach, and brought to a sudden halt as his feet touched sand. Just disembarking from a barge were several officers of obviously high rank, from their cocked hats and the amount of gold braid at breast and shoulder of their uniforms. Leading them was a tall, thin-faced man wearing the blue frock coat and white breeches of a British admiral. He carried no sword, but instead a telescope under his arm, which he now waved at the burning city. "Hot work, eh, gentlemen?" he said. "Hot work. What's this? I had no idea Japanese grew to such a size."

"Begging your pardon, Admiral, sir," said the marine sergeant, saluting. "This is no Japanese. This is the American renegade we was told to look out for. Freeman, sir."

"Taken alive, by God," the admiral cried in delight, and stood before Ralph. "Yes, indeed, he has the look of a rascal about him. And he was pretending to be Japanese, eh? Meaning to save his skin, if he could. Well, well. You, sir, are a murdering scoundrel, by all reports. I shall have great pleasure in sentencing you. Yes, indeed. Secure him over there, Sergeant. We'll have the court-martial the moment I return from my tour of inspection. It was on this beach, by all accounts, that he performed the worst of his crimes. Thus it is a fitting place for the matter to be settled. You hold him here, Sergeant. Yes, indeed. Let him sweat awhile. And have that fellow Matheson brought ashore. We'll do it properly." He tapped Ralph on the chest with his telescope. "Can't have you complaining about a lynching, eh, even if it's what you deserve. But when I hang a man, I like him to know he's had a fair trial.

Oh, yes, you'll have a fair trial, Mr. Freeman. And *then* we'll hang you."

"Miss Gray!" Admiral Kuper raised his hat and bowed. "My dear, dear Miss Gray. You may be sure of the deepest sympathy and devotion of every man of my fleet, nay, of every man, woman, and child in Great Britain, and of their wholehearted admiration for the tremendous courage and fortitude you have displayed during the two years of your terrible captivity."

Alison stared at him.

"This is Admiral Kuper," whispered the marine officer. "Our commanding officer."

"You . . ." Alison looked at the burning city, listened to the cries of the victorious marines. "You commanded this to happen?"

"My dear Miss Gray," Kuper said, "my orders were to exterminate a nest of vipers. A nest of vipers who have shamefully mistreated *you*, Miss Gray. This I have done. Without the loss of a man, I may say," he added proudly.

"You have murdered women and children," she shouted.

"She's not well, sir," the marine officer hastily explained. "I think her misfortunes may have addled her brain."

"Well," Kuper remarked, "it would be surprising had they not."

"And now Ralph . . . Captain Freeman?" Alison asked, her voice brittle. "You intend to murder him as well?"

"The man who has used you worse than any other, as I understand it? Who is a traitor to his country and to white people everywhere? Believe me, Miss Gray, I only wish I could hang him for *every* crime he has committed."

"You . . ." She kept her temper with an effort. "Am I not allowed to speak in his defense, Admiral? As I am the only witness to what actually happened."

"Ah . . ." began the officer standing on Kuper's right, but the admiral gave a quick shake of the head, and he bit off what he would have said.

"Of course you may give evidence, Miss Gray," Kuper

said. "If you feel able. Remembering that you no longer
have anything to fear from this man or these people.
Now, Dr. Clarkson, I feel that Miss Gray would probably appreciate a cordial, and also some less barbaric
clothes to wear. Can you attend to that?"

"Of course, sir. Miss Gray, if you will come with
me . . ."

"And I shall look forward to the pleasure of your
company for luncheon, Miss Gray," the admiral said.

She hesitated. "And Ralph?"

"Oh, he will be fed," the admiral promised her. "But
we shall have the trial as soon as we have eaten. Do not
fret. It will all be done by this evening, and then . . .
then, Miss Gray, we are going to take you home to
England." He raised his eyebrows as she gave him
another stare, and sighed as the doctor led her away.
"Poor child, indeed. Quite gone. But she shall tell us
whatever she pleases, gentlemen. Oh, indeed she shall."

"Yes, but if her evidence—"

"Her evidence will be meaningless," Kuper said.
"Matheson is the key. And I shall turn it in the lock. I
will swear to that."

"You can sit down," the sergeant said kindly. "For
the last time, eh?"

Ralph sat on the sand, felt the sweat trickling down
his shoulders. Of course it was already very hot, as the
sun soared above the mountains to the east, brought a
vivid sharpness to the scene, the smoke rising above
Nariaka's burning palace, and from his city as well,
contrasting so intensely with the calm of the blue sea,
the quiet peace and prosperity represented by the long
row of anchored warships. But he was perspiring more
with an awareness that he was probably in greater danger now than at any moment since he and Alison and
Aya had been recaptured on the Inland Sea—and there
was not likely to be any providential interruption this
time.

And he had no idea how it had happened. It had
never occurred to him that *anyone* in the outside world
had any idea where he even was, much less than he commanded Nariaka's guns. Had Ito and Inouye used his

name on their second embassy? He supposed that was certainly possible. But even so, he was being treated as guilty of something far more heinous than laying a Japanese gun.

The thought of Frémont brought back other memories. "Can you tell me who won the Civil War?" he asked.

"The Civil War? Oh, you mean between the states in America," the sergeant said. "Why, it was still going on when last I heard. Seems they'll be fighting for years yet, that lot. But you don't want to worry about them, son. There's no American, Federal or Confederate, wouldn't hang you on sight, by all accounts."

Four years, and still fighting. Ralph wondered what sort of country would be left at the end of it. His knowledge of history reminded him that England, the land of his forebears, had never been the same after the Great Rebellion. As if it mattered. He began to feel an increasing sense of hopelessness as he sat on the sand for upward of an hour, watching one or two injured marines being brought down for transportation to the ships—they seemed to have suffered burns and bruises from falling timbers more than sword cuts— and watched, too, more and more men coming ashore from the ships. One of these wore civilian clothing, and came up to him, staring at him for several seconds.

"This is the scoundrel, Mr. Matheson," the sergeant said. "But I don't reckon you should be talking to him here."

"I ain't talking to him here," Matheson said, and walked away again.

Ralph supposed he had to be a newspaper correspondent, although he looked more like a seaman. But now he was worrying about what might have happened to Alison. Yet the officer commanding the advance party of marines had seemed prepared to treat her as a lady rather than a prisoner—which was important, because, quite apart from her own safety, Alison was the only witness to the fact that he had committed no crime to which he had not been forced.

At last things started to happen. A boatload of sailors had erected a large tarpaulin at one end of the beach, to form a makeshift marquee, and here several side drums were being placed, close together, and covered with a dark cloth, while chairs had also been brought from the ships and arranged behind the extemporized table. To this shade there now came the admiral and his senior officers to enjoy a meal, a very tasty meal, Ralph estimated, watching the wine bottles being opened and the cheese and sweetmeats being passed around; to his great relief, he made out Alison seated among them, wearing a gown obviously very hastily cobbled up by the ship's sailmaker, but being entertained with much laughter and witty talk. She kept turning her head, obviously trying to find him, but could not locate him behind his guard of marines. But there was at least one worry removed, and soon even some of his discomfort was ended as his wrists were untied to allow him to eat as well, although his food consisted of a lump of salt pork, a very hard biscuit, and a mug of water which had been laced with rum. It was the first time in three years that he had eaten anything other than delicate Japanese food or drunk anything but sake and plum wine, and he found it revolting. But necessary, he supposed, to keep up his strength for the coming ordeal.

Which was upon him almost as soon as he had swallowed the last of the rum; a marine officer brought the guards to attention, and Ralph was marched across the sand, to stand just inside the blessed shade of the tarpaulin and gaze at Admiral Kuper, who was delicately wiping his hands with a linen napkin. Seated to either side of the British admiral were the senior French and Dutch officers, helping to form the panel of three judges required by military law, but clearly only Kuper mattered.

"Ralph!" Alison was on her feet. "Oh, Ralph, are you all right?"

"So far," Ralph told her.

"Ahem," remarked the admiral. "You'll understand that you must withdraw out of earshot, Miss Gray, until you are called upon as a witness. We must be proper about these matters. Oh, proper."

A midshipman stood at Alison's elbow, and she bit her lip as she looked at Ralph, and then allowed herself to be escorted down the beach.

"Now, then," Admiral Kuper said, "it is a hot day and we do not wish to waste any more time than we already have. Bring the prisoner forward."

Ralph was marched forward again, to stand immediately in front of the drumhead table.

"Read the charges, Mr. Hallinan," requested the admiral.

A British naval lieutenant stood up, a sheet of paper in his hand. "Ralph Freeman," he said, "you stand before this court accused of the following crimes: first, that on 18 March 1860 you did feloniously murder one Jefferson Hardy, in the city of San Francisco, in the United States of America; second, that you did then abscond from the said United States of America to the country of Japan, where you entered the employ of the notorious brigand and pirate known as Nariaka of Cho-Shu; third, that you aided and abetted the pirates of Cho-Shu in their murderous assault upon the officers and crew of the English vessel *English Rose* on 3 April 1861; fourth, that you did command the guns of Shimonoseki in firing upon a French and American squadron which sought redress against the pirates of Cho-Shu for earlier crimes against their nationals; and fifth, that you did command the guns of Shimonoseki in firing upon the allied fleet this day commanded by Admiral Sir Frederick Kuper. How plead you, guilty or not guilty?"

Ralph gazed at the judges, and past them at the yellow beach and the blue sea, all still overhung by the smoke pall from Shimonoseki. And felt angry. These people, who knew nothing of what he had experienced and suffered, and over what he had triumphed, were out to destroy him, with smug self-righteous arrogance.

Well, he thought, I'll go down fighting, if I go down at all.

"In the main, I plead not guilty," he said. "It is impossible to answer all of these accusations in a single breath."

Lieutenant Hallinan looked at the admiral uncertainly. "I have never heard such a plea. But," he added brightly, "I have a friend waiting here, Lieutenant Browning, who is prepared to undertake the defense. Perhaps, if Mr. Freeman were to consult with his lawyer . . ."

"For God's sake," Ralph said. "How can he defend me, when he knows nothing of the facts, and when we have not even discussed them together?"

Kuper sighed. "I knew this was going to waste a deal of time. But we are not fools, to be hoodwinked by you, sir. I suppose you will require a remand, that you can brief your advocate. I will have none of that. You claim you cannot answer all these charges together? Very well, sir, we will take them one at a time. We will be fair to Mr. Freeman, Mr. Hallinan, and permit him to hang himself at his leisure. Now, Mr. Freeman, do you deny having shot down in cold blood one Jefferson Hardy, in San Francisco, on the early morning of 18 March 1860?"

"I do not deny shooting Jefferson Hardy, sir," Ralph said. "But it was in self-defense. And I should like to question your jurisdiction over an event which took place between American citizens on American soil."

"I have never yet met a murderer who did not claim self-defense," the admiral observed. "As for jurisdiction, Mr. Freeman, it may interest you to know that the American ambassador in Edo specifically requested and authorized me to make that charge against you. Were it not for the private war your people are having, there'd have been an American squadron with us today. But no matter. The prisoner has pleaded guilty to the first charge, Mr. Hallinan. Now, sir, do you deny having come to Japan to serve the brigand Nariaka?"

Ralph realized that whatever he might say was going to have no effect whatever. Only Alison could save him now. Yet he had to continue to make the effort.

"I can hardly deny coming to Japan, sir," he said. "As I am here now. But I must point out that to the people of this country Lord Nariaka is not a brigand, but a daimyo, the equivalent of an earl in your country, I would say."

"You would, would you? The prisoner has pleaded guilty to the second charge, Mr. Hallinan. Write it down. Now, Mr. Freeman, do you deny having taken part in the massacre of the survivors of the wreck of the *English Rose?*"

"I do, sir. I did all in my power to prevent it, and nearly lost my own life in doing so."

Kuper gazed at him for several seconds, then glanced at the paper again. "Do you deny firing into the French squadron last year? A squadron which included an American vessel?"

"I fired on the French ships, sir, because I was forced to do so by Lord Nariaka. I did not fire upon the American vessel."

"It is true that no damage was sustained by the American ship," said the French officer on Kuper's right.

"Which is surely a matter of mere chance and bad gun laying," the admiral observed. "The prisoner pleads guilty to the fourth charge, Mr. Hallinan. And finally, sir, do you deny firing upon my fleet this morning? And more especially, my flag of truce?"

"I fired upon your flag of truce, for which I am heartily sorry, again at the command of Lord Nariaka, and after protesting most strongly at such an action. I did not fire upon your fleet, Admiral Kuper. I did not have the time."

"I am glad you have a sense of humor, Mr. Freeman," Kuper said. "The prisoner pleads guilty to the fifth charge, Mr. Hallinan. Now, Mr. Freeman, you have pleaded guilty to four charges, any one of which carries the death penalty, as crimes against either your fellowmen or against your own race, your own people. However, the charge upon which *I* wish to hang you is the third one, that of murdering helpless English seamen, upon, I understand, this very beach. Now, sir, as you are going to hang anyway, why not be a man and change your plea upon this score?"

"I am not guilty," Ralph said, raising his voice. "I am guilty of none of the crimes of which I am accused, because I acted under duress. I can prove my innocence."

The admiral sighed again. "I intend to give you that opportunity, Mr. Freeman. I will not have a false conviction upon my conscience. Mr. Hallinan, your friend will after all have to play his part."

"I will conduct my own defense, sir," Ralph declared.

Kuper shrugged. "As you wish. But you will abide by the rules of this court. Mr. Hallinan, you may produce your first witness."

"I call James Matheson," Hallinan said.

To Ralph's surprise and dismay, the man who had inspected him on the beach was brought forward, to stand a few feet to his left while the oath was administered. He could not understand what part the fellow could possibly have to play.

"Now, then, Mr. Matheson," Hallinan said, "*we* know who you are, but the prisoner may not. Would you kindly state your name and station, as it is relevant to the facts of this case."

"My name is James Matheson," the man said, "and two years ago I was the second mate of the bark *English Rose*."

"The *English Rose*?" Ralph cried. "But . . ." He bit his lip.

"You were going to say, Mr. Freeman?" the admiral inquired.

"I supposed there had been but one survivor of the *English Rose*, sir."

"Quite so. You supposed there was but one witness alive to your nefarious deeds. But you were wrong, you see. Tell us about that night, Mr. Matheson."

"Well, sir, we struck just . . ." He hesitated, getting his bearings, and then pointed. "Over there, by that outcropping of rock. The sea was something fierce, but the beach, this beach, sir, was only a short distance away, and the skipper, Captain Gray, may God rest his soul, said we should have a go at it. There were all these fellows wearing nightshirts on the beach, you see, and we thought they would come into the water to help us. So off went the lads, and Captain Gray sent his own daughter, tied to a life belt, to give her something to hold on to. Well, sir, you can imagine our feelings when we saw the first lads to reach the shore immediately chopped to pieces by these yellow devils. We realized the fate to which we had sent Miss Gray, and the fate for which we were destined ourselves. Well, sir, Captain Gray was beside himself with grief and anguish. He didn't want to live anymore, anyhow, and just threw

himself overboard. I don't think he reached the beach.
I think he drowned."

"But what did *you* do?" Lieutenant Hallinan asked.

"Well, sir, it seemed to me that I might as well drown
as be cut to pieces, so I stayed with the ship while she
broke up, and I took the time to lash myself to the
mizzen boom, and as luck would have it, sir, when the
stern finally broke away, I was washed out to sea with
the spar rather than toward the shore."

"And thus you survived."

"Well, sir, I was like to have drowned, or died of
hunger and thirst. But I was still lucky, sir, in that two
days later I was picked up by a Chinese junk sailing
down for Shanghai. They cared for me, sir, and I was
eventually able to regain Hong Kong, and thence
England."

"Where you told your terrible tale," Hallinan agreed.
"Now, Mr. Matheson, during the time you were clinging to the ship on those rocks over there, you could see
the beach quite clearly?"

"Oh, yes, sir."

"And you saw what happened to your shipmates
quite clearly?"

"Oh, yes, sir. The water was red with blood."

"Did you see what happened to Miss Gray?"

"Well, no, not exactly, sir. There was a lot going on."

"But did you that afternoon see anyone whom you
might recognize, if seen again."

"Oh, yes, sir."

"Have you ever seen one of those men again?"

"Oh, yes, sir."

"When, and where?"

"Standing right beside me here, sir." He pointed at
Ralph.

"You are quite sure of this?" Hallinan asked.

"I never forget a face, sir. I saw him clear."

"And what was he doing?"

"Why, sir, he was running up and down the beach
like everyone else, chopping with a great sword, and
whooping like the devil. And smiling while he did it."

"Thank you, Mr. Matheson," Hallinan said. "I have
no further questions."

"Thank you, Mr. Matheson," the admiral said. "You may stand down."

"Do I not have the right to cross-examine?" Ralph asked.

The admiral raised his eyebrows. "Why, I suppose you do, if you insist upon it."

"I do insist, sir. Mr. Matheson, were you really the second mate of the *English Rose*?"

"Why, I . . ." Matheson's face reddened, and he looked at the admiral.

"Do you really expect anyone here to believe," Ralph went on, "that after having been saved from the wreck in a somewhat miraculous fashion, you have spent two years doing nothing more than endeavoring to return to this beach, on the off chance of discovering me here so that you could accuse me of taking part in that crime?"

"Now, Mr. Freeman," Kuper said, "this won't do at all. No, it will not. You are allowed to cross-examine on matters relevant to the matter in hand. Not to conduct an investigation into the affairs of the witness."

"Not even when I suspect the witness to be perjured, sir?"

"Mr. Matheson is not perjured, Mr. Freeman. If it will set your mind at rest, his story has been accepted by everyone who has heard it. He has not spent two years waiting to return to this beach. He has spent that time sailing out of Hong Kong. But when it was decided to undertake this expedition, he was invited to accompany us."

"On the off chance of discovering me here," Ralph remarked.

"Oh, no, Mr. Freeman. We knew you were here. Everyone in Edo, perhaps everyone in Japan, speaks of Freeman San, the gunner of Cho-Shu. Our only fear was that you might be killed in the bombardment. Now, if you are finished with this witness . . ."

"I have not, sir. Mr. Matheson, let us accept that you are what you say you are, for the time being. In that case, your memory of what happened on that terrible day two years ago appears to be so vivid I have no doubt at all you can remember what time it was when the *English Rose* struck the rocks?"

"Well . . ." Matheson looked at Hallinan. "It were in the afternoon."

"What time of the afternoon?"

"Well . . ." Another look at Hallinan.

"I think I am right in saying that you are still under oath, Mr. Matheson," Ralph pointed out.

"Well, it were late afternoon."

"In fact, it was past dusk," Ralph said. "And you could see very little. I put it to you that you could hardly make out the beach, and that you have no idea what was happening on the shore because you could not see that shore."

"Are you suggesting that the crew of the *English Rose* was not murdered, Mr. Freeman?" the admiral asked.

"No, sir. I am sorry to say that the crew was murdered. I am merely attempting to establish that this man does not know whether or not *I* was on this beach, and that he cannot know, because he couldn't see, and that in fact he has never actually seen me before in his life until he met me on the beach this morning. Which, sir, must throw a considerable doubt on *any* testimony he may deliver."

"I was there," Matheson insisted, "and I could hear. Those screams will be with me to my dying day."

"You must have very keen hearing, Mr. Matheson," Ralph said. "My memory of that night is that it was blowing better than forty knots of wind, from the ship to the shore. If it had been blowing the other way, toward you, the *English Rose* would never have stranded in the first place. In any event, are you suggesting I was screaming with terror as I murdered people?"

"They was murdered," Matheson insisted. "And you was there."

"Thank you, Mr. Matheson," the admiral said. "I am sure Mr. Freeman has made his point. Would you take your place over there? Call your other witness, Mr. Hallinan."

Hallinan turned to look at the waiting marine sergeant. "I call Miss Alison Gray," he said.

*   *   *

Alison's face was pale but composed. She stood where Matheson had, but did not look at Ralph as she took the oath in a low tone. Then she glanced to her left, at the spectators, and saw Matheson.

"Matheson?" she asked in bewilderment. "But . . ."

Ralph's heart gave a curious lurch as he saw Kuper smile. With one word, and quite inadvertently, Alison had destroyed his every hope of proving Matheson a liar.

"Saved from the sea, Miss Alison," the mate said. "Saved from the sea. And here now to save you from this devil."

"I think we should get on," Admiral Kuper said in a mild tone, still smiling his pleasure at the way things had turned out, the success which had attended his maneuver of not allowing Alison to see her old sailing companion until this moment.

"Now, Miss Gray," Hallinan said, "may we take it that you recognize this man?"

"Of course I do," Alison said. "That's Mr. Matheson, my father's second mate."

"And was he on board the *English Rose* when she struck?"

"Yes," she said. "I thought he had drowned."

"But as you see, he survived, to return and point the finger of guilt against this murdering rascal."

"No," Alison cried. "No, that is not true at all. You must—"

"Miss Gray," Hallinan interrupted, "we have explained to you that your terrible ordeal is over. That you have nothing to fear, from this man or any other in Japan. Do you understand this?"

"I . . ." Alison changed her mind as to what she would have said. She was beginning to understand, as Ralph had earlier, that these men were not going to listen to protestations. She nodded. "I understand that."

"All we require from you," Hallinan went on, "are completely truthful answers to whatever questions may be asked you."

She nodded.

"Well, then, we have been told by Mr. Matheson that

your father's ship struck on that outcrop of rock over there. Is this correct?"

"Yes," she said.

"And that Captain Gray, your father, gave the command to abandon ship and make for the beach, and that he sent you with his crew, clinging to a life belt. Is that correct?"

"Yes," she said. She knew there had to be a trap coming, but for the moment she could not figure out what it might be. It was necessary to concentrate very hard, try to forget that Ralph was standing beside her and that it was his life now at stake.

"I know this memory must be intensely painful to you, Miss Gray," Hallinan said. "But I must now ask you to tell the court *exactly* what happened to you when you reached the beach."

Alison drew a long breath as the events of that dreadful night clouded across her brain. "I was seized by a man," she said.

"Can you identify this man?"

"Yes. But he is not here."

Hallinan frowned at her. "Are you sure, Miss Gray?"

"He is not here." She allowed her voice to become more emphatic. "He was a Japanese. Cannot you all understand? I was seized by a Japanese named Munetake, who would have struck off my head. He was prevented from doing so by Captain Freeman. Captain Freeman saved my life, and afterward he risked his own in an endeavor to help me escape. He is innocent of all the charges you have brought against him."

She had seized the initiative, at the cost of a small lie which was yet essentially a truth; if it had been Ralph and not Munetake who had actually taken her from the water, the samurai had yet intended her death before he had realized who and what she was.

In any event, Hallinan had been taken aback by the vehemence of her outburst, and turned his head to look at the admiral.

Kuper leaned forward, looking like a kindly if slightly irritated uncle. "Miss Gray, as I have already said, there is not a man in this fleet who does not feel in his heart a bitter sense of outrage and disgust at what you have experienced, held in this den of iniquity for two long years. We are here to help you. We *will* help you." His tone indicated that they would do so whether she wanted them to or not. "And as the lieutenant has said, we intend to make sure that no harm ever comes to you again. I know how confused must be your emotions at your sudden deliverance, how deep-rooted must be your fear of this man and of the devils for whom he worked. I therefore do not wish to keep you standing here for one minute longer than is necessary."

"You don't *understand*," she cried. "Mr. Freeman—"

Kuper held up one finger. "Do me the courtesy of allowing me to finish, Miss Gray. As I was saying, I intend to ask you five brief questions, to which you may safely answer yes or no. Will you do that for me?"

"Well, sir, I—"

"Just yes or no, Miss Gray. First, when you reached the beach, were your shipmates being murdered by the Japanese?"

Alison gazed at him. Suddenly she knew she was beaten, because he would play the game only according to *his* rules. "Yes," she said.

"Second, was Captain Freeman with the Japanese on the beach?"

"Yes, of course he was, or he could not have saved me. But—"

"Yes or no, Miss Gray. Third, did Captain Freeman give the order to fire into the French and American fleet last year?"

"Yes, but—"

"Fourth, did Captain Freeman give the order to fire on my flag of truce this morning?"

"Yes," Alison shouted. "But—"

"And last, Miss Gray, and this question will require a somewhat more detailed answer, you say that Captain Freeman saved your life on the beach, and afterward. May I ask what has been your relationship with Captain Freeman these past two years?"

Color scorched Alison's cheeks as she stared at him.

"I know the question disturbs you, Miss Gray," Kuper said gently. "But it must be answered."

Alison raised her head. "I . . . I have been his wife."

Kuper leaned back. "You are married to him? You were wed in a church? By a priest?"

"No, of course not," Alison said. "There are no churches, no priests, in Cho-Shu. I was given to him, and . . ." She bit her lip, realizing what she had just said.

Kuper smiled in triumph. "You were *given* to him, as I might give you a new gown or a bauble to hang about your neck. And thus for two years you have been forced to submit to this monster, to acquiesce in his every whim, his every crime."

"That is not true," Alison cried. "I love him." Her head half-turned, her cheeks again flaming; it was not a statement she had ever actually made before, even to him. "I . . . I bear his child."

"Then, madam, our sympathies are redoubled. But you are free of him now. You may stand down."

"I beg your pardon, sir," Ralph said. "I have the right to cross-examine Miss Gray, surely."

"What, do you hope to terrify her all over again?"

"I wish to ask her but two questions," Ralph said quietly.

Kuper sighed. "Oh, very well. Remember, Miss Gray, that there is no longer any reason for you to be afraid of him."

"Miss Gray," Ralph said. "Alison. Have I ever offered you any violence, of word or deed?"

"Oh, no, Ralph," she said. "Oh, no."

"And when I fired into the French fleet, as when I fired on the flag of truce this morning, what would Lord Nariaka have done had I refused to obey his command?"

"He . . . he would have had my throat cut," Alison said.

"Thank you," Ralph said.

Kuper gazed at him. "Do you really expect this court to believe that, in this year of 1864, such a barbarous pressure could possibly have been brought to bear on you, Mr. Freeman? Even by a rascal like Nariaka?"

"It is what would have happened, Admiral. And what do you really find so repellent about such an idea, when you seem ready to believe everything else of these people?"

Another long stare. "Even supposing it were true," the admiral said at last, "do you expect us to believe that the possibility of Miss Gray dying would have had any effect on your decision, if you had feared losing and being faced with the consequences of your crime? Thank you, Miss Gray."

"He has done nothing *wrong*," Alison screamed as she was half-dragged from the tent.

"Well, sir," Kuper said, "it seems to me that your guilt has been established beyond any reasonable doubt, and by the testimony of the one witness who might have been supposed to be favorable to you. As I understand it, your defense is based upon the fact that you saved Miss Gray's life and continued to act the traitor to your race and your country in order to preserve that life. Mr. Freeman, I believe that you did save Miss Gray's life. But I also believe that but compounds the horror of your crime. I suggest that, tiring of the dubious pleasures of yellow flesh, and faced with the opportunity to secure a young woman of your own kind, and as comely as is Miss Gray, you prevented her death in order that you might satisfy the urgings of your lust. As indeed you have done, as she has testified. You thus added rape and abduction to your other crimes." He glanced left and right at the other two judges, who nodded in agreement. "So, then, have you anything more to say before I pass sentence upon you?"

"Only that you are a master at twisting evidence," Ralph remarked.

"As you are one of the most brazen scoundrels I have ever encountered. And one of the biggest cowards. I have been to that fortress up there, Mr. Freeman. I have looked upon such a holocaust of self-destruction as I trust I shall never see again. But to choose death rather than surrender is at least an honorable way of atoning for one's crimes. You lived with these people, shared their lives and their villainies, and then refused to die with them at the end. Perhaps you thought you could thereby save your miserable life, by sheltering behind a helpless and frightened woman. But we have found you out, sir, and you stand convicted upon all five charges made against you. My sentence is that you be taken from here back to those battlements you have disgraced, that you be held there under guard for a period of eighteen hours so that you may reflect upon your crimes, and that tomorrow morning you be hanged from those selfsame battlements, and your body left to dangle there until it rots, as a reminder to these yellow brigands of the fate that will be theirs should they ever dare to murder an Englishman, or a Dutchman, or a Frenchman, or an American, again, until the end of time."

"Miss Gray?" The man wore a long black cloak and a clerical collar, and stooped in the entrance of the tent she had been given for the night.

Outside she could hear the tramp of the marine sentry, and indeed, see him from time to time through the open flap doorway; she was under guard, not because Sir Frederick Kuper supposed her an enemy, but because she was regarded as insane and capable of injuring herself.

Well, she supposed, was he not right? Had she not been insane for at least two years, in imagining that one day a British fleet would come steaming to her rescue?

To end, in fact, the only true happiness she had ever known, by returning her to a life of lonely misery after hanging the only man she had ever loved, or ever could love—and the father of her unborn child.

So whom would she now dream of seeing arrive in Shimonoseki to rescue her from the British? To rescue Ralph. They would have to be mighty quick about it.

And now this priest was here to offer her comfort and hope. And interrupt her thoughts.

"You will forgive this intrusion at what I know must be a difficult time for you, Miss Gray. My name is Collins." He sat beside her on the mat, seemed to wait for her to say something, and sighed. "I know how confused you must be by all these events," he said. "And I can only promise you that within a few weeks, nay, a few days, even a few hours, once the fleet has sailed, tomorrow, Cho-Shu will be nothing but a bad memory."

Alison turned her head to stare at him, and then looked down at herself.

"Ahem," the Reverend Collins remarked. "Yes. That is in fact the main reason for my visit. The babe, be he boy or girl, is one of God's innocents, as are you, Miss Gray. I know how much you have suffered. I know how much you must look forward to resuming your place among your own people, with your head held high, how much you mean to give your unborn child every opportunity in life, and how much you must fear the stigma which will attach to him, and to you."

Alison continued to stare at him, frowning, but only half-listening to what he was saying. There could be no hope for Ralph, and therefore none for herself, either, or the child. The two of them were alone against the entire world. That was made plain. Except in Kagoshima. There he had friends, and powerful friends, too, who would certainly take them in, and allow them to live and be happy, even if it meant never seeing an English or an American face again. Kagoshima! The Satsuma! The most powerful clan in Japan, it was said, save for the Tokugawa themselves. If only a Satsuma army would appear at the strait, eager to turn the tide of battle; it had been sent for.

"So what I would like to suggest to you, Miss Gray," Collins went on, "is that . . . well, I know it is presumptuous of me, but I have discussed the matter with the admiral, and he entirely agrees . . . well, that it might solve a great many of your problems were you to be married."

"*Married*?" He had jerked her back into the present.

"Oh, I meant to Captain Freeman. That way, you see, you would return to the world a widow rather than a . . . well, you would be entirely respectable. As would be your child."

"Married," she muttered. To Ralph. Of course she wanted that. Of course. . . . She could then weep over his corpse as a widow, as the priest had said. She realized she had not wept at all yet. The tears were there, pent up behind the anger and the outrage which were her principal emotions at the moment. And the sense of helplessness. Because of course the Satsuma were not coming; they would know by now it was too late.

If only there were some magical fashion in which she could gain Ralph, and fly across the strait, and . . . She gazed at the parson.

"It would be an entirely private affair, of course," he was saying. "Just myself, and two witnesses . . . no embarrassment could possibly be caused. And it could be done right away. I know there have been no banns, but in these circumstances the admiral is prepared to issue a special dispensation. And frankly, Miss Gray, if there is a slight irregularity, a slight doubt as to your *legal* status as a wife, I would regard that as irrelevant in all the circumstances, as well. What do you say?"

Thoughts seemed to be clamoring through her brain, jostling each other so hard she found it difficult to separate them. And it was terribly important to do so. Because . . . Fly, fly like a bird. Not forever, but for long enough. And then swim like a fish. She *could* do that; she had swum like a fish ever since she had first fallen in love with the rivers of her native Galloway. And no doubt Ralph could as well.

A private ceremony, priest and two witnesses. But the witnesses would be armed guards, and they would be allowed no time alone together, either before or after. Except . . . She gazed through the doorway of the tent at another priest, this one more obviously so, who knelt alone on the sand, a French soldier beside him, hearing the confession of the man. As other soldiers waited their turn to rid their consciences of whatever crimes they had committed this day.

It could be done. But even to think of it was madness. She was a nineteen-year-old girl, and these were her people. No, not anymore. Thus she would be turning her back on them forever. If it worked. If it did not work, she might very well find herself hanging beside Ralph. But did she want anything different? That was how it had begun. That was how it should end. That, or mangled bones at the foot of the battlements, or drowned bodies swept out through the Strait of Shimonoseki—or Kagoshima, and freedom, and love.

And eternal damnation for pretending to be what

she was not? But she did not fear the judgment of heaven in this matter. She *knew* the angels were on her side.

"Miss Gray?" Mr. Collins asked anxiously.

She turned her head and smiled at him. "I thank you for your most kind suggestion, Mr. Collins," she said. "And would indeed be greatly relieved to be able to take advantage of it. But unfortunately, Captain Freeman and I are both Roman Catholics, and I cannot believe he would wish to be married by a priest of any other denomination, with his soul about to be thrust into the hereafter. You would not, by any chance, have a Catholic priest with your fleet?"

The sun set behind the Strait of Tsushima, plunging the afternoon into gloom, immediately relieving the summer heat. But doing little about the stench which pervaded the castle of Shimonoseki. The flames had died down by now, and the palace of Nariaka was nothing more than a burned-out shell. Some of the bodies had been pulled clear by the marines, but then had been thrown back into the dwindling fire by orders of the admiral. To bury them all would have been a task beyond the capabilities of his force, unless he were to remain here a month, and he was clearly in a hurry to be away. It occurred to Ralph that they might all be just a little ashamed of the massacre they had launched, less even by the weight of their bombardment than by the mere infliction of defeat. Certainly no member of the fleet could have had any concept of the meaning of mass seppuku, or hara-kiri, as the Britishers called it, before today.

Perhaps he had not either, for all he had known it was *there*. And perhaps Kuper was right, and he should have taken that "honorable" way out, in preference to sitting here staring at the ocean, his hands tied behind his back, two marine sentries sitting a few feet away, smoking. In preference to sitting here waiting to die when that sun next appeared.

But that way would have also involved Alison's death. Now she would live, and hopefully prosper. As would his son. His son. The last remnant of Ralph Freeman in the world. He had nothing to reproach himself with. He had to believe that, had to believe, too, that whatever he was going to encounter tomorrow morning, there would be Someone Else who would believe that also.

His supper was the same salt meat and biscuit, the same watered-down rum, or grog, as the marines called it. His guard was changed. "You'd best try to sleep," one of the new men recommended, not unkindly. "No use in lying awake brooding on it."

Sleep, Ralph thought. That is all I have left to do, sleep forever. And dream of Alison, and the escape they had been going to make, and the life they had been going to live, somewhere, and . . . He opened his eyes at the sound of footsteps, and gazed at her, again wearing her kimono, as if she had found the Western gown uncomfortable after all this time. She was accompanied by a tall man wearing the robe and cowl of a Catholic priest.

"What's this?" demanded the marine, getting up and presenting his rifle. His companion also rose, rifle at the ready.

"Peace, my son," said the priest, speaking English with a foreign accent.

"But who are you?" the first marine demanded.

The priest threw back the cowl from his head. "I am Father Mansour, from the French flagship. Here, I have written permission to visit the prisoner, signed by your own admiral."

The two marines struck matches to peer at the scrawled handwriting. "Seems all right to me," one said.

"Thank you," Father Mansour said. "We are here upon a mission of mercy. I understand that you are of the true faith, my son," he said to Ralph.

Ralph gazed at him with his mouth open, and then at Alison, standing at the priest's shoulder and giving a desperate nod. "Why, yes, Father," he lied, hoping his Methodist ancestors would forgive him. "So I am."

"Then I am here to offer you words of comfort before you begin your last terrible journey," the priest said. "But more. This young woman has come to me and explained *her* terrible situation. I cannot expect her ever to forgive you for the horrors you have perpetrated upon her, but at her request I would beg of you to grant her the boon of marriage before you depart this life. Then you will at least have made her a widow rather than leave her as a concubine, and the child she carries in her belly will not have the name of bastard."

And he had hoped, in some strange way . . . But for what? Even had she considered helping him, what could one woman do? Yet there was no reason for anger. Had he thought of it, he would have proposed the idea himself.

"Willingly, Father," he said.

"Then do you kneel beside him, Miss Gray," the priest said. "And you, soldiers, will act as witnesses."

"Well, if this ain't the strangest thing I ever did see," remarked the first marine to his compatriot. But both men were plainly delighted; here was something to tell their messmates. And five minutes later Father Mansour was pronouncing Ralph and Alison husband and wife.

"I will not ask you to kiss the bride," the priest said. "Indeed, I am sure she would not wish it. But you have the pleasure of knowing that you have at least performed one generous act in your life. And now—"

"There is one thing more, Father," Alison said, and Ralph gave her a quick look; her voice had trembled, just for a moment, whereas earlier it had been quite calm.

"Yes, my child?"

"I think it would be fitting if my husband were to confess, Father," Alison said.

"Why, that would be *most* fitting," the priest agreed. "Are you willing to make this final atonement, my son? It will ensure you a happier reception in heaven."

Ralph's heart was pounding so hard he was sure the priest could hear it—or more important, that the marines could. Because now he knew that Alison had something in mind. She had always played such a passive role, bending before each storm as it had overtaken her, that he found it difficult to imagine what she might have planned. But he knew that he must go along with her. "I would be happy to confess, Father," he said. "But I will not do so in front of these men."

"No one would expect you to," the priest said. "Is there somewhere we can go, where this man may relieve his conscience in private?"

"Well, I don't know about that," said the marine.

"His hands are tied," Alison said. "He can be no danger to anyone."

"She wants a minute alone with him." The second marine grinned. "What the hell, Reilly? They can't *do* nothing."

The first guard hesitated a last time, and then shrugged. "There's that wall still standing, over there. I reckon you could go behind that. No further, mind."

"That will do very nicely," Alison said, leading the way.

"But . . . do you mean to attend the confession?" the priest asked in surprise, following her, Ralph at his shoulder.

"Should I not, Father? He is my husband now, before God. I have a right to know the true extent of his guilt, and to know that he understands it too, and accepts responsibility for it. Have I not?"

"Well . . . I suppose you do," the priest said thoughtfully.

They had now rounded the charred buttress and were for the moment out of sight of the marine guards. "I think this is the place to stop," Alison said, and stepped against Mansour, to let him see the short sword she had taken from the inside of her kimono, and which she now held against his breast. "If you move or cry out, Father," she said, "I will kill you. Please believe me."

"My dear child," Mansour said. "Do you have any idea what you do?"

"Yes, Father," she said. "And do not suppose, after having spent two years with these people, I do not understand the use of knives."

"And you would risk so much, to save a man who has shamefully misused you?"

"A man who has magnificently loved me," she corrected. "Now, haste."

"Alison . . ." Ralph said, his brain spinning.

"We *must* be quick," she said, and with a slice of the knife severed his bonds. "Take off your kimono, Ralph, and you take off your robe and cowl, Father. You will change clothes."

"I think we had best do what the lady says, Father," Ralph said, and a moment later he was wearing the cowl and robe.

"Now, Father, if you will lie on the ground, Ralph will bind you. I'm afraid he will have to gag you as well, but it will be for only a little while. I have brought some additional cord." This, and some folded cloth to make the gag, she produced from the flap of her kimono.

"My child," Mansour said, "you are committing more than a crime. In assaulting a priest, in deceiving him into assisting your nefarious schemes, you are committing a deadly sin. Be sure that you will suffer divine retribution."

"Then you must pray for me, Father," Alison said. "I mean to escape with Captain Freeman or die beside him."

The priest hesitated, and then shrugged and lay down without a word, while Ralph bound and gagged him.

"They'll find him in a matter of seconds," he pointed out. "Alison, are you sure you know what you're doing? They'll likely hang you right beside me."

"That at the least I intend," she said.

"But where can we go, even supposing we can escape the fortress?" he asked. "From what was said at the trial, every man's hand is against me."

"Not the Satsuma," she said. "And you will be doubly welcome for bringing the news of this disaster and putting them on their guard."

"The Satsuma? But . . ." He looked at the waters of the strait, silent and deep.

"It is not far," Alison said. "Can you swim it?"

"I suppose so."

"And are you afraid of heights?"

"I've never really thought about it."

"Well," she said, "there are only two men out there. And it will have to be several minutes before any others can be summoned to the battlements. I think we have a fair chance. It has to be better than waiting to be hanged."

"But . . . the child . . ."

"Must take his chances on *my* survival, Ralph. I do not intend to bear him without his father. Will you not risk all, with me?"

"Willingly." His heart swelled. He wanted to take her in his arms and make her understand how much he loved her, how much he valued her now, more than he had ever supposed. But now was not the time.

Together they walked around the buttress and toward the guards, taking care not to hurry. "Don't forget the accent," she whispered.

"The man Freeman wishes a moment to pray," Ralph said, doing his best to approximate Father Mansour's speech. "I beg you to grant him that."

"We'll give him a minute, Father," said the man named Reilly. "He didn't have much to confess, eh?"

"And he didn't have much of a kiss and a cuddle either," said the other man with a chuckle.

Ralph followed Alison across the courtyard, inhaling the stench that had been Shimonoseki for the last time, thinking for a last time of Nariaka and Katsura, and even Munetake, who would no doubt roar with laughter from his ronin hideout, supposing he still lived. And then thought of Ito and Inouye, two good and loyal men, cursed by having to serve a vicious lord, but yet prepared to serve him to the death, because that was the way of the samurai. What would *they* say at the news of the destruction the lord of Cho-Shu had brought upon himself?

They reached the inner drawbridge, and the two guards had already faded into the darkness, identifiable only by the glow of their pipes. "Now," Alison whispered, and in the same instant whipped off her kimono and dropped it over the edge, to float gently down to the sea; beneath it she wore only a cord around her waist, into which she had thrust the short sword. Then she swung herself over the rail and climbed down onto the supporting struts, a sliver of white flesh in the gloom.

Ralph threw Father Mansour's robe behind the

kimono, and followed her example, joining her on the cross strut, where the breeze plucked at their hair and raised goose pimples over their flesh. Here they were six feet beneath the bridge itself, and forty feet above the moat. But the moat . . . "There are rocks down there," he whispered.

"Yes," she said. "So we must wait." Clearly she had planned their escape to the last detail.

They did not have to wait very long. There came a shout from the battlements, and then another, and then a stream of explanations and accusations from Father Mansour, but in his agitation he spoke in French and the marines clearly could not understand him.

"There's only one way they could have gone," Reilly bawled. "We'll get them. And when I lay hands on that bitch . . ."

He ran for the drawbridge, at the same time firing his rifle into the air. A moment later both men's boots crashed on the wood above Ralph's and Alison's heads, and the two marines were pounding across the outer courtyard, firing their rifles and shouting, of all things, "Stop, thief!"

"No, no," Father Mansour cried, trotting behind, tripping and stumbling in the unfamiliar kimono, and at last remembering to speak English. "The sea, the sea."

Ralph swung himself back over the bridge. The priest checked, and peered at the naked man looming in front of him. "But, mon Dieu . . ."

"Sorry, Father," Ralph said, and hit him on the point of the chin. The priest went down as if poleaxed. Alison was already running back across the courtyard and gaining the outer battlements, overlooking the strait itself, and thus facing away from the warships. She stood there for a moment, then threw up her arms and dived. A moment later Ralph also stood on the battlements, inhaling the night air, remembering that the sea was fifty feet down. Then he also threw himself into space.

—9—

THE SAMURAI

The water was cool, and, to Ralph's relief, deep. He had jumped holding his nose, whereas Alison had dived, but even so he went in some twenty feet, had lost the last of his breath when at last he struggled back to the surface. "Where are you?" he gasped.

"Here," she said from the darkness, only a short distance away. "Swim beside me."

He struck out, and soon lost his breath again. Water splashed in his face, and he all but sank, then felt her hand touch his shoulder.

"You must not hurry," she said. "It is a long way, and the tide will do most of the work for us. It is rising, will carry us inland, and more, toward the southern shore. I have observed this often from the palace veranda, and thought, were we to wish to escape, it would have to be done on the rising tide."

She had thought these things, and observed, and planned, and kept her secret, until necessary.

"Turn on your back," she now commanded, "and use your feet, until your breath returns."

He realized that she knew as much about the sea, and survival in the sea, as he knew about cannon. He obeyed, gazed up at the night, and at the walls of the fortress as well, already a long way away and drifting sideways as he looked at them. Up there were flaring torches and splashes of exploding rifles, as well as bugle calls and indistinct shouts. "They'll send boats in here," he said.

"That also will take time," she said. "Just keep swimming. Just keep swimming, slow and easy. If we do not splash, they will never find us in the dark."

Without her, he would have drowned. But then, with-

out her, he would have hanged. Alison Gray—a young
girl, a young *lady*, who had seemed to possess only the
virtue of survival.

"I owe you my life," he said.

"As I owe you mine," she replied.

The lights and the noise had faded. Now they heard
only the signal guns being fired from the ships at sea.
Sending, or recalling? There was a good chance the
British might suppose they would drown.

And there remained a good chance the British might
be right. Ralph's legs seemed to be filling with lead,
and he kept thrusting a foot downward, hopefully, and
finding nothing but water. Desperately he raised his
head to look at the southern shore; it still seemed a
very long way away.

Alison had observed his agitation. "Don't think of the
distance, Ralph," she said. "Don't think of your weariness.
Think of other things. Happy things. We'll get there."

He thought of them, and of the son they would have,
of the great happiness they would enjoy. Where? It
could only now be with the Satsuma. But the lord of
the Satsuma was a more honorable man than Nariaka,
and besides, he knew that, wherever they were and, he
thought, whatever their circumstances, they would be
happy now. How could they not be, so long as they
were together?

His foot struck something, and he felt a rush of
blood through his veins as he supposed it might be a
shark or some other predator of the deep. But Alison
was standing beside him. Now it was a matter of forcing his exhausted legs to carry him through the shallow-
ing water until they stumbled onto the beach, to collapse
on their faces.

But almost immediately Alison was on her knees
again. "We must get inland," she said. "They will look
for us on the beach."

He followed her up the slope and into the trees.
Thorns pricked their feet, occasionally tore at their
flesh, but she would not stop, went on for several
hundred yards before again dropping to her knees.
"As soon as it is daylight, we'll look for water."

"Alison . . ." he said, kneeling and then lying beside

her. But there was nothing more to say, because there was so much to be said. "Where did you learn to dive and swim like that?"

"I was born in Galloway, in Scotland," she said. "I have been swimming ever since I can remember. And I swam even more when I lived in Hong Kong." She smiled at him. "The water is warmer there."

There was something more that had to be said now, after all. "Those are your people out there. They would have taken you home."

She rolled onto her back, her head pillowed on her hair. "You are my people, Ralph. And my home is where you are."

"Alison Gray," he said, "I love you." And realized that it was the first time he had ever actually said that to her, or to any woman.

"As I love you, Ralph Freeman," she said. "As I want just to be your wife. Am I truly your wife?"

"I'm not sure, legally. But I would say so."

"And will we be able to live together in peace, now that Nariaka is dead? Say that we will."

"We will, Alison. Once we get to Kagoshima."

They rested until daylight, sheltered by the trees and bushes where they lay. Their hands touched each other, and from time to time they raised their heads and looked at each other in the darkness. They wanted nothing more.

"Are you sure you didn't hurt yourself?" he asked. "That was a great dive."

She smiled. "You're worrying about the baby."

"And his mother."

"Neither is likely to die, save of hunger and thirst, perhaps." She watched the first light begin to sweep across the sky. "Let's be on our way."

They topped a rise and looked back at the sea, at the smoke pall which still hung above Shimonoseki, and at the ships, clearly preparing to put to sea as the boats ferried the last of the marines from the shore. No doubt among them were Reilly and his friend, bound for the punishment cells. But Kuper was not wasting any more time in seeking the fugitives.

They realized they were not alone; people stood around them, also staring at the departing fleet—but equally interested in the two naked barbarians.

"You are from Shimonoseki," said one old man who wore a long gray beard. "You are the white man who fires the guns. We have heard of you. And now you have swum the strait? That is a mighty feat."

The women gazed at Alison in wonder.

"We must hasten to Kagoshima," Ralph explained, "to warn Lord Shimadzu what has happened in Shimonoseki. That fleet may be bound there next."

"We will help you," the old man said.

They were taken to the village, and given rice to eat and water to drink, and kimonos to wear. The people had no weapons, but here in the land of the Satsuma there was no need for weapons. Then two of the young men were appointed to guide them to the town and castle of Kumamoto, the northern bastion of the Satsuma, where they were told they would find horses. The journey on foot took several hours, and they were both near fainting with exhaustion when they finally arrived, Ralph indeed carrying Alison the last few miles, his fears for both her and the baby she carried increasing with every step.

But in Kumamoto they were welcomed, and she was immediately taken by the women to eat and rest. Ralph was led before the general commanding the city, Hayashi Mitsusada, with whom, to his great pleasure, he found Ito. Messengers had apparently been sent on to Kagoshima, and in anticipation of their return with the necessary orders from Saigo Takamori, Hayashi was in the process of marshaling his men to march to the aid of the men of Cho-Shu.

Together the two samurai listened in horror to Ralph's tale; they had in fact heard the gunfire in the distance but had assumed the men of Cho-Shu were giving as good as they received.

"But . . . *all* are dead?" Ito inquired.

"It is difficult to say," Ralph told him. "I think many of the samurai escaped. Those who remained must all have died. But there is no need for you to follow their example," he hastily added as he saw how his friend's mind was working. "Inouye San certainly escaped, and is probably on his way to Edo now. And will he not find Lord Nariaka's son there, and therefore a new lord for you both to serve?"

For it was the age-old custom of the shogunate to require at least one son of each daimyo to live in Edo, as a guarantee of loyalty.

Ito's face brightened. "Yes. And he is but a boy. He will need advice, and support. I must go . . . Inouye San's family, do you know what became of them?"

Ralph shook his head.

"I will find out," Ito said. "*We* will find out, Freeman San."

"No," Ralph said. "I am going to Kagoshima."

"To offer your services to the Satsuma?"

"That's right. Saigo Takamori has long promised me employment. You know that I was never more than a prisoner in Shimonoseki. Well, it seems that I have little choice now about remaining in Japan, at least until I can clear my name with my own people. But I will remain here with men who will treat me as a man, and not an object to be used. You'll not stop me, Ito San."

Ito hesitated, and then sighed, and shrugged. "How can I? You are not one of us. You are not even a samurai. And I know there is much truth in what you have said. Your treatment by Lord Nariaka has long been a cause of concern to me, and to Inouye San as well." He held out his hand, Western style. "May good fortune attend you always, Freeman San."

Ralph squeezed the proffered fingers. "And you. But we will meet again, surely."

"I look forward to that day, Freeman San," Ito said.

Hayashi had been listening to the conversation, and was obviously pleased. "If it is your decision to go to Kagoshima and take service with my lord, Freeman San," he said, "then I shall accompany you, as I can do nothing now to help the men of Cho-Shu. We will depart tomorrow morning."

"I think we should depart now, Hayashi San," Ralph said. "The sooner Lord Shimadzu knows what has happened at Shimonoseki, the better."

"You are right, of course," Hayashi said. "We should make all possible haste. I will see to the horses immediately."

"My wife is exhausted, and she is with child," Ralph went on. "May she remain here with your women until I can send for her?"

Hayashi looked at Ito, who shrugged. "Of course, Freeman San, if that is what you wish. Now, let us depart."

But before the horses could be saddled, they watched a squad of mounted men galloping over the hills toward the fortress, pennons flying in the breeze, shouting their dreadful news long before they reached Kumamoto itself. "Haste," they shouted. "Haste. To arms. Have you not heard? Kagoshima burns."

"It is not possible," Ralph said. "The fleet cannot have gotten there already. It was only weighing anchor this morning."

"Then this is another fleet," said the hatamoto commanding the messengers. "Twelve great ships, exploding fire and smoke. There was nothing we could do against them."

"And you say the city is destroyed?" Hayashi demanded.

"Not destroyed," the hatamoto said, looking a trifle ashamed of his earlier overexcitement. "Because of the situation of Kagoshima, the barbarians could not come close enough, and we prevented them from landing. But the city burns, and the barbarians were still firing on it when we left. General Saigo has sent us to say that the men of Satsuma are unable to go to the aid of the men of Cho-Shu, but rather require all the aid that can be sent from Shimonoseki, as well as from Kumamoto."

Hayashi looked at Ralph.

"Shimonoseki *is* destroyed," Ralph said.

"Then we are lost," the messenger proclaimed.

"We are never lost," Hayashi declared. "Not while we have breaths in our bodies. I will march on Kagoshima with every man I can spare. Freeman San, will you accompany me, or have you changed your mind about serving my master?"

Ralph hesitated but a moment. As he had told Alison

on the battlements, he did have nowhere else in the world to go, if the Americans too were breathing vengeance against him. Even if the Satsuma were about to be destroyed, he had to fight with them. And if there was the slightest chance of their surviving the battle . . .

"I will march with you, Hayashi San," he said. "But give me a moment to bid farewell to my wife." He hurried to the women's quarters, where indeed Hayashi's wife and daughters as well as Alison were waiting anxiously to learn the news. Briefly he told them of the catastrophe. "You understand, my dearest love, that I must get to Kagoshima as rapidly as possible. If in some way I can assist them, then our welcome will be the greater."

"Of course I understand, Ralph." She forced a smile. "I wish I could come with you, but I would only be a hindrance, and I *am* still very tired. But, Ralph . . . do not delay in sending for me. I love you."

He kissed her, for the first time as his wife, his heart swelling all the time with the thought of the marvelous creature who had so strangely come into his keeping, and then he and Hayashi galloped in front of Hayashi's army, sending their horses soaring over the hills of Kyushu, riding all through the night, until soon after dawn they looked down on the city and fortress of Kagoshima. And saw with relief that the flags of the Satsuma still flew above the citadel and that if parts of the city were smoldering heaps of ashes, most of it had been saved. Because unlike Shimonoseki, Ralph realized after the most brief inspection, Kagoshima was truly impregnable. Not by virtue of its fortifications, which appeared to be on the same antique lines as those of the Cho-Shu stronghold, and thus equally vulnerable to modern artillery, nor, he presumed, by virtue of its cannon, which were probably no less antiquated, but because of its superb position. Whereas Shimonoseki stood on an open promontory, Kagoshima rested two-thirds of the way up Kagoshima Wan, a vast inlet rather than a bay, which penetrated some forty miles into the heart of the island; from where the pair of them sat on their horses, they could not even see the ocean. Most of the inlet was several miles wide, certainly at the seaward end, and thus easily accessible to enemy vessels, and indeed they could see the masts of the British squadron, which was anchored in the distance. But at Kagoshima itself the water narrowed to a passage barely half a mile wide, and was commanded by a bluff opposite the city; this too had been fortified to make an almost impassable barrier. Inland of the city the bay again widened, into a saltwater lake, where the Satsuma fleet had been gathered in perfect safety.

But that the Japanese had here also had the worst of the engagement could not be doubted; it was difficult to make out any damage at all in the distant fleet.

Ralph and Hayashi kicked their exhausted horses on again, clattered down the cobbled roads, excited people scattering before them. The drawbridge was lowered for them, and they galloped into the outer court of the castle.

"Freeman San?" Saigo Takamori himself hurried toward them, escorted by a group of samurai. "You bring no good tidings." His own face was grim, and he wore full armor, as did his companions.

"Shimonoseki is fallen," Ralph said. "Nariaka is dead, with many of his samurai. The fortress is destroyed, the city burned."

"You fought the guns?" Saigo demanded.

"I did not have the time," Ralph said. He had not yet decided his attitude. "We fired two guns only, and then were overwhelmed by their fire."

Saigo nodded. "Shimonoseki is too exposed. And perhaps Nariaka deserved his fate, as it is his evil deeds which have brought this disaster upon us. But at least he died with honor. No man can condemn him for that. We—"

"But have you not repulsed them?" Hayashi asked, looking at the distant fleet; the British were certainly no longer firing.

"Repulsed them?" Saigo gave a snort of anger. "Yes, Hayashi San, we have repulsed them. But we have also surrendered."

Ralph and Hayashi stared at him in total disbelief, and total consternation as well. Because if the Satsuma had surrendered . . .

"I know what you are thinking," Saigo said. "How can I and my people stand before you in such disgrace. Lord Shimadzu has made us swear to live and seek our revenge upon the true author of all our misfortunes." He pointed to the north. "The shogun, who has opened the gates of Japan to the barbarians, who was permitted these misfortunes to overtake us."

Ralph scratched his head.

"He is right, Freeman San," Saigo insisted. "I thought as you, at first. The barbarians sailed as close as they could, and lobbed fire shot into our fort and our city. They started many fires, but they could not reach us to defeat us, and when they sought to land their soldiers, our samurai repulsed them, drove them back to their boats. We could have held them for days, perhaps weeks. But Lord Shimadzu ordered us to parley. We thought then that he was an old man who would disgrace us. But that was not his reason. He surrendered in the name of the shogun, because the shogun had sent him a messenger expressly commanding him to do so, to accept the British terms and agree to the indemnity. It is the Tokugawa who bear the burden of this defeat, and it is the Tokugawa who will pay for it. And when that is done, when Japan is again strong and prepared to meet the invaders ... But you ..." He clapped Ralph on the shoulder. "Your lord is dead. Will you serve a new lord?"

"That is why I am here," Ralph agreed.

"Then come with me. Lord Shimadzu will be pleased to see you. Had we had you here, we might not even have had to obey the shogun, eh?"

Ralph and Hayashi walked beside him over the inner drawbridge. "I did not do very well at Shimonoseki," Ralph reminded him.

"Yes. You lacked the guns. We lack them too. But we will get them, Freeman San. Oh, we will get them. And we will use them, too. One day the foreigners will rue their arrogance. One day."

Samurai gathered to stare at them as they climbed the stairs toward Lord Shimadzu's audience chamber. The scene very naturally reminded Ralph of Cho-Shu, but there was a considerable difference. These men were all angry at having been forced to surrender to the British, even if their lord had found so ingenious a method of absolving them, and himself, from all blame in the matter. Thus there were few smiles to be seen. But there was also a complete lack of the tension which had been so obvious among the Cho-Shu people. Shimadzu suffered none of the moods and uncertainties of Nariaka. A samurai in Kagoshima could feel that his life and his property, and his future, would be secure, except in the most grave of circumstances. Shimadzu ruled entirely by the law, and the law had been handed down for generations, the law of bushido, known to every samurai. In that they could securely rest their hopes and their ambitions.

And he was about to become one of them. It occurred to Ralph that he had a feeling of coming home, even if this was the first time he had ever set foot inside the place. Here he *would* find honor.

The doors were opened, and he knelt before his new master. "Truly are you welcome here, Freeman San," Shimadzu said. "Would you could have been here yesterday, and the day before. But no matter. The past is the past. Only the future matters. It is to you and General Saigo that the future of the Satsuma must be entrusted. The future and the *honor*, Freeman San. Now . . ." He raised his head with a frown as there was a disturbance outside.

"He is here," someone was shouting. "I am told he is here. I *know* he is here. And I will face him *now*."

Forgetful of protocol, Ralph leaped to his feet to face the door. For the voice belonged to Munetake.

The doors swung in, and Munetake stood there. Like Saigo, he still wore full armor and carried both swords and a spear. "Freeman," he said, his voice now little more than a whisper. "Freeman!"

He had not changed at all in two years. Two years, Ralph thought, in which I had supposed him dead, and put him altogether from my mind.

"What is the meaning of this intrusion, Munetake San?" demanded Lord Shimadzu mildly.

"My lord," Munetake said, bowing low, "when I came

to you, a masterless ronin, you took me in because of your great and generous spirit and because you knew of my prowess with the sword. You did not seek to learn the reason I left Lord Nariaka's service." He pointed at Ralph. "This man, my lord, this barbarian, is the cause of my disgrace. When we quarreled, Lord Nariaka forbade us to fight, forbade me to save my honor, because he knew I would kill this man, and he deemed him too valuable to die, on account of the guns. But this was not the law of bushido, great lord. I refused to accept such a decision, and then my Lord Nariaka threw me out, turned me into a ronin. But I was not the one disgraced by his action. It was Lord Nariaka who disgraced himself, and the barbarian."

"And so you came to me," Shimadzu said quietly and thoughtfully. While Ralph waited. But presumably Shimadzu, who lived by the law, could come to only one decision. How often had he dreamed of facing this man, sword in hand, and thus avenging all the hideous wrongs he had done to Alison. But those dreams had faded with the passage of time. Now he was aware only of how tired he was. And after two years, he held no enmity, even for Munetake. He doubted he would be able to summon the mental strength to kill him, even if he possessed the physical strength. Or the skill.

If only these people could understand, he thought, that he and Alison wished only to find rest, and peace, here in Kagoshima. Alison, he thought in sudden alarm. She would be waiting for his summons. Thus, if he had to fight, he had also to win.

"You must tell me the cause of your quarrel," Shimadzu was saying, "before I can judge it."

Munetake hesitated, then squared his shoulders. "It was over a barbarian woman, great lord."

"Over a *woman*?" Shimadzu was clearly astounded.

"A barbarian woman, great lord," Munetake repeated carefully. "She is not as other women. She was given to me, as my slave, and I used her. But this man saw her and coveted her and stole her away. I took her back, but instead of executing them both, or even returning the woman to me and executing the man, as was the law, Lord Nariaka gave her to the barbarian, on condition he command the guns of Shimonoseki."

"A sad tale," Shimadzu observed. "Lord Nariaka has truly brought the wrath of the gods upon himself by his intemperate meddling with the laws of our land. But it is done now, Munetake San. Lord Nariaka is dead. Shimonoseki is destroyed. And this woman who has caused so much mischief is undoubtedly also dead. I therefore command you—"

"Not so, great lord," Hayashi said. "The woman lives, and lies at Kumamoto waiting to come here to Kagoshima."

Ralph caught his breath as Shimadzu looked at him and then at Munetake.

"She is *mine*," Munetake said. "By all the laws of bushido, the woman is *mine*. She was given to me. I have served you faithfully and well, Lord Shimadzu, for more than two years. It was I who yesterday morning led the samurai who repulsed the British attempt to land at the north cove. I did these things, great Lord Shimadzu. I have served you according to the law of bushido. It is by that law that I live, that I fight, and that I shall die, when my time comes."

To Ralph's horror, the samurai gathered around were nodding their heads in agreement.

"My lord," he protested, "the woman is now mine. She was given to me by Lord Nariaka, and yesterday we were married."

Shimadzu raised his eyebrows. "Yesterday?"

"The day before, my lord," Ralph said. "I have lost track of time, these last few days, my lord. But it was done by a Christian priest."

"That is no marriage." Munetake sneered.

"This is a sad business," Shimadzu again observed. "It is even sadder that two great and famous warriors should quarrel over a mere woman. I had no part in the original quarrel, in the original dispositions." He looked around his warriors. "It might be supposed that the simplest solution would be to let them fight. But for two great warriors to duel to the death over a woman— that is not the law of bushido. Yet must I follow the law, as far as I am able." He looked at Ralph. "You say you and the woman were joined in marriage by a Christian priest the day before yesterday?"

"Yes, my lord," Ralph said, relief starting to surge through his body.

"As Munetake has said, that is not a ceremony which would be recognized in Japan. Yet it is obviously meaningful to you, Freeman San. Therefore I would ask you one question, which I require you to answer truthfully, as you are an honorable man. In the beginning, was this woman, as Munetake San claims, given to him by Lord Nariaka?"

"Why, yes," Ralph said. "So she was. But the circumstances—"

"The circumstances are thus irrelevant, Freeman San," Shimadzu said, his voice soft. "The original gift of Lord Nariaka takes precedence over any later disposition he might choose to make, and over any marriage ceremony. How may a man, even a lord, give today, and take that gift away tomorrow? If a samurai is to die for some crime, and commits seppuku, then are his women and his chattels free to be disposed of, or, if he dies in disgrace, then are his women also to be executed. This is the law. Lord Nariaka has no power to change the law. Only Munetake San may now give this woman elsewhere. Do you agree to release this woman, Munetake San?"

"No," Munetake shouted. "Never. She is mine. She was given to me. She—"

"As you say," Shimadzu said, even more sadly. "She is yours. That is the law of bushido. She is yours, and must be returned to you. That is my ruling in this matter."

For a moment Ralph could not believe his ears; only the sudden savage smile on Munetake's face convinced him that the words had actually been spoken.

"No," he said. "No," he shouted, looking from left to right, for support, and finding none, reaching for his empty belt in a gesture of despair—he had not supposed he would need a weapon in the land of the Satsuma. "It cannot be," he cried, and hurled himself at Munetake.

Men surrounded him, grasping his arms, dragging him away from his foe, forcing him to his knees before Shimadzu, while Munetake drew his sword.

"Are you mad?" Hayashi asked him. "Lord Shimadzu has given his judgment."

"It cannot be," Ralph shouted again. "My lord, great lord, you do not understand. This is a white woman, used to different treatment than a Japanese. Her life with Munetake was a long torture, and will be again. You cannot do this."

Shimadzu sighed. "I understand your grief, Freeman San. I have heard of how barbarian men treat their women almost as goddesses, and yield to them in all things."

"Well, then . . ."

"But yet must I obey the law of the land. Even I, Freeman San. Or perhaps it would be more true to say I more than any other. The woman is Munetake's. To take her from him would be to make me a common thief."

"She is my wife," Ralph cried. "She is carrying my child."

Shimadzu frowned. "Is this true?"

"It is true," Ralph said. "I swear it, by everything I hold sacred."

"This is truly a sad case," Shimadzu said. "Munetake San, in all the circumstances, can you not prevail upon your heart to let this woman go?"

"She is mine," Munetake growled. "I will never let her go."

Shimadzu stared at him for several seconds, but the big samurai refused to lower his gaze; he certainly did not lack courage.

"If that is your decision, then that is an end to the matter," Shimadzu said.

"No," Ralph shrieked, heaving against the restraining hands, throwing them off, reaching his feet, and being brought down by the weight of several of the samurai. "Never!"

"But yet," Shimadzu went on, "as this is so exceptional a case, there are certain courses upon which I must insist."

"The woman is mine," Munetake said again.

Shimadzu inclined his head. "That is accepted. But as you are so determined to possess her, Munetake San, then shall she be yours forever, or until the day you die. I would not have her your slave. I understand you have no wife."

Munetake stared at him. "I wish no wife. I will marry no barbarian, and no *Christian*. The woman is mine, by law."

"Yes," Shimadzu said. "And as you well know, I cannot command whom you marry, or whether you marry at all. But I will not be gainsaid in this matter, Munetake San. It is clear to me that this woman is no mere honin, to be used as such. She is certainly wellborn and educated, fit to be the wife of even a hatamoto. If you will not marry her, then I command you to take her into your home as your chief concubine, who will have pride of place over all other women in your house, and in whose care will be placed all your domestic arrangements. I also demand that from this day forth you treat her with the respect and honor due to a wife. And more, the respect and honor due to a wife who comes from a different civilization from our own. She is not to be beaten, Munetake San, ever again. That is a decree from your lord. And this child, when it is born, will be regarded by all men, and more especially by yourself, as your own, will be raised and educated as your own, will be loved and respected as your own. This is my decree."

Munetake gazed at him for several seconds. Then he bowed. "It shall be as you decree, great lord."

"Then I am pleased. As will be Freeman San, when he recovers his senses, I have no doubt. Now, leave this place, Munetake, and go for your woman. Do not return here for a season. I appoint you to command my castle and fief in Hokkaido. Go there with your people, and serve me well. Until I send for you again."

Another bow, and then a long stare at Ralph, and Munetake left the room.

"I will write down what I have commanded," Shimadzu said, "and you will accompany Munetake San to Kumamoto, Hayashi San. There you will acquaint the barbarian woman of my decisions and my instructions, so that she will be left in no doubt of her situation, but also her prerogatives."

Hayashi bowed.

"You cannot," Ralph shouted. "You cannot allow this, Lord Shimadzu."

"I have done all that I can, Freeman San," Shimadzu said. "And perhaps more than I should. This woman will be treated with honor from this moment forth."

"You *believe* that?" Ralph spit at him. "Honor? From Munetake?"

"She will be treated with honor," Shimadzu repeated. "And now, it is time for you to come to your senses. *You* are showing no honor, no manhood, in thus demeaning yourself over a mere female, even a barbarian female."

"She is my wife," Ralph moaned, and raised his head. "At least let me go to Kumamoto to say good-bye to her, to prepare her for what is going to happen."

Shimadzu shook his head. "You would merely seek out Munetake and wish to kill him. But he would kill you, Freeman San, even were your action not a breach of bushido. And if you did succeed, and carried off the woman, what then? You would have become a ronin, an outlaw, and every man's hand would be against you. No, no. You will remain in Kagoshima until you have recovered your true character."

"Do you suppose I shall ever do that?" Ralph shouted. "Do you suppose I shall not kill Munetake the next moment I lay eyes on him?"

Shimadzu sighed. "Take him away," he said. "Take him away and lock him up." He raised one finger. "But where he can do himself no damage. He is demented. For the moment."

It took a dozen samurai to force Ralph down the stairs and hold him quiet while one of the powder stores—chosen because of the thickness of the walls—was emptied of its contents. No mattress was given him, for fear he might smother himself, but food and drink were placed in the room, and a change of kimono—

although the girdles had been carefully removed so that he could not strangle himself, either.

His incarceration was supervised by Saigo himself. "Truly," he said, "it grieves me to see a man so driven from his senses by desire for a woman. But you will recover, Freeman San. And then I look forward to talking with you."

"What about?" Ralph snarled. "Do you suppose I would lift a finger to help you, or any Satsuma man, any Japanese man, ever again?"

"You will recover," Saigo said again, and left the room; Ralph heard the bolts being driven on the outside of the door.

And could collapse on the floor in a paroxysm of the most utter despair. Munetake would already be halfway to Kumamoto. By dawn tomorrow he would be there, and Alison, starting from her couch to see what message her husband had sent her, would be seized and . . . He dared not allow his imagination to carry him any further, because that way *was* madness.

But what way was not? Could he exist for a moment, thinking of Alison in Munetake's arms? Without even being allowed to prepare her for that fate himself? What could she suppose, save that he had abandoned her like a coward rather than fight for her? After she had risked her life for him, had turned her back on her own people for him. After they had sworn their undying love for each other.

He wanted to hurl himself against the door time and again until he knocked all the senses from his brain. But did not. Slowly his wild despair began to recede, to be replaced by a slow, cold-burning fury. Alison would know that what had happened was beyond his power to prevent. But Alison, also, with that marvelous reserve of spirit which she possessed, would refuse to despair, would accept whatever tortures might be inflicted upon her, sure that one day, however long it took, her husband would again come for her. Had they not been separated before, twice, as it had then seemed, forever? And yet had found their way back together again? What could now prevent him from regaining her, were he only as patient and as determined as might be required? He was again a prisoner, but a prisoner of a man who, like Nariaka, valued his services, and would never execute him—or he would already have done so after his insubordination of today. And Munetake also served the same master. Perhaps he *was* being sent to Hokkaido, the most northern of the three islands of Japan, but yet was he serving the Satsuma, and they must one day meet again. And when they did ... that day must he be ready, Ralph resolved. Ready in every way. For that day would he live, when at the least he would be avenged, and at the best ...

He ate the food and drank the sake, and lay down and actually slept dreamlessly, so great was his exhaustion, and awoke to find the door open and Saigo Takamori standing above him. "Sleep is a great healer of wounds," the general observed, "especially those of the mind."

Ralph sat up cautiously. He certainly must not betray his resolve; his problems at Shimonoseki had nearly all stemmed from his too-open opposition to Nariaka. "As you say, Saigo San," he agreed.

Saigo waved his hand, and the door was closed on them. Saigo squatted in front of the white man. "I would have you know how much my heart aches for you, Freeman San," he said. "When I first met you, I thought, here is a man with whom I would be proud to be a friend. Now, again, I would be your friend."

Ralph gazed at him, and the general sighed.

"Lord Shimadzu would be your friend as well, Freeman San. He did what he had to do. You will understand, one day, if you do not already, how slender a thread holds our Japanese society together. I have read and heard much of your society in the Western countries. It is not for me to criticize other ways, however much I may dislike or disapprove of them. In your culture, as I understand it, a man is ruled by his wealth, his money. His very honor is bound up in that. I have heard of men who have committed seppuku in your lands because they could not pay a debt or because their business had failed. To a samurai that would be unthinkable, and the merchants, they know nothing of honor anyway. Yet perhaps a society controlled by personal wealth is

easier to manage. A man's prowess is there for all to
see; he is either rich or poor, or richer or poorer than
his neighbor, and the neighbor knows these things.
Here in Japan, we deal in intangibles. Oh, it is easy to
know when a man has acted the coward in the field.
But samurai do not often act the coward in the field.
And no man can tell the innermost workings of a man's
mind, the true glory of his spirit, or the true debase-
ment of his nature, until and unless it is put to the test.
Honor is not something that can be worn on the sleeve.
Yet must it be preserved, at all times, for it is sacred.
How can this be done, and be known to be done, by all
men? This problem taxed our forefathers many years
ago, and thus the law of bushido was devolved by them
for our guidance. Bushido is the sacred law that gov-
erns every action, and indeed should govern every
thought, of a samurai. Woe to the man who breaks that
law. Nariaka of Cho-Shu was known as one such, whenever it suited him. Great lord as he was, he was hated
for it, and now perhaps it has brought him to his death.
We of Satsuma believe in bushido. And by the laws of
bushido, Freeman San, there was nothing else Lord
Shimadzu could have done yesterday."

Ralph gazed at him.

Saigo sighed. "You are still angry. This is natural.
But this anger you must overcome. As you are a man,
as you are a warrior, as you will be a samurai, and a
leader of samurai, you have more important things to
do with your life than mope over a woman. But if you
wish a wife, Freeman San, then I would honor you
above all other men."

Ralph frowned at him, not at all sure of his meaning.

"Come with me," Saigo said.

The door was opened, and the guards stood back to
allow them through. Saigo led Ralph into the palace
gardens, where the cherry blossoms were just coming
to life in the morning sunlight, and birds were singing,
and the flowing water which was ever present in a
Japanese garden rustled by. A place of great beauty
and great peace. A place such as he had hoped to walk
in with Alison. The thought brought tears to his eyes.

And a place of female laughter. Saigo touched his

lips with his finger and showed Ralph where to stand, against a hedge, through which he could look without being seen. To gaze at five young women walking together, their kimonos a blaze of color, their glossy black heads shaded by equally brilliant parasols. They talked, and they giggled, each a picture of animated beauty. For as it was early morning, and they had no idea they were being watched, they wore no makeup, and as they were clearly very young and unmarried, he could see that their teeth were a gleaming, natural white.

"They must never know that you have seen them in dishabille," Saigo whispered. "But I would have you look on them in their natural state."

"Who are they?" Ralph asked.

"They are my nieces, Freeman San. The youngest is twelve, the oldest eighteen. One of them will be your bride."

Ralph stared at him in amazement. "My *bride*?"

"I would have it so, Freeman San. Everything I have seen of you, and everything I have heard of you, convinces me that you will be a worthy member of the house of Saigo. And thus I would have it so."

Ralph shook his head. "You know I cannot agree to that, Saigo San. I am already married."

"Not anymore," Saigo said. "And you have never been married, by Japanese law, Freeman San. Besides, the barbarian woman is now lost to you forever. Do you not realize, my friend, that once she is Munetake's chief concubine, for her even to smile upon you would give him the right to strike off her head?"

"To . . . But I thought Lord Shimadzu commanded that no harm was to come to her?"

"He did, as far as he could. As Munetake's chief concubine, she will control his household, rule his other women, mother all his children. To be a chief concubine is a position every bit as responsible as to be a wife. In addition, Lord Shimadzu has forbidden her ever to be beaten, and a man normally does have the right to beat his woman if she displeases him in any way. To belong to a samurai is also a post of great honor, however, especially when the husband is so famous a

swordsman as Munetake. Your barbarian has nothing
but a life of wealth and contentment in front of her, so
long as she acts the wife. But should she ever even
suggest adultery, which amounts to betrayal of her
lord, then she is worthy only of instant death, and no
one, not even Lord Shimadzu, could then save her
life." He rested his hand on Ralph's arm. "I have spoken thus frankly with you because you deserve to know
the truth, and it is very necessary for you to know the
risks you will take, for her, should you ever endeavor
to see her again. For both your sakes, you must forget
her. And that can only be done in the arms of another
woman. I would be happy to call you nephew, Freeman
San, the moment you become a samurai."

"That is exactly as the barbarian related it to me,"
Hayashi told Munetake. "Riding this very way, but
twenty-four hours ago."

The two men walked their horses over the hills toward Kumamoto, their escorts following a discreet distance behind, and Hayashi had talked all the way, while
Munetake had ridden in silence.

"So you will understand, Munetake San," the general
continued, "that in addition to manly lust, this Freeman
no doubt feels he owes the woman his life. And indeed,
she would appear to be an exceptional female, in her
strength, of body no less than mind. A great prize." He
glanced at the big samurai, but Munetake continued to
stare at the road in front of his horse.

"Which you have now secured," Hayashi observed.
"And should have, and enjoy. Munetake San, you and I
have been friends for many years. I knew you and
loved you when you still served Nariaka of Cho-Shu,
and when you came to Kyushu, a masterless ronin, it
was I took you in, and I led you before Lord Shimadzu
and begged him to employ you. In your happiness I
find much of my own. And therefore it grieves me to
see your spirit downcast. I feel that you have been
hardly done by, and would assist you if I may. You are
to go to Hokkaido. That is far away, yet will you thrive
there, I know, and regain the full confidence of our
lord. But it *is* far away, and it will be months, perhaps

years, before you are again summoned to Kagoshima. Years in which you may well bend this woman to your will. If it will assist you, and you wish it, I will not read her the whole of Lord Shimadzu's message."

Now Munetake's head did turn.

Hayashi smiled. "Thus would I disobey my lord. But Lord Shimadzu is not the man he once was. Or he would not so tamely have accepted the shogun's command to surrender to the barbarians. You are a great and mighty warrior, and you do not deserve to be hindered by a ruling no man has ever heard before. For however strong, however brave, however resourceful this woman may be, as she was described to me by the barbarian man, she is still a woman, and should be treated so. Think well on this, Munetake San; Kumamoto lies over that next hillock."

Munetake gazed at the road once more. If he was depressed, it was less because he knew that at this moment Lord Shimadzu looked on him with disfavor than because for the first time in his life he was aware of a certain confusion in his emotions. Emotions were not a weakness he had ever allowed himself, as a samurai and a famous swordsman. Hatred of one's enemies, love of honor and glory, pride in one's strength and ability—those were the emotions proper to a samurai. Thus it had been easy to hate Freeman the barbarian, simply because he was the bigger and stronger man, and because he knew secrets, such as his mastery of the guns, which were his alone. In Freeman, Munetake, whose dream was of carving a fief for himself in the coming revolution—as had been done by more than one lowborn warrior in the past; the immortal Hideyoshi, indeed, the greatest warrior in Japanese history, had risen from the son of a cowherd to be kampaku, regent for the shoguns, by the strength of his right arm—had instinctively recognized a determined rival.

And thus it had been easy to extend that hate to the woman Freeman wanted. The fact that she was different from any other woman had only slowly penetrated his consciousness. There was more of her than he had ever known previously in a woman, and her mind had resisted him, whereas he had never before doubted

that he could bend any woman utterly to his will as he
chose. She had presented a challenge, at once to beat
but also to *love* into submission. And that last evening
he had felt himself to be near succeeding—and yet an
hour later she had fled with Freeman, her mind still
unconquered. Thus he had hated her equally with the
man, had deliberately given her to the honin, had deliberately anticipated her being sliced into a thousand
pieces.

That had not happened. Instead, through her and
Freeman he had become a ronin, to nurse his hate in
bitter solitude until the Satsuma had taken him in. Still
had he hated, and dreamed of revenge, and now it was
his. He knew Hayashi was right, and he could take the
woman to Hokkaido, hundreds of miles to the north,
and there torture her with all the refinement he could
imagine, and listen to her scream, and watch her writhe
. . . and simply report to Kagoshima that she had died
of a fever or in childbirth. There would be no one ever
to betray him.

And then she would be gone. He would never look
upon her like again. Because during his years of exile,
when he had dreamed of her—and he had often
dreamed of her—it had not been of beating her or
torturing her, but of that wealth of soft white beauty
moving against him. He wanted her for himself, Freeman forgotten. And now there was more. This was a
woman who had defied her own people, had risked all,
and finally had dived fifty feet and swum across the
Strait of Shimonoseki to save the life of the man she
loved. Munetake was not sure *he* could swim the Strait
of Shimonoseki.

He had read and heard of women such as that. They
occurred in the histories, to stand at the shoulders of
their warrior husbands. But he had never met one
before, nor had he heard of one living. Until today.

And she was his, to do with as he chose. Whatever
disfavor he might be in with his lord, he was surely the
most fortunate man on earth. In the sheer possession
of her, he had utterly conquered Freeman. But also in
the sheer possession of her, if he could win from her
the faithful love she was obviously capable of bestowing,

and the strength which flowed from that love, then all things were possible, all heights attainable.

They topped the rise and looked down on the fortress of Kumamoto. "Hayashi San," Munetake said, "I am honored and delighted by your friendship, and your offer. But I would not have you go against the wishes of your lord, any more than I would do so myself. You will read Lord Shimadzu's full message to the barbarian woman. Omitting not a word."

"Horses!" Alison ran to the window, but it was again growing dark, and she could only just make out the men.

"That is my husband," Mrs. Hayashi said at her shoulder. "But the other man . . . He is very big."

"Ralph." Alison turned to face the door, knowing that a moment later he would be standing there. The past two days had been the most utter torment. They had strained their ears to listen to the rumble of the guns, and heard nothing. She had walked in the garden with Hayashi's daughters, pretending to be concentrating upon picking flowers, and all the while had listened and attempted not to think. If there was no firing, Ralph had to be safe, and had to be coming back to her, or at least sending for her—provided only he was welcomed by the Satsuma. But how could he not be welcomed, how could . . . ?

The door opened, and Hayashi stood there. He embraced his wife and then bowed to Alison. "I bring a message from Kagoshima," he said.

"From Ralph? My husband?"

"From Lord Shimadzu himself. You will please kneel?"

Alison hesitated, glanced at Mrs. Hayashi, who gave her a reassuring smile and knelt herself, and then obeyed. She half-closed her eyes in painful anticipation, and then closed them altogether as the words slowly issued from Hayashi's mouth. They seemed to come from a very long way away, and their substance beat on her brain like drops of rain. She lost all feeling in her legs and arms, and was aware only of the baby rolling in her belly, as if he too could not comprehend, could not believe.

She listened to movement, and opened her eyes. Hayashi and his wife had left the room, and in their place Munetake stood in front of her. And the door was closed.

Alison heard her own breath rasp as she half-fell over, and still sitting, pushed herself across the tatami mats. A weapon! There had to be one somewhere; but Munetake had even discarded his. Yet she had to discover something with which to destroy herself quickly and irrevocably. Because clearly Ralph was dead and their brief dream of happiness had been, after all, only a dream. By turning her back upon the British fleet, she had prolonged his existence by exactly three days, and brought her own down to a similarly short span.

Munetake smiled at her. "I would have you know," he said, "that Freeman San refused to accept the judgment of Lord Shimadzu, and would have fought until he was killed. But he was seized and imprisoned. He will live, and no doubt prosper. But you will not look on him again."

He took a step toward her, and Alison discovered that her back was against the wall. She was helpless, trapped with a man who would begin by beating her until she would be unable to move, and then ... She watched his hand coming closer, and waited for it to drive into her hair; she scarcely breathed, and she wanted to vomit. She wanted to scream, too, but she was afraid to utter a sound.

The hand picked up her own, and slowly drew her to her feet. "You carry a child," Munetake said. "Thus I cannot love you. Because the child is now mine, and I would not harm you. I *shall* love you when the babe is born. But we have a long way to travel, you and I, and we must go slowly, so that the babe is not harmed. I have my people preparing a litter, and we will depart as soon as we have eaten." He released her, went to the door, and held it open. "Come and eat, Alison."

He pronounced her name in three distinct syllables; clearly he had been practicing. And he was holding the door for her. And his touch on her fingers had been as gentle as any she had ever known. Yet he was Munetake, who had beaten her, and raped her again and again. She glanced at him, and felt the heat in her cheeks.

He smiled at her. "I will *love* you," he said again. "As soon as you are able. Now, come. You are my woman."

The thought was impossible. Having lost Alison, Ralph had no desire to look upon another woman until she was restored to his arms. And if he could look on a Japanese woman ever again, would she not only remind him, every moment of the day or night, of Aya's smile and quiet charm, and thus of Aya's head rolling in the dust?

Yet Saigo had reminded him that in endeavoring to regain Alison there could be no room for failure—and even more, that there would be no refuge for him in Japan afterward, even if he succeeded. The Satsuma were his only friends now, and he would be turning his back on them. Thus this time his plans must be *very* carefully laid indeed, and thought through beyond any mere settlement with Munetake.

And thus it could be no part of his plan to quarrel with Saigo or with any of the Satsuma samurai, who were intent only upon honoring him. Of course, in order to use him. He did not delude himself on that point. For every samurai in Kagoshima, indeed in all Kyushu, was filled with a burning anger at the humiliation which had been inflicted upon them, less by the British, as they saw it, than by the pusillanimity of the shogun. To avenge themselves was the sole consideration all Satsuma warriors held, from this moment forth, however they might dissemble with true Oriental politeness. Ralph watched from a secluded window when, a month after the bombardment, the British warships were allowed to anchor off the citadel, and the British envoys came ashore to receive their blood money—which had to be paid mainly in rice. They were greeted with bows and smiles, as the shogun's representatives, who had traveled south from Edo to oversee the transaction, were also greeted respectfully and with every honor. Only when one of the samurai was caught in an unguarded moment could the tight lips, the flashing eyes, the barely suppressed hiss of anger from the flared nostrils betray the consuming rage felt by all.

The truth of the matter was not lost on the British, Ralph was sure. He did not suppose it was lost on the shogun's representatives either. But white men and Tokugawa also dissembled, and drank the health of the mikado and Queen Victoria of England, and smiled, and kept their thoughts to themselves.

It was not only the Satsuma clan and the scattered remnants of the Cho-Shu who now hated the shogunate. It was difficult to suppose anyone in Japan still respected or venerated the Tokugawa as they had in the days of the immortal Iyeyasu, the victor of Sekigahara, the true founder of the greatness of his house, two hundred and fifty years before. Eight generations was too long for one family to hold supreme power without the sanction of divine right; it was perhaps too long even *with* such a sanction, if European history was anything to go by, Ralph thought. And certainly the growing unrest that was spreading through Japan, which accelerated following the British triumph at Shimonoseki and Kagoshima, and in the consequent approach of a civil war which would set every man against his brother, and in which Lord Shimadzu and Saigo Takamori were clearly planning to rely heavily upon the skill and experience of their master gunner, he saw his best hope of regaining Alison and his son—for although no news came to him from Hokkaido, as the summer dwindled into autumn and then winter, he had to face the fact that she would soon be giving birth, to Munetake's child, by law. Thus if he spent almost every night in a turmoil of misery and mental torture, he sprang from his couch every morning the more determined to become a samurai as soon as possible. That alone would give him the power of movement and personal freedom he needed. And more, to make himself the most Japanese of men, and to rise in the councils and the estimation of the Satsuma, until he could rise even above the law of bushido.

Thus he practiced his arms, and he studied Japanese history and legend, and he told Saigo what was required to make his army into a modern fighting force—

and was listened to with far more interest and attention than he had ever received from either Nariaka or Katsura, and he smiled upon Saigo's nieces, from a distance. To be Japanese meant to dissemble, and to smile frequently, and at other times to maintain an impassive lack of expression, regardless of the raging hell that might be inside his brain.

And with the Satsuma he planned for nothing less than a total revolution. It would not be regarded as a revolution when it happened, of course—unless it failed. When they would all die, anyway. Revolution was unthinkable against the empire of the mikado, the Son of Heaven; what was possible was to convince the mikado that his shogun was betraying the country. Thus it was necessary to gain possession of the emperor and to depose the shogun in his name. It was all a great charade, in which Ralph could not help but wonder what the helpless, aging demigod in Kyoto thought of it all—if he even knew what was happening, for apparently the emperor by tradition paid very little attention to temporal affairs, and confined his judgments to religious matters and to deciding who had written the finest poetry of the previous year. But that the Tokugawas would resist any attempt to replace them as shoguns was not doubted by anyone. They knew the precarious grasp they retained upon power; Iyemochi's cousin and predecessor, Iyesada, had been murdered at the very gate of his palace, officially by a band of lawless ronin, but it was well known the ronin had been in the pay of some dissatisfied daimyo, and the name of Nariaka of Cho-Shu was often mentioned as the instigator of the crime. Thus Iyemochi never went abroad unless adequately guarded, and he maintained a powerful and well-equipped army; the Satsuma indeed suspected that part of his reason for dealing with the barbarians at all was to obtain Western weapons, the better to overawe the recalcitrant daimyos. And the emperor, in his royal seclusion at Kyoto, was similarly protected by a Tokugawa army.

But Saigo was not lacking in resource, and neither was his master. Having appeared to accept their defeat by the British with good grace, the Satsuma now even encouraged foreigners to visit Kagoshima, and open markets there. These again were mainly British, who brought news of the ending of the American Civil War and the triumph of the Northern states and therefore the Union—and also the word that Ralph Freeman remained a criminal and a renegade, abhorred and wanted by all Christian men. But these same men were also anxious to consult with him as to the best way of approaching the Japanese in business matters, arriving as they did with their stovepipe hats and their mustaches and their gaping wonder at the strangeness of Japanese life, which was revealed to them with open-handed generosity by their hosts, so that there were highly respectable London merchants who spent entire days in the bathhouses, surrounded by giggling honin girls or boys, and even transacting business from that damp but sexually exhilarating intimation of paradise.

And in return, they brought guns. Rifles and revolvers to begin with, but soon even modern cannon. Not Dahlgrens, to be sure, but field pieces of the kind Ralph had commanded in the army and with which he was utterly familiar. Soon he disposed of two batteries, with which he thought he could dominate any looming battlefield. Saigo was delighted. "I see the future crowding upon us, Freeman San," he said. "So now it is time for you to become a samurai."

The pain was over, and the discomfort. And the baby lay in Alison's arms, while Munetake smiled at her. "Freeman was the father?" he asked. "You are certain of this."

"Yes," she said. "I am certain."

"Then the boy will be tall and strong. He will be a worthy son of Munetake. We shall call him—"

"Jeremy," she said.

They gazed at each other. She had picked the name out of the air, determined that her child would bear a Christian name. But also once again to discover her true situation. For six months now she had lived in this bleak northern castle, during an equally bleak northern winter: snow lay on the ground outside, even at the end of March. And for those six months she had been treated with the utmost courtesy by her master, the utmost reverence by her maids and servants, none of whom seemed to have any doubt *she* was their mistress. But those six months had been understandable: Munetake wanted this child.

Now the child was born, and seemed healthy. Now her figure was already sinking back into its original shape. "I will *love* you," he had said, apparently certain she would welcome his advances. But would she not? Would she dare not, in the first place. But the second consideration was far more worrying. She would never see Ralph again. Lord Shimadzu had said so, and Munetake had told her so often enough during this winter. This was to be her life from now on, and she must either die or make the best of it. But how could she die, now that she had the child to care for?

And she knew what Munetake could do for her, too. As did he.

Yet she had to be, and remain, her own woman. She could not understand what had brought about the change in her master's attitude to her; she could not believe he was so subservient to *his* master's wishes. Now he studied to please her, whereas before he had studied to hurt. Because of the child? Now was certainly the time to find out—and to find out, too, what was going to be the pattern of her life.

Munetake smiled at her. "Jeremy," he said, again using three very distinct syllables. "He shall be called Jeremy, as you wish it so." He knelt beside her on the mattress and pushed sweat-damp hair from her forehead. "There will be other sons, Alison. My sons. Our sons. We will give *them* Japanese names."

"Our first responsibility," Saigo explained, "must be to make you *look* like a samurai, at the least."

For the ceremony, which took place in the great chamber of Lord Shimadzu's palace, and was attended by a large number of samurai, as well as by the lord himself, Saigo, acting as sponsor, was assisted by one of his young nephews, Togo Heihachiro, barely eighteen years old, but one of Ralph's most promising gunner officers, and an interesting and attractive personality, for he dreamed only of ships and the sea, of great voyages and greater naval battles—ambitions he was unlikely to achieve in a Japanese junk, Ralph supposed. Now he was on hand to remove Ralph's kimono and show him where to sit on an extra tatami mat placed in the center of the room, back straight, arms folded. At his side knelt another young samurai, holding the tray on which were the various accessories necessary to the coming ceremony. And now Saigo and Togo both sat in front of him, each having beside himself a large lacquered box. From the waiting assembly there was no sound.

"It will be a lengthy business," Saigo said, "as we must in one morning complete a ceremony which takes place on several occasions during the life of a Japanese. To begin with, Freeman San, while we shave a child's head up to the third year, from the fifteenth day of the eleventh month of that year his hair is permitted to grow. Whereas yours would seem to have been shaved within these past five years."

In fact, although both Aya, at his command, and Alison, from a desire to have him looking at least partly like the American he was, had cut his hair quite regularly, and he had shaved his beard almost every day since arriving in Japan, Ralph considered that he looked unnaturally shaggy. "We do not shave our heads at all," he said. "But we keep our hair cut short. At least our menfolk."

"Why?" asked Togo.

"I suppose for cleanliness. We in the West do not practice bathing quite so regularly as you in Japan."

Saigo shook his head sadly. "Let us proceed. I have chosen your position carefully, you understand, Freeman San, for it is important that you face the most auspicious point of the heavens for this ceremony."

"Which is that?"

"I have consulted the various tables and have decided that northeast is the most appropriate. This will bring you fortune. Now . . ." He took a pair of scissors from the waiting tray, knelt in front of Ralph, reached forward, and gave three snips of the scissors at the hair on Ralph's left temple, then three snips to the right, and then three snips in the center. Next he replaced the scissors on the tray and took instead a large piece of cloth, which he placed on Ralph's head like a wig, arranging it to begin on the forehead, and carrying it back so that it hung down behind. He then took from the tray a piece of fish and seven rice straws and attached them to the bottom of the cloth, tying them into two loops with a length of string. "There," he said. "Your hair is now suitable for acceptance by the gods. Now we must drink to your fortune. You will come and sit on my left hand, Freeman San."

For in Japan the left hand was the position of honor, unlike in the West; a man seated on the left hand could not impede the drawing of the sword, should it become necessary, and would also act as a guard for the weaker side.

Togo was smiling. "You *should* sit on his knee, Freeman San, but I am afraid you would press him to the floor. Remember that you are but three years old."

Ralph sat beside Saigo, while a young samurai brought forward a small lacquered table, which he placed in front of the general; another came forward with a bowl of rice.

"This has been offered to the gods," Saigo explained, and carefully took some of the rice from the bowl and placed it on the table in the corner nearest Ralph. He now took the food sticks from his waistband and placed three grains of rice, one after the other, in Ralph's mouth. While this was going on, another youthful warrior brought in five cakes of rice meal, and with these Saigo also pretended to feed Ralph, without actually placing any of the food in his mouth. "Now you may resume your seat."

Ralph returned to face them, while a tray was brought forward on which there were three wine cups, each hardly larger than a thimble. Saigo drank from each of the cups in turn, and then presented the first one to Ralph. There was not quite sufficient liquid left to wet his lips. The second cup was also presented, and then Saigo took another pair of food sticks from his sash. "These I give to you, Freeman San, for your use in the future."

Ralph examined the sticks in wonder. They were quite exquisitely made from the finest ivory, and on the top of each one was carved a tiny replica of a cannon, perfect down to the last detail. "Why, Saigo San, I do not know how to thank you."

Saigo placed his finger on his lips and shook his head.

"Of course, I forgot, I am but three years old."

Saigo now gravely presented the third cup, and Ralph again drank. One of the samurai youths was hovering with a fresh tray on which there were three more cups and a small dish of fried fish.

"Three times," Togo whispered. "But only pretend to drink."

Ralph nodded, sipped from each of the cups, and passed them to Saigo, who drank in turn. Each man then broke off a piece of fish and ate it.

"And now, Saigo Takamori, on behalf of this child," Togo said, "I present you with this robe of white silk." As he spoke, he took the garment from his box.

"Surely I should have purchased that," Ralph said in dismay; it was clearly a most expensive gift.

"It is my responsibility," Togo explained. "I am acting as your godfather. We have now completed the first ceremony. Shall we take a little walk while the room is prepared?"

Ralph removed the cloth from his head, put on his kimono, and then went onto the veranda with the other samurai, among whom, on this special occasion, even Lord Shimadzu mixed freely and without undue ceremony—it was difficult to imagine Nariaka ever unbending so far. But ten minutes later Togo announced that all was ready for the second stage of the ceremony, and they returned inside. Now a checkerboard had been placed on Ralph's mat, and on this he took his seat. Saigo delved into his box. "It would now be, in normal circumstances, the fifth day of the eleventh month of the fourth year," he explained. "You have aged a year, and I present you with this." He held out, across both his arms, a most splendid outer kimono, in pale green, on which were embroidered storks and tortoises, fir trees and bamboos.

"What a marvelous piece of work," Ralph remarked. "No doubt the emblems are symbolic?"

"Oh, indeed," Saigo agreed. "The stork and the tortoise are emblems of longevity; it is said the stork lives for a thousand years, and the tortoise for ten thousand; we pray that you may be similarly blessed. The fir trees, being evergreen, are symbols of an unchanging, virtuous heart. And the bamboo is symbolic of an upright and straight mind. These things we already know that you possess, Freeman San."

"I thank you, Saigo Takamori," Ralph said.

"And with these," Saigo said, once more opening his box, "I give you the hayama." He produced a pair of the loose, baggy trousers which the samurai wore under their kimonos when not in armor, to distinguish them from the bare-legged peasants. "And also this sword and dirk, made of wood."

Ralph accepted the gifts, as the young samurai once again brought forward the trays, to resume the wine ceremony. This time Togo's gift to Saigo was a piece of gold embroidery, another vast expense, Ralph supposed.

"Truly, Togo San, this business seems costly," he remarked, as once again they strolled on the porch.

"Because it is an occasion of great importance in a man's life, Freeman San. Indeed, there are only two more important: the day of his marriage and the day of his death. But do not suppose you will escape the expense; you will have to provide all of this for your own sons."

For my own sons, Ralph thought. Had I any. Should I ever have any. Or at least any I can call my own.

Saigo had observed the expression on his face. "But that lies in the future," he said. "Which no man may foretell. Come, let us complete the ceremony."

The actual shaving of Ralph's head was performed by another of the samurai, who was skilled in the art, and worked with great speed, removing all the hair except for three patches, one on each temple and one in the center, and leaving also a long lock of hair attached to Ralph's forehead, and then combing out the tress which extended from the crown of his head.

"Now you have achieved the age of fifteen," Saigo said, "and are ready to enter upon a man's estate and his responsibilities. Come, let us drink to your fame as a samurai."

This time the waiting tray had only a single earthenware cup, but it was a large one. Saigo drank three times, and passed the cup to Ralph, who also took three sips.

"Now come and kneel over here," Saigo instructed. Ralph obeyed, and Saigo moved behind him, for all the world like a lady's hairdresser, and gathered the long hair falling from Ralph's crown to tie it on his head in a reasonable facsimile of a true topknot. "Now bend forward from the waist," he commanded. Ralph obeyed, so that his head all but touched a willow board held by one of the elder samurai. He watched Saigo out of the corner of his eye, with some apprehension, as the general drew his short sword, while with his left hand he gathered the forelock and pulled it forward so that it lay on the board. There was a quick movement of Saigo's arm, and the sword struck the board, and indeed bit into the wood. Ralph jerked upright, and watched his hair lying in front of him.

"By God," he said, "I had almost thought my head was on the block."

Saigo was carefully folding the forelock into a piece of paper decorated with the black-and-white paintings of cannon. "You will keep this in a safe place forever, Freeman San," he said gravely. "So that it may bring eternal good fortune upon you and your family. And when you die, let it be buried in your coffin, to protect you throughout the afterlife."

Ralph took the folded paper with due deference. It seemed to have as much significance as any of the ritual undergone in a Christian church, with the difference that in Japan a man was his own judge, bound to observe his honor and thus his courage at all times, bound to create his own fortune, not only in this life but also in the afterlife. Two different ways of expressing the doctrine of free will, perhaps.

And he realized that, despite his determination to hate these people, the certainty that he would one day

have to betray them and fight them, he was impressed
and even affected by the ceremony, and the honor
which was being done to him.

More wine was now brought, and the drinking became general, while the samurai, led by Shimadzu
himself, came forward to embrace Ralph and wish him
long life and good fortune.

"But no man can truly be a samurai until he is properly equipped," Shimadzu remarked. He clapped his
hands, and one of the young men hurried into the
room with the most superb set of armor. There was a
shield, round and thick, and an iron helmet, lined with
buckskin, with a flap of articulated iron rings which
would droop below his shoulders. The visor was made
of thin, lacquered iron, with a removable nose and
mouth piece. Like all Japanese helmets, there was also
a false mustache, huge and bristling, to add to the
terror of his appearance, as the mouth was twisted into
a ghastly grimace for the same purpose. But this was a
far cry from the leather helmet which had been given
him to wear at Shimonoseki. And worked in the center
of the front piece was once again the replica of a
cannon.

"My lord," he said, "I am overwhelmed."

"I had it made especially for you," Shimadzu said
with simple pride, "because I know you will wear it with
honor."

The helmet itself was about three feet in height, and
in the top there was a hole into which fitted an orna-
ment like a pear.

"That is what your enemies will aim for when they
swing at your head," Saigo explained.

"No doubt," Ralph said thoughtfully, examining the
armor itself, for here again, unlike the suits he had
been shown in Shimonoseki, the breastplate was composed of thin scales of iron, over which he would wear
a chain-mail surcoat. His arms, legs, abdomen, and
thighs would be protected by plates joined with woven
chains, and there were great loose brassards to be worn
on his shoulders. There were also greaves for his legs,
but apparently he would wear his normal sandals beneath them. Perhaps a samurai thought it dishonorable

to cut at an opponent's feet. Certainly Munetake had never done so during their hours of practice. But could anyone, even Munetake, perform those tremendous leaps when clad in such weight?

Munetake! The very thought made his body suffuse with rage.

The entire suit, including the helmet, was painted green, and laced and bound with iron clamps and cords of silk, decorated with gilt tassels and glittering insignia, principally, the cross and bit of the Satsuma, to leave an enemy in no doubt as to whom he served. "Truly a spectacular piece of equipment," he said.

"Now for what you will always carry into battle," Togo said, and produced a satchel which contained several layers of thick paper, with an adhesive side, which meant that each layer had to be peeled off from the next.

"These are for binding up your wounds," Saigo explained. "Every samurai carries a supply of these. The paper will be laid over the wound, to which it will immediately stick. It is then wrapped around the limb, or left flat, should the wound be on a flat part of the body. If it is desired to wet the wound, then the water can be added without disturbing the paper, for it will soak through."

"And the paper will not aggravate the injury?"

"On the contrary," Togo said. "It has healing powers of its own."

"Next," Saigo said, "here is your bow."

This was very like the weapons used by the men of Cho-Shu, although here again the quality was far superior. The oak had been most carefully chosen, that was obvious, and on either side it was encased in a semicylinder of split bamboo, black where it had been toughened by fire. The three pieces had been bound into a whole with withes of rattan, and the result was a weapon of remarkable lightness, and with even more remarkable elasticity. The string was hemp. He thought that with such a superb weapon he might even be able to send an arrow as far as a Japanese, a failing in the past which had caused his Cho-Shu mentors to smile. As if he would ever dream of using a bow in battle, when a Colt revolver could hang from his belt—one of the first requirements he had made Saigo obtain for the Satsuma army had been a supply of revolvers, although the samurai showed very little aptitude in their use.

"And the arrows." Togo produced a full quiver, again beautifully decorated. "We have given you a selection of the most deadly. They all have their names. This one, for instance, is called the turnip head, from its shape."

"I doubt it would pierce this armor," Ralph said.

"It is not intended to, Freeman San. Its purpose is to make a singing noise as it passes through the air. A volley of these arrows is decidedly alarming to the enemy, as a warning of what will follow. No doubt this one is more to your liking." He showed Ralph a bolt with a two-edged barb but a nearly blunt point. "This is called the willow leaf, and is intended to knock a man from his horse."

"This," Togo said, handling a similarly shaped arrow, but with sharply serrated edges, "is known as the bowel raker."

"Very apt," Ralph agreed. "And this?" From the quiver he drew the plainest of bolts.

"The armor piercer," Saigo said. "*That* will puncture your breastplate, Freeman San, if properly aimed."

Ralph examined the arrow. The barb was made of steel, and the shaft of cane bamboo. The string piece was horn, whipped on with silk. The Cho-Shu men had used similar weapons, and had had to aim very true even to penetrate leather armor.

"And now, the sword," Togo said, and with great reverence laid the weapon across his left forearm, the hilt toward Ralph. It was identical with the weapons first shown him by Ito and Inouye, and clearly of better quality than those with which he had practiced in Shimonoseki—again, it carried the name of the famous Masamune.

"It would be a good idea to give your sword a name of its own," Saigo said. "That your enemies may know of it, and fear it. Mine is called the Silken Death, because the blade is so sharp it will even separate a piece of floating silk."

"Then mine had best be called the Noise Maker," Ralph said. "For I doubt it will ever do more than whistle harmlessly through the air."

"Do not suppose so," Togo said. "That weapon is the guardian of everything a man should hold sacred. It took Masamune sixty days of labor and prayer to forge."

"Prayer?"

"He had to pray for guidance with every inch of the blade, every design on the hilt. This is not just a weapon, Freeman San. It is your soul, as of this moment."

"Is it not said," Saigo remarked, "that one's fate is in the hands of heaven, but that a skillful fighter does not meet with death?"

"And also," Togo added, "that in the last days, one's sword is the wealth of one's posterity?"

There was no suggestion of humor in either face. Here, Ralph realized, he *was* in the presence of a religion.

"And yet," he could not stop himself saying, "is not the day of the sword, and the arrow, and the armor coat, forever dead, now that cannon and rifles rule the world?"

They stared at him.

"The day of the sword can never be dead, Freeman San," Saigo declared. "Then would the day of the samurai also be dead, and how could that ever be?"

For all his desire to learn, his open approach to the world, he remained what he had been born, a Japanese nobleman, Ralph thought. And thus he would carry an inescapable burden to his grave.

But now Saigo was smiling. "It is not a subject for us to differ on, Freeman San," he said. "And certainly not on this day of days. Come, you are now a samurai, and more, a hatamoto and a general of artillery. We can do nothing more for you until you have the opportunity to display your skill. But we can make you happy. This very night will you be married."

"Married?" Ralph cried.

Saigo's smile broadened. "Of course. It is all arranged."

—10—
THE HUSBAND

The thought remained impossible, but it was equally impossible to refuse the ceremony, for it had all been arranged, without a word to him.

"We have chosen for you my third niece, Suiko," Saigo explained. "She is just sixteen years of age, and is at once comely and talented. And, Freeman San, when she was told the name of her chosen husband, she expressed great pleasure. But she is also a little apprehensive, at once of your stature and your barbarian customs. Not that she knows what these are. But I would beg of you to use her gently."

"Use her?" Ralph cried. "My dear Saigo San, if you really do wish me to marry your niece, then I must be honored and pleased to agree. But you know that I can never accept her in my bed."

Saigo looked grave for a moment and then smiled. "That is for you and Suiko to decide, and for fate to arbitrate, Freeman San."

"I know of these things," said Saigo Shona. She was seventeen years old, and soon due to be married herself; like her elder sister, Shikibu, also betrothed, she was somewhat put out that Suiko should actually be leaving their home first. But this was the will of their Uncle Takamori, and no one was prepared to dispute that.

So now she soaped her sister's back slowly and thoughtfully, paying particular attention to her secret valleys—for these above all else must smell sweet this night. And she teased, with more than a hint of malice. "You have seen him," she pointed out. "You have seen how he towers above ordinary men. Do you not suppose he is that size all over? I have spoken with the

279

honin women who bathe him. They say when he rears he could support the heavens. They say when he enters you his tip will come out through your mouth, if the mere entry does not split you in two."

Suiko shivered, and knelt with head bowed, legs pressed tightly together.

"I too have spoken with the honin women he has used," Shikibu said. "And they say it is his delight to lie on his woman and crush all the breath from her body. And worse . . ." She lowered her voice into a whisper. "They say he uses your *mouth*, and wishes entry there, with his *tongue*."

Suiko raised her head in alarm, gazed at her sisters for some sign of a smile. Such things were surely not possible. But they were possible. And soon, within a matter of hours, they would be happening to her.

She had been terrified from the day, only a fortnight ago, that her Uncle Takamori and her father had told her of their decision. She had of course known for over a year that she was approaching a marriageable age and that she would be wed as soon as her sisters had completed their own nuptials. This was the inevitable fate of any Japanese young lady. It was also the most important and irrevocable step she would ever take in her life, for it would mean forsaking her father's house and her own family for another. From the moment her wedding ceremony was completed, she would be a Saigo no longer, and her family would have no claim on her and no rights over her—those claims and those rights would belong for the rest of her life to her husband and his family.

These too were things she had known since puberty, and accepted. If she had prayed at all concerning them, she had begged that her husband might not be too much older than herself and able to smile, that he might not beat her too often and would live to a ripe old age, and that she might bear him many strong and healthy sons. These things would ensure her prosperity no less than his. How he would use her, what they would do in the privacy of their bedchamber, were not matters to concern her.

But to be presented to an alien who might have come

from one of the planets for all she knew, a monster of a man, and so suddenly ... Uncle Takamori had explained some of it to her. "This man would become one of us, Saigo Suiko," he had explained, taking her on to his lap as he used to when she was a little girl. "And we, your great Lord Shimadzu and I, wish it so. He is a mighty warrior, and will serve us well. But he must be made to feel welcome here, to feel this is his home. This will be your task. I have talked with your father, and your sisters, and because the matter is an urgent one, we have decided to disobey the rules for this one occasion, and marry you immediately. This is for the sake of the Satsuma, which I know you hold as dear as I do myself."

She had bowed her head in reverence. From her earliest memory it had been instilled in her, as it was instilled in all Satsuma, that the clan was the center of their lives, and that without the clan they were nothing. And at least she had been reassured that the American was going to be taken into the clan as a Satsuma samurai. Because sometimes the daughters of great nobles *were* required to marry outside their own people, for reasons of alliances. That was a fate she could not possibly contemplate.

She sat in the hot tub and soaked. So what fate was there to contemplate? A stranger, an alien, a monster. A man she had never met, whose voice she had never heard, whose face she had seen only from a distance. It would be her responsibility, her only responsibility for the rest of her life, to rule his household to his satisfaction, to support him in all things, to satisfy his lusts, or if unable to do so herself, to see that they were satisfied ... and above all, to bear him strong and healthy children. These would have been her responsibilities no matter whom she married. She had known this from her earliest moment, had been educated to it, and had accepted it.

But with a monster ... She raised her head to gaze at her mother, who stood by the tub smiling at her. And apparently able to guess her thoughts. "He is but a man," she said. "If he is more than a man, then he is a friend of your uncle. That can be no bad recommendation, Saigo Suiko. Now, come and dress, and go about your duty."

As Ralph had no home of his own in Kagoshima as yet, the wedding took place in Saigo Takamori's own town house, where everything had already been arranged. As it was dark when the ceremony was due to begin, flaring torches filled the courtyard, to form an avenue of light from the gate to the porch. On either side there had been fires lighted, to make the courtyard as bright as day. And now that the hour approached, the blenders of the rice meal had taken their places, two men and two women, one pair sitting on either side of the path, their mortars ready.

The whole household waited, Saigo's wife smiling at the suddenly nervous Ralph to reassure him. For waiting too there was a long tray on which two silken robes lay, stitched together. "One of these was your present to Suiko, three days ago, when you became betrothed," Saigo had explained during his necessarily brief synopsis of what the ceremony would consist. "Now it is returned, with hers added."

"I should be very angry," Ralph had said. "I do not doubt I will be. In my country, a man does not become betrothed without even knowing it. And you well know the burden I carry, Saigo San, which it would be dishonorable of me to forget." He was learning how to carry a point with his hosts.

Saigo smiled. "In Japan, marriages, at least among samurai, are usually arranged, Freeman San. But anyway, it was necessary to do it thus, or you would have argued and resisted, as you have just admitted. And as in your eyes your reluctance to abandon the memory of the barbarian woman is honorable, it is therefore respected by me and by my people. But we wish you to be one of us, in every way, and we are doing all in our power to bring that about."

And did he not wish the same thing? Ralph asked himself. Therefore anger did not come into it at all. Only playacting, and dissembling, and a determined resistance to the very real feeling of belonging which was creeping over him. So he made himself inspect the wedding presents sent to him by Saigo Kiyotake, Saigo Takamori's brother, the father of the bride. These consisted of a ceremonial girdle, a fan, five pocketbooks, and a sword, and had been placed in the bridal chamber, which was composed of three rooms converted into one by the removal of the inner screen walls, and newly decorated, by order of Saigo himself. The presents, the girl's to Ralph, and his to hers, apparently selected by Saigo's wife, were both displayed, and the bedclothes had already been laid; even the lacquer basin for washing had been placed on the floor, while a tiny shrine containing an image of the family god of the Saigos had been installed above the bed.

And in front of the mattress, in the position of honor, waited the towel rack, with its full complement of heated cloths.

The erotic suggestion in the room was quite overwhelming. Ralph sweated as he waited with Saigo for the arrival of the litter. And he did not even know which of the girls she was. But whichever one, she was just sixteen, while he was twenty-nine, and knew too much.

Saigo smiled at him. "You are anxious, Freeman San. This is good. An anxious husband is a fruitful one. Be sure that your bride will also be anxious."

He was content, as he had said, to leave the consummation to Suiko, and to fate, with complete confidence. And was he not right, despite all? But thoughts kept crowding Ralph's mind, carrying him all the way north to Hokkaido. As Japanese men did not apparently use their women during pregnancy, Alison would have been granted a certain respite by Munetake . . . but by now she would have given birth. And thus would now know her lord.

Except that she had known her lord already, and hated and feared him for it.

"She comes," Saigo said. They did not go outside, but the door was open, and they could see the litter approaching through the main gate. Saigo Kiyotake came first, with his wife. They walked up the path between the flaring torches, both dressed in their finest clothes, and paused at the steps to the porch to congratulate each other. Behind them walked two of Saigo Kiyotake's manservants, carrying between them a huge bowl of clam broth. This had apparently been made from clams Saigo Takamori had sent to his brother, on Ralph's behalf, the previous day, and was solemnly presented to Saigo Takamori in the doorway of the house.

Now the men and women on each side of the path commenced pounding the rice in their mortars, moving with careful emphasis, each stroke a timed function. For the bridal litter was coming through the gate. And now, too, in the porch, two of the Saigo women each lit a candle, one standing to the left and one to the right of the corridor leading to the bridal chamber.

Slowly the litter, borne by four of the Saigo male relatives—among them Togo—and completely enclosed by the decorated draperies, came across the courtyard. As it passed between the rice blenders, those on the left of the path handed their bowls to those on the right, and the contents of the two bowls were mixed together.

The litter reached the steps to the porch, and here it was laid on the ground. The curtains were parted, and Saigo Suiko stepped out. She wore a white silk robe with a lozenge pattern, made from the bolt of cloth Saigo Takamori had sent her as a betrothal present on Ralph's behalf, over an underrobe, also made of white silk. A veil of white silk hung from her head, so that only the crown of her black hair was visible as she slowly came up the steps between the bowing women, who, as she reached them, passed the left-hand candle over the right, allowing the two wicks to be brought together and extinguished.

Ralph and Takamori, as well as all the assembled Saigo relatives, bowed low as Saigo Suiko came down the corridor toward them. For this occasion she was the most noble person present—to her both the deference and the place due to her rank. She swept past them, her face hidden beneath the veil, and was escorted into the room and beyond, to a small chamber set aside as a dressing room, by two of her Saigo aunts. When she had straightened her gown and renewed her paint, she reentered the room and mounted the steps to the dais, where she took her place upon an embroidered mat.

Takamori touched Ralph's elbow, and he went forward, discovering that his heart was pounding as if it would burst its way out of his chest. There was something uncannily compelling about marrying a girl whose face he had never properly seen and whom he had never addressed in his life, especially when he was already married, before God.

He reached the dais and took his seat immediately below Suiko. As instructed by Takamori, he did not glance at her, but turned to face the room as the assembled relations came in and took their places before them, and the ladies prepared for the ceremony.

Two covered trays had already been laid upon the dais. Between them was a lacquered table on which were fowls, fish, and two sake bottles, together with the inevitable three cups, and two kettles for warming the wine. The ladies now knelt before the couple and handed them dried fish and seaweed to eat, accompanying each dish with a short speech in which they praised the beauty, industry, and virtue of Suiko and the manhood, valor, and fame of Freeman San, and promised the assembly that here was a union which would endure as long as Japan itself endured.

While they knelt thus, two married females each took one of the wine bottles to a lower part of the room. Two handmaids also took down the kettles, to be heated. The ladies attached a paper model of a female butterfly to one bottle, and a male butterfly to the other. The female butterfly was then removed and laid on its back, and wine poured from that bottle into one of the kettles. The male butterfly was now placed on top of the female, and wine poured from the male bottle into the same kettle, after which the mixed wine was poured into the second kettle, which was then placed on the floor beside Ralph.

Meanwhile, the maids were arranging small lacquered tables before each person in the room, before Suiko, and before Ralph, and before the two girls who were acting as bridesmaids, and who Ralph now decided were Suiko's two elder sisters; it was impossible to be sure beneath the white paint which coated their faces. And now at last Suiko removed her veil; but her face too was a gloss of white paint and red lips, behind which only the black eyes were alive. She never looked at Ralph, remained gazing in front of her at the table.

One of the maids placed the three cups, one inside the other, in front of Ralph, while another brought the empty kettle to set beside the waiting full one. As instructed by Saigo Takamori in his hasty lesson only an hour earlier, Ralph sipped twice from the first cup and then poured some wine from the full kettle into the empty one. He next poured wine into the cup, filling it rather more than before, and drank half of it. The maid took the cup to Suiko, who finished what remained of the wine and then in turn poured some from the full kettle into the empty one.

Condiments were then served, and the wine ceremony repeated, this time starting with Suiko, and using the second cup. Then the third cup was served, beginning once more with Ralph. This done, he saw Takamori beckoning him, and rose and left the room for the porch, still without looking at the girl, until he was outside. "Where is she going?" he asked, as he saw her, escorted by the two married ladies, also leaving the room.

"To change her gown," Saigo said. "So come, you must do the same." He escorted Ralph into a dressing room. "It is actually more of an excuse to permit the family and the ladies to eat, as they are not all sustained by the emotion of the moment. They will be given special soup, made of fish's fins, and a cup of wine to drink, to give them strength for the rest of the ceremony."

"To give *them* strength," Ralph muttered, accepting a change of dress from a waiting manservant.

Who closed one eye. "Truly my lord Freeman, it is enough to make a man wonder if marriage is worth it, when there is a geisha house in every town."

Once again Ralph sat on the mat below Saigo Suiko, this time drinking clam soup and eating a preparation of rice, while the women placed two earthenware cups, one gilded and the other silvered, on a tray. Inscribed on the tray was a map of the island of Yakasago, in the province of Harima, on which there was a pine tree known as the Pine of Mutual Old Age. At the root, apparently, the tree was single, but toward the center it split into two stems, and this twin-stemmed tree was a symbol that the happy pair would reach mutual old age together, while the evergreen leaves denoted the unchanging constancy of their hearts. Drawn under the two stems of the tree were the figures of an old man and an old woman, to represent the spirits of the world.

Another wine ceremony, and then the wedding feast itself, beginning with soup made from carp—according to Saigo, the most expensive fish in all Japan, but an indispensable part of a wedding banquet—followed by twelve dishes of sweetmeats, and then three courses, the first of seven dishes, the second of five, and the third of three dishes. During the meal Suiko and Ralph were each taken out twice to change their garments, and at the end Suiko put on the second of the silk robes he had given her as a betrothal present.

But at last he found himself sipping the cup of green tea, while the guests murmured discreetly among themselves, and Saigo Takamori smiled at him from across the room. It was time. Nearly. He watched Saigo Kiyotake and his wife rise and bow toward their daughter, and then toward Saigo Takamori and his wife, before going to the door to take their leave. He wondered why they had not bade farewell to him.

Once again the tea, sipped decorously. The room was nearly quiet. How far from the boisterous speechifying and toast drinking of an American wedding. He could feel the girl, close to him, could almost hear her breathing, even if so far as he knew she had not yet looked directly at him. But they were married, and the wine was having a powerful effect upon his senses, just when he wished to be sober and able to bolster his resolution.

Togo Heihachiro was rising and smiling and beckoning Ralph. He got up in turn, bowed to his wife, and to Takamori, his foster father for this occasion, and his wife, and to the handmaids and guests, before following Togo outside. "I had thought Suiko would leave first," he whispered.

"Not so, Freeman San, for now we have our duty to perform."

"You mean I do not stay in the same house as my bride?" Ralph demanded, feeling acute disappointment even as he reminded himself that this would be the best of all solutions to his problems.

"In due time, Freeman San. In due time. First, we must pay a visit to your mother- and father-in-law, for you will see little of them in the future."

"Why should I not see a great deal of them, Togo San, as we live in the same city and they are Suiko's parents?"

"As of now, they are no longer even related to her," Togo said gravely. "Now she is your wife, she has become part of you, Freeman San, and is the lady of your house. Think well on this. It is a great step for a young woman to take, to abandon entirely her natural relatives in favor of another's. A great step in any circumstances. But in normal circumstances she is at least assured of a large new family who would protect her honor and guard her children. But you, Freeman San, have no family, at least in Japan. Suiko has taken a deep and serious step, for now she too is alone in the world, saving her lord."

Good God, Ralph thought. That aspect of things had not occurred to him. To be alone with Alison in this world of strife and honor, of blood and courage, had seemed the most natural thing in the world. But this sixteen-year-old child of whom he knew nothing?

He watched the Saigo servants at work. The two trays used at the feast had been brought to the porch and were now being loaded with fowl and fish and condiments before being placed in a long box for transportation down the hill. Five hundred and eighty rice cakes had also been prepared, and these were placed in lacquered boxes, to follow the rest of the food. Behind them came the presents which Ralph had personally to present to his parents-in-law, amounting to seven men's loads, as representing his status as a hatamoto. They included a sword and a silk robe for Saigo Kiyotake, and a silk robe for his wife, and also presents for his new cousins-in-law, chosen with great care by Takamori and his wife.

"Truly, my head is spinning," Ralph said as he and Togo started down the hill behind the porters. "And what happens at the house of Saigo Kiyotake, Togo San?"

"Why, you will go through the wine-drinking ceremony with Kiyotake and his wife."

"I was afraid you might say that." The night was already beginning a slight spin around his head.

"Do not fret; Suiko must at this moment be going through the same ceremony and exchange of presents with Saigo Takamori and his wife."

"And how long will this take?"

Togo shrugged. "Perhaps an hour. Perhaps longer."

"And then I return here?"

Togo smiled. "Indeed you will, Freeman San. But not immediately to retire. For you must then await a return visit from Saigo Kiyotake and his wife."

"For *another* wine ceremony?"

"That is correct."

"By God, Togo San, when do I get to see my wife alone? Supposing I can *see* at all."

"You have all your life to see her alone, Freeman San. But do not be impatient. There will even be time for that tonight."

How vast the room, of a sudden, for the mattress had been laid at the farthest end away from the doorway, beyond the two opened walls, and seemed at a greater distance than that encompassed by Lord Shimadzu's audience hall.

The girl knelt, her body arched forward, her forehead close to the floor. Her brief enjoyment of power was over; now she was alone with her lord.

"Do not kneel to me, Suiko," Ralph said. "Never to me."

Her body slowly raised itself. She wore, so far as he could see, a single robe of white silk, and knelt beside the mat on which they would sleep. On which they would consummate their marriage, if he dared. But after what Togo had said to him, would it not be compounding crime upon crime *not* to take her? She was his. She could belong to none other, now. If he spurned her, then she had nowhere to go at all, no man or woman to call her friend.

Beside her on the floor was a tray bearing a cup of sake. She gazed at him, her eyes black pinpoints in the whiteness of her face. Her face itself was expressionless. He crossed the floor slowly. In fact, at this moment he felt no desire. He felt old enough to be her father.

She watched him approach. "May I serve my lord?" she whispered. Her voice trembled. The composure was, after all, only the depths of her paint.

He halted at the dais. "I will serve *you*, Suiko."

He reached for the cup, lifted it to her lips. Her hand came up and closed on his, and was as quickly withdrawn. She sipped the wine, watching him all the while.

"My lord has but to command," she whispered.

He shook his head. "I had no wish for this to happen this way, Suiko."

She gazed at him, and he took the cup from her hand, drank in turn. If ever he needed wine, it was now.

"Do I, then, not please you, my lord?"

"Please me? I am sure you are the most pleasing girl in all the world, Suiko. I meant that in my country a man is at least granted permission to make his own proposal of marriage."

"For what reason, my lord?"

"Why, because if he is a man of any sensibility, he will be able to discern whether or not his future wife would have it so."

"And he would be concerned with her wishes, my lord?"

"With common folk, yes. Where property or station is involved, not necessarily."

"We are not common folk, my lord," she said. Clearly she was well aware of her station in life, as a daughter of one of the oldest and most famous houses in the land.

"I know that, Suiko," he said. "And yet it matters

naught beside the fact of you. Did you come to me willingly, Suiko?"

"Willingly, my lord. With great happiness."

But her eyes had flickered just a little, to betray her words. She had been as afraid of him as he of her.

He took her hands, drawing them from the sleeves of the kimono. So small, so delicately formed. And now indeed his heart was pounding. "I am a stranger to Japanese customs, Suiko." Which was not altogether a lie; he *was* a stranger to the bed manners of the upper classes. "I would wish my wife to share in my customs as I am prepared to share in hers."

"You have but to command, my lord," she said again. Now her eyes were watchful. What new and strange and perhaps terrible fate was he about to inflict upon her? The bodice of her robe rose and fell more quickly. What lay beneath it? What beauty? What treasure? And he had done no more than touch her hand.

He stroked her chin, and her eyes flickered. He gripped her chin and heard the intake of her breath. Perhaps she expected to be throttled. Still holding her chin, he brought her face forward. Her eyes widened, the pupils dilated. But she would submit. Submit to whatever he wished, because she had been trained only for that.

His lips touched hers. Her eyes were an inch away, gazing at him, wider than ever. He moved his lips against hers, inhaled her breath as it came from her nostrils, felt the lips parting as he touched them with his tongue, and withdrew it in haste; he had forgotten that her teeth would be black and that her lip rouge would have a taste of its own.

Suiko gazed at him, a faint line creasing the white paint between her eyes. "My lord . . . ?" she whispered.

"Why do you blacken your teeth?"

"Because I am married, my lord. It is to signify my fidelity. Tomorrow I will shave my eyebrows."

"Shave your eyebrows? What I have just done, does that please you?"

"I am here to please *you,* my lord."

"No," he said. "I would not have it so. I would have it for both of us, equally. But there is something I would

like you to do for me. Suiko, would you wash your face,
remove your paint, take the blackness from your teeth?
Will you do that for me?"

Still the unblinking gaze. "I will do whatever you
wish, my lord. But the teeth, I cannot cleanse them
utterly."

"Nevertheless, do what you can. Now, Suiko. I ask it
of you."

"Yes, my lord." She knelt over the basin of water.
Her back was turned to him, her body only a wisp of
life in the huge empty room. His. The thought kept
returning to him with increased force. His. Absolutely.
The realization, the understanding, reached down from
his mind into his belly . . . and there met the thought
that Alison also belonged—to Munetake.

And yet, never could, entirely. Any more than he
could possess Suiko to the exclusion of any other, Alison would never *belong*, but would wait, and pray, and
hope, and *know*, that one day . . . But that thought was
already overlaid with the insidious certainty that she
was lost to *him*, at least for a long time, and that it was
six months and more since he had known any woman,
and that this girl had to be *made* his, or be cursed and
humiliated for the rest of her life. And of all Japanese,
she at the least had done him no harm.

He placed his hands on her thighs, moved them
upward and forward. Beneath the silk there were
small, hand-filling, hard-pointed mounds. Beneath the
silk.

His fingers released her girdle, parted the kimono
while he knelt against her. Her hands scooped water to
her face. Did she shiver? Was the water cold, or was it
the touch of his fingers as they slid inward, to reach the
firmness of the belly, stroke down to thigh and groin,
move in again, to jungle and gateway, prison and
paradise.

"My face is clean, my lord," she whispered.

And wet. His hands moved backward, bringing the
robe with it. He knelt, away from her, the robe in his
hands. She rose to her feet, her back still to him, aware
of her nakedness, went down the steps to reach the
towel rack, dried her face with careful pats, hesitated,

and turned to face him. Perhaps consciously, she inhaled, to swell her chest, sucking her belly flat. Her midnight hair drifted forward over her left shoulder, lay in strands around her nipple. Thus framed, the face was small and exquisite, forehead and nose and mouth and chin fitting into a tiny mold of utter perfection, presently tightly composed. Nor was her face alone her source of beauty. Beneath the small breasts and the lurking love forest were delicate stems, neither long nor strong, but entrancingly youthful. Here was no breathtaking femininity, compared with Alison, or perhaps even Aya; but here was an eternal sweetness, a gentleness, such as he had never known, and not expected ever to find, in this harsh land. And she was his wife.

"Come," he said.

She knelt beside him. And looked beyond him to the shrine. Now she bowed from the waist and gave two quick claps with her hands.

"Why do you do that, Suiko?"

"To summon the kami of the shrine, my lord, that I may pray to him for his protection."

"Do you fear me, Suiko?"

"No, my lord. Not if it is in my power to make you happy."

And this time he thought she might be telling the truth.

"Then have you prayed?"

"Yes, my lord."

"Then give me your tongue."

She hesitated again, opened her mouth, waited, and thrust her tongue forward to be kissed and sucked, caressed with his own. Now she did tremble, but she did not withdraw.

"In Japan," he said, "men and women do not kiss each other's mouths. Why is that?"

She gazed at him.

"Is it not stimulating, Suiko?"

"Yes, my lord."

He sighed. She would not resist him, even in his thoughts. And so, suddenly, he felt frustrated and incapable, all over again. She *was* beautiful. No question about that. An utterly beautiful child, and an utterly innocent one. And yet he could not accept what she was so willingly prepared to give, without fear and without anger, without haste and without reluctance.

Or was it the image of Alison, constantly rising before his eyes, that left him only half a man?

"Does my lord wish to ... to kiss again?" she asked. She was bewildered. He was her husband, but she could see the conflicting emotions in his eyes, perhaps feel the anger emanating from his body.

"No," he said almost harshly. "Not now. Lie down, Suiko. On your back. Stretch your arms above your head and spread your legs as wide as you may."

Prostrate yourself, he thought. But she obeyed, without question. Before him then, in her person, was all Japan. The daughter of a line of samurai warriors, at his feet, his to do with as he wished.

Gazing at him with anxious, watchful eyes, wishing only to anticipate his desires. To please him.

And she he could not hate. This delicate beauty had nothing to do with the tyranny of Nariaka, the lusts of Munetake, not even the unchanging rigidity of her uncle's views upon life. She was only a girl who wanted to make him happy and who was now his responsibility for the rest of their lives. No matter what happened, no matter how he intended to implement his other plans, she would remain his, and thus his responsibility, for as long as she lived.

It was not a burden he had intended to accumulate. But what a marvelous, sweet-smelling, and devoted weight to carry. He knelt between her legs to take possession of his bride.

She could feel his anger, as nowadays she so often felt his anger, as he surged into her and climaxed, his fingers tight on her breasts with frustration. She could not tell him, she did not wish him to know, how close he had come to fulfilling his dearest dream. And hers? But that was an admission she would never dare make, not even to herself.

She could not even tell if her inability to feel was deliberate, or just there. She wanted to feel, often enough. But she feared to surrender. Not to surrender, never to surrender, was more than loyalty to the memory of what had been, and what might, one day, be again. It was also a knowledge that every time he came to her, and it was at least once a day, and sought to conquer her, and failed, she was being herself, her own woman—however much with every day she could sense the closeness of an explosion which would again have her writhing on the floor while he stood on her hair and tore her buttocks to shreds.

Yet his control was amazing, to one who had known him uncontrolled. It was as if the desire to possess her was paramount to any other, far greater than any frustrated urge to hurt. Now he threw her on her back, as he often did when he was finished with her. But this evening, to her surprise and concern, he remained kneeling above her, taking an ankle in each hand to spread her legs, held above his shoulders, and smiled. It was an angry smile, and his fingers hurt her flesh. She caught her breath, realizing that she might at last have caused his patience to snap.

"What do you dream of?" he asked. And when she did not reply, but gazed at his reawakening desire, he smiled again, and answered himself. "But this I know. You are a fool, Alison. The past is the past, and the future is the future. Do you not know that messengers arrived this morning from Kagoshima. Among other things, they told me that Freeman has wed, the daughter of Saigo Kiyotake, Takamori's niece."

She caught her breath, and knew her eyes had widened. Her brain wanted to reject his words as her body had rejected his love. But she knew it was not a lie. It was against his code. Rather had he waited for the right moment to tell her.

"I know this girl," he said. "Saigo Suiko. She is the loveliest of Takamori's nieces, and they are all lovely. In the arms of Saigo Suiko, even Freeman will soon forget all about you, my Alison. Even you."

Still holding her legs apart, he entered her again, for the first time as Ralph might have done, and more, releasing her legs, he sank onto her and into her, as Ralph might have done, while his mouth sought hers.

Her brain spun into a kaleidoscope of fears and desires, dreams and nightmares, even as she knew that she could no longer resist him.

That she no longer had any reason.

But that she *had* to resist him, now and always, until she could be avenged.

III
THE
EMPEROR

—11—

THE LOVERS

In the mornings, the sun rose out of the limitless ocean to the east and sent its rays beaming over Kagoshima Wan, brought the huge inlet to life, glinted from the sails of the fishing boats as they hauled their nets within the shelter of the headlands or more boldly put out into the heaving ocean. And at dusk the sun sank beyond the mountains of the west, into the China Sea, disappearing into the immense Dragon Empire of the Manchus. Immensity, to either side. And in the center, the bustling happiness that was Kagoshima, and indeed, all the lands of the Satsuma.

No doubt the memory of the British bombardment, of the humiliation of paying the indemnity, lingered, certainly in the minds of Lord Shimadzu and Saigo Takamori and their samurai. But they were Japanese warriors, content to watch and to wait, to listen and to learn, never to endanger their ambitions by a single hasty action. And thus they were forced to give a pretense of happiness. It was difficult to suppose they were playacting all of the time.

Certainly the common people, the sailors and fishermen, the despised merchants, the laboring honin and eta, were happy. After spending several years in Cho-Shu, Ralph would not have believed this possible, had he not seen it with his own eyes. Down in southern Kyushu, far removed from the constant internecine squabbling of Honshu, and more especially of Edo, where Tokugawa Iyemochi still clung to precarious power, life maintained an equable quality, in keeping with the unceasing revolutions of the sun which dominated all things. It had been so for centuries, ever since the Satsuma had ceased to war with the Tokugawa after the Battle of Sekigahara, and had instead become one of the props of the shogunate. That the prop had lost its foundations was not readily apparent to anyone. The British bombardment had been a unique disaster, but it had not been the physical catastrophe for Kagoshima that it had been for Shimonoseki, and it could be classified with the last serious earthquake—and even these natural mishaps were far less common in the south than in the north—or the last eruption of Mount Aso, whose snow-clad peaks dominated the southern island, in the same way as Fujiyama did Honshu. Aso gave expression to the entire ambience of Kyushu. It was an active volcano, there could be no doubt about that; it rumbled constantly, and often enough smoked. Yet within its immense eighteen-square-mile crater there were eleven villages and a patchwork of brilliant green fields. One day Aso would explode, and houses would be destroyed, and perhaps people would be killed. But that would be an act of the gods. Until it happened, and after it happened, the people of Kyushu would continue to fish, and farm, and be happy in their eternal sunlight.

So how could someone who had never known such perfection not also be happy, whatever the memories and ambitions tugging at his heartstrings? How could a husband not delight in the most tranquil, willing, and beautiful of wives? How could a father not delight in the babies she bore, the first a son, almost exactly nine months after their wedding night; the second a girl, eleven months after that. The boy they called William, after Ralph's grandfather, a name Suiko found great difficulty in pronouncing. The little girl they called Maureen, after Ralph's mother, which she found easier, but still did not understand. Yet she would never question the decision of her lord.

Then how could a samurai, a hatamoto, not be happy, when he was wealthy, and had a house of his own outside the castle, and was as free as air to come and go as he chose? When he had that water-whispering garden which he had always found the most attractive of Japanese creations? When he had an interesting and even exciting daily task to perform, for the Satsuma samurai, unlike the men of Cho-Shu, were eager to learn the ways of Western tactics and even drill, and flocked to volunteer for the rifle regiment he was forming, whose ranks were limited only by the number of weapons they could procure? And when he had friends such as Saigo Takamori, who watched him drilling his men with increased satisfaction, or Togo Heihachiro, who would practice with the cannon until he dropped, but who also delighted to take Ralph sailing in the bay, fishing for prawns and crabs, whenever they felt like a holiday.

In fact, Ralph used none of his freedom, his wealth, his growing power, to travel. He had no desire to go even as far as Shimonoseki, where the young lord of Cho-Shu, Yoshimune, was rebuilding his citadel and his city under the guidance of his trusted advisers Inouye Bunta and Ito Shunsuke; Ito was apparently now general of the Cho-Shu army. But Shimonoseki, even those two good friends, evoked too many painful memories.

And north of Cho-Shu there were the lands of the Tokugawa, where he was known, and not, by repute, loved. That he was now serving the Satsuma was apparently known the length and breadth of Japan, and both the British and the American consulates in Edo repeatedly demanded his surrender, demands which Iyemochi duly passed on to Shimadzu. And which the Satsuma lord, for all his visible aging, ignored. "If the barbarians wish Freeman San so badly," he told the shogun's envoys, "let them come and get him. They will not find us so easy to defeat this time."

Probably an idle boast, Ralph feared, but neither the British nor the Americans wished to undertake another war, apparently, however briefly, simply to gain possession of a common criminal who was in any event doing them no harm at the moment. Among the Americans, indeed, who came to Kagoshima on business, it was possible to discern a growing revulsion at having ever taken part in such brutal punitive expeditions, even if only by proxies; the United States government, alone of the Western nations, returned its share of the Satsuma indemnity to Japan for the founding of an English-speaking college. This, no less than the Satsuma faithfulness to him, Ralph found very gratifying, even if he knew that his own people would still hang him if they could, and that the Satsuma would still use him *when* they could. It was this last fact which was not lost upon the shogun, and which made it probable, according to Saigo Takamori, that were he ever to venture to Edo privately, he would never return, but his body would be found lying in some ditch, clearly set upon by bandits.

But even if Tokugawa Iyemochi had been prepared to welcome him with open arms and a safe conduct—which was the more important—Ralph would not have wished to go north privately. Because north of Edo, and the island of Honshu, lay Hokkaido.

News filtered south from time to time, but it was mainly political. A samurai did not discuss his personal affairs with anyone. Yet Ralph felt that had anything untoward happened to Alison, he *would* have heard. In this he found some reassurance, yet whether she was well, and whether she was happy, or at least contented, any more than whether she had given birth to a son or a daughter, or had done so again for her new lord, and above all, whether she still thought of him, still waited for him to come to her rescue, and still dreamed of him doing so, could only be answered by his imagination, his mood. Accomplishing that ambition seemed to lie as far in the future as ever. Because it could be done, he had realized almost from his first day in Kagoshima, only as part of a general upheaval which would plunge the country into civil war, and in which all things might perhaps be possible. Certainly, should such a thing happen—and the Satsuma were almost openly preparing for it—Shimadzu and Saigo would need to call upon all of their forces, and Munetake would have to join the Satsuma armies. Whether he brought his barbarian concubine with him or whether he left her behind would make little difference then. Ralph dreamed of Munetake dead, whether killed in action or by his hand was immaterial to him, and thus Alison abandoned to be claimed. Traditionally, favorite concubines did not survive the deaths of their masters—he would never forget that dreadful day in Nariaka's audience chamber—but Alison was not Japanese, and neither was he, and if he had led his riflemen to victory for the Satsuma, he did not think Saigo would stand in his way. In those circumstances, he did not think Saigo would condemn him even if it had been he who actually killed Munetake. He was in any event prepared to risk that.

And Suiko, who loved him, or at least served him, with such entire devotion? That was a dilemma hardly to be contemplated, but which he prayed to be able to resolve when the moment came. Because the moment, the war, had to happen first. And as sunrise succeeded sunrise, he grew less certain that it ever would. It was difficult to imagine this peaceful country bursting into red and bloody anger. He had no doubt that Saigo and his lord were planning as carefully as himself, and waiting as patiently as himself—no one *could* doubt their hatred for the shogunate, and their determination to overthrow it, one day—but no man could tell just *what* they were waiting for. And as day drifted into week, and week into month, and month into year, with his domestic happiness and prosperity multiplying all about him, even the memory of Alison began to fade. So, then, he was the most miserable of creatures. She had saved his life, and abandoned the chance to return to her own country and her own people, simply to be with him. And he had sworn eternal love, and protection, and honor. And now found his happiness in the arms of another woman. Easy to say that he had absolutely no alternative. That for him to have challenged the Satsuma then, and thus died, would not have changed Alison's situation in the least. That for him to have rejected Suiko after their marriage would merely have left her bereft of human companionship. And that like the Satsuma, he was still planning, and watching, and waiting. The fact was that with every day he was growing older and more set in his ways—as perhaps Alison was growing more set in hers. And with every day his determination weakened a little further, the contentment with his present lot grew a little stronger, and his feelings for Suiko ripened into something very close to love.

But yet they were all waiting. And for those who wait with sufficient patience, the right day always arrives.

Ralph was drilling his riflemen on an autumn morning in 1866 when Saigo Takamori galloped up to them, having clearly driven his horse all the way from the castle. "Cease this playacting," the general shouted. "The day is here. The news has just reached us from Edo. Tokugawa Iyemochi is dead. The shogunate is vacant. The day of our revenge is here."

So there was the answer to the question which had been puzzling him for two years, the event for which Saigo and Shimadzu had been waiting. And yet . . . "A most fortuitous occurrence," Ralph remarked to Saigo as they rode together back to the castle. "I understood that Tokugawa Iyemochi was not an old man."

"Not an old man at all," Saigo agreed. "And by repute, a healthy one." He gave Ralph a sidelong glance. "Still, no human being can properly understand the workings of fate."

Which left Ralph in no further doubt that the unfortunate shogun had been assassinated, whether by a Satsuma hand or merely with Satsuma approval was not relevant—like all Japanese, Saigo did not regard political assassination as in the least dishonorable.

"But will not another Tokugawa be made shogun in Iyemochi's place?" he asked.

"Undoubtedly this is what the Tokugawa will intend," Saigo agreed. "But still, there must be an election, however sham in reality, and these things take time to arrange. Besides, such are the workings of fortune in this instance that Iyemochi has no son, not even a close cousin, to whom the family may turn. There is only one Tokugawa prince left, of an age to succeed, and that is the lord of Mito, Yoshinobu. And he is but a boy, and of a weak and pleasure-loving mind. He is called Keiko by his friends. And even by his enemies. Messengers have already gone to Lord Yoshimune of Cho-Shu. Were the men of Cho-Shu and the men of Satsuma to arrive in Edo together just before the election, then it may be possible to bring about a decisive result."

He did not elaborate on just what decisive result he had in mind, and Ralph's own brain was in any event already soaring toward the possibilities suggested by their conversation.

"No doubt Lord Shimadzu will summon *all* his samurai, from all over Japan," Ralph suggested.

Saigo gave him another quick glance. "That remains to be seen, Freeman San," he said. "It is still necessary to hurry slowly."

In fact, for all Saigo's excitement on that first morning, there was very little evidence of haste at all. It was almost as if, having arrived at the decisive moment, as they saw it, the Satsuma leaders were now suddenly afraid of taking the decisive step.

Ralph was invited to attend their council of war and listen to the problems that had to be surmounted, as expounded by Lord Shimadzu. "For although there can be no doubt that most samurai hate and fear the shogunate, and know that it is the Tokugawa who have inflicted this great and dishonorable burden of foreign interference in our affairs upon us," Shimadzu said, "yet are our enemies sanctified by two hundred and fifty years of power, by the apparent confidence of the emperor, and supported by their innumerable brothers- and fathers- and cousins-in-law, all of whose power rests upon a continuation of Tokugawa rule. We of the Satsuma are entitled to attend the election of a new shogun, like all daimyos, and we are entitled to be accompanied on our march by a reasonable company of our samurai, as are all daimyos, but not by an army. If we march north with all our power, with all our cannon"—he glanced at Ralph—"then will we be declaring our intentions to our enemies, who will unite against us before we may even reach sight of Edo."

"But if we march north with only our personal attendants," Saigo objected, "even if we have the men of Cho-Shu beside us, the Tokugawa will be able to marshal greater forces against us, and our efforts will be in vain."

"There is the problem," Shimadzu said, looking around the faces in the room.

"If I may speak, my lord," Ralph said.

"Your words are awaited, Freeman San," Shimadzu said.

"First, my lord, I would ask, is it truly your intention to overthrow the Tokugawa once and for all?"

Shimadzu gazed at him, face expressionless. "It is our intention to restore the honor of Japan," he said. "If it can be done."

"Knowing that the Tokugawa hold your youngest son hostage, in Edo?"

"My son will know his duty, when the moment comes," Shimadzu said.

To die, Ralph thought, without a tremor crossing his father's face. But what else had he expected? And having received such an answer, could he now do less than provide this stern old man with the victory he sought?

"Then, my lord," he said, "I would ask you this: if, as you say, your march north can only be attended by your personal bodyguard, how many men would this be?"

"I would say we could take five thousand men without arousing undue suspicion."

"And the Tokugawa would have no reason to mobilize against five thousand men?"

"Not without themselves making men suspicious as to *their* motives. It is well known that they would like to destroy us. No, no, they must follow the same strategy as ourselves, that of allowing some *accidental* spark to ignite a conflagration."

"Which they can do, and will do," Saigo said gloomily. "They have no *need* to mobilize an army. There are at least fifteen thousand Tokugawa samurai permanently mobilized in Edo."

"Five thousand men may defeat fifteen, if properly led," Ralph said. "And properly armed. And properly supported. And will we not also be supported by the bodyguard of Lord Yoshimune of Cho-Shu? May I suggest, Lord Shimadzu, that in your personal bodyguard you include myself and my regiment of marksmen. If we march with our rifles concealed, no one will know we are armed with anything more than swords and bows. And may I further suggest that you prepare your artillery to follow, with the rest of your army, on an appointed day, with all possible haste, so as to join us after we have reached Edo, so that when we have gained the initial victory, we will then be able to bring overwhelming force to bear upon your enemies before they can do the same. In this regard I would urge you to send messengers north to Hokkaido and to your other fiefs and allies, requiring them also to march on Edo at a certain date."

Shimadzu looked at Saigo.

"I follow your strategy, Freeman San," Saigo said. "But all will depend upon our gaining that initial victory. If there is a *spontaneous* outbreak of hostilities between ourselves and the Tokugawa, it will doubtless take place among the houses of Edo. Edo is the greatest city in the world, and stretches for miles on every side, away from the Tokugawa stronghold. Will your riflemen be effective in such conditions? Will it not after all come down to men and swords, in which weight of numbers is everything?"

"My riflemen will be effective, my Lord Saigo," Ralph promised.

Saigo gazed at him for several seconds. Then he said, "So be it. We will adopt your plan, Freeman San. Remembering that all our heads, yours included, will roll if we fail."

The honin girl bowed almost to the floor. "The lord comes," she said.

Alison nodded, and took the little boy from her breast, to hand him to the waiting wet nurse. She was just having to surrender the feeding of the child altogether, after a little over two years. She was pleased about that, having found a suitable substitute—but then, she was also pleased that her milk had lasted so long and so well.

She had in fact nothing to be displeased about. Her lord was returning from exercising his soldiers, but she had nothing more to do than stand and prepare to bow as he entered the room; she did not even bother to fasten her kimono, as he would certainly immediately wish to *un*fasten it again. Her girls were doing all the work, hastily heating the sake, bringing out the clean kimono for him to wear, while others were already preparing the bath he would wish to share with his concubine. She had accomplished all of this order and discipline, again thankful to the years she had managed her father's house in Hong Kong. Command came naturally to her.

But so many things came naturally to her. Had anyone told her, even five years ago, that she would complete her life as the concubine of a Japanese hatamoto, she would have supposed it the most dreadful of nightmares, just as had anyone even hinted what she might have to endure before reaching these almost calm waters, she would undoubtedly have fainted. Yet she *had* endured everything. Everything she supposed could ever have been inflicted upon any woman who had ever lived—not least the loss of the man she loved, not to death, which might have been acceptable, but to another woman. No news ever came north from Kagoshima, except for various military or political suggestions. But the very absence of news presupposed that Ralph must be happy in the arms of his Saigo wife. And how could he not be, supposing a Japanese woman could supply one iota of the erotic stimulation of a Japanese man?

So Ralph had forgotten all about her, as was inevitable, and she must find her own salvation where she could. This she in fact desperately sought to do, even if it meant accepting Munetake. She knew he desperately wanted a son, and she was concerned at their inability to conceive, because she had not conceived during the fortnight she had belonged to him five years before, which suggested a lack in him. And, strangely, she *wanted* to give him a son. If she was as resolved as ever she had been to preserve at least her mental inviolacy, and never reveal anything of the physical pleasure he undoubtedly gave her, from time to time, and even more never to allow a single endearment ever to escape her lips—if she was, indeed, resolved to hate him for what he had done to her to the very moment of her death, as that moment seemed to lie a long time in the future, during which time this bleak, windswept northern enclave was to be her home, then the more children she could have, the better. Children would not only provide her with protection as her beauty faded, but they could even become instruments of revenge. But above all, they would provide her with legitimate objects to love, and how her soul cried out for those.

And now that she had ceased feeding Jeremy, she thought it might at last be possible. It had to be possible.

Munetake stood in the doorway, an always dramatic figure in full armor, while his servants unfastened the straps and took away his helmet, and the girls hurried forward with the cup of sake, and Alison bowed from the waist, as was required from a concubine in the presence of her lord, bending until her body was parallel with the floor before straightening again.

He nodded toward the bathhouse, and she followed him, frowning; he was not usually quite so abrupt. He said nothing while they were washed, but stared at her with his deep-set black eyes. He did not speak until they soaked in the hot tub and a wave of his hand had sent the girls to the far end of the room.

"I have received a messenger from Kagoshima," he said.

She was immediately watchful, while her emotions were held in suspension—she had no idea what might be coming next.

"I am to leave Hokkaido, with all my force, one week from today," Munetake said. "And march on Edo."

"Edo? But . . ."

"It is to do with the death of the shogun. Lord Shimadzu means to settle the matter once and for all."

"You mean . . . civil war? But, my God . . ."

"We will either win, and the Satsuma will assume the shogunate, or we shall lose, and be forced to seppuku," he said, still staring at her. "Freeman also, because he will certainly be there."

"Freeman?" Now she could hardly breathe.

"You still dream of him, Alison. Which is why you never dream of me."

"I . . ." She could feel the color flaring into her cheeks. "He is the father of my son."

He continued to stare at her for several more seconds.

Then he stood up and stepped from the bath. "Would you like to accompany me to Edo?" he asked. "And see Freeman? For the last time?"

"War," Suiko said sadly. Maureen was still at her breast, and her figure was still plump from carrying the child; William crawled and rolled at her feet. "I will pray for you, my lord. And pray, too, that you will be away for only a season."

"Only for a season," Ralph promised. "And it may not even come to that, Suiko. We may triumph without firing a shot. Who can tell the workings of fate?"

"Return to me, Freeman San," she said. "Return to me."

Which very nearly made him wish to stay. But his whole being was filled with a tremendous glow of anticipation. For how long had he waited for this moment? Why, since his first arrival in Japan, six years and more ago. Nearly seven now, for the move to the north had had to be carefully timed, and the daimyos had been informed by messengers from Edo that the election to the shogunate would not take place until six months' mourning had been observed for Iyemochi. That meant, in effect, the following spring, which would be the spring of 1867. And thus the Satsuma armies did not commence their march until the end of February, by Western reckoning. It had been the longest winter Ralph had ever spent.

But it had been spent well. He was a soldier, at last being called upon to use his professional skill, and in a manner concerning which he need not feel any pangs of conscience. He was going to fight Japanese, and for how long had he wanted to do *that*? That, such were the paradoxes which seemed inescapable from his life, he would be fighting against a government which he was sure in his heart was pursuing the right course for this island empire, and a course which should prevent crazy tyrants like Nariaka from ever again rising to power, could not overturn his contentment. He could assuage that aspect of conscience with the reflection that any man whom the Satsuma backed for the shogunate had equally to be a man of conscience and intelligence and broad-mindedness. And either way, he did not care. Here was the turmoil he had wanted for so long. He would be killing Japanese rather than Englishmen or Americans. And in that turmoil he would surely be able to seek out Munetake. And then at last go north to Hokkaido?

That consideration alone made him unable to meet Suiko's gaze as she presented her lips for the kiss she knew he would wish before leaving. Because even if he went north, and regained Alison, he must yet return here for his child bride and his children before he could leave Japan. Suddenly, as the possibility had become almost a reality, it was not something to be thought about anymore. His business was to concentrate on the matter in hand, on achieving the victory that the Satsuma expected of his Western knowledge. And how he looked forward to a fight, on his own terms.

Perhaps his confidence inspired the whole army. The Satsuma samurai bristled with anticipation as they marched north, pausing at Kumamoto to give Hayashi the necessary instructions; fast riders had already been sent galloping to Hokkaido. The plan had been very carefully drawn up by Saigo and himself. No one was to move for four days after their departure; then the remainder of the Kagoshima forces were to march for Kumamoto, including the artillery, which Ralph had placed under the command of Togo Heihachiro, for all his youth, and there camp. Such a movement would obviously be overseen by the Tokugawa spies who were well known to infest Kyushu, but as yet they would have nothing positive to report to their masters in Edo. And meanwhile, the daimyo would be hurrying north, with his bodyguard.

Two days after reaching Kumamoto, the entire Satsuma army, under the command of Hayashi, was to begin its march on Edo, hopefully accumulating the Cho-Shu army as well, to create a force of perhaps thirty thousand men. *Then* the spies would go fleeing for the shogun's capital, to tell the Tokugawa clansmen what was impending, that the Satsuma and the Cho-Shu intended to settle this election by force of arms, but Saigo calculated that the fastest messenger could not get to Edo before Shimadzu and his advance guard. Meanwhile, by then Munetake and his northern army would also be approaching the capital. His move could obviously not be calculated with accuracy, as no man could tell how long it would take the messenger from Kagoshima to reach him. But the messenger should already be there, they knew as they left Kumamoto behind them, and in commanding the northern general to march one week later, they were timing the concentration as best they could—Munetake's march south from Hokkaido would take only a quarter of the time needed to travel from Kagoshima. So that not more than a week after Shimadzu had arrived in Edo, the entire Satsuma force would be assembled, to give a mighty backing to their lord's decisions. If the plan worked, it would have been a masterpiece of concentration. If it miscarried, Lord Shimadzu and Saigo Takamori, with their American adviser, would be left with just their bodyguards to face the entire wrath of the Tokugawa.

But included in those bodyguards were the twelve hundred riflemen under Ralph's personal command. He knew nothing, at least by personal experience, of any other Japanese army, save for the undisciplined Cho-Shu horde, but from everything he had heard, he doubted there was a force to match his in the entire empire. They were his trump cards.

Boats were waiting to ferry them across the Strait of Shimonoseki, to look upon the once stricken city, already rebuilt as Inouye had told him it was so easy to do. The fortress had been less simple to repair, and the destroyed palace was still being recreated. But here was young Lord Yoshimune, and *his* advisers, and their retainers, making another five thousand men, ready to march behind the Satsuma.

"Now we have an army," Saigo said.

"Now we have accumulated a rabble," Ralph said. As Ito admitted, having watched Ralph's regiment on the road for a day.

"Truly, Freeman San," he said, "your soldiers remind me of American infantry. I wish the men of Cho-Shu were more inclined to discipline and training."

"It requires patience," Ralph told him. "But also

understanding. Discipline alone will never carry the day." He embraced Inouye. "Your family?"

"Survived," Inouye said.

"But you cannot find it in your heart to forgive me for leaving Shimonoseki for Kagoshima."

"I do not know, Freeman San. I believe you have done well by the Satsuma, and the gods know you were not fairly treated by Lord Nariaka. And if now we march together to save Japan . . . who am I to cavil against the whims of fate? A Japanese could not have done what you have done, without being borne down by the weight of abandoned honor. But you are not Japanese. And no doubt you were sent especially to us, to lead us to a new and greater Nippon."

"If they no longer love you, Freeman San," Saigo explained, "I doubt it is because you abandoned the flag of Cho-Shu for that of the Satsuma. It is because you failed to defeat the British fleet. If you gain the day against the Tokugawa, they will again hail you as a brother."

The journey to the north took considerably longer than Ralph had anticipated; he was not yet used to the true size of this land, or the slowness with which a Japanese samurai army marched, with lengthy stops for meals and the necessity of finding luxurious quarters for the two daimyos each night. They marched by the sea to begin with, following the coastal road to the east, along the southernmost edge of Honshu, from Shimonoseki to Hiroshima, thence to Fukuyama and Okayama, before, after a fortnight, they beheld the flags flying from the great citadel of Osaka. Osaka had once been the chief city of Japan, in the days of the great Toyotomi Hideyoshi, before the Tokugawa had come to power. It lay at the very head of the Inland Sea, and yet close to a passage to the ocean, and in addition was only some twenty miles south of the imperial capital of Kyoto itself, on the shores of Lake Biwa. Thus it was the very nerve center of the entire empire, as its castle was the greatest in the land, rectangle within rectangle of high stone walls, separated by deep moats, and at the center, a huge keep. Here the last of the Toyotomi, Hideyoshi's famous wife Yodogimi and her son, had fought the final battle of the great civil war against the Tokugawa and lost, two and a half centuries before. Now the garrison flew the golden fan of the Tokugawas themselves, gazing down at the marching southerners.

"But they cannot interfere with us," Saigo told Ralph. "We are entitled to attend the election."

"What would happen," Ralph asked, "if we were to turn aside now, and march on Kyoto, and seize the person of the mikado? We could be there by tomorrow morning, if we hurried."

"Then the garrison would certainly fire upon us. And do not forget that Kyoto is also ringed with Tokugawa troops. And more important, that they would speak in the emperor's name when they commanded us to lay down our arms and commit seppuku."

"And you would feel obliged to obey, even knowing it was your enemies speaking, rather than your king?"

"That is a situation I would rather not have to face," Saigo admitted. "Certainly it would have a serious effect upon our people. You speak of a king, Freeman San. But we are talking of the mikado, who is the Son of Heaven, and acknowledges only the great Sun itself as his superior. No, no, it is necessary to bring down the Tokugawa first."

"In the name of the emperor."

"How else may we wage war?"

"Knowing that the Tokugawa will also claim to be acting in his name?"

"Any man may claim anything he likes, Freeman San. But only the shogun himself, having been duly elected by the daimyos, and accepted by the emperor, may henceforth act in the emperor's name without his written consent. Thus if we can either bring them down or force them to withstand a siege in Edo castle, before a new shogun can be elected and accepted by the mikado, they will just be ordinary men, like us, and may be opposed, and defeated."

It all seemed a rather semantic exercise to Ralph; not the least of the questions he would have liked to ask being how a being who exercised such total theoretical power over the lives and even the thoughts of his subjects had not in more than five hundred years ever attempted to exercise that power physically. Here more than anything else was an example of that tradition which held the Japanese in such a terrible grip, and which the Tokugawa shogunate was actually attempting to change, not realizing that it must perish together with all the other aspects of the past if Japan was truly to move into the nineteenth century.

Again, he reminded himself, not his concern. Now, as they marched more to the northeast, to Nagoya, came evidence that it was not yet summer in the northern islands. The nights were cold, and there was the occasional sharp frost; he had almost forgotten what frost was like, and more than one of the samurai was frozen to death. But from Nagoya they again followed the coast, actually swinging southeast for a while, to Hamamatsu, before once more marching east, for Shizuoka. Now huge mountains, the Hakone range, loomed on their left hand, and rising above even these was the eternally snowcapped peak of Fuji, twenty thousand feet and more in height, Japan's eternal monument. While at Kamakura, where they arrived soon after, Ralph gazed in wonder, as the samurai knelt in awe, before the huge Daihatsu Buddha, greatest of Japanese manmade monuments. Here was history leaping at them from around every corner. But from Kamakura they could look across the water at land to the east. "Because we are in a bay," Saigo explained. "Edo Wan. That village in the distance is known as Yokohama. Beyond are the walls of Edo."

They had been on the road a month since leaving Kogoshima.

The greatest city in the world, Saigo had claimed, and Ralph had not paid much attention, accustomed as he was to the Japanese habit of regarding everything in their island empire as the best. Yet as they marched along the shore, looking at the houses and the pagodas which seemed to fill the entire landscape beyond, he wondered if the general might not have been more accurate than he had supposed. Certainly no city *he* had ever seen, from New York through Dodge to San

Francisco itself, had ever suggested such a teeming metropolis; he had counted Shimonoseki and Kagoshima sizable towns, but Edo made them appear as villages. And it was entirely open, so far as could be seen.

"That is not actually so, of course," Saigo said. "The Tokugawa built a wall to enclose their city, many years ago. But the city has grown and overflowed the wall."

"And that is the wall we must enter?" Ralph asked.

"That certainly," Saigo agreed. "After wending our way through the houses you see there. But it is the inner wall, the wall which surrounds the palace and citadel of the Tokugawa itself, that must be our goal."

A time to think. Because the general's comment back in Kagoshima had also been more right than he had supposed. Certainly once their ten thousand men, or an even greater body, got lost in those narrow streets, they would necessarily lose all cohesion as a fighting force.

"Will they let us in, do you think?" he asked Saigo.

"They must," the general said. "We come in peace, do we not?" His face was blandly expressionless, but then he frowned as he looked toward the houses again and saw issuing from them a large body of men, certainly armed—the morning sun was glinting from their lance heads—and accompanied by a battery of artillery; above their heads waved the emblem of the golden fan. "What can this be?" he inquired at large, and urged his horse forward, to where Lords Shimadzu and Yoshimune rode together. Ralph followed more slowly, watching the army in front of them debouching into the open space before the first of the houses. And it *was* an army, some twenty thousand men, he estimated. But it was the artillery which mattered. If it were properly handled.

A herald rode out in front of the Tokugawa some two hundred yards and there drew rein and waited for the Cho-Shu and Satsuma forces to come to a halt. Saigo Takamori himself went forward, having conferred with his lord, while the armies waited, staring at each other, perhaps half a mile apart. Saigo spoke with the herald for several minutes and then turned his horse and rode back to the waiting daimyos.

"Well?" Shimadzu demanded. "How dare they bar my way? Am I not to attend the election?"

Saigo's face was a picture of dismay. "The election has already been held, several months ago."

"Already held? But . . . the mourning . . ."

"Was ignored. It was decided at a meeting of the Tokugawa that affairs in Japan were at too critical a stage to leave the country without a head for six months. Therefore an election was held there and then, and Keiko"—his voice was loaded with angry contempt—"was chosen. Only Tokugawa kinsmen were present. But apparently they had sufficient daimyos for legality."

"It is nonetheless a fraud," Inouye declared.

"Certainly," Saigo agreed. "But it has been accepted by the emperor."

"We have been outwitted," Yoshimune grumbled.

"Why were we not informed of this election?" Shimadzu asked.

"They say that we were. They do not know what has happened to the messenger."

"And we know that is a lie," Shimadzu said angrily. "Well, we shall make our objections plain. Tell those fellows to stand aside. We shall pay our respects to this new shogun of ours."

"The shogun wishes no respects at this time, my lord," Saigo said. "His men have orders to bar us from the city. He says to tell you he will receive his daimyos one by one, as he sends for them, and that he will have no bodies of armed retainers enter Edo. He says to tell you that if you urgently desire to pay your respects at this time, then you are to enter the city alone and unarmed, under Tokugawa escort. He guarantees you safe conduct."

"And you believe him?"

"Very probably he is telling the truth, my lord. For what could you do, alone and unarmed, and with no samurai at your back, save agreed to his commands?"

"We have been outwitted," Yoshimune said again. "The Tokugawa have been too clever for us. It was ever so. Now we can only go home again."

"And raise the standard of revolt?" Shimadzu asked,

chewing his mustache. "The shogun will command the emperor, and we will be nothing more than rebels."

Ralph urged his horse closer. "The alternative is to act now, my lord."

Shimadzu stared at him. "You would have us challenge twice our number, and armed with cannon?"

"I do not think they understand the use of cannon on a battlefield, my lord," Ralph said, gazing at the Tokugawa force. For instead of massing their six guns for use as a battery, able to command any part of the field on which they might be trained, the Tokugawa had adopted the tactics of three hundred years before in Europe, when gunnery had been in its infancy, and placed one piece every hundred yards, thus covering their entire frontage but throwing away all of the advantage possession of the guns should have bestowed.

Shimadzu was looking at Saigo.

"You think we can defeat them, Freeman San?" Saigo asked.

"I have no doubt of it, my Lord Saigo, provided we adopt the correct tactics."

"Will we not still be rebels," Yoshimune asked, "supposing we are alive to answer for it?" He was definitely Nariaka's son.

"No, my lord," Inouye said, he and Ito having joined the council of war. "Not yet. The command to withdraw was issued in the name of the shogun, not the mikado."

"And does that *matter*?" Ralph cried in sudden impatience with these endless semantics. "My lords, we are here to accomplish a purpose, and that purpose depends on a victory in the field. Let us worry about the legalities afterward. If we win, *we* decide the law. If we lose, then are our lives forfeit in any event."

The Japanese looked surprised at his outburst. But Saigo smiled. "As you say, Freeman San. How should we arrange our forces?"

"On a front broad enough to match theirs," Ralph said. "And then advance as rapidly as you can."

"But . . ." Ito looked thunderstruck. "That will involve each man of ours opposing two of them. We shall be swallowed up."

"That is what our enemies will certainly assume," Ralph said. "And it will be one of ours to *three* of theirs. I will hold my riflemen in reserve, on the right wing. And when you are spread so thin, those cannon will be even less destructive."

"And you will remain in reserve?" Saigo asked, frowning.

"I will mass my people on your right wing, my lord. And we will gain the day for you. Trust me."

Saigo gave him another long stare and then trotted off to make his dispositions, followed by Ito, sadly shaking his head. The Satsuma and Cho-Shu forces were slowly brought into line, amid a tremendous clashing of cymbals and blowing of conch shells, which was reciprocated from the ranks of the shogun's army, as they realized that the southern samurai meant to challenge them. A messenger could be seen galloping back to the city.

"He seeks reinforcements," Ralph muttered. "Haste, Saigo Takamori. Oh, haste."

His riflemen were in column behind him, twelve hundred strong; at his command they kept their loaded rifles slung on their shoulders and revealed only their bows to the enemy, who had observed this concentration, whereas the rest of the southern army was so widely dispersed, and now detached a body of archers, some two thousand strong, Ralph estimated, to repel their charge. Which but made his task the easier.

Now at last Saigo was ready, and took his place before his troops, dismounting, as was customary—the Japanese had little concept of the use of cavalry as an offensive arm—and drawing his long sword. The signal was given, and with a mighty shout of "Banzai!" the Satsuma and Cho-Shu men loosed off their arrows, filling the air with the whistling of their shafts, and then immediately starting their armored advance behind their missiles. Instantly the Tokugawa replied with their own arrow storm, but so far as Ralph could see, and as he had expected, very little damage had been done to either side. But now the swords and spears were out, as the lines approached each other for the hand-to-hand combat which was so dear to the samurai's heart, and which the Tokugawa, with their immense superiority in numbers, anticipated with the utmost confidence. Besides, now the cannon were exploding, and the iron balls came bouncing over the ground, and these did kill and maim; despite the thinness of their ranks, several of the Satsuma warriors were scattered to and fro by the deadly iron.

Ralph estimated the two sides would close in about one minute. "Now," he shouted. "On the double."

His riflemen gave a great cheer, threw away their bows, and ran forward. This was the moment the Tokugawa left wing had anticipated, and they immediately loosed an arrow storm; a hail of shafts whistled about the riflemen, and one bolt struck Ralph on the helmet with a force which for a moment left him dizzy. But it did not penetrate, and only a handful of the Satsuma fell. The rest were unslinging their rifles, and as they had been taught by Ralph, they immediately formed two ranks, the front one kneeling and the second one standing. But only the kneeling men presented their rifles, as the Tokugawa bowmen in turn discarded their weapons and drew their swords for the charge.

"First rank, fire!" Ralph shouted, and watched in horror as the storm of lead, fired at what was, for a rifle, almost point-blank range, swept through the enemy ranks; the two thousand men dissolved as if struck by a typhoon. "Second rank, advance," Ralph commanded, again taking his place at the end of the line, as the standing samurai stepped past their kneeling comrades for some six feet before themselves kneeling. "First rank, load," Ralph ordered, and the samurai who had already fired stood to reload. "Second rank, fire!"

Their immediate opponents having been scattered, the rifle corps now enfiladed the Tokugawa position, and the storm of six hundred bullets swept through the center of the shogun's army like a gigantic mowing machine. Armored bodies tumbled this way and that in their flying blood, and even the advancing Satsuma stopped to gaze in wonder at the destruction being wreaked before them.

"First rank, advance," Ralph called, voice now hoarse. "Second rank, load. First rank, fire!"

Once again the hail of bullets swept through the Tokugawa ranks. The entire left and center had by now broken up, several hundred men lying on the ground, the remainder hastily retreating toward the shelter of the houses, for all the shouts and commands of their officers.

The rest of the Tokugawa had virtually abandoned facing the oncoming spearmen, to wheel their force to face the tremendous threat on their left, but the inexorable advance of the riflemen, firing volley after volley, was too much for them. They did not lack courage. A regiment of armored warriors actually charged, swords waving, only to be mowed down long before they could even cover the quarter of a mile remaining between themselves and the deadly rifles. Others vainly fired their arrows, and a few even had sufficient presence of mind to use their rifles, but their efforts were uncoordinated and their aim poor. The field commanders could tell that all was lost, and gave the command to withdraw, and the withdrawal very rapidly became a rout, the samurai racing back for the safety of the city and the wall. Now Saigo gave the order to charge again, and his spearmen ran forward to complete the victory.

"Cease firing," Ralph commanded. "Load your pieces."

The samurai stood together, chattering among themselves and echoing the shouts of "Banzai!" which were swelling up from the throats of the rest of the Satsuma, while the conch shells wailed to recall the spearmen; Saigo was too good a general to wish his men to become dissipated among the houses.

Ralph's horse was brought forward, and he mounted to canter across to where Shimadzu and Yoshimune waited, and where Saigo was now coming, while the paean of victory continued to spread across the field.

"That was well done, Freeman San," Shimadzu said. "I have never seen an army defeated so quickly and by so few men. Oh, that was well done. What would you have us do now?"

"We have done all we can in the field, my lord," Ralph said. "And to send our people among the houses would be to cast away all our advantage. Now we must wait for our support to arrive. Although it may be possible to treat with the shogun now, while his forces are in disarray."

"Treat?" Inouye demanded. "How can we treat? We have rebelled. We have defeated him in the field. We can settle for nothing less than his abdication."

"He knows we cannot get at him inside Edo," Yoshimune commented, gloomy as ever.

"Then we wait," Shimadzu said, his face gravely composed and expressionless, even though he must be sure that his youngest son was at this moment being executed. "As Freeman San says, we can do nothing more, until the arrival of the rest of our army, to convince this Keiko that we are the stronger and shall gain the day. Our task now must be to prevent any messengers leaving Edo to summon the Tokugawa to Keiko's rescue. Indeed, we must prevent any word of what has happened here today from reaching the rest of Japan, in order that . . ." He frowned as a hatamoto came hurrying up, to bow beside their horses.

"My lord," he said. "A mighty army approaches from the west."

They turned, to stare at the approaching host, for winding over the coast road from Kamakura was certainly a vast force, and above them waved the emblem of the golden fan, together with the rising sun of Japan.

"The army from Osaka," Saigo muttered.

"And that of Koyoto as well," Inouye said. "They must have followed us."

"Why should they do that?" Shimadzu snapped. "They had no cause. Unless we were betrayed." He looked left and right.

"My lord," Ito cried, pointing. "Look, look there."

For in the center of the approaching mass, and somewhat out in front, was a very richly caparisoned group of horsemen, riding under the national flag only, but also carrying the white banners of mourning. Shimadzu's eyes narrowed. "It cannot be," he muttered.

"It cannot be. But . . . Saigo Takamori, form up your men. Freeman San, yours too. Form ranks."

"To give battle, my lord?" Ralph asked.

"To receive them," Shimadzu said. "Those men bear the marks of the mikado. But here, at Edo . . ." He fell to chewing the ends of his mustache.

Ito had already galloped off, to call his men to attention, followed by Saigo. Ralph could do no less. He did not understand what was going on, save that apparently the emperor was himself taking a hand in this quarrel. But why, when he had never done so before? And anyway, as he was marching with Tokugawa guards, he surely intended to intervene on the side of the shogun. Ralph was aware of a curious lightness in his chest. He had not considered the possibility of defeat. But even his twelve hundred riflemen could not beat so large an army; he estimated there had to be not less than fifty thousand men on the road. And commanded by the mikado in person—he had been assured that could never happen.

Orders were given, and the mighty host came to a halt, banners waving in the breeze. For several seconds there was almost complete silence, save for the snorting and pawing of the horses; then a herald rode out from the imperial ranks. "Lord Shimadzu of Satsuma," he cried. "Lord Yoshimune of Cho-Shu. Advance and submit to the Son of Heaven."

Ralph stared at the group of horsemen. One had moved a little in front of the others, and certainly sat his horse like a king. But he was hardly more than a boy, and the emperor was supposed to be an elderly man.

Shimadzu and Yoshimune were obeying the summons, slowly walking their horses forward, then bringing them to a halt a few yards in front of the mounted youth.

"We seek the Son of Heaven," Shimadzu said.

"I am he, Lord Shimadzu," the boy said. "Have you not heard? My father is dead."

"Dead, Prince Mutsuhito?" Yoshimune asked. "We had not heard."

"You know now," the prince said. "My father died at the very moment you and your samurai passed by Kyoto, a fortnight ago. Thus I have succeeded him. And what do *I* hear, that you war upon the shogun?"

Shimadzu and Yoshimune exchanged glances, and

then they dismounted together and performed the kowtow, an act which was immediately copied by all of their troops, and that moment, Ralph supposed, as he followed their examples, spelled their surrender and the ending of all their hopes, with seppuku to follow.

"Rise, Lord Shimadzu," Mutsuhito said. "Rise, Lord Yoshimune. I heard the sound of gunfire as I was on the road."

Again the two lords exchanged glances. "The shogun would prevent our entry into Edo, Majesty," Shimadzu said.

Mutsuhito looked past them. "I see no Tokugawa soldiers barring your way."

"We dispersed them, Majesty."

"With so few men? You must tell me of this. And justify your deeds, if you can."

"Majesty, we have been bedeviled by the shogun." Shimadzu's voice grew stronger as he realized that he had not yet actually been condemned for rebellion. "As all of Japan has been betrayed by the Tokugawa."

Mutsuhito gazed at him for several seconds. Then he said quietly, "I know of this, Lord Shimadzu. I think it was the knowledge of Tokugawa trickery which drove my father to his grave. And I knew that there would be war between the Satsuma and the Tokugawa when you reached Edo and learned what had happened. Which is why I followed you."

Shimadzu stared at him, then looked past him at the ranks of Tokugawa soldiery.

Mutsuhito smiled. "These men march for the mikado, for Japan, regardless of their flags. Come, now, Lord Shimadzu, Lord Yoshimune, will you not do the same?"

"But, Majesty . . . the shogun . . ."

"There will be no more shogun," the emperor declared, still speaking quietly, but his voice reaching to every corner of the field. "The shogunate has served its purpose, perhaps for too long. As I am emperor of this land, as I am the Son of Heaven, as the burden of this empire and these peoples now rest on my shoulders before the gods, I have decided to resume the authority of my forebears. Come, Lord Shimadzu, Lord

Yoshimune, will you march for Japan, instead of merely for the Satsuma and the Cho-Shu?"

Shimadzu was clearly too terrified to speak, and Yoshimune too shocked. Ralph realized that he was witnessing the greatest revolution in Japanese history, without quite understanding it. He looked at Saigo, but the general seemed equally thunderstruck at the thought of ending two and a half centuries of tradition by a word. It was Inouye Bunta who broke the spell of indecision. He drew his long sword, pointed it at the sky, and shouted, "Long live the mikado, the Son of Heaven, in whose name we live and breathe and march."

His voice echoed across the field, and was taken up by all the Satsuma and Cho-Shu troops. "Long live the emperor."

"Long live the emperor," Shimadzu cried. "Long may he rule over us."

"Ralph Freeman," said the Emperor Mutsuhito, speaking, amazingly, almost perfect English, "I have heard a great deal about you. Rise, Captain Freeman, or should I now call you general?"

Ralph slowly raised himself from the kowtow, and then, at another movement of the young prince's hand, stood, aware that every eye in the vast room was upon him. And it *was* a vast room, the audience chamber of the Tokugawa shogunate, created by Tokugawa Iyeyasu himself two and a half centuries ago, surrounded by the famous singing floors, made of loosely fastened timbers, against which were set nails in the joists, so that every footfall, as it caused the boards to sag, was recorded by a gentle scrape, and thus no man could approach the Tokugawa councils without betraying his coming.

The Tokugawa were here themselves, today, dressed in their finery, even if their faces were at once grim and confused. They had clung to power for so long, at least partly because they had been unable to conceive of no way they could give up that power without at the same time losing their lands and their lives. But here was a seventeen-year-old boy deposing them by a mere word, and at the same time expressly forbidding them to consider seppuku. "The time for those things is past, except where personal honor is concerned," the emperor had declared. "You and your families have served the empire faithfully and well for eight generations. But now the empire has need of *me*, and so you will step aside."

Words any one of the boy's ancestors could have spoken, at any time in the past two hundred and fifty years, had they dared? Probably not, and survived, Ralph reflected. Mutsuhito happened to have a backbone his ancestors had lacked, and at seventeen he also had the circumstances, a Satsuma and a Cho-Shu army which he had been sure would support him, and which in turn was about to be reinforced by vast reserves, as undoubtedly he had also discovered. Yet the courage and the determination to act, while still in mourning for his father, when indeed he had but succeeded a matter of hours before, indicated the character he had somehow inherited from a line of puppets. It was there in his face, a strangely old face for so young a man, in which the wisps of mustache and beard which he was obviously trying to grow clung oddly. But *of* his determination, and of his purpose, there could be no doubt, nor of the care with which he must have prepared for this moment, while yet a child. Apart from the way in which he had learned to speak English—and acquiring an English tutor must have been his idea—for this occasion, to which not only the daimyos and their generals had been invited, but also the representatives of the foreign powers which maintained embassies or consulates in Edo, he had discarded the kimono and the armor displayed about him, and wore instead a perfectly tailored Western-style uniform, blue jacket and white trousers, which made him look the least regal man in the room—from a distance. Only the eye, and the voice, and the manner, indicated the born ruler of men.

"That you speak to me at all, Majesty, is sufficient honor," Ralph said, also in English.

Mutsuhito regarded him for several seconds. Then he observed, "You have learned to be a Japanese. By necessity, Captain Freeman?"

Ralph glanced at the British and American consuls-general, heads close together as they whispered at each other; could they really recognize the big man in the green armor and with the shaved head, for all the paleness of his skin? "By necessity, Majesty."

"And yet you have done well," the emperor said. "Which is the true mark of greatness. We shall see what can be done about this necessity, Captain Freeman. Unless you would choose to remain in Japan."

Ralph hesitated. How to say: "I cannot leave this land, Majesty, even were I permitted to do so, without another man's woman"? Because that *would* be betrayal; he would never be able to look in a mirror again. But Mutsuhito could not break the law, his law, any more than Shimadzu had been able to. Only by *changing* the law, and thus by destroying the entire structure of bushido, could the emperor interfere. And why should he wish to do so for an American renegade?

Now the emperor smiled at his confusion. "Be sure, Captain, that as long as you do choose to remain, you will be welcome here. I have been hearing an account of this battle you have won for your lord with your rifle corps. I would hear more of it, from your own lips. When we have more time."

His head inclined, and Ralph understood that his particular audience was at an end. He had been almost the last to be called forward, as Mutsuhito had spoken with everyone of importance, one after the other.

"Yet *were* you called, Freeman San," Saigo reminded him. "The mark of greatness is upon you. The mark of greatness is upon us all. I feel that this day Japan has suddenly awakened, as from a long sleep, ready to face the future. With a boy like this to lead us, with his energy and determination and courage, we shall yet show the barbarians that unless they would be our friends, and learn to respect our ways and our customs, and our laws, we shall seize our own destiny. Do you not agree, Freeman San?"

"I am sure the emperor has only the greatness of Japan in his mind," Ralph said with true Japanese imperturbability. The audience was at an end, and the dignitaries and the daimyos were drifting away, while

Shimadzu and Yoshimune on the one side, and the Shogun Keiko and his nearest relatives on the other, stood close to the young emperor, to hear what he would say to them privately. Ralph went onto the veranda, singing very loudly now from the numbers of men walking over it, and gazed at the great compound of the Tokugawa stronghold, the pagodas and the palaces, the statuary and the exquisite gardens, and gazed too at the soldiery pouring into the city, the men of Cho-Shu and the men of Satsuma, no longer resisted by the Tokugawa even if the ex-shogun's samurai glowered at the invaders in frustrated anger. Everything had happened too fast for these simple, honor-bound warriors to appreciate or understand. Now they could only take refuge *in* that honor, which commanded men to obey, and obey, and obey.

No doubt Japan was, as Saigo had suggested, about to awaken from a deep sleep, but Ralph could not help but wonder if the awakening would be a happy one for the samurai. Even for Saigo Takamori.

And then he ceased to wonder at all, as he watched a Satsuma banner riding by, and made out the tall figure of Munetake, leading his army down from Hokkaido to the support of his lord. At Munetake's side there rode a figure no less tall, erect and slender, and undoubtedly female, concealed from the vulgar gaze by a heavy veil.

—12—
THE DECISION

Ralph's heart seemed to constrict. Because there could be no doubt. Munetake had, after all, brought Alison with him. And their son? It was all like an impossible dream come true.

Yet common sense and reason quickly returned, prevented him from rushing out onto the street to see her again—and have her see him. It was still necessary to be very careful. Perhaps it was more necessary than ever to be careful. But that he would see her, again hold her in his arms, he never doubted. And that he would never let her go again, he also refused to doubt.

It was first of all a matter of waiting, and watching, and regretting that he had no trustworthy servant, as once he had been able to rely on Aya. But he had deliberately refused the intimacy of a single personal attendant since joining the Satsuma, instead used several honin men in rotation. This had been dictated partly by the girl's memory, indeed, the certainty that one day he would have to betray such a friend, but also by a reluctance to make a close friend of any Japanese, in his anger. Now he had no one to spy out the land for him. He could only walk the streets of Edo, knowing how conspicuous a figure he was, lost in apparent wonder at the size of the city, the industry of its inhabitants, being greeted in awe and wonder himself, as the man who had overthrown the might of the Tokugawa in a few short minutes, and always listening, and considering. Finding where Munetake's force was encamped was a simple matter; like the rest of the Satsuma army, it was outside the city. Even finding the lodgings within the walls which the hatamoto had taken for his personal use was simple. Getting to Munetake's woman would be the difficulty.

But by now she would know that *he* was also in Edo. And thus would know, too, that he would come for her.

"He is a hero," Munetake said. "A famous man. It is said he defeated the Tokugawa single-handed. I had not supposed he would be able to do it."

Alison knelt before her master, as it was her duty to do, head bowed. She was aware of a feeling of abeyance, almost as if her mind were hovering above her body, afraid to reenter its natural home . . . until Munetake said it could?

Because there was so much that mind had to grasp. In the beginning, she had been the victim of an apparent savage, without a spark of humanity or gentleness about him. Then he had reappeared as a very gentle man, a man of understanding, and if not of softness, not of harshness either. She had been unable to understand this, had waited for a sudden reversion to type. For four years.

Yet she had never doubted that he was still a simple samurai, as bound by tradition and duty as any of his class. If this provided him with immense strength when in adversity, she also had felt it indicated a certain rigidity of thinking, which was a weakness. This past month she had begun to wonder about that as well. He had obeyed his lord's summons to the letter, and with his army had marched from Hokkaido exactly seven days after receiving his instructions. But he had not hurried, had indeed proceeded at a very measured pace, answering her queries with the unanswerable reply that what happened in Edo depended upon the will of the gods.

Now she knew better. He had deliberately delayed, anticipating a battle which the Satsuma must lose, from sheer disparity of numbers. Thus a battle in which Ralph Freeman might be expected to die. This she could appreciate. But also a battle in which Saigo Takamori and Lord Shimadzu would perish. Because she had suddenly realized that hatred of Ralph was by no means the beginning and end of his life. Here was no ordinary samurai, but a general who had begun to consider what prizes might be his were he left in command of the only existing Satsuma army.

A terrible thought for a loyal samurai. An even more terrible thought for a loyal samurai's concubine, supposing her lord ever learned of her suspicion. And now, an irrelevant thought, because the Satsuma, thanks apparently to Ralph, had won. And Munetake was not pleased.

"Are you not happy for him?" he asked.

"I must be happy for the triumph of the Satsuma, my lord," she replied.

He gazed at her so intensely that she raised her head.

"He will wish to see you," Munetake said. "He will *come* to see you. He will suppose that, now he is the favorite of both the mikado and Lord Shimadzu, all things will be possible to him."

"But when he comes, you will still have the right to kill him," she said quietly. She had known from the moment he had insisted she accompany him, when she would have remained in Hokkaido, what he intended, and even more when he had insisted she bring Jeremy with her, despite the winter weather.

And she was utterly helpless. More helpless, at last, than even Munetake suspected, because she had not yet told him what she suspected of herself.

"I will behave with honor," he told her. "I could claim his head. That is my right. But I will challenge him to meet me, sword in hand. He will accept that challenge, because he is a brave man."

There was no suggestion of praise in what he said; it never occurred to Munetake that any man would not be brave and would still be worthy of a challenge. Yet was he certainly right about Ralph.

"And you will still kill him," she said.

Munetake smiled. "Of course. I am the greatest swordsman in Japan. And Freeman . . . I taught him all he knows, such as it is. And it is nothing." His smile faded. "This distresses you. I would not distress you, my Alison. Yet it must be done, both to make you dream of me and because he is a dangerous man. Not only to me, but to the Satsuma. I know this. I feel it in my bones."

Alison hesitated—but there was no alternative. Especially now. She drew a long breath. "If he is dangerous, it is because he is here at all, my lord. And he is only here because of me. If you will permit me to see him, and tell him that I no longer love him, that I am your woman now and always, then he will depart, and cease to be a danger to anyone, and you will not have to fight him. I would beg this of you, my lord."

He frowned at her. "*See* him? You mean, speak with him? You expect me to permit that? He may touch you."

"My servants touch me every day, my lord." She raised her head to stare into his eyes. "My son will remain with your people, as hostage. And you will have my word, not only that I will return to you, my lord, but also that I will return *your* woman, as I have never been before."

The emperor sat on a dais in the Tokugawa audience chamber, but on a chair rather than a tatami mat; Ralph wondered if such a thing had ever been seen before. Around him, standing rather than kneeling, were grouped the great daimyos, as well as the ex-shogun, Tokugawa Yoshinobu, Lord of Mito—Keiko was not in fact a great deal older than the boy who had so rudely deposed him.

In front of the dais were gathered all the hatamotos and lesser daimyos; like their betters, they also stood, unable to resist shuffling their feet and glancing at each other in mystification at this totally un-Japanese method of conducting an audience, at this total lack of respect, as they saw it, for the august figure of the mikado. Ralph was at the very back of the throng, close by the doors, conspicuous because of his height. There was only one other man in the room even remotely as tall, Munetake, standing only a few feet away. Occasionally they turned their heads to look at each other, and Munetake would smile. Undoubtedly his act in bringing Alison with him had been sheer bravado and provocation; Ralph felt even Saigo knew this. But

Munetake's reputation for bravado and provocation was known throughout Japan, and was admired by most—it was in keeping with his reputation as the finest swordsman in the land. And besides, a man could do what he wished with his concubine—even take her on a campaign.

Thus if the big samurai had clearly been momentarily put out to learn that Ralph had gained another triumph, now he could again flaunt his own victory to the world.

And Ralph could do nothing but smile back, in public. Even as his heart pounded and the blood seemed almost to burn as it hurried through his arteries. He had not wasted the three days since the arrival of the northern Satsuma, had discovered that Alison was allowed a considerable amount of personal freedom and spent a portion of each day in the Edo markets, attended by but a single maid. He had encountered her there yesterday. They had exchanged nothing more than a quick glance, but the color in her cheeks had indicated she knew that he would not let her drift away without seeing her again, without speaking with her. And without rescuing her?

She would be there again this afternoon, if she wished any of those things to happen. And meanwhile, he was in the process of making other necessary arrangements. Now it was a business of *daring,* and strangely, of daring to face the woman more than any physical risks that might be involved. Because suppose she had *not* understood what had happened at Kagoshima, his helplessness, and thus had *not* forgiven him, remembered him only as the man who had hideously betrayed her?

An immense rustle spread through the chamber, and several men instinctively knelt—for to the amazement of all present, the emperor himself had gotten to his feet, and now advanced to the edge of the dais. As he looked over the assembly, those samurai who had knelt hastily stood again.

"My lords," Mutsuhito said, speaking in his usual quiet, but intensely clear voice. "My samurai! I have invited you here today because I know how many of you will be concerned at the events of the past few days. I would wish to set your minds at rest, and more, to enlist you upon my side in the great tasks which lie ahead of us." Another pause as he looked from face to face in front of him, to their great embarrassment. There was hardly a man present who would ever have seen an emperor before, much less have been in a room with him and listened to him speak.

"First," Mutsuhito went on, "I would have you know that in acting as I have done, I intend no disrespect to the shogun or to the great family whose name he bears. The Tokugawa have been the sure heart, as well as the strong right arm, of Japan for two hundred and fifty years. They ended a long period of internecine strife between the daimyos, because my ancestors, the then Sons of Heaven, lacked the strength themselves to do so."

The samurai gasped. No one had ever dared criticize even a dead mikado before.

"And so well did Iyeyasu and his great successors manage our affairs," Mutsuhito said, "that my more recent forebears were content to let them continue to deal with the day-to-day business of government. My own father was so disposed. But he saw, as we all can see, that it is the present and the future with which we have to contend, and not the past. We all know that the weight of the barbarians is pressing heavily upon our land. We have all our own differing concepts of how this threat should be met and repelled. It has come to us in Kyoto, many times in these last ten years, how divided were our daimyos on this subject, as it came to us also that the shogun could no longer command the undivided support of the people of Japan. This is our first necessity, to restore the unity of our people, of our samurai, that we may face the barbarians with a single front. We have discussed the matter with the shogun, and he willingly agrees that he should abdicate his responsibilities and retire into private life."

The silence was so acute it was possible to believe that no one in the room was even breathing. The eyes of the Satsuma and Cho-Shu men gleamed with triumph, as those of the Tokugawa were clouded with dismay, but now was no time for shouts of victory or cries of defeat.

"His excellency, Lord Yoshinobu, will resume the dominion of his lands of Mito," Mutsuhito said. "But more, as a retired shogun, as the *last* shogun, he will be accorded every honor that can be paid him by a grateful state. As of this moment, he is prince and elder statesman of Japan. Lord Yoshinobu in his gratitude would refuse these titles. More, he would renounce his very estates. And this gift we are pleased to accept, as revealing to ourselves a true and contrite heart, and a willingness to serve our great purpose. May his example shine as a beacon to all of my people. To all of my lords."

The emperor's head turned slowly to look at the daimyos grouped on his right, who exchanged glances, before Lord Shimadzu came forward to kneel before the boy who had taken such sudden control of all their destinies. "There is no daimyo in Japan, Majesty," Shimadzu said, "who is more loyal and devoted than myself, than all of my samurai. My lands are yours, in deed, Majesty, as they have always been yours in spirit."

"And mine," cried Lord Yoshimune, kneeling beside Shimadzu.

"And mine!"

"And mine!"

All the daimyos in the room were kneeling to make this extraordinary declaration.

Mutsuhito smiled. "We thank you, loyal subjects," he said. "And we accept your gracious gifts. These lands are now ours, by deed. But were they not always ours, by deed, and *law*? Our great ancestor bestowed them upon his sons and grandsons, for are not all of you also descended from our own great ancestor? That the fiefs of Japan have come to be regarded as the personal property of the daimyos is a mistake of history. Glad indeed am I that this mistake has now been corrected."

The kneeling lords exchanged glances, as did their samurai. They were just realizing that in their enthusiasm they had reduced themselves to poverty.

Mutsuhito continued to smile as he gestured them to their feet. "But fiefs have to be ruled, and how may we govern without your support and advice? Arise, my lords. I give you back your lands, to be held in fief of my goodwill. Be sure that such laws as I shall decree for the better organization and government of this realm will meet with your utter approval. As for Lord Yoshinobu, he also will receive back his lands, and the respect of all men. In only one matter will we yield to his desire to surrender his every right. Prince Yoshinobu would abandon this city of Edo, his ancestral home, and retire forever to his estates. This we are prepared to permit him to do, for it is in our mind that Kyoto, hallowed as it is, is yet not a suitable capital city for a Japan which is about to take its place in the community of nations. It is too far from the sea. Edo is here, with a magnificent natural harbor, and with the knowledge of government already within its walls. We now declare that from this moment forth, Edo will be our capital and our residence. And we further declare that Edo will have a new name. As Kyoto was, and will remain, the western capital, so do we rename this Tokyo, the eastern capital of Japan."

The samurai shuffled their feet, uncertain what had just happened, while Ralph again found himself marveling at the cool arrogance and political skill of this boy, who had just removed all the daimyos' power in law, returning only the substance, which, given the Japanese total respect for the law, could be withdrawn at any time. *To be held in fief of my goodwill.* And who was now calmly appropriating the ancient seat of the Tokugawa, and at the same time eliminating the memory of Iyeyasu's city from the minds of men.

"But that is all in the past," Mutsuhito said. "It is the future that more concerns me. We face, as I have said, a great and many-headed challenge. I have given this matter much thought and have come to certain decisions. The first is that if we are to rise above the level of mere servants of the white people; if we are to regain true jurisdiction over our own laws and customs, it must be the will and therefore the purpose of *all* our people, not merely of a few daimyos and their retainers. In this, as in all things, we must not be afraid to borrow from the barbarians, for assuredly there is a *source* of their strength, which we must discover and put to our own use. Thus I would form a government which shall express the hearts and minds of all my people, whether

samurai or scribes, merchants or . . ." For the first time
he hesitated, seeking to change his mind about what he
would have said. "Or daimyos," he finished. And then
once again stared from face to face, daring anyone
present to challenge him. "This is intended as no insult
to my samurai, yet must I make my intention clear. For
at least a part of that barbarian strength which is proving so obnoxious to us is the strength of money, money
to build great ships and employ great armies, and money
to buy great guns. We in Japan have far too long
despised money. We have made do without it for
centuries. Now it is necessary, for our future. Thus the
farmer and the manufacturer who can create wealth,
and the merchant who can order it and use it in the
international marketplaces, will be as important to the
future greatness of our country as the finest soldiers in
the world."

This time there was at last a murmur of protest,
instantly quelled as the emperor searched with his eyes
for the malcontents. Ralph observed that Munetake
had ceased to smile.

But Mutsuhito continued to do so. "When one com-
mences to put on a suit of armor," he said, "which will
make one invulnerable to anything an opponent may
do, it often happens that a strap is pulled too tight, or
that the iron of breastplate or greave scratches the skin
and causes a momentary discomfort. Yet once the ac-
coutrement is complete, how safe and secure do we feel,
and how comfortable as well. We are now engaged in
the process of arming all Japan, my samurai. *You* will
have to lead that process. You must have firm foundations upon which to plant your feet as you advance to
glory."

Once again he had entirely captivated them, and
there were nothing but nods of approval to be seen.

"Thus, as I have said," the emperor continued, "I
would have a parliament elected, as they do in the
barbarian countries, in which will be represented the
artisan as well as the samurai, the scholar as well as the
merchant. The exact form that such a parliament will
take, the form that the elections will take, you may
leave to myself and my lords to decide. I would but

have you know what is in my mind. And be certain always of the purpose behind my decisions, which is only that Japan should at the earliest possible moment throw off this tutelage which has been imposed upon us. Thus I come to the rest of my intentions. We know, and if we did not, we have received sufficient salutary lessons in the past five years to teach us, the strength of the barbarians in military matters. Only a few days ago a barbarian, commanding the troops of the Satsuma, was enabled to overcome a vastly superior force simply by understanding modern weaponry better than his opponents. These barbarians are not braver men than we, my samurai. There is no braver warrior in the world than a Japanese samurai. But it is a simple fact that no warrior, however brave, can oppose only a sword to a rifle capable of striking him down at half a mile's distance. Just as the strongest fortifications in the world are useless against red-hot shot lobbed over the battlements. But there is more. The mere possession of such weapons, the knowledge of how to fire them, is not sufficient. It is the knowledge of how to do this to the best advantage, again as the Satsuma have proved to us this last week, that matters. I have considered this matter long and hard. We must learn how to equal the best. And we may only do that by employing the best to teach us. It is my intention to create an army which will be the finest in the world. How may we do that? By employing officers of the army which is at present considered the finest in the world to teach us. We shall ask the French government to lend us military instructors. But we also intend to create the finest navy in the world. Thus we shall ask the British to lend us naval instructors, and more, to build our battleships for us, until we can build our own. Yet must we match the barbarians in spirit, also, and in what they call civilization. They contend that our laws are outmoded and out of keeping with modern thought, modern opinion. Our laws have stood us in sufficient stead for long enough, my samurai. Yet is there nothing that cannot be improved on this earth. To this end we have considered all the legal systems presently in use, and have come to the conclusion that that of Italy provides the fairest concept of justice we have been able to discover. We shall therefore send to Rome for lawyers to examine our legal system, with a view to reform, where it may be necessary."

They gaped at him. They had long lost their breaths at the sweeping nature of the measures he intended.

"But bringing foreigners to Japan is only half the battle ahead of us," the emperor said. "It is not sufficient for us to learn their techniques. We also need to know *them*, to understand the secrets of their lives. For two hundred years the Tokugawa, in their wisdom, forbade any Japanese to travel abroad on pain of death, for fear what they might learn in other lands would disturb the even tenor of our lives here at home. This was what undoubtedly would have happened, and what will happen. But it is now necessary *for* our lives to be disturbed, here at home, as it is going to happen anyway. The shoguns understood this, ever since the coming of the Americans, twelve years ago. And thus during the last ten years the law against travel has been abrogated, but still only official embassies have been permitted to visit Europe and America. We would alter that. We would wish as many Japanese as possible to travel, for as far as possible. We would have our young men attend the British and French naval and military colleges, that they may know what is being taught there, as we would have our scholars attend their universities, and our doctors attend their medical schools, and our lawyers attend their courts, that we may discover everything that makes the barbarians strong." He smiled. "And perhaps some of the things that make them weak. We have much to do, my samurai. The future calls us, and the prize is great. What lies ahead will not be easy of accomplishment, and it will not be to the liking of us all. Yet *must* it be done, for the sake of our children and our grandchildren. My samurai, my hatamotos, my daimyos, will you follow your emperor into the dawn of a new age for Japan?"

The cries of "Banzai!" continued to ring out long after Mutsuhito and his lords left the chamber, and the hatamotos gathered in the gardens to exchange their

views and try to order the thoughts which tumbled
through their reeling minds.

"A fine speech," Inouye declared, and for the first
time since the fall of Shimonoseki, he embraced Ralph.
"His majesty intends to bring American liberalism home
to Japan. I know it. And I welcome it. I have long felt
how sad it is that many of our most acute brains are
prevented from playing any part in governing our
country, simply because perhaps they might not be the
sons of samurai."

"And to send our young men abroad, that is a splendid concept," Ito agreed. "Truly will we see a new
nation arising. And you played a great part in bringing
it about, Freeman San. You must be a proud man
today."

Ralph supposed he was right; he wondered if the
emperor could have risked being quite so forceful, so
early in his reign, had the Tokugawa not just suffered a
signal defeat. And he also knew that Ito and Inouye
were good fellows, representative of all that was best in
the samurai, and that they were genuinely pleased at
the way things had turned out. Well, so was he. Or he
would be, when he had the time to think about it. And
when, he knew in his heart, he had overcome the slight
feeling of pique, or was it concern, that the emperor,
having paid tribute to his skill, had not then invited
him, and perhaps other Americans as well, to help train
the new imperial army of which he had spoken. But if
Mutsuhito had not taken to him as perhaps he might
have wished, the omission had at least simplified any
doubts he might have had about what lay ahead. Right
now he wished only to escape and gain the bazaars; the
emperor had kept talking for far too long. He smiled at
his friends, and made his excuses, and hurried across
the trampled grass, and encountered Saigo, just leaving
the palace.

"Well, Saigo San," he said. "A momentous day."

Saigo did not look half so happy as Ito and Inouye.
"Momentous indeed," he agreed. "The boy would accomplish a revolution with words."

"Do you doubt he means to carry out his intentions?"

"No, Freeman San, I do not doubt that for a moment. What I would question is the *meaning* of his intentions."

"I would say you may rest easy on that score, Saigo San," Ralph said. "His every sentence indicated his determination to deal with the barbarians as rapidly as possible."

"You think so?" Saigo inquired. "Does he not know that every word he spoke today will soon be reported to the British consul, and the American?"

"I am sure he does know that, Saigo San. And perhaps intends his words as a warning to them. But at the same time, in calling upon them to assist him in modernizing Japan, he is offering a powerful temptation. They will feel they will also have the influencing of this new Japan. And think on this, Saigo San. Try to imagine how long and how deeply his majesty must have thought on these matters, to have so complete a program ready so immediately. He is but seventeen years old. At what time did he start considering the problems of Japan? Ten, twelve? Or even before then? Has any emperor in the past had a European tutor? And more, try to imagine at what age he made the decision that he would end the shogunate the moment he became emperor. Because this has been no hasty action. This has been too long planned. And this must have been *his* decision alone. Even if his father saw to his education and planted these thoughts in his mind, knowing that Japan was approaching a decisive moment in her history, *he* cannot have expected to die at this moment, and no father could recommend to a seventeen-year-old son so bold a course, when his grasp of affairs could only improve with waiting a few years. Saigo San, I would say to you that we are dealing with no ordinary man here."

Saigo regarded him for several seconds; then he gave a brief smile. "We are dealing with a god, are we not, Freeman San?" The smile faded, the face resumed its more normally sardonic expression. "He would have had you in his service, also."

"Me?" Ralph's heart gave a curious leap.

"Oh, indeed. Are you not the most famous barbarian

in Japan at this moment? But I would not let him take you."

"*You* refused, Saigo? Why?"

"Because, Freeman San, your home, and your place, lies in Kagoshima. With the Satsuma. Who can tell when we shall need you again?"

Ralph frowned at him. "Against whom? There is no one left to fight." His frown deepened. "Unless you would tilt against the emperor himself."

"The emperor, for all the stature that he clearly possesses, is but a boy, as you have just reminded me," Saigo said. "And thus is liable to be influenced by older, perhaps less wise advisers. This is a matter which must be closely watched by all responsible men. He said a great deal today, and not all of it makes my heart jump for joy. He wishes, he says, to drive out the barbarians. This is my sole reason for living. And I do not argue with him when he says that to achieve this, Japan must become a modern state, must have guns and ships to equal the Europeans'. I do not even argue that to accomplish this it may be necessary to smile on them for a season and accept their tutelage, again, for a season. And I accept that purchasing weapons and munitions will cost money, and that therefore money must be created in greater quantity than we have ever thought necessary before. For this it may well be necessary to exalt the merchant somewhat, perhaps even ask his advice in business matters. Perhaps it is even possibly worthwhile to ask the opinions of scribes and poets, although Japan has survived well enough in the past without the aid of such impractical dreamers. These steps may all be necessary; however it may also be necessary to walk amid such imponderables with the greatest of care. But there are other things his majesty said, or perhaps did not say, which concern me greatly. You understand that I speak in complete confidence, between you and me, Freeman San."

"Of course."

"Well, then, I would ask you to consider *this*. What word was it his majesty left unsaid, and inserted 'daimyos' in its place?"

*   *   *

Ralph left the citadel for the streets of Edo. Saigo
had not in fact made any comment he might not have
made himself. What *had* Mutsuhito had in mind? Or
who? Because, dared he think of a word, the attitude of
the samurai to the honin and the eta was very similar to
that of the white men of America's South to the Negro.
But that thought was incomprehensible. What possible
value could Mutsuhito hope to gain from including a
honin in his parliament—not to mention the storm of
discontent such an act would arouse. On the other hand,
if he intended truly to liberalize his country, well, surely
not even the samurai could grumble if he attempted
somewhat to alleviate the lot of the unhappy slaves—at
least, perhaps, remove them from their masters' powers of life and death over them. This would certainly be
in keeping with, in fact be necessary for, a nation attempting to become a modern, civilized power.

And no matter what Mutsuhito had almost said, or
even what he intended, the possibility that in certain
circumstances Saigo might actually take up arms against
his emperor, under whatever specious disguise, was
absurd; for one thing, Shimadzu would never let him.

And after all, Mutsuhito had asked for *him*. The
thought gave him a warm glow. As if it could ever be.
As if his plans were not already well laid. As if all Japan
would not soon hate him.

"Mr. Freeman?"

He had arrived at the appointed street corner, close
by the markets, surrounded by bustling Japanese. And
Mr. Coates from the American embassy was waiting for
him.

They strolled side by side, the armored samurai and
the gray-suited Yankee. They both came from Rhode
Island. "I suppose you have an idea why I asked for
this meeting?"

"I've a notion you'd like to leave Japan," Coates said.
"I have to admit that I can't altogether see why, Captain.
I'd say you have a pretty good setup here. A hero, and
all. And a wife and children too, I understand. And a
good position."

"I would wish asylum for my family as well," Ralph

told him. "Provided there will be asylum for myself, of course."

"There's the problem, Mr. Freeman. There's no statute of limitations on murder. Or treason."

"I can prove that I did not commit treason," Ralph said. "And I shot Hardy in self-defense. All I ask is a fair trial in a proper court of law."

Coates plucked at his lower lip.

"I can also provide the State Department, and the War Department, with a great deal of very important information about the intentions of the Japanese," Ralph continued. "Everything here is not as it seems."

Coates shrugged. "We're beginning to appreciate that. Well, Captain, I'll put what you say to the consul general. I doubt he'll be able to make a decision without referring to Washington. But that's going to take some time."

"No good," Ralph said. "The decision must be made now. If I am going to leave Japan, it must be within the next two or three days. There is an American vessel in the harbor now. That is the ship I would have to travel on."

Coates frowned at him. "What's the rush, after seven years? Sure, I don't imagine you're the most popular man in the world with the Tokugawa, but they'd not dare try to do anything about it right now."

"I am not afraid of the vengeance of the Tokugawa, Mr. Coates. The rush is simply that there is someone I mean to take with me. Someone who is currently here in Tokyo, but will not remain here very much longer. Once this person leaves Tokyo, my reason for returning to America no longer exists."

"We're talking about a woman?"

"That's right."

"The Englishwoman? The one you saved on the beach? And who got you away from the British?"

"That's right," Ralph said again.

"Well, well. Seems to me you're bucking a whole lot of laws and customs, Captain. We've heard she's married to a samurai."

"Not married," Ralph said. "She was *given* to him."

"Really? Well, I can appreciate why you would want to leave Japan." Coates pulled his nose. "Captain, I'm

going to do my damnedest for you. I watched that
battle last week, and it was the prettiest piece of work I
ever saw. What's more, I think you told that court-
martial the truth. I think, having watched you at work,
that if you'd wanted to hit that American ship back in
sixty-two, you'd have done it. And you'd have given the
British a bit of what-for, too, if you'd had the intention.
As for Jefferson Hardy's death, well, there do seem to
be a whole lot of unanswered questions about that. You
let me talk with the consul general. Meet me here
tomorrow, same time, and I'll give you his answer. But I
would say you could start making plans for tomorrow
night." He held out his hand.

Ralph squeezed the fingers. "Thanks."

"It'll be a pleasure. There's just one more thing; what
about the little lady down in Kagoshima?"

"I'm not forgetting her. She's my wife, and she's also
Saigo Takamori's niece. No matter what I do, she won't
be harmed. Nor will anyone stand in the way of her
leaving Japan when I send for her."

Coates nodded thoughtfully. "You just want to
remember, Captain, that bigamy is one crime there
won't be any pardon for back in the States."

But those were details. Important details, to be sure,
but no more than details, compared with the getting of
Alison away from Munetake, away from Japan. His
heart seemed to be jumping about his chest in anticipation as he entered the bazaar. It was incredible that he
should be going home after seven years—and yet that
mattered absolutely nothing compared with having Alison once more at his side.

He strode past the stalls selling sweets and stalls selling animals, stalls selling bolts of silk and chests and
boxes made of lacquered wood, and stalls selling little
jars of creams and unguent boxes made of porcelain
and decorated with the most exquisite cloisonné work,
all blues and greens and purples. Then there were
sandal sellers and girdle sellers and sword sellers, mixed
in with the inevitable jugglers and fortune-tellers, who
would spin a metal cylinder containing about twenty
different fortunes wrapped around spindles, and invite

you to take your pick. That all Japan was thus reduced to having one of twenty possible characters and futures did not seem absurd to anyone, and besides, if the fortune did not please you, you could always visit a pagoda, where there was sure to be an avenue of sacred trees, and by tying your fortune to a branch, make the reverse of what it had said come true. Trees in the vicinity of temples were always covered with little bits of white paper, almost like extra blossoms. But this was the Japanese way, to make one's own fortune, by whatever means came to hand. It was not a subject in which Ralph wished to dabble today, because today he *was* making his own fortune.

And mixed in with all the trade and all the chicanery were hairdressers and surgeons, dentists and chiropodists, all performing their skills with a total lack of hygiene or of privacy, and all inflicting suffering which was endured without even a grimace by their various clients and patients. Dogs barked and ran to and fro, birds chirped from their cages, and everywhere the brilliant colors of the rustling kimonos and the gently twirling silk parasols dominated the scene. Except where an occasional samurai marched through the center of the throng, hissing nostrils and stamping feet, eyes flashing from side to side as he dared any of the lower orders even to meet his eyes.

Ralph wondered if, even after the emperor had perhaps called some of these merchants and vendors to his parliament, they would ever be able to look a samurai in the eye. Well, he thought, *he* neither hissed nor stamped, nor perpetually challenged, but there was no one in all Tokyo who did not know who the tall white man in the green armor was, and who did not seek to bow low before him.

But he sought only a single figure, and there she was, buying silk, her maid at her elbow. He stood behind her and said, "Alison."

She turned. Today she wore no veil, and her hair was dressed in the Japanese style, gathered in a huge auburn bun on the top of her head. He had almost forgotten what she looked like, and would not have recognized her but for her hair and her height. Now he wondered how he could ever have lost the instant image of that lovely face. Nor had she changed. He looked for lines of worry or distress, of misery and of pain, and could not find them.

"Captain Freeman," she said. "What a fine samurai you make. And what a great warrior you have become." She spoke in English. Nor did her maid show any alarm at his appearance, but merely withdrew a few steps. He had been expected.

"Captain Freeman?" he asked.

She gazed at him, twin spots of pink gathering in her cheeks.

"You knew I would come for you," he said.

"I knew you would come, Captain Freeman."

He gazed at her, his arms threatening to move of their own volition, to embrace her, to hug her against him. She gazed back at him, her face expressionless, save for the flush.

"If you watch where I go," he said, "and follow discreetly, I will lead you to a house where we can be alone together."

"I do not think that would be either safe or wise, Captain Freeman."

"Alison . . . do you know what happened two years ago?"

"Munetake has told me of it. I think the truth. I know that you were prevented from returning."

"And you still hate me for that?"

"I do not hate you, Captain Freeman. I know how you fought, and I can imagine your despair; I have felt something of that. But anyway, a woman does not hate the man she loves, no matter what he does. I told you once that I love you. I love you still."

"Oh, Alison . . ." Now his arms did move.

She shook her head. "But it can never be, Ralph."

She had called him Ralph, and there were tears in her eyes. "You mean because I am married? Alison, I was married to you before I ever laid eyes on Saigo Suiko. That was a marriage I had to undergo, to preserve my life, and yours. Alison, if we love each other . . ."

Now at last her expression changed. Color flared

into her cheeks, and her nostrils flared. "It cannot *be*, Mr. Freeman."

"Because of the risks which are involved? Listen to me, Alison. It has all been arranged. I have made my peace with the United States government. At least, they have promised me a fair hearing, and I can ask for nothing more than that. If you will come with me tomorrow, we shall be on board an American ship tomorrow night, where no Japanese may ever touch us. We shall be going home to America, Alison. Home to resume our lives together. To *begin* our lives together." He watched a tear roll down her cheek. "We can do it, Alison. We will do it."

"And the children?" she asked.

He frowned at her.

"We have a son," she said. "A little boy with your eyes and hair and nose, Ralph. I have called him Jeremy."

"Jeremy? My God. Oh, Alison. But . . . where is he?"

"Here, in Tokyo."

"Then you can bring him with us. Alison—"

"I have also, in my belly, another child."

He bit his lip. "Munetake's?"

"By law, they are both Munetake's. By nature, they are both mine. But I promise you that your son is in every way treated as the son of a Japanese hatamoto and as a future samurai himself. You need have no fear for him. And I am sure that one day you will be proud of him. As no doubt you will be proud of your legal children."

He stared at her, while his stomach filled with lead. As he had known without admitting it to himself, two years was too long a time. But he could not just abandon his dream so quickly. "Do you think I care about Munetake's child?" he asked. "As you have just said, it will also be *your* child, and therefore mine. *I* will educate it to the best of my ability, and treat it as my own. Alison, we will be able to work it out. But *you* are the key to the situation. You are the one who must be gotten to safety. You and Jeremy. Believe me, there will be no problem with *my* children. I have done Lord

Shimadzu and Saigo a great service. I am sure they will do everything in their power to assist me."

He dared not mention Suiko.

"I am sure they would assist you, as far as they could," she said. "But not to break the law. And the children, my children, are Munetake's by law, Ralph. To take them away from him would be a breach of bushido." She saw the expression on his face, and rested her hand on his arm, at the same time glancing left and right at the interested passersby, observing the two barbarians in Japanese dress, holding such an animated conversation. "Ralph, please listen to me and try to understand. I love you. I think I loved you from the moment I set eyes on you, in San Francisco, ten years ago. Certainly I learned to love you in Shimonoseki. Those two years when you were able to come to me once every week will remain the happiest of my life, always, and that I was able to help you at the end, and we were able to be married, still remains the greatest treasure of my life. I will always love you. But fate has decreed that we should travel in opposite directions. Ralph, forget about me. I know you think it impossible now. But as you have survived in the past, so will you survive in the future. As you say, you have done a considerable service to your lord. And all Japan is now changing. There will be no more civil wars, and there will be no more foreign bombardments. Thus there is no need for you to stay here. You say you have made your peace with your government. Ralph, if you cannot accept what fate has mapped out for you here, then go home. Leave this place, where you have never been happy. Turn your back on it and on everything that has ever happened here. Live again, as what you are, an American officer. And *be* happy."

He stared at her. "I could almost believe you are trying to tell me you have found happiness with Munetake," he said.

She would not lower her eyes. Instead she raised her chin defiantly. "Yes," she said. "Yes, I have found happiness with Munetake. I bear his child. I . . . I love him."

"I do not believe you," he said. "You are lying. He

has some hold over you, and you fear him. Leave Japan? Leave *you*? As long as you remain in Japan, so shall I. And one day we *will* be together again."

"That cannot be," she cried, for the first time raising her voice and giving a quick flush as heads turned toward them. "It can never be. Ralph, I shall never look upon your face again. Believe me, for the sake of God."

She turned and walked into the crowd.

He stared behind her, quite unable to believe his eyes or his ears, every instinct crying out for him to rush behind her, and seize her, and carry her by force if need be to the American consulate, if he had to fight every inch of the way.

But there had been no indecision in what she had said. He had been expected, and she had determined on what she would say and do. Because she feared for him. Of course. She feared that Munetake would seek him out and cut him down, as he would by law be entitled to do. Indeed, as her maid had overseen the entire meeting, was it not possible that Munetake was also lurking around some corner, and that she had been only playacting, to save both their lives?

Well, then, why not seek out Munetake and challenge him? Seize one of his servants, as he himself had explained how to do, and cut off the poor man's head, and stick his ko-kotana, nestling in his waistband, in the fellow's ear, and have the head delivered to Hokkaido. Would Saigo, who would not even let him go to the service of the empire because of his value to the Satsuma, condemn him, and risk losing his services?

Except in order to save his life. To face Munetake, sword in hand . . . Were it pistol in hand, now, things would be different. That would not be a duel, it would be murder. And would it not also be murder to face him with a sword? His own murder?

Now he did walk like a samurai, striding past the stalls, sending people scurrying from his path, while his hand closed on the hilt of his sword. He was rich, he was famous, he was healthy, and he was happily married, and he yearned for the one thing he could not have.

And he was afraid. Could that possibly be true? It could be explained, but only to himself. He was not afraid of dying, sword in hand, facing the monster who had so distorted his life. He was not even afraid of the moment of death, the sharp pain that would follow the cut of the sword. But he was afraid to die and abandon not only Alison and Jeremy, the son he had never seen, but also Suiko and William and Maureen, while there was yet a chance of saving them all, for a better and happier life. It was not a point of view that would be appreciated by any Japanese, or indeed by many Americans either, he supposed. But yet was it a Japanese point of view. To wait, and watch, and time his move, however long it might take for the right moment to arrive. For what was a year, two years, five years, ten, even? If they loved, and they did. And ten years gave time for a great many things to happen. And a great many things *would* happen, he had no doubt at all, under the impetus given by the new emperor. Alison thought there could be no escape for either of them, at least no escape which would permit them to live and love as they both wanted—and, again the coward, he had been unable to admit that he planned to take Suiko as well. There the fault was entirely his. Because where *could* they live, and be accepted, on such terms? He was not a Mormon. So that had to be worked out as well, in a more careful fashion than he had done so far.

So she could wait as well, without even knowing she was doing so. As would he. But he could not wait in Tokyo, seeing Munetake every day, and perhaps seeing her as well. Knowing she was there. That was too acute a torment for the most patient, the most determined of men.

"There is nothing more to be done here," he told Saigo next morning. "We, you and your lord, have accomplished everything that you dreamed of, and more. You have no more need of me at the moment. I would take my riflemen and return to Kagoshima. I have been away too long."

"And you find the presence of Munetake and his wife too great a temptation?"

How much did he know? Ralph refused to lower his gaze. "Why, that too," he agreed.

"It is always sad," Saigo remarked, "when a man cannot be content with the things a bountiful fate has bestowed upon him, but must always seek after forbidden fruit."

"And have you, Lord Saigo, never sought after forbidden fruit? Do we stand here now because you and your lord have always been content with your lot?"

Saigo studied him for several seconds, as was his habit, before replying. "You are too bold, Freeman San," he said at last. "Did I not love you as a brother . . ."—he smiled—"as a *nephew*," he added, "then I suspect I would hate you as a rival. But you have my permission to take your riflemen and go home to your wife. I know she awaits your coming."

Ralph bowed and left the room. On the veranda he saw Munetake, walking with some other hatamoto. The two of them had not exchanged a word in all the week they had been together in Tokyo. They had only gazed at each other and smiled. Almost like lovers, he thought. Now they did so again. Because now he could no longer doubt that Munetake knew of yesterday's meeting, as he had known it was *going* to happen, before it had taken place, and therefore had probably even known what his mistress had been going to say—why else would the maidservant have been totally unconcerned? Thus *he* could have been caught in the act of approaching another man's woman, had Munetake chosen, and been cut down without any man daring to interfere. But that might have been to incur the disfavor of Saigo and Shimadzu, however justified the deed. Munetake had preferred to demonstrate his total triumph by the utter mastery he had established over Alison.

Ralph turned away and went down the steps, gave the order for his men to assemble, for his horse to be saddled. But he could not leave Tokyo without first returning to the corner by the bazaar, where Coates waited.

"Great news, Captain," the secretary said. "The consul thinks like I do, and everything has been arranged. We didn't think you'd want to make your move in daylight, though, so the captain of the *Margarita* is expecting you sometime tonight. The tide will be right at one o'clock tomorrow morning, so try to be on board by midnight."

"My thanks, Mr. Coates," Ralph said, "but forget it."

"Eh?" Coates was astounded.

"I've changed my mind," Ralph said. "Seems I'm going to become a Japanese, after all."

—13—

THE REBEL

"Freeman has left Tokyo," Munetake announced. "But not Japan. He has returned to Kagoshima. You knew of this?"

"No," Alison said.

"You broke your word to me."

"No," she said.

"What did you say to him?"

"That I loved you, and was content with you, and that I would never leave you. As I promised to say."

"And he accepted this?"

"No. So then I told him that I carry your child."

Munetake stared at her, brows drawing together into a frown and then slowly clearing again. "This is true?"

"A samurai's woman does not lie, my lord."

She had been kneeling before him. Now he held her elbows to raise her and gaze into her eyes. "Then am I the happiest man in the world," he declared. "You have made me so, Alison. It was wrong of me to distrust you. I know you for what you are, a pearl among women." He held her close, Western style, as he knew she liked. "And do not suppose it is your lot merely to be the concubine of a hatamoto all your life. What has happened here this last week is but the beginning of a revolution, an upheaval in the affairs of men such as no Japanese has ever seen before. It will set man against man, and even brother against brother. I know these things, I feel them in my bones."

"You paint a somber picture, my lord. What, then, will become of us?"

Munetake gave a great shout of laughter. "It is at such times that a man truly makes his own fortune, by his courage, and his wisdom, and the strength of his own right arm. Toyotomi Hideyoshi was one such, who rose to power the last time Japan was so convulsed. My courage and my wisdom are not inferior to his, and my right arm is the strongest in the land. Truly, for me it will be a time of greatness." He hugged her, and then released her. "And for you," he said. "Because you will stand at my side, always."

She bowed her head. "As my lord wishes."

Munetake walked to the door, and there stopped and turned to face her again. Now his frown was back. "Did Freeman not ask you to run away with him? Did he not tell you that there was an American ship in the harbor waiting to give him, and you, passage back to the United States?"

"Yes, my lord," Alison said. "He told me these things, and asked me to run away with him."

"And you refused? Ha. You were sensible, my Alison. Because I knew of these things, and I had my people waiting to cut you down, cut you both down, on the very quayside, had you tried it."

He closed the door behind him, leaving Alison gazing at it. Yes, my lord, she thought as tears rolled down her cheeks. I knew that also.

It was early May before Ralph regained Kyushu, and there it was high summer. But then, it was always high summer in Kyushu.

Lord Shimadzu had of course sent messengers home the moment his victory had been gained over the shogun's army, with news not only of that but of the amazing aftermath. The people of Kyushu, like the people of all the fiefs through which Ralph passed on his way home, were totally uncertain as to what such an immense change in their lives could possibly mean. The mikados had not merely lived in seclusion since the beginning of the Tokugawa shogunate. Their eclipse as physical rulers of the empire had happened long before even that, and dated back to the year 858 of the Western Christian era, when the Fujiwara clan had gained complete dominance over the imperial family. But even before then the pernicious habit of early abdication and subsequent minorities had become

commonplace. Down to that momentous year, the retired emperors had themselves in most cases acted as
regents for their sons or nephews; but increasingly
often the retiring mikado had preferred to devote himself to poetry and meditation, and the regency had
been placed in the hands of an uncle or cousin. In 858,
the Fujiwara, married closely into the imperial house,
had merely turned a farce into a legality, by remaining
as regents even after the then emperor, Seiwa, had
attained his majority. Thus the revolution that had just
taken place was actually the overturning of one thousand years of custom and imperial eclipse.

Fujiwara Motosune had not been the first shogun.
The title had not been considered in those far-off days.
He had called himself kampaku, which meant, simply,
regent. And in fact the Fujiwara had always ruled from
the imperial capital, which they had removed from
Nara to Kyoto, and had worked very closely with the
emperors, both actual and retired. It was not until the
Fujiwara strain had itself weakened, and after a bitter
struggle for supremacy between the Taira and Minamoto
clans in the twelfth Christian century, that the regent
himself had been rendered ineffectual. But because of
the Japanese reverence for history and tradition, the
title had been retained; only now, as well as an emperor and a regent for the emperor, there was to be
someone who ruled for them both. The victor in the
great civil war, Minamoto Yoritomo, whose brother
Yoshitsune was the most revered soldier in all Japanese
history, had had to find for himself a new title, and this
he had done by calling himself Barbarian Subduing
Great General, or, in Japanese, Sei-i-tai-Shogun. Thus,
if the possession of the title had changed families several times in another series of civil wars, and the immortal Toyotomi Hideyoshi, not being of noble blood, had
even for a while suspended the shogunate and had
ruled simply as military dictator before his death had
resulted in the triumph of Tokugawa Iyeyasu, the system of government which had just ended had itself
obtained for very nearly eight hundred years.

Until swept away almost in the twinkling of an eye,
the wave of a young man's fist. Ralph supposed the

only possible analogy in the Christian world would be for a teenage pope to be elected in Rome, and for him suddenly to assume a temporal role and announce himself to be emperor of all Europe. Such a concept was almost impossible to envisage. What had happened was no less difficult for the Japanese to imagine. And yet, certainly in Kyushu, where the shogunate had for so long been an object of hatred, the momentous event was welcomed. Too much so, Ralph feared. Mutsuhito was by rights a god, as his ancestors had all also been Sons of Heaven. But they had been moribund, uninterested Sons of Heaven. Now of a sudden the god had descended from his heaven and was walking the earth. Clearly there was nothing he could not do. At least in the eyes of his people. What would happen when they found out that he was but a man after all?

Thoughts which had to concern him now, as he had made his decision. This was to be his land, no doubt for the rest of his life. Therefore these were to be his people, their problems his problems—and their god king, his shining beacon, as well.

As if such things as kings and reforms, ambitions and even dreams, should concern a hatamoto who was a national hero, at least in Kyushu, and who had the soft arms of Saigo Suiko to welcome him home.

"I dreamed that perhaps my lord would not return."

She knelt beside him, naked, as she knew he liked, and gazed at him with that unblinking interest which was so disconcerting.

"I told you that I would."

"And yet I feared. I would have liked to be at your side, my lord, to watch you scatter the Tokugawa." The shogunate might be a thing of the past, but she could still fill her voice with hatred and contempt when she uttered the name. She had been born a Saigo and a Satsuma, and educated to be nothing else.

"It was a bloody business." He laid his finger on her chin, as he knew *she* liked, and with his other hand ruffled William's hair. Suiko had even come to permit this most un-Japanese way of pampering her children.

Jeremy, he thought, was a year older than William.

No, the difference was a year and a half. He would be attempting to walk, and talk.

Suiko was frowning. "You do not wish to speak of it?"

"I will, if you wish."

"But a shadow crossed your face," she insisted.

His head turned sharply. How much did she *know*? Only what Saigo himself might have chosen to tell her. Or her sisters? Presumably all Kagoshima knew at least about the beginning of the business. "I am a man with many memories, Suiko. Not all of them are happy."

"I have no memories," she reminded him. "Save of you, and me. Of us."

"Of us." His fingers slid around her neck into her hair and gently brought her face down to his, to be kissed. "There will be many more of those, Suiko," he said. "And they will all be pleasant ones."

"And you will go away no more, my lord?"

"No more, Suiko. You have my word."

"Until Lord Saigo has need of you to fight another battle," she said, nestling her head on his shoulder and reaching across him to give the little boy an admonitory pat; he was fond of attempting to join in their embrace.

"Not even then, my sweet Suiko," Ralph promised her. "There is no one left to fight."

"Those tactics you employed outside Edo," Saigo Takamori said. "I have been thinking about them a great deal, Freeman San, and frankly, I do not see how any army could have withstood them. How do your barbarian armies not destroy each other totally in seconds?" He had returned from Tokyo as filled with restless energy, and equally restless plans for the future, as ever.

"Because no modern barbarian army would confront its enemy standing in parallel lines at a distance of no more than half a mile," Ralph replied. "They used to, in the days when they were armed only with muskets, which could fetch no more than half that distance. Nowadays, battles must be fought from cover, and by maneuvering. Do not mistake me. The loss of life in a modern battle is far greater than in any ancient one. Certainly among the victors."

Saigo nodded thoughtfully. "I can see that. In a Japanese battle, nearly all the dead are killed in the pursuit, after one side has broken and fled. But if both sides have rifles ... if they take cover, as you say, and just fire away at each other, how does one side ever win?"

"It is not quite so simple as that, Saigo San. The ultimate victory still rests with the side which finally charges home and drives the other army from its position or puts it to flight. This is where artillery and maneuvering come in. Artillery to blast great holes in your opponents' ranks, and thereby create a weak spot, and flanking marches to get around behind him, or at least threaten to do so, and thereby force him to withdraw from his prepared position. The concept of a battle being fought in the course of a few hours in a single day is gone forever. Battles now continue over several days at a time, each general maneuvering to place his enemy at a disadvantage."

"It sounds more like a game of go, than a battle," Saigo grumbled.

"Except that it is being played with the lives of men," Ralph reminded him. "And sometimes even of countries. And that, at the end, it is the general who makes the decision to charge home at the right moment who carries the day."

"Yes," Saigo said, frowning. "And these Frenchmen whom his majesty is employing to train his armies, they will know of these things?"

"Undoubtedly. The French have long been the most famous soldiers in Europe. Do you know what they call your Toyotomi Hideyoshi in Europe? The Japanese Napoleon."

"I have heard the name Napoleon," Saigo admitted. "He was a Frenchman?"

"I think, technically, an Italian. But a Frenchman by adoption. He was the greatest soldier of modern times."

"The greatest *European* soldier," Saigo corrected him. Ralph smiled and bowed.

"The entire concept of an imperial army is strange to

us," Saigo went on. "There has not been such a thing in Japan for a thousand years."

"You must have had a unified force to repel the Mongols?"

Saigo shook his head. "We fought as we have always fought. The daimyo in whose territory the enemy sought to come ashore, which in the case of the Mongols happened principally to be Cho-Shu, repelled them; it is from those days that the tradition arose of slaying all men who attempt to land on the shores of Cho-Shu. Certainly the then lord of Cho-Shu called upon his allies for assistance; there were Satsuma warriors on the beaches outside of Shimonoseki for that battle, but each daimyo led his own troops independently of any other. At that time, of course, the shogunate was weak, and Japan was ruled by the Hojo family. But they did little. The nearest approach to a national army in recent times was when Toyotomi Hideyoshi decided to invade Korea. He led a vast force, composed of men from all the clans. But the clans marched under their own banners and were commanded by their own generals."

"And Hideyoshi failed of his purpose," Ralph pointed out.

"He died before he could complete his project," Saigo said severely.

"Of course," Ralph agreed. He had forgotten that failure was not a word which could be used in Japan, except immediately before the performance of seppuku. "But yet, Saigo San, a national army is an essential in a modern state."

"Why?" Saigo asked. "For Japan at least, I should have thought a national navy was even more important."

"Does his majesty not intend that also?"

"Then why an army as well? I am sure *he* does not mean to invade Korea. And if the navy were strong enough to defeat any attacking force at sea, well, the daimyos could take care of those who came ashore, as they have done in the past. These things concern me, Freeman San. They concern me very much." He clapped Ralph on the shoulder. "But the Satsuma, at the least, will also have a modern army, eh?"

*   *   *

Saigo was suspicious of the whole concept being presented to him, whereas the rest of his people, even including Lord Shimadzu, were overcome with wonder. But Lord Shimadzu clearly aged with every passing day. Keiko had not, after all, executed his younger son—revealing a streak of humanity, a lack of ruthlessness, which no doubt accounted for his easy acceptance of his enforced abdication—and there were other youthful lords waiting to rule Kyushu in his place. But no one could doubt that the great general was the one who would have the power. Shimadzu had raised Saigo from a hatamoto to be commander of all the Satsuma armies, and the Satsuma were the greatest of all the clans. Perhaps that was why he was suspicious; he saw his greatness being eclipsed—the emperor, equally jealous of his prerogatives, had not invited Saigo Takamori to be commander of the imperial army.

And what could Saigo's protégé do, in turn, save drill and train and educate the Satsuma army against an event which was unthinkable? And writhe in agony whenever he dreamed of Alison. Or indeed of the home which he now doubted he would ever see again—and had no desire ever to see again, save on his own terms.

And be happy, at least momentarily, holding Suiko in his arms. Within six months of the fall of the shogunate, she was again pregnant.

And within six months of the fall of the shogunate and the assumption of temporal power by the mikado, they became aware of the far-reaching effects of the reforms he had so casually introduced.

They watched, from the battlements of the citadel, the Rising Sun banners of the entourage approaching. An imperial embassy headed by . . . Inouye Bunta?

"Prince Inouye, if you please," Inouye said, but he smiled as he spoke. "His majesty would match the barbarians, where it seems princes are common enough."

"And you have left the service of Lord Yoshimune?" Ralph asked in wonder.

"Both Ito and I have done so, on invitation from his majesty."

"Then Ito is also a prince?"

"Of course. Ito is going to command the imperial navy. I also have been given naval rank—that is, I am an admiral, because I have sailed upon the oceans. But my duties will be more land-bound, I can promise you that."

"And Lord Yoshimune does not object?"

"Lord Yoshimune is proud that we have been singled out," Inouye explained. "For how may a man do more for his country than serve his emperor in person?"

"You have not told us whether or not we should kowtow before you," Saigo remarked dryly.

Inouye gave him a bow. "You will not, General. The kowtow is a thing of the past."

"Because it is not practiced by barbarians?"

"Partly."

"And have you come this great distance to tell us that we are no longer Japanese, but barbarians in disguise?"

Inouye frowned at him, then glanced at Ralph. Clearly he had not anticipated such hostility. "I have come here to inform Lord Shimadzu of certain reforms which his majesty has promulgated, and in which he hopes and anticipates the men of Satsuma will fully participate."

"But not to kowtow to our lord," Saigo said.

Inouye gazed at him. "No," he said at last. "Not to kowtow to your lord."

"His majesty has decided upon a number of decrees," Inouye told Lord Shimadzu and his assembled hata-motos. "Which he would have me relate to you, confident that they will please you, as steps in creating the greater Japan which is the dream of all of us." He paused and looked over the anxious faces, smiled at them. Inouye had an especially benevolent face, increased by the growing whiteness of his mustache. Mutsuhito had clearly chosen his representative with his usual care.

"His majesty wishes me, first of all, to make clear to you that these decrees are but interim measures, pending the summoning of the first Japanese parliament. Writs for this are at present being prepared, but it will take some time for his majesty and his advisers to complete their task, and his majesty is anxious to press ahead with such measures as are necessary to ensure the future prosperity of the empire."

He paused, and again surveyed the faces in front of him, which were registering total stupefaction; there was no one present, save Ralph, and Inouye himself, who actually had the slightest idea what a parliament even meant.

Inouye continued. "Second, it is his majesty's wish that his reign be known as 'Meiji,' or 'Enlightened Rule.' "

This time the samurai could smile their approval. The naming of a reign was more in keeping with the traditions by which their lives were governed.

"Now, as to the decrees themselves," Inouye said. "It is first of all his majesty's desire that the imperial presence be maintained in all the islands and all the fiefs of the empire. The reason for this"—another bland smile—"is very simple. It is to ensure that, should there ever again be a quarrel with any barbarian country, our enemies will understand that they do not deal simply with the men of Cho-Shu, or even the men of Satsuma, but with the might of a united Japan, and thus they will require to think twice before perpetrating any more outrages such as the bombardment of our cities. To this end . . ."—he appeared to consult his notes, although obviously he knew by heart what he had to say—"his majesty requires Lord Shimadzu to withdraw his garrison from the fortress of Kumamoto, so that it may be occupied by imperial soldiers."

There was a moment of complete silence; then the hisses began, and Saigo stepped forward. "How can this be, my lord *prince*," he said. "Kumamoto has been in the hands of the Satsuma since time began. It guards our northern approaches."

"Against whom, General Saigo?" Inouye asked softly. "There *is* no enemy north of you, only fellow Japanese."

Saigo glared at him, and then turned to Shimadzu.

"It is an imperial command," Shimadzu pointed out. "I will send the necessary orders to General Hayashi."

"It is to be occupied by imperial troops?" Saigo

demanded. "Where are these troops? *Who* are they? The banner of which clan do they fly?"

"His majesty would introduce no nothern *clans* into the heartland of the Satsuma, General," Inouye said. "This force will be recruited from soldiers of all clans, who are coming forward in their thousands to volunteer to march for the mikado and for Japan. Why, any Satsuma samurai so wishing will be welcome."

He looked around their faces, and received only stony stares in reply.

"You say this is going to happen all over Japan, Prince Inouye?" Shimadzu asked.

Inouye bowed. "That is so, my lord. There will be imperial garrisons in one castle in every fief."

"Then we accept the imperial decree," Shimadzu said, silencing his own men with his look.

"His majesty never doubted your loyalty, my Lord Shimadzu," Inouye said. And once again consulted his paper. "It is also his majesty's wish, as he outlined in his speech in Tokyo, that the most promising of our young samurai should travel abroad to learn the ways and the skills of the barbarians. He has already held discussions with the British and French consuls, and they are pleased to agree. Places will be made available in the British naval colleges and on British ships, and in the French military academies, for any Japanese officer recommended by the emperor. It is his majesty's earnest hope that each daimyo will supply him with a list of recommendations, that these young men may commence their training at the earliest possible moment." Again he was greeted with nothing but stony silence. "I can hardly emphasize too strongly the immense opportunity that is here being presented," he said. "And the benefit which will accrue to the empire as such young men, trained in the best of Western arms, grow to maturity in his majesty's service."

"I will consult with my young men," Shimadzu said.

Inouye bowed and read his paper. "And third, my lord, it is his majesty's imperial command that, commencing with next year's harvest, all rice produced in Japan will, in each fief, be delivered to a central store, so that the entire rice production of the empire may be coordinated and used to its best advantage."

Another complete, stupefied silence. This time it was Shimadzu himself who raised the obvious objection. "But what will we live on, Prince Inouye?"

Inouye smiled. "On money, my lord."

"Money?"

Inouye's face took on the expression of a kindly uncle explaining a very simple mathematical problem to a backward nephew. "His majesty is not going to *seize* your rice, Lord Shimadzu. But his minters are at this moment preparing a national currency, which will be known as rin, sen, and yen. There will be one hundred sen in each yen, and there will be one hundred rin in each sen. The yen will be related in value to the national currencies of the barbarian nations. Thus the imperial commissioners, of whom I will be one for Kyushu," he added reassuringly, "will set a value upon your rice crop, and will pay you for it, in money. Thus nothing will have changed, except for the better. For whereas, my lord, you are presently allowing a hatamoto eighty koku of rice a year, you will now allow him, shall we say—the figure has not yet been determined—one hundred and sixty yen a year, that is, two yen for every koku of rice, which is what you will have received from the government. Think of the advantages of this, my lord. Your hatamoto at present can only exchange his surplus rice in Kagoshima itself, for such goods as are obtainable in Kagoshima. Also, he must exchange a whole koku; there is no means of subdividing it. Thus he goes to a farmer and says, 'I will give you a koku of rice in exchange for a year's supply of meat,' regardless of the fact that this farmer may deal only in poultry, and another only in pork. In addition, outside of Kagoshima, and even more, outside of Japan, his wealth is useless. Nor can he save it against some future project. But *money* can be spent anywhere in the world, and in whatever denomination may be required. Also, it can be saved. It can even earn interest, as is paid in the barbarian countries. I do assure you, my lord, that the advantages of possessing money are immense."

The samurai, and their lord, could only stare at him in continuing incomprehension.

"Fourth, my lord," Inouye continued, "it is his majesty's decree that a uniform system of justice be practiced throughout the length and breadth of the empire. Eminent Italian lawyers are already on their way to Japan to advise his majesty in this great task. For the time being, however, and in line with the requirements of the barbarian countries in these matters, the apprehending of criminals, and even more, the sentencing of them, is to be the jurisdiction only of courts of law, no matter what class the criminal may come from. These courts, my lord, will be appointed by you, as daimyos of Satsuma, and indeed, you may sit on them yourself, if you so choose. But the decision as to whether or not a man may be punished, or a woman, can only be made in such courts, and never arbitrarily, on the spur of the moment, but only after evidence has been heard and guilt established beyond the semblance of a doubt. Of course, the laws of bushido will still obtain, to be administered by you, my lord." Another pause, another inspection of the faces in front of him. "Continuing this theme, to a logical conclusion, and while recognizing that the samurai are, and will always remain, the sure right arm of the Japanese power, his majesty decrees that all class distinctions be now abolished. Especially does this apply to the word 'slave.' As of this moment, the word is forbidden."

"Did you say *all* class distinctions, Prince Inouye?" Lord Shimadzu inquired.

"Among commoners, my lord," Inouye reassured him. "The daimyos retain their ancient rights and privileges, and ranks, save where they may be elevated to a princedom."

Shimadzu gazed at him, no doubt reflecting that this had just happened to his inferior, Inouye himself.

"But below that rank?" Saigo inquired.

"His majesty wishes all his subjects to be Japanese," Inouye said. "That is the greatest glory to which any man may aspire. There is no reason for one Japanese to step aside because another approaches, or to be afraid to enter into the company of any other Japanese and sit with him."

"You would have the farmers and the artisans bear arms?" demanded one of the other samurai.

"If they require to do so, certainly."

"And what of the honin and the eta?" Saigo asked, his voice menacingly quiet.

"The decree applies to them too. Them more than any other, since whereas they were slaves down to yesterday, now they are slaves no longer."

"Then we are no longer to have servants?"

"Of course you will have servants," Inouye told him. "The honin will be your servants. But they will not be your slaves."

Saigo snorted. "Where is the difference, my lord prince?"

"Why, simply that, whereas you now allow one koku of rice for the feeding of each of your honin, you will in future pay him a wage. But there *is* a greater difference than that." He drew a long breath. "A servant may seek employment wherever he chooses, wherever he thinks conditions, or wages, may be best. A slave may not. The honin are now to be considered as servants, not as slaves."

The samurai stared at him.

"Almost, one would suppose this law would permit honin to leave one fief and go to another, in search of better reward," Shimadzu said mildly.

Inouye took another long breath. "That is exactly what the law intends, my Lord Shimadzu."

"But—"

"His majesty would remind the daimyos," Inouye said, "that they are no longer absolute rulers in their own fiefs. That they voluntarily relinquished such absolute powers in Tokyo not a year hence. Indeed, my lord, it is his majesty's fifth decree that the term 'fief,' and the ancient meaning of that word, be now abolished forever."

The samurai gasped. It was the first time Ralph had ever heard such a collective sound of surprise from these normally impassive throats.

"The areas formally known as fiefs will now be called

ken," Inouye went on. "That is, they will correspond to what in barbarian countries are called prefectures. Henceforth the daimyos, while they may retain their ancient titles for as long as they live, will be known as prefects, that is, agents for the carrying out of the will of their imperial master. And will remember at all times that it is the imperial word which is law. Thus will we take another step toward realizing his majesty's determination that all Japan will become one country, in every way, instead of remaining a patchwork quilt of almost independent princedoms, with movement between the various boundaries restricted by guards and local tariffs."

"You will be telling us next that your lord of Cho-Shu will lose his right to collect dues from ships using the Strait of Shimonoseki," Sagio remarked.

"Lord Yoshimune has already surrendered that right, General Saigo, at the imperial command. And he is no longer *my* lord. My master is the emperor, who is the master of us all."

Once again he had silenced them as their brains tried desperately to grasp the full import of what was happening. Only Saigo seemed capable of speech.

"On that same day in Tokyo which you have just recalled for us, my lord prince," he said, "his majesty repeated several times that it was his sole wish and intention to drive away the barbarians and all of their pernicious influence upon our affairs. Yet do we now perceive that he is intent merely upon turning us into a copy of all the barbarian nations lumped together."

"His majesty seeks the strength to carry out all of our desires," Inouye said. "The strength of unity, the strength of one people. While achieving that strength, why, it is necessary for us to be humble. For a while. I can promise you that he has not lost his purpose." Inouye smiled at them. "And finally, his majesty wishes it announced throughout the empire that he intends to take a wife. Your new empress will be the Princess Ichijo Haruko."

Once again the stunned silence.

"Princess?" asked Shimadzu.

"The Ichijo are not of imperial blood," Saigo growled.

"Are not *all* daimyos of imperial blood, somewhere in history?" Inouye inquired. "In any event, the rank of princess has been conferred upon the Lady Haruko by his majesty, personally."

"Is not the lady older than his majesty?" Shimadzu asked.

"Perhaps, my Lord Shimadzu. But this is not a matter which can be discussed." His gaze swept them all. "Shall I offer his majesty the congratulations of the Satsuma?"

"This is a most serious matter, my lord." Saigo Takamori knelt, with his hatamotos behind him, before Lord Shimadzu, quivering with anger. "It is obvious to me that we are become the victims of a vast conspiracy. I wonder you did not seize this upstart Inouye and behead him for the insults he directed at you."

"Why do you not stand, Saigo San, to address me?" Shimadzu inquired gently. "As it is to become the custom?"

"I do not stand before my lord and master," Saigo declared. "My lord, listen to what I say."

"I cannot, Saigo San. You are speaking treason. As for Prince Inouye, he was but obeying his emperor. He is a brave man, and an honest one."

"My lord," Saigo begged desperately, "hear me. I mean no treason. But the facts are obvious. His majesty is but a boy. Clearly he has fallen into evil hands. The Tokugawa are still thick around Tokyo, and now that the imperial court has been removed there, his majesty is entirely in their power. And clearly that of the Ichijo as well. Why, *they* are not even daimyos of the first rank, and now one of their daughters has been made a princess. If his majesty wishes to take an empress from among his people instead, as has always been done, from the imperial house itself, why did he not come south, to Kyushu, to the greatest daimyo in the land?"

"One gathers that it was a personal choice," Shimadzu said. "No doubt the lady is of great beauty, and as you say, his majesty is young and no doubt in a mood to appreciate beauty."

"He did not come to your house, my lord, because he

was prevented from doing so," Saigo insisted. "Just as he is promulgating decrees which could have been written by the Tokugawa themselves. Or even the barbarians. What we have heard today is but double-talk, such as a barbarian might have uttered. Prince Inouye announces that the daimyos' rights and powers are unchanged, and then calmly tells us that the daimyos *have* no rights and powers any longer. And in another breath lets slip that the title of lord of Satsuma exists for your lifetime only, my lord. What of your sons, left with nothing, no land, no rights, not even a title to inherit?"

"Hush, Saigo San," Shimadzu said. "We are samurai. Our duty is to serve the Son of Heaven in every matter and in every way. If his majesty were to appear in this chamber at this moment and command us all to don our armor and march into the sea until we drowned, would we hesitate? I will hear no more talk of this seditious nature. Whatever his majesty has decreed, then it shall be so, for the greater good of our country." He stared from face to face, and Saigo dropped into the kowtow, his shoulders hunched in recognition of the reprimand.

"If I may speak, my lord . . ." said Togo Heihachiro.

"I await your words, Togo San," Shimadzu said.

"With your gracious permission, my lord, I should like to volunteer to have my name put forward to the emperor, that I may attend a British naval college."

"You," Saigo said, pointing, "are a silly, traitorous boy."

They walked in the citadel gardens, the younger hatamoto as usual waiting on the words of the great general, but on this day clearly disturbed.

And Togo did not lower his eyes. "My lord," he said, "I beg to differ. His majesty has indicated a course of action which he wishes us to take. I am but doing my duty. Believe me, it grieves me to leave my family and my friends, to leave Kagoshima, yet cannot I help but believe I am serving the imperial purpose, which must be the goal of every samurai. I would ask you to withdraw these accusations, sir."

Saigo gazed at him for several seconds and then gave

a great shout of laughter. "Will you confess to me that your heart is really bounding with joy at the thought of travel, of visiting faraway lands, of perhaps standing on the deck of one of those great warships you so admire?"

Togo flushed. "I will not deny these things, Lord Saigo."

"Then you have my apology," Saigo said. "Go, and enjoy yourself. But return with knowledge, Togo San. Study, and watch, and listen, and *prepare*."

"I shall heed your words, Lord Saigo," Togo said, eyes shining with delight.

"Who can blame a young man for looking on the world as his oyster?" Saigo demanded of Ralph, as they walked, now alone together. "I did, once, and my oyster was much smaller than what lies in front of Togo."

"Then you are not as angry as you pretend to be," Ralph observed.

"I never pretend, Freeman San. I *am* angry. But more than that, I am disturbed. No one, not even a god, can take a thousand years and crumple them in his fist and toss them over his shoulder. His majesty hurries, too far and too fast. Or perhaps," he added with a smile, "I should say that his advisers do that. Who knows what will happen next? With more and more barbarian customs being introduced, we may even reach a stage where a *woman* might leave her master, as a honin can now abscond so easily. Or is that what you are waiting for?" He frowned as he gazed at Ralph, and clapped his friend on the shoulder. "I did but jest. But, Ralph, do you truly still yearn after her?"

Ralph gazed at him in amazement; no Japanese had ever before addressed him in a European fashion.

"Can Suiko bring you no happiness?" Saigo asked.

"Suiko brings me more happiness than I deserve, Saigo San," he said. "Yet a man who can utterly control the urgings of his heart is a cold and lifeless creature."

"And you love the red-haired barbarian still," Sagio mused. "And now you have before you the example of the emperor, who would marry for love rather than honor and duty. I sometimes feel the world is turning upside down about us. Freeman San, my heart bleeds for you. As it did in the beginning. And I have no words of comfort, save to remind you that as we are men, and samurai, we must bear misfortune with the same steadfastness as we bear success. The gods know there will be sufficient misfortune for us all to bear in the next few years. We can but pray that his majesty does indeed know what he is about, and follows his own counsel, and not that of ambitious ministers."

"That you will pray for that, and trust in it, Saigo San, is surely the best news I have heard this last year," Ralph said.

Saigo smiled. "And your wife is pregnant? We shall make a samurai of you yet, Freeman San. I do pray, and trust. But I trust more in this simple fact, that as long as his majesty abides by the law of bushido, and knows that the ultimate strength of his kingdom lies in the hands of his samurai, as it has always done, then no matter what mistakes he may make, the future of Japan is secure."

Was not Hokkaido the bleakest place on earth? It had not always seemed so. But the summer following Alison's return from Tokyo was dull and wet, and autumn seemed to set in early, with the promise of the winter gales and snow already upon them.

Last year had been no different. The bleakness was in her heart.

She had saved Ralph's life, because it was the most precious thing in all the world to her. Yet he had remained in Japan, and was clearly still dreaming, and even planning—to commit suicide? She could see no other way for him.

She had not entirely lied to him in describing her life with Munetake as satisfactory, and even, on occasion, happy, in her possession of Jeremy and of a considerable personal freedom. The misery lay in having to submit to him whenever he wanted her, and he wanted her nearly every night. That at the least was no longer possible, as her belly became swollen and he took his pleasure with his honin women. And incredibly, she realized that she missed him. At least his company. Because she had nothing more. Munetake had at least provided a certain *event* every day. Without him, life was as

bleak as the landscape and the weather. Having of
necessity adopted Japanese ways and customs, and having enjoyed them in Shimonoseki, she dabbled in painting and in needlework, with no talent. She ordered her
household like an absolute tyrant, determined that
Munetake would never find fault with it—this was simply a personal pride—but even the insidious pleasure
of *acting* the tyrant was absent, because the girls would
have been surprised had their mistress acted any other
way. But in addition to her boredom, having more time
to observe, and to think, she also found herself beginning to fear. She knew Munetake now for what he was.
In many ways, indeed, she could recognize the spark of
ambitious greatness in him, where such ambition is not
hindered by absurd notions of loyalty or gratitude. He
was a samurai, and he believed in the laws of bushido,
utterly. But he had also been a ronin, cast out by his
original master, and to the Satsuma he paid no more
than lip service. He served them faithfully and well, but
only until a better cause came along. And the best cause
of all was that of Munetake.

A philosophy, and an ambition, which could take
him very far, or simply as far as seppuku or the gallows,
leaving his servants, and certainly his chief concubine,
equally to suffer. How odd a fate it would be for her to
die at the side of a man she loathed, because of being
regarded as his lover in the eyes of the world.

But reaching to him as a human being, seeking more
than the mere composing of her mind to resist his
caress, was not practical, because he did not wish it. He
adored her body, and she had come to understand
that in some way he regarded her as a symobl of success and even good fortune. But he was also well aware
that she hated him, and thus had no doubt she would
betray him if she could. Despite Tokyo. Because Tokyo
could be simply explained: she had given him her word,
and she had feared for Ralph's life. It would never
occur to Munetake that any human being would break
his or her word. But if the opportunity were to arise
when she had *not* promised fidelity . . . Thus he would
permit no mental intimacy, no relationship other than
that of their bodies.

Thus she had to depend more than ever upon the companionship of Jeremy, which would surely grow, and of the child in her belly, whose stirrings were so full of promise. She was becoming, she realized, even more Japanese than she suspected, in that her children were to be the center of her life. But because of Munetake's ambitions, and his distrust of her, she now began to fear for them. That he would expect his sons to follow him and die for him could not be doubted, the moment they were old enough to do so. But even before then, should his plans go awry, she could not doubt he would take his children to hell with him. So she watched him with a frown as he stamped into the bedchamber where she lay, glaring at the scroll he held before him.

"Truly Japan is collapsing about our ears," he shouted. "There is to be no more koku. Can you believe that? In its place, there is to be money. Money, as if we were all a hovel of merchants. Money! I know nothing of money. My samurai will surely desert me, and we shall dwindle and starve."

Alison stared at him, while a tremendous joy seemed to burst from her heart. She had kept her father's books. "I understand about money, my lord," she said.

He frowned at her. "You?"

She knelt, despite her bulk. "Let me see to it for you, my lord," she said. "It will be my pleasure, and I will see that you are not robbed."

He knelt beside her. "A woman who understands about money?" he asked in wonder. "Truly, you are a treasure, my Alison. What should I do without you?"

"May I, my lord?" she begged. "May I?"

"Why, if you wish it that badly, of course you may. Once you have had the child."

"Then shall I be happy, my lord," she promised him. For if she hated him and would always hate him, if she *had* to hate him in order to preserve her self-respect, yet could she now also be a wife as well as a mother. And perhaps preserve her sanity as well.

Suiko's second daughter, named Shikibu after Saigo's wife and her own eldest sister, was born at the end of the summer of 1868. She was a plump child, too plump perhaps for Suiko's slender body. The delivery caused much anxiety to the surgeons, and even more to Ralph. "I think we have sufficient of a family, my sweet," he told her; contraception was a very widely and skillfully practiced art in Japan.

For suddenly she was too precious a burden to lose. Alison had told him to forget her and find happiness, but he had not intended to obey her. Yet it was inescapable in Kyushu. Despite the evidence that times were changing, and for the worse. Not on the surface. There was progress, even if the summoning of the parliament was postponed from year to year. The emperor clearly wished to wait until the samurai, likely to be overconservative in their approach to modernization, could be at least balanced by a sufficient number of merchants and farmers—and these had first of all to be educated to equality, and then *made* equal. A momentous step which would take no less careful preparation.

But the Satsuma regarded the postponement of the parliament as a victory for good, traditional sense—they might not approve or enjoy many of the decrees issued by the emperor, but they were at least used to being ruled by decree. And soon enough the entire nation was being distracted by the imperial wedding, which was celebrated with great splendor. Indeed it was a momentous occasion as Lord Shimadzu, accompanied by his lords and ladies, took the road to Tokyo. It was the first time that Ralph and Suiko had traveled together, and it was a delightful experience—could he but for a moment have rid his mind of the dread excitement he felt at supposing that Munetake and Alison might also be there. As it turned out, they were not, and he was able to discover no reason for their absence, and was left with a wildly overactive imagination which ranged from supposing Alison ill, or Jeremy, to the more reasonable suggestion that Shimadzu had forbidden Munetake's attendance just because Ralph would be there.

So he must swallow his disappointment and enjoy Suiko's delight when, before the entire assembly, which included representatives from all the Western countries as well as America, the emperor paused for a brief

word with the famous Freeman San, general of the
Satsuma.

The wedding, as such things often do, took some of
the tension out of the air; it gave men other things to
think about than their own troubles, made those troubles somehow less urgent. Even the occupation of
Kumamoto by a token force of imperial samurai suddenly seemed less important. In fact, events in the rest
of Japan seemed very remote down in Kyushu. No
barbarian instructors traveled south to drill the men of
Satsuma; the barbarians were there for the imperial
purpose, and the Satsuma already had a barbarian
adviser. They could afford to smile, Ralph among them,
when in 1871, following the defeat of the French by
the Prussians in far-off Europe, the French military
attachés were hurriedly returned to Paris and replaced
by Germans. But reports from Tokyo, gleaned mainly
from Prince Inouye, suggested that neither Germans
nor French were having any great success in whipping
the northern samurai into a modern fighting force; it
seemed that the Japanese warriors were reluctant to
exchange their colorful kimonos for the uniforms their
new mentors wished them to wear, and of course they
would not consider abandoning their swords for rifles
and bayonets, or their tempestuous charges in favor of
disciplined maneuvers. Thanks to the example shown
them by Ralph's riflemen outside Tokyo, they *were* becoming more prepared to exchange the bow for a
firearm, but of course even rifle fire, unless controlled
by volley and delivered en masse, was hardly more
effective than bowshot.

Well, Ralph thought, all of those things he could
have told them, had they thought to ask. And even
more, he could have told them how difficult it was
going to be to get the samurai of different clans to
march and train and fight together when for centuries
they had been at least rivals, if not actual enemies.

But these were matters for imperial concern. They
did not affect the country as a whole. It was eventually
the necessity to pay for the upheaval Mutsuhito had
brought about that reached down into the calm of
Kyushu. Ralph first became aware of what was happen-

ing when no meat was served him for a week, only fish. "Are there no fowl left in Kyoto?" he asked.

Suiko bowed before him. "There are fowl, my lord, but the farmers are demanding such ridiculous prices for their products that I refused to buy."

He frowned at her. "Explain."

"Well, my lord," she said, "five years ago, one koku of rice was sufficient to secure a supply of chickens, two a week, for an entire year. When the koku was abandoned for money, we paid two yen for the same supply, to the same farmer. But now he says that two yen is not sufficient. Two yen will buy only one fowl per week for a year. If we wish more, we must pay *three* yen."

Ralph scratched his head.

"This has never happened before, my lord," Suiko said severely. "In all history, since the dawn of time, one koku of rice has been worth at least one hundred fowl per year. These farmers have grown above their station, and should be punished. Before the reforms," she added darkly, "you would have gone to his farm and struck off his head."

"I shall have to discuss this with Lord Saigo," he said. "Let us be thankful there are still fish in the sea and that sake is made from rice."

He did not actually take the situation too seriously, but only a fortnight later the deteriorating financial condition of the country was brought home to him even more forcibly one morning as he practiced swordplay with William, now six years old and fiercely aggressive. For when they rested, sweat gleaming on their naked shoulders, it was to find his six personal honin waiting to speak with him.

"We can no longer live, my lord," said their spokesman, performing the kowtow even though that ceremony was no longer officially recognized. "On the two yen which honorable master pays us with such generosity. But two yen no longer purchases the necessities of life. Our wives weep and our children wail because their bellies are empty. My lord, if you will forgive this unpardonable insolence, I am deputed by my fellows to beg you to search your heart and discover if you cannot find another yen for each of us, lest we and our families starve."

"I understand your situation, believe me," Ralph said. "But the fact is that I also am feeling the pinch. I mean, my income has not been increased to match the rising cost of food, and I have no spare yen at all. Why, my table even lacks meat, except on special occasions. We must tighten our belts and wait for better times."

The honin exchanged glances. Then the spokesman said, "You will forgive me, my lord, but we cannot see our families dwindle. My Lord Freeman, we beg your leave to seek our fortunes elsewhere."

"To . . . Well, I certainly cannot *stop* you leaving my service," he said, realizing that these poor devils had probably never had meat on *their* tables in their lives. "But where will you go? Is not the entire country suffering from this inflation?"

Another exchange of glances. "We have heard, my lord, that there are merchants in the north, and farmers, too, who are paying four and even six yen a year to faithful and capable honin. When we tell them that we are come from the service of the great Freeman San . . ."

"They'll very likely offer you ten yen," Ralph agreed. "Well . . . the best of luck." He smiled. "I wish I could do the same."

But that was a lie. He had no real desire to go to Tokyo and work for the emperor, even for an increase in his stipend. Tokyo was to be too much in the center of things, to begin asking himself too many questions—and perhaps to suffer too many temptations. There was indeed, as Saigo had suggested might happen, a movement toward even freeing women, and more especially, concubines—supposing a discarded concubine, or worse, one who had fled her master, could ever find a man to take her on. But a man was still allowed but a single wife, and it was not possible for him to put aside the mother of his three children, who had never done less than love and obey him. Besides, Alison, so far as he knew, was making no move toward leaving Munetake. Because obviously she would not be allowed to take her children—he had no idea how many she now had—and therefore, for them, nothing had changed.

They were doomed to travel in parallel grooves, but never even to touch, unless a miracle happened, and until that did happen, as Saigo had said, his home was in Kagoshima, with his wife and children, and his heart should be there too. However often it wandered off to Hokkaido, for Munetake was apparently now stationed there permanently, Saigo being well aware it might be too disruptive to bring him, and therefore his family, back south.

But Hokkaido, in their circumstances, might have been the moon.

"What can I do?" Lord Shimadzu asked. His back was bowed now, his voice thin, and his hair was entirely gray. He seemed afraid to look his samurai in the eye, or he was afraid of what he saw in those eyes. For Ralph was not the only one to be finding that the incomes which had been more than sufficient when paid in rice were quite inadequate when reduced to money. "I have made representations to Prince Inouye and suggested to him that the value of our rice crop should be increased, and he has told me that this is impossible, that the empire is finding great difficulty in financing its progress as it is, and that all surplus money must go to that purpose."

"Progress." Saigo Takamori sneered.

"He speaks of schools and colleges, as well as guns and rifles," the old man said.

"And uniforms," Saigo said. "How many thousands of yen are being paid for uniforms, which no one wishes to wear?"

"It is the decree of the emperor," Shimadzu said, and there, as usual, the matter ended. Yet Ralph took his next opportunity to discuss the growing crisis with Inouye himself, as they were once again on terms of intimate friendship such as they had known when first he had come to Japan; Inouye indeed made it plain that he regarded Ralph as his only friend in the lands of the Satsuma, and never visited Kagoshima without calling at Ralph's house for a game of go and a jug of sake, prepared on these occasions by Suiko herself, before

she would shepherd the children from the room to
leave the two men to themselves.

"I will tell you frankly," the prince admitted, "that
things move slowly, and are costing much more than
we had anticipated. His majesty would have a fleet of
modern battleships . . . but the cost, Freeman San. We
are talking of hundreds of thousands of English pounds.
When you consider that the rate of exchange has been
fixed at ten yen to the pound sterling, you will have
some idea of the millions we are discussing. Yet a navy
we must have. Thus the money must be found."

"While the country starves."

Inouye shook his head. "The country is a long way
from starving. I have it on good authority that the
farmers and the merchants have never been so prosperous. As for the honin . . . do you know, despite our
stringent financial requirements, there are even rumors
that certain honin are preparing to stand for election
when the parliament is summoned? Can you imagine,
one of your servants standing next to a samurai before
the emperor?"

"He is hardly likely to be one of *my* servants," Ralph
pointed out. "As I am reduced to less than a dozen.
Inouye San, I am sure you are right, and the country
prospers, despite the inflation. But only where a man
may go out and earn. Those who are on fixed incomes
are suffering, and will suffer more. I do not talk of
myself alone. I talk of all the samurai, everywhere."

"The samurai," Inouye said thoughtfully.

"You are one yourself," Ralph reminded him.

"My income comes from the emperor."

"Because you have been summoned to his service.
Not all samurai have been that fortunate. And what are
the rest to do? They are forbidden by tradition, by the
very laws of bushido, from earning a living."

"Of course. They are the retainers of their lord, and
their fortunes must rise or fall with his. But if you
mean that the samurai of the Satsuma are suffering
most of all, and I can tell you that they are, it is because
they are so stiff-necked. Why will they not join the
imperial army? There they would receive far more
than their present incomes. And they would be serving

the emperor, who is the greatest lord of all." He pointed. "Why do you not set them an example, Ralph? His majesty would be pleased to have you. I wager he would give you a command, the imperial artillery."

Ralph smiled. "You tempt me, Inouye San. But my place is here. The Satsuma gave me a home when I was a fugitive, and they have heaped honors and distinctions upon me. As long as they need me, I shall remain in Kagoshima."

Inouye studied him. "Good and faithful Freeman San," he said at last. "But why should the Satsuma, why should Saigo Takamori, wish you to stay? Why does he continually prepare to fight? I must warn you, Freeman San, that men like Saigo are dangerous. They will not move with the times. He will not let you serve the emperor. I happen to know he will grant none of his samurai permission to take service with the imperial army. And these are the finest samurai in the empire. Why is Saigo holding them back, save for some scheme of his own?"

"I don't think you need worry about Saigo," Ralph said. "He is a very conservative man; I will not argue with that. But he is a patriotic Japanese, and he worships the emperor. And besides, he has the restraining hand of Lord Shimadzu ever on his shoulder. I should think you need only give him more time, that is all. But it cannot help but concern him to hear his samurai grumble, and to observe their distress."

"Time," Inouye remarked. "The empire has no time. The emperor has not sufficient time. I will tell you this, Freeman San. His majesty will not stand still and wait for the samurai to realize where their true duty lies. Laws already lie drafted, just awaiting his signature . . . but those are state secrets. Yet must I beg of you, Freeman San, as you mean to live in Kagoshima for the rest of your days, persuade your general to accept what is happening, and quickly."

"He seeks to frighten us," Saigo Takamori said. "Let Mutsuhito pass whatever laws he likes. He dare not, even the Son of Heaven, tamper with the laws of bushido. He said so himself, and Inouye has repeated it. He has taken our honin away from us. Now he would hope to crush us into accepting these new ways by reducing our incomes, perhaps by starving us. He will not succeed. Samurai are not to be crushed. And we have his promise that one day Japan will march against the barbarians. Who does he suppose will do that for him? The honin?"

But only a few months later they received word from Tokyo decreeing that, as the samurai—especially, the imperial announcement said, the *southern* samurai—had not come forward in sufficient numbers to create an imperial army large enough for the requirements of the empire, from the following year *all* male Japanese between the ages of eighteen and twenty-five were required to enroll in the armed services, unless specifically excluded by name.

"It is called conscription," Ralph explained to the thunderstruck samurai. "And is in fact practiced by all European countries to fill the ranks of their armies. Only the British, and of course the Americans, do not resort to this, the British because they are an island people protected by their great navy, and we Americans because we have no need of such measures except in time of actual war."

"Well," Saigo said, "if it is a law . . ." He looked over his warriors. "You young men will have to obey it, I suppose. Provided you always remember that you are men of Satsuma and that your lord has first call upon your service." But he held Ralph's arm to take him aside. "This is a badly worded document, Freeman San," he said. "One would almost suppose, reading it, that more than just samurai are intended."

"I'm afraid that is just what it does mean," Ralph said. "Inouye warned me of this."

Saigo frowned at him. "You are saying that his majesty would enroll the sons of merchants and farmers alongside samurai in the army?"

Ralph sighed. "The sons of honin and eta, also."

"That is not possible."

"It is possible, and it is happening. You must understand, Saigo San, that it is the intention of your emperor to sweep away the old Japan forever. Whether he is right or wrong to do this, I do not know. But *he* believes he is right."

"My young men, training alongside a honin?" Saigo cried. "*Sleeping* alongside a honin? Why, it is possible, according to what you say, that a honin might obtain a command."

"I should think that is very possible," Ralph agreed, thinking of Aya and all the other very intelligent honin he had known.

"That shall never be," Saigo declared. "Not over a Satsuma samurai," and he immediately rescinded the permission he had earlier given for his young men to go north. When Ralph reminded him that conscription was a law, he merely snorted. "So let his majesty send an army of *honin* down here to arrest us, if he dares."

"Why do all men wander about with such long, grim faces?" Suiko asked Ralph that evening. "Does not the sun still shine, my lord? Are not our children healthy? Do we not still find comfort in each other's arms?"

They had been married eleven years. And in the context of each other's arms, of the health of their children, of their domestic bliss, they had been eleven marvelously happy years. Even his own health had remained almost perfect. It was impossible sometimes to consider that he had now lived in Japan for sixteen years, that he was about to become forty, that his life had so strangely slipped away from him, living and working—and loving—in the strangest of worlds. The most fascinating of worlds, too, although a world in which he had never belonged. And yet in which, from time to time, he had been so very happy.

And Alison had now lived in Japan fourteen years, eleven of which had been spent with Munetake. How many children would she have had by now? There had been a dream, which he knew now could never be realized. In a month's time he *would* be forty. An age when all the romantic challenges of youth suddenly take on somber hues, and gentle hills over which a man might once have galloped at full tilt suddenly become unscalable precipices. If a man lets them.

But Alison, after eleven years . . . Jeremy would almost be ready for induction as a samurai. As was William.

He found he was sleeping badly. It was more than an awareness of time past, and insufficient time to come. More even than a wondering where his life would end, and if, as seemed most likely, it were to end here on this mattress in Kagoshima, with Suiko attentive at his side, whether in his last moments he would smile, or weep with frustration. More than either of those, it was a feeling of approaching doom, a certainty of catastrophe. For all of his grumbling, Saigo had never before openly defied the emperor.

So it was possible to be happy in the bleakness of Hokkaido. Happier, no doubt, than it would have been possible anywhere else. In many ways Hokkaido was very like the Scotland Alison remembered from her girlhood, and that, she was realizing, was a very long time ago. She was in her thirty-second year and had become a matron.

A very Japanese matron, for all that she kept her lord's accounts in English, only translating into Japanese, a tedious language to write, the essentials for him to grasp. She sat at her desk, in her kimono, with her hair piled on the top of her head. She wore no makeup, as she had always refused to do so, and he had never insisted.

She formed her letters and her words with careful strokes; she enjoyed her work. But she also enjoyed writing itself, and had taken up keeping a journal, in English, into which she could record her most intimate thoughts and feelings, sure it would never be read by anyone. This was an escape for her occasional moods of lonely bitterness or angry frustration at what might have been. But the moods themselves were growing more and more infrequent as each uneventful year followed each uneventful year.

Had anyone told her ten years ago that she would spend probably the rest of her life in this windswept castle, she would have been horrified. But she had had such thoughts before, and she had survived many worse things than Hokkaido in the winter. Now she no longer ever wished to leave. To leave, to go south, to reenter the world of polite bows and smiles, of tea ceremonies and fluttering fans, was also to reenter a world of memories and temptations, and therefore of dangers. Of dangers greater even than Munetake's vengeance now, because Ralph had surely forgotten all about her. This she knew had to be so, but as long as she did not have the proof of it, she could dream.

It was better to keep her happiness on a more earthly plane. As they had known each other, in the fullest sense of the word, for so very long, Munetake no longer came to her every night. But she enjoyed sleeping alone, and he came to her often enough, and could still make her, for a few brief seconds, the happiest woman in the world. That *he* was not happy was obvious. He fretted at the restrictions imposed upon him by the money shortage, and he fretted even more as year succeeded year and the explosion he so desired did not take place. Because he was approaching fifty. "Before he was my age," he would storm, "Hideyoshi ruled Japan."

No doubt he was doomed to die frustrated. She knew little of what was going on in the country as a whole, but it seemed clear to her that the new emperor had a very firm grip on affairs, and however much the samurai might grumble, they were in no position to do anything about it. She only hoped and prayed that his angry frustrations did not affect her boys, because here was the true source of her happiness. Jeremy was now eleven years old, and Harunari eight. There had been no others, but she had not wanted others; one of each nationality was sufficient. Both would of course become samurai; Jeremy's head had already been prepared, his hair long and flowing, waiting for the ceremonial shaving and the removal of the forelock; Harunari was not far behind. And both, as Munetake's sons, lived for the sword and bow, the horse and the chase. Sometimes she feared for them, and was reassured by Munetake's own confidence, and that Jeremy was going to be the large adult Munetake dreamed of was obvious.

She begrudged him none of his dreams, so long as he never led the two young men off to war, and misery, and death. But war, and misery, and death, were all he dreamed of, and thus she felt her heart constrict as she watched him stride into her chamber, smiling. He had not smiled for some time.

He waved a piece of paper at her. "Orders from Lord Saigo. We are to hold ourselves in readiness for action."

"Action? Against whom?"

"He does not say. He says that affairs are moving toward a crisis, that he may need all my strength at any moment, and that therefore I must prepare my men. To march south." He grinned at her. "You will accompany me."

"I? But . . ." She did not wish to march south. Oh, how she wanted to march south. But that would be to allow dreams to become perilously intertwined with reality.

"You will accompany me," he said again. "It is the moment I have been waiting for. A moment when there will be fortunes to be made, and accounts to be settled. And you are my fortune, Alison Gray." He rested his hand on her head. "Besides," he said in a lower tone, "Freeman will also take part in this war, whomever it may be against." His fingers tightened, squeezing the hair from her scalp in a way he had not done since the early days in Shimonoseki.

Tears started from her eyes, but they were not of pain. She was realizing how brittle a thing is happiness, how simple to destroy.

The lords of Satsuma, with their generals and their hatamotos, stood together on the battlements of Kagoshima and watched the imperial party approach. "Ten, fifteen men," Saigo remarked. "More words. I begin to think that we are ruled by a man who imagines words will accomplish all things. Let us go down, Freeman San, and listen to what dread punishment Prince Inouye seeks to inflict upon us."

Lord Shimadzu was now so old and infirm he could not even sit, but had to recline on a litter in the center of his dais, his samurai grouped at his back, to face the imperial envoy.

Inouye allowed no suggestion of benevolence to cross his face this day. Nor did he speak to them personally, but preferred to read from the document he held in his hand.

"Be it known," he said, "that as certain samurai in various parts of the empire have failed to respond to the imperial command that all men, of whatever rank or ancestry, between the ages of eighteen and twenty-five, should report for training in the imperial army, it is the will and decree of his majesty that the class of Japanese warriors hitherto known as samurai shall no longer exist."

There was not even a hiss. No doubt everyone in Kagoshima had seen cracks in the sky for the past ten years, but today the heavens were definitely falling.

"In this regard," Inouye went on, "the pensions hitherto paid to the samurai as warrior retainers of the daimyos shall be abolished, and the former samurai shall seek their livelihoods by toil and by serving the emperor, as do all other men. Further to this, the distinctive marks of the samurai shall no longer be seen in Japan. The shaved skull and the topknot are by decree illegal from this moment forth." To prove his point, he removed his hat to reveal that his own hair had been allowed to grow, while the samurai tress had been cropped. That *did* bring a gasp.

But he was not finished. Now he did raise his head from the paper to utter the most dread words Ralph supposed any Japanese had spoken in a thousand years.

"It is further decreed that the wearing of two swords, the traditional badge of the samurai, shall from this moment be forbidden by law."

The ensuing silence was broken by a sudden choking sound, and Lord Shimadzu fell forward and rolled from his litter and down the steps of the dais.

—14—
THE CAMPAIGN

Saigo knelt beside the man who had given him greatness. "Lord Shimadzu is dead," he said, and raised his head to look at Inouye. "You have killed him, with your *words*."

Inouye's face was stony. "He was an old man, and ripe to die," he said. "And perhaps he is fortunate, in dying now, before he can see the disgrace of his people." He walked to the doorway, where the other nobles of his entourage waited, and beckoned Ralph.

They went outside together. "You are the only man of sense here, Freeman San," he said. "I beg of you, instill some of that sense into Saigo Takamori."

Ralph shook his head. "I doubt any man could do that now, Inouye San," he said. "The rights of samurai are all these men had left."

"They have brought this catastrophe upon themselves," Inouye said. "More than that, they have brought it upon all the samurai in Japan. Do you think it has been easy for any of us? Do you think I did not hope and pray that his majesty's program could be carried out without resorting to such a dreadful measure? It is the men of Satsuma who have forced this upon us, who have brought us to this disgrace. The emperor is angry with them, Freeman San. Only by submitting utterly to his decree will they mitigate that anger. Tell them this."

"And if they will not?"

Inouye sighed. "Then his majesty will destroy them. Japan will *be* one nation, Freeman San. Ruled by the emperor. On this he is determined. If they would not see their city burn, their wives and children die, they must submit, Ralph. Tell them that." He rested his hand on his friend's shoulder. "And think deeply on that yourself, old friend."

The conch shells wailed, the cymbals clashed, the bugles played a dirge as Lord Shimadzu of Satsuma was laid in his grave. The last of the daimyos, Ralph thought. The old man had been truly that, just as, in his unwavering justice as well as his unfailing good humor and generosity, he had been about the best of them as well. It was tempting to hope that his heart had failed before the fatal words had been spoken, before he had heard the death knell of his people.

Now there was only grimness. The imperial party had gone, and Kagoshima mourned. And the hatamotos gathered around Saigo Takamori. Even the young lords did that. Only Saigo counted, now.

He had prayed long, and knelt long in thought. Now he paced the audience chamber, not speaking to a soul, for more than an hour. Now was not a time for decisions, for actions; tradition demanded a lengthy period of mourning for the dead lord. But time was no longer upon the side of tradition.

At last he faced them. "General Hayashi," he said, "you will prepare the army for war. Send a messenger north to Hokkaido and tell General Munetake that I wish him to bring his force south with all possible haste. Every samurai, mind. The fief will have to be abandoned." His face twisted. "It is apparently no longer ours, anyway. The messenger, and others you will send to Tokyo and to Kyoto, will proclaim loudly that Lord Shimadzu is dead and that it is the duty of all Satsuma samurai to travel to Kagoshima for the mourning. Inouye Bunta will be telling a similar tale, and thus no one will doubt that it is the truth. Thus no obstacles will be placed in the way of Munetake's march." He sighed. "Would that we could recall Togo and those who have sailed across the oceans so easily. Then, General Hayashi, you will mobilize. General Freeman, you will form your artillery into whatever force you think fit, and select a hatamoto to command it. I would have you take personal command of the rifle regiments, as you did at Tokyo." For a moment he almost smiled as he recalled the completeness of that triumph; then the sternness returned. "We have the advantage of knowing our plans, and of *time*," he told them. "Time to mourn our lord, as he would have wished us. No move will be made against us until our mourning is completed and a new lord of Satsuma is installed. By the time *that* happens, I wish us to be in Tokyo. Now, go, my hatamotos, and prepare your men. And let no one but the messengers *you* send, Hayashi San, leave Kagoshima."

Ralph remained behind. His heart was leaping with anticipation; Alison was coming south at last. She was coming to Kagoshima, while the world of the Satsuma was . . . falling apart?

But he had other responsibilities. "I would know what you have in mind, Saigo San."

"Why, to restore the integrity of the empire," Saigo told him. "It is obvious, it has been obvious for ten years, that far from ever intending to act against the barbarians, his majesty is acting *with* them, and against us. Why else has he surrounded himself with men like Inouye and Ito, who are well known to the barbarians and eager to promote their interests? And it is equally well known that it is the samurai whom the barbarians have been determined to destroy, from the beginning. Now, when all is prepared, they think they have forced the emperor to issue the final decree which would destroy us. Well, they will discover that a samurai cannot be destroyed by mere words and decrees. He must be conquered in battle, or he must triumph."

"And you really suppose you can triumph over the imperial army?"

"What army are we speaking of, Freeman San? An army of honin? Can you imagine ten, a hundred, even a thousand honin daring to stand before a single samurai, sword in hand?"

"If all were armed with swords, perhaps not. But these honin will be armed with rifles, Saigo San."

"Do we not have riflemen, Freeman San? *Samurai* riflemen, and led by *you*? Do we not know that the imperial forces are a rabble? And may we not be certain that when our banners are seen, and our cause is heard, even the imperial samurai will hurry to our side?"

"To live as rebels?"

"To live as true Japanese. I have in mind a quick campaign, Freeman San. A *lightning* campaign. We will first move on Kumamoto. There is but a handful of men in the garrison. We shall sweep them aside like chaff. Thus we will again secure ourselves from invasion. Then the straits. The men of Cho-Shu will never prevent our passage. Then a march north, while we send a fleet of war junks up the Inland Sea to protect our flank. The fleet will distract the garrison at Osaka while we pass it and bear on Tokyo. Our goal must be the emperor's person, that in his name we may undo the many mistakes that have been made, the many wrongs that have been perpetrated, that we may show the barbarians the true resolve of Japan."

"And if I tell you that it will not work, Saigo San? That even if you reach Tokyo, with every southern samurai at your back, you will still be defeated?"

"How can we be defeated, if we have all the southern samurai at our backs? Such a thing has never happened in all history."

Ralph sighed. "Saigo, we are not dealing with history now. We are dealing with the present. In the past your wars in Japan were fought only between samurai. How many samurai are there in the entire nation? Half a million? I doubt so many. But there are some *thirty* million Japanese, of whom not less than five million will be males capable of bearing arms, and these will be standing behind the emperor. Odds of ten to one."

"Honin." Saigo sneered. "Merchants. Farmers."

"Armed with modern weapons. Believe me, Saigo San, my European ancestors went through this same upheaval only a few hundred years ago. Then the armored knight and his bowmen ruled the field. But with the coming of gunpowder, the armored knight was swept away. More, in every country, a whole generation of aristocrats, of samurai, if you like, was swept away, because however brave, however skillful, and however wellborn, each man was still at the mercy of a farmer hiding in a ditch with a gun. Will you not learn from the experiences of others, Saigo San? Surely that is all the purpose history has."

Saigo stared at him for several moments; then he said, "You are painting a picture of the death of the samurai, Freeman San. I do not believe that you are right. I do not believe there is a honin in Japan would dare level a rifle at a samurai, much less stand before him on a field of battle. I believe we shall conquer, so long as our hearts remain those of samurai. But if I am wrong, and you are right, then we shall die, with our swords in our hands, as did our ancestors. We shall permit no man, not even an emperor, to take away our swords."

"Even if such a course means the destruction of everything you have created here? Of your wives and children, your fathers and mothers?"

"A samurai cares nothing for possessions," Saigo declared. "As for our families, are they not composed of samurai, the mothers and wives of samurai, the children of samurai? Believe me, Freeman San, they would not *wish* to live as no better than honin."

It was tempting to suppose he might be suffering from advanced megalomania. But that was not so, Ralph knew. Saigo Takamori represented all the virtues of old Japan, since time began. And all the virtues too that he thought necessary to the continued glory of the nation. He was not prepared to live in any other circumstances.

Nor did Ralph suppose he was at all inaccurate in his judgment of his followers. So where did that leave a man who had no such weight of tradition on his shoulders, either to bear him down beneath its load or to bolster his refusal to accept the slightest change? And a man who was yet married to the daughter of a samurai, and had samurai children?

Suiko was well aware of what had happened, and of what was going to happen; there could not be a living soul in Kagoshima who was not aware of the situation. She sat beside him with a bowed head, made a single remark. "Be sure it is again a short campaign, my lord."

"Suiko . . . suppose I told you that I hope and pray there will not be a campaign at all?"

She raised her head. "The emperor will never rescind a decree, my lord."

"I know that. Thus the Satsuma will have to accept it."

"My lord? How may a samurai live, when he is not a samurai? How may a samurai not carry the two swords which are his birthright?"

"The two swords are a symbol of a dead age, Suiko. Believe me. Men as good as samurai live in my country, America, but they neither have to carry two swords nor have to make other men get out of their way to prove it."

Her face seemed to close. "My lord does not understand the ways of the Japanese," she said.

"I have lived sixteen years with your people, Suiko. It is the Satsuma who do not understand the way the world has of changing. Suiko, there is no way the army of the Satsuma can defeat the emperor. They can only die. Is it sensible to die for the sake of two swords and a topknot?"

"My lord does not *understand*," she said, hissing the last sibilant, like any male samurai might have done, and rising to leave the room. It was the first time she had ever revealed the slightest displeasure to him regarding anything he had said or done in eleven years.

"They are only honin, Father," William cried. "Of course you will beat them. You will bring us their heads."

He had no doubts. It was difficult to imagine any Satsuma clansman with doubts. Perhaps Togo Heihachiro might have had doubts, because he was the most levelheaded of them all. But Togo was in England, serving on a British warship.

Ralph lay awake all night, on his back, his hands beneath his head, Suiko breathing gently at his side. But she slept with her back to him; she was still displeased.

The messengers had already left to ride north and summon Munetake and his samurai to the aid of their lord. If he was to abandon the Hokkaido fortress,

Munetake would certainly bring Alison and his children here to Kagoshima, to share in the holocaust which would be the inevitable result of defeat in the field—Saigo Takamori would never surrender. And with the knowledge and skill of his barbarian adviser, he might even be able to prolong the struggle, to defend Kyushu for a lengthy period. Ralph did not doubt that a surprise attack would regain possession of Kumamoto, and thus turn the whole of Kyushu once again into a Satsuma stronghold. They grew sufficient rice down here to sustain the population, and there were sufficient arms and ammunition for a lengthy campaign. Besides, with Kyushu safe, Saigo *could* then strike north. He was probably right in anticipating the support of a large number of Cho-Shu samurai, certainly if he gained an early victory. With such an army he could perhaps even carry war and rapine to the very gate of Tokyo. Only ten years ago, Ralph remembered, he had welcomed that thought.

Because then victory had been a possibility; it would still have been a quarrel between samurai and their lords, not between a dying breed and an entire people. Now the deed would only be the more terrible for having been delayed. He had read everything he had been able to procure through the American consulate and his friend Mr. Coates, of the war in the States, the way the South had been crushed out of existence. He had no regrets for that. He was a Northerner born and bred, and had he been there he would have served with Grant's army. Yet he could feel pity for a proud people who had been so humbled. And they had been Christians fighting Christians. When the burden of defending their plantations had become intolerable, and however bitter it may have been, they *could* lay down their guns and say, "Enough." They had not feared for their women and children.

Such a civilized outcome could not obtain here. Even if the emperor might be willing to pardon rebels against him—which no Japanese ruler, emperor, regent, or shogun, had ever done before in a society where the only acceptable penalty for rebellion was death—the Satsuma would never accept such humiliation. If they

lost, as Saigo had said, they would die, taking their
women and children with them.

He chewed his lip. How could it be avoided? Only by
the coldest, most calculated, most brutal act of treachery.
Treachery against men who had befriended him, against
the woman he had married, the children he had
fathered. Because without his American adviser, Saigo
would surely know the odds were against him. And
were his American adviser marching with the emperor,
he would have to realize that he stood little chance even
to make a successful defense. And with, say, the fortress of Kumamoto reinforced and made impregnable,
and an immense imperial army stationed in Shimonoseki,
with perhaps an imperial fleet at anchor at the southern entrance to the Inland Sea, and another off
Kagoshima Wan, even Saigo would know that he would
not even be able to *move* without being strangled on the
first day.

What would happen then? Undoubtedly Saigo would
wish to take his own life, swearing curses against his old
friend. If that could be prevented . . . But the fact was,
that even if it could not, the rest of the Satsuma would
live. They would not have been defeated in battle.
They would not even have formally rebelled and then
surrendered. They would merely have accepted the
imperial decrees and broken their swords.

That was the only practical approach to the situation.
That indeed was the path of duty, if he would save the
lives of Suiko and the children, however they might
hate him for it. But the awareness of duty was com-
pounded by another, far less sensible and noble thought.
Munetake was coming south, committed to rebellion. If
he encountered an imperial force determined to stop
him, he would at once be an outlaw, with a price on his
head, with the privileges of his rank withdrawn.

Would he then, Ralph thought, betray his friends,
his people, of eleven years, merely to avenge himself
on Munetake and regain possession of Alison? Such a
consideration was unthinkable. Yet it had to be faced.
Because for the first time in his life since the death of his
parents, the call of duty, and the call of desire, and the
call of humanity were all pointing in the same direction.

*   *   *

Suiko could feel the man against her, moving restlessly, occasionally even touching her flesh tentatively. He was awake, and supposed her asleep. No doubt he wished she would also awake, turn toward him, and end their first-ever quarrel with an embrace.

Their first-ever quarrel. Because Japanese ladies did not quarrel with their husbands; they bowed low and accepted their master's will. Only in matters of honor was it conceivably possible to differ with a husband, and when one was a lady, and therefore married to a samurai, there could never *be* a question of honor.

She was married to a samurai. But one who did not accept the tenets of that near-religion in their entirety. She had known this from the beginning, and feared it. And been lulled into a sense of false security by his personality, his obvious strength. He had used her strangely, with never a harsh word or a blow, an obvious reluctance even to enter a room before her, as was his prerogative. These things had been strange and disturbing; her sisters had chided her about them. But he had been her husband, given to her by Saigo Takamori himself, and she had been bound to accept his ways.

Besides, such ways had been enjoyable. She had more freedom, more power, within the walls of her house than any other woman in Japan, she supposed. Her instincts told her this was wrong—but she could not help but enjoy it.

As with their children. Too often he treated them as friends rather than as a parent should. And this disturbed her. But that they adored their father and would do anything for him could not be doubted. Thus he had gained what every Japanese father sought—by love rather than example and discipline.

Then what had she gained? She had come to him afraid. And with reason. His ways had been even stranger than she had feared; even after eleven years of marriage she still trembled when he would come down on her with all of that immense weight—even if she seldom was allowed to feel it. But in sex, as in all things, he was the very reverse of a samurai; he was gentle.

Indeed, this was the word he prized above all others; when she had asked him, since there were no samurai in America, what he would be considered there, he had replied, "I would hope, a gentle man."

She had not seen how it could be possible to respect, much less honor, a man who so deliberately eschewed all the masculine virtues. And yet there could be no doubt that Saigo Takamori, all the Satsuma samurai, all the samurai in Japan indeed, and even the emperor himself, regarded Freeman San as a most formidable warrior, a man to fear, and to copy where possible. But Ralph himself did not seem to want respect and emulation, certainly not from her. He wanted, he had said often enough, her love. She had not known what to reply. Japanese ladies did not *love* their husbands, as they might love their brothers and fathers and sons; they *respected* them, as they honored and obeyed them.

Yet had she not succumbed? Was it possible to live with a man for eleven years, to share his bed for that time, to have him whisper endearments and desires, and know nothing but softness and charm, and not respond? She had not wanted to respond. She had always known this great weakness in his character would eventually bring disaster upon them. She had hated herself when she had whispered endearments back, however she had meant them at the time.

Now that disaster had nearly come upon them. It had not, and would not, of course. Even Freeman's distorted sense of honor would never permit him to be a coward or to betray the Satsuma in any way. Yet had he revealed his true weakness, and for the future she must be on her guard. Her husband, the man she had so nearly come to love, did indeed have feet of clay.

Whatever he intended, it would have to be undertaken alone. Clearly it was not possible even to warn Suiko, much less attempt to take her and the children with him. She had illustrated her attitude too well last night. She was a Saigo and a Satsuma, and no matter how much she loved him—and he did not doubt that— she would never change her allegiance. But for that very reason he had no fears for her safety, unless the

Satsuma went down in battle, and this was what he was determined to prevent. But by the same token, she would not, she could not, agree with what he was about to do; she would even, he was sure, feel obliged to stop him if she could.

Yet, when it was all over, he was equally sure she would bow her head and accept the will of her lord in this as in all matters. Good and faithful Suiko.

So he held her in his arms a little tighter than usual, and kissed her a little more tenderly than usual next morning as he took his leave. And he hugged his children more anxiously. But they too would survive when he returned in triumph.

He exercised his artillery, drilled his riflemen, as usual; the Satsuma soldiers were not being allowed actually to mourn their dead lord. These were his men, trained to the ultimate, and he now disposed of no less than three regiments, nearly three thousand strong. They had little in the way of preparation to make for any coming conflict; they were always in a state of readiness. And they too would hate their beloved general for what he was about to do. Almost there were tears in his eyes as he dismissed them at midday and then rode north, as he often did, either to exercise his horse or to inspect the land over which one day he might have to fight—more necessary than ever in present circumstances. Certainly no one questioned what he was doing. No one had any reason to suspect Freeman San of treachery.

Not until he was out of sight of Kagoshima did he kick his horse into a canter, sending him across the fields toward Kumamoto, feeling a curious lightness of mind that he was, for the first time since he had thrown himself from the battlements of Shimonoseki behind Alison, doing exactly as he wished to do, what he knew had to be done. And at the same time there was a great heaviness in his belly, because what had to be done so involved his personal honor and the integrity of his friends.

It was dusk before he reached Kumamoto, where the lanterns glowed and the imperial sentries looked down on him. He had not been to the north since the royal wedding several years ago. That had been before the introduction of uniforms, and now he gazed in surprise at the smart blue jackets and white breeches, the white gaiters, and the blue caps with the red bands. Now it was he in his green armor who was the archaic figure. But were these men samurai or honin? It was impossible to tell. Every man carried a rifle and a bayonet, and there was not a sword to be seen, except conventionally in a scabbard on the thigh of the officer who greeted him. "Freeman San! Welcome to Kumamoto."

"I seek your commanding officer," Ralph told him.

The lieutenant frowned. "You have a message from General Saigo?"

"I am on imperial business," Ralph said, and a few minutes later was in the office of General Kodama, dapper and smart, who gave him a brief bow, while his eyes remained watchful; no doubt Inouye had warned him of the looming hostility of the Satsuma.

"General!" Ralph returned the bow. "May I ask the strength of your garrison?"

"You may ask, Freeman San."

Ralph sighed. But he had to anticipate this attitude. "Very well, General, let me put it another way. Have you sufficient men to hold the Satsuma army, should it move to the north?"

Kodama stared at him.

"Because that is what is going to happen very soon," Ralph said, refusing to lose his temper. "General Saigo has determined to resist the abolishment of the samurai. He is determined to march on Tokyo and seize the person of the emperor, as soon as he can mobilize his forces. He will eventually dispose of twenty thousand men, I would estimate. Can you defend this castle against such an army? They possess rifles and modern cannon."

"You, are telling me this, Freeman San?" Kodama stroked his chin. "Is it permitted to ask why?"

"Because I think the emperor is right in what he does, and because I would save Japan from the horrors of civil war. Listen to me, General Kodama. It is my purpose to ride for Tokyo and inform the emperor of what is happening. Now, I do not think General Saigo will move against you until he is fully mobilized and has called in all his samurai. This will take some weeks, and I would hope you will be reinforced by then. But he does possess artillery and three regiments of riflemen, ready to march at a few hours' notice. These he may send against you the moment my flight has been discovered, hoping to overwhelm you by the speed of his assault. Should he do so, you *must* hold him here. Because, General, if he takes Kumamoto, he will hold all Kyushu, and the emperor will overcome him only by a great effort and much bloodshed. If he fails to take Kumamoto, then he can never invade Honshu, and more, he will not even possess this island. His majesty will be able to meet him here and save the rest of the empire from war."

"My orders are to hold Kumamoto for the emperor," Kodama said. "I will carry out my orders."

"These men of yours are honin or samurai?"

"They are Japanese soldiers," Kodama said stiffly.

Ralph sighed. "Well, then, General, will you take some advice? This castle of yours will not stand a bombardment. The enemy must be kept at the maximum range of their guns." He went to the window, looked out. There was an early moon, and visibility was good. Kumamoto itself stood on a slight hill, south of which the ground dipped into a deep hollow, before again rising to another hill, almost as high as that of the castle, and about two miles away. Ralph pointed. "You should make that rise your perimeter. I know you have not many men, but if they were to dig trenches in which they could conceal themselves, they should be able to resist a force many times their own size."

"My orders are to hold Kumamoto, General Freeman," Kodama said again. "I do not need to be told how to fight. I will hold this fortress as long as I live, and I shall not survive its fall."

Ralph chewed his lip in frustration. Like all samurai, Kodama could envisage no greater loyalty, no greater service, than the sacrifice of his life. If he lost that serving his emperor, then he would have carried out his orders to the best of his ability. He could not imagine that he might still have failed, by dying either unnecessarily or too soon.

"Well, General," he said, "try to stay alive as long as possible. By whatever means you may. Believe me, the empire depends on that. Now, will you let me have a fresh horse?"

Kodama's face was coldly impassive.

"General," Ralph said, "I must be across the Strait of Shimonoseki by dawn."

Kodama nodded. "Undoubtedly the Satsuma will send behind you," he remarked with some satisfaction.

"Undoubtedly," Ralph agreed. "However, that is not my only reason for haste. I seek Prince Inouye, to march with me and a detachment of imperial troops from Cho-Shu, to intercept the men of the northern Satsuma. General Saigo has sent messengers to Hokkaido, summoning the rest of his people to Kyushu."

"The messengers passed through here yesterday morning," Kodama said. "It is right that the men of Satsuma should attend the mourning for their dead lord."

"That is but a subterfuge," Ralph told him. "General Saigo means to concentrate all his strength. General Munetake must be intercepted and his people dispersed."

"How may you attack men who wish only to mourn their lord?" Kodama asked. "That is not the law of bushido."

"Even when you know it is a trick?" Ralph cried.

Kodama got up from behind his desk. "I will lend you a fresh horse, to see Prince Inouye, if that is your desire." His voice was loaded with contempt.

What more could he have expected? Ralph wondered. Kodama was very definitely a samurai, who believed in the values of his forefathers, even if he now served his emperor in endeavoring to turn those values upside down. He would have nothing but contempt for a man who would so betray his adopted clan, regardless of the treason they intended.

But *his* business remained first of all the interception of Munetake; he could worry about the contempt afterward. And *that* depended upon finding Inouye.

He was unlucky. Inouye was not in Shimonseki, having, Ralph was told, hastened north to report to the emperor. To tell the monarch that the Satsuma undoubtedly would resist the law abolishing the samurai, but also, as Lord Shimadzu was now dead, there was no great need for haste in preparing the measures against them, because of the mourning period. Nor was the commander of the imperial garrison here any more helpful than Kodama. But Ralph was able to obtain another fresh horse and to gallop on. There *was* still time, he kept on telling himself. Besides, for all his pretended indifference to Kodama, he was well aware that by now Saigo would indeed have sent assassins after him. And so, after ten days of hard riding, he came to Tokyo.

He went straight to the house occupied by Inouye, as he knew he would not readily gain admittance to the emperor. The prince was sipping green tea with his wife—he having removed his main residence from Shimonoseki to the capital—in his garden. He gazed at Ralph in total amazement, then sent Mrs. Inouye away as he listened to what his friend had to say. When Ralph had finished, he thought for several minutes. "You have but taken my advice," he said. "And yet, I never supposed that you would. And how I wish that circumstances could be different. They will call down curses upon you, Ralph. You know this?"

"At least they will be alive to do so," Ralph said, accepting that even Inouye would wish to consider the personal element first, however great the import of his news.

"I wonder," Inouye said. "You think they will not fight, knowing that the emperor is aware of their plans? They are samurai, Ralph, and what is more, they are desperate. They will fight."

"Then we must defeat them, utterly and quickly, and in the field," Ralph said. "Before they can shut themselves up in Kagoshima."

"If Saigo does not resolve on such a strategy from the beginning."

"He will not," Ralph said. "He holds the imperial army in the most utter contempt, and his entire strategy is based on the offensive, on somehow gaining possession of the emperor and acting in his name."

"We must hope that you are right." Inouye gave a sad smile. "And that he is not. But your own wife and children . . ." He shook his head.

"She at the least—"

"Will hate you more than any other," Inouye said. "She is a Saigo."

"Then you condemn what I have done," Ralph said bitterly.

Inouye shook his head again. "I but marvel at your determination, your courage. Your loyalty, if you like, to Japan as opposed to one clan. Once I told you that no Japanese could have done what you had. Now I must hope and pray that all Japanese will one day possess such steadfastness. But I cannot help but grieve for the personal catastrophe you are risking. Come. We must see the emperor."

Mutsuhito, on hearing that Inouye had the gravest of news to impart, canceled his afternoon council and received the pair of them alone. He too listened to Ralph's words in silence, and he too gazed at him for several moments when he had finished speaking, while Ralph returned the look. The young monarch was clearly tired, and for all his youth there were worry lines clustering beside his eyes and lips. He was not finding the path he had chosen an easy one. But now he smiled. "Perhaps," he said, "it is best that these discontents, these hatreds, are brought out into the open and decided once and for all. We thank you, Freeman San, for your loyalty. Be sure we shall never forget it." He looked at Inouye. "Can our army cope with this rebellion, Prince Inouye?"

Inouye bit his lip. "If Saigo Takamori can throw twenty thousand men into the field, and hope to gain more . . ."

"Can we not more than match him? Have we not fifty thousand men under arms?"

"Half-trained," Inouye said. "And . . ." He looked utterly disconsolate.

"And once they were honin," Mutsuhito said softly.

"What is more, your Majesty," Inouye said, "many of the Satsuma will have been trained by General Freeman."

Mutsuhito looked at Ralph. "Well, General Freeman?"

he asked. "Or, having warned us, would you prefer to stand aside from this conflict?"

"It is my purpose to end it as soon as possible," Ralph said, "with an imperial victory. I admit that I have trained the Satsuma. But at the least I will know what they are most likely to do."

"Then you will accept a commission?"

"Gladly, your Majesty."

"As commander of a brigade of foot?"

"Preferably not, your Majesty."

"Of course. That was an insult. You will command our field artillery."

"Your Majesty . . ."

Mutsuhito frowned at him. "Is artillery not important?"

"It will be, my lord, most certainly. But as Prince Inouye has said, there are many factors here to be considered. First, that the Satsuma army will be composed only of samurai, with all the strengths but also the weaknesses that are thereby involved. Yet it will also include three regiments of riflemen and four batteries of field artillery. These I have trained myself, and if General Saigo's dispositions are not faulty, they will match anything your people can do."

"And mine are composed entirely of honin." Mutsuhito glanced at Inouye again. "Will honin stand against samurai, Prince Inouye?"

"This we shall have to discover, your Majesty."

"At risk of the empire," Mutsuhito observed, and sighed. "Well, we must mobilize every man we can raise, and march south."

"To mobilize will take weeks, perhaps months, your Majesty," Inouye said. "And the moment we begin, even should it be during the mourning period, General Saigo will know of it and take the field."

"Are you suggesting we should do nothing, but await his assault here? Allow him to overrun half Japan?"

Inouye looked at Ralph, who was snapping his fingers with impatience.

"We must act *now*, your Majesty," he insisted. "The key to the situation is Kumamoto. It lies across the Satsuma line of march, and it is an imperial sally port in the very heart of Satsuma territory. There is no way in which Saigo Takamori can cross the Strait of Shimonoseki and march on Tokyo, leaving Kumamoto in his rear, in hostile hands. If you were to dispatch a small field force at this instant, without mobilization, to travel south as rapidly as possible and reinforce General Kodama, and hold Kumamoto at all costs, then you will have a bastion against which the Satsuma may throw themselves in vain, while you mobilize your main army."

"And this is what you would command?"

"If your majesty would agree. I know Saigo Takamori. I know the way his mind works."

Mutsuhito stroked his chin. "Have you any idea, General Freeman, what would be your fate were the Satsuma to capture you defending Kumamoto?"

"If I did not think I could hold the fortress, your Majesty, I would not attempt it. But there is more. If you can dispatch such a force now, I would also be able to intercept a force of Satsuma samurai who have been summoned from Hokkaido. That is some five thousand men, your Majesty. Their loss would be a severe one to Saigo Takamori."

"As would the loss of their general, Munetake, the Cho-Shu renegade," Inouye observed.

Mutsuhito glanced at him. How much did these two men share in their knowledge of him? Ralph wondered.

"What force would you need, Freeman San?" asked the emperor.

"If I can have a brigade of riflemen, and horses for them, as well as a battery of field artillery, your Majesty, I believe the Satsuma can be held, pending your mobilization. The horses are to enable us to reach the vicinity of Lake Biwa with all possible speed, for General Munetake will have to be stopped there, before he can get south of the lake and pass Osaka. Once that is done, your Majesty, if you would command a fleet of ships to be made ready at Osaka, to take my brigade south, then we could reach Kyushu in less than a week, as against a fortnight should we have to march the whole way."

Mutsuhito gave him another long look and then rose. Both Inouye and Ralph immediately bowed. The emperor walked to the door at the rear of the room, opened it, and looked out past the two guards standing there, at the palace gardens, where for so long the Tokugawa had walked in stately power. After a few minutes he closed the door again and turned back to face them. "The only force readily available," he said almost to himself, "is the Imperial Guard, which is now being organized. It possesses the elements you require, and indeed has two batteries, not one. But I must warn you that it is composed of half-trained honin, General Freeman." He smiled. "I should say half-trained peasants. They have never faced samurai in battle. They have never in their lives done more than scurry aside and bow low whenever a samurai has even approached them."

"Perhaps, your Majesty," Ralph said, "they have never been given the opportunity to do more."

"Now, do you know, that is a point of view I had not considered?"

"But, your Majesty," Inouye protested, "if you send the Imperial Guard away from Tokyo . . ."

"I will be unprotected in my capital, Prince Inouye? At least until the remainder of the army can be mobilized. But yet *will* I be protected, by the love of my people. My honin." He came across the room and held out his hand. "I give you your command, General Freeman, and wish you every fortune. A fleet will be waiting for you in Osaka. If you can hold Kumamoto for a month, I promise to be there with every man I can raise."

Ralph squeezed the imperial fingers and hoped Aya could somehow know of this moment, when the safety of the realm was being placed in the hands of her people. "My authority?"

Mutsuhito glanced at Inouye. "Officially, General Kodama must remain in command. You understand me, General Freeman?"

"Of course, your Majesty." For the sake of the future, the rebellion must be crushed by Japanese soldiers led by Japanese generals.

"But I will give you a letter instructing Kodama to take your advice in all things relating to the defense of Kumamoto."

"And have I anything to offer General Saigo and his people, should the occasion arise?"

Mutsuhito turned away for a few moments. "Saigo Takamori is a rebel against his emperor. I will not demand his seppuku; I would like to feel those days are behind us. But he will have to leave Japan forever. As for the Satsuma, they have but to obey the imperial decree to live and be happy."

There were no bugle calls, no clamorous messengers. Speed and silence were the weapons here. Ralph and Inouye rode to the encampment of the guard, only a mile south of the city. Here there was a German colonel, Rupprecht Helsinger, who read the imperial orders with a grave frown and then raised his head. "You would pit these few thousand men against twenty thousand samurai?"

"We have but to hold," Ralph said. "And it is possible that they may not even attack us in time. Besides, the very fact that our enemies *are* samurai increases our chances. We are a forlorn hope, Colonel. You know what that is?"

Helsinger grinned. "I am a soldier, sir. We can march at dawn."

"We will march when the horses are assembled," Ralph said.

Which was not until the following afternoon. It was a long, tedious wait, when there was so much to be done. But it was worth it. They would travel twice as fast, mounted, and he spent the day in acquainting his gunners with what he would require of them. The artillery, even though it might be no more than two batteries, was his only hope of gaining any ascendancy over the Satsuma.

And with the horses there arrived a uniform for Ralph, to replace his green Satsuma armor. It was seventeen years since he had worn Western uniform.

Inouye also returned, to clasp his hand. "I begged permission of the emperor to accompany you, Ralph, and he has given it. But only as far as Shimonoseki. I am to make sure the men of Cho-Shu do not attempt to stab you in the back."

"That is more than half the campaign, old friend," Ralph cried, and raised his head. There were crowds to watch the mounted infantry march out, but no man save the three commanders had any idea where they were going. It was given out as merely a training exercise. So rapidly, indeed, had events transpired, that the only fact known to the good people of Tokyo, who necessarily would include several Satsuma agents, were the death of Lord Shimadzu and the treacherous flight of the barbarian from Kagoshima. Upon this Ralph was heavily counting, that Saigo, sure in his reverence for tradition, would not believe *any* force would be dispatched against him before the mourning period was up, no matter what lies Freeman might disseminate.

But first, Munetake and Alison. Until that was done, Ralph was only half the general everyone supposed him to be.

"What route would he take from Hokkaido?" he asked Inouye.

"I do not think, even relying upon the mourning period, that he will wish to march close by Tokyo," Inouye said. "So he will take the north coast road. That is also the shortest."

"But he must pass close by Lake Biwa, where the land narrows," Ralph said.

"Indeed he must," Inouye agreed. "It is simply a matter of deciding whether he will travel northwest, that is, remaining by the coast, or southeast of the lake, to gain the coast of the Inland Sea below Osaka. There he will soon be in Cho-Shu territory, and he will know at the least no attempt will be made to stop him." He smiled. "If he comes southeast, it will be to cross Sekigahara, the Plain of the Barrier. That is the most famous battlefield in Japan."

"Where the Tokugawa secured power two hundred and fifty years ago," Ralph said. "I have heard of it. But so has Munetake. Yet we must cover each route. I will take five hundred men and one battery and hasten ahead to cover the northern road. You follow with the remainder, and occupy the Plain of the Barrier. Should Munetake come against you, then send for me immediately. But, Inouye San, all you must do is defend. Keep your men under cover and repel Munetake with rifle and cannon fire until I arrive."

"Be certain I shall do nothing more than that," Inouye said. "But you think he will take the northern road?"

Ralph nodded.

"And you hope to stop him with five hundred men?"

"We will have the advantage of surprise, and he will have no cannon." He clapped Inouye on the shoulder. "Besides, *I* will send for *you* the moment I discern his intention."

He hurried his men by forced marches across the hills north of Lake Biwa. It was high summer, and there was little rain; the roads remained solid. They made good progress, flooded through the passes, Ralph galloping ahead with his immediate staff, seeking some sign of movement on the coast road, and finding none.

Then he looked out to sea and saw the fleet, coasting south before the light northerly wind. His force was equipped with the most modern aids to warfare, and from his belt, hanging beside the Colt revolver, was a pair of powerful field glasses, with which he could easily make out the flags on the junks; they flew the cross within the ring of the Satsuma.

Alison had not been at sea since that dreadful day in 1861. It was sheer bliss to sit on the afterdeck of the junk and feel the motion of the hull beneath her, the wind rippling through her hair.

Neither Harunari nor Jeremy had ever been on a ship before in their lives, and both were obviously terrified, for all Jeremy's hissing and stamping to prove his courage. He modeled himself, clearly, on his foster father, which was reasonable, even if disturbing. What was less easy to understand was his complete lack of interest in his past, in the reasons for his paler skin and greater stature than the average boy of his age. Yet the sea was surely in his blood. And how many other things besides?

When *would* he begin to ask questions? And what would she answer? Because soon he was going to see his father for the first time. There could be no avoiding that, as Ralph was clearly a very important man in the Satsuma army. And now there was no question about the inevitability of a war. Which it was impossible to imagine the Satsuma winning, as they seemed determined to take on the entire rest of Japan. She did not think even Munetake expected victory, however much he certainly expected to survive, and even salvage a great deal from the wreckage.

But Ralph, being Ralph, would go down beside his friend Saigo, fighting gallantly. Leaving behind him ... Her heart throbbed most painfully. If she was afraid of facing him on such an occasion, how could she face his wife? And he had children, also. To meet, knowing they were on a collision course with disaster ... She had allowed herself to dream that in the catastrophe all things might be possible, Munetake might be dead, and Saigo too, but she and Ralph would survive, with Jeremy ... which was why she had given Munetake the benefit of her advice, to his delight: she had wanted only to gain Kagoshima.

But now she knew there were too many other people involved in her dream for it ever to come true. Saigo Suiko—the very name suggested beauty and sweetness. Could she possibly dream of *her* dead? And the children? She did not even know their names.

"Look there." Munetake had been standing at the rail, scanning the coast with his binoculars. Now he beckoned her to his side, allowed her to use the glasses to see the sun reflecting from the bayonets of the men gathered there. "Imperial troops," he said. "Just as I supposed."

"But how could they know?"

He shrugged. "Treachery. There is always treachery. But we have given them the slip. Thanks to you. I will give you credit to Saigo Takamori, my Alison. I certainly would not have thought of using the sea to turn their flank." He snapped his fingers. "We shall be in Kagoshima before they can even reach the Strait of Shimonoseki. I have outwitted them." He hugged her against him. "I shall always outwit them, my Alison, with you at my side. Not even the emperor can match us." He grinned at her. "Not even Freeman."

"You fight for the same side," she reminded him.

"Do we?" he asked, and gave her another squeeze. "When we fight, it shall be for possession of you, my Alison. And I will win then, too."

"Munetake is not a seaman. It just never occurred to me that he would use ships," Ralph confessed to Inouye and Helsinger as they rode south. They could still see the sails, but hull-down now; the breeze remained fresh and the horses had to rest every night—the ships did not. While his stomach seemed as lead-filled as his brain. He had begun with a failure. Alison would not even know what he had attempted. She would be anticipating, or perhaps fearing, meeting him in Kago-shima, knowing that they were embarked together on the most dread of adventures.

"He still cannot sail right around Kyushu and reach Kagoshima and disembark his men before we gain Kumamoto," Helsinger pointed out. "Not as we also intend to use ships. If your theory is right, and Saigo will not launch an assault until after Munetake's arrival, by forcing him to take to the sea we will still have accomplished our purpose."

Ralph found Inouye gazing at him. The Japanese knew there had been a personal reason for the attempted interception. They walked together that evening after supper, just the two of them, surrounded by the encamped brigade. The honin laughed and sang as they drank their sake and polished their rifles and bayonets; in the darkness, the barrels of the cannon gleamed.

"They are good men," Ralph said. "I think we have the makings of a fine army here, Inouye San. Provided only they do not become overawed at the very thought of facing samurai, then all things are possible."

"I am sure you are right, Freeman San," Inouye agreed. He was waiting for the question which he knew Ralph wished to ask.

Ralph sighed. "When Shimonoseki fell, Lord Nariaka committed seppuku, and with him, his women."

"I know," Inouye said.

"Is this customary?"

"It has often happened before," Inouye said cautiously.

"Had you been present, would you have felt called upon to do so?"

"Perhaps."

"And would you have required the sacrifice of your wife?"

"Tradition says that this is the correct thing to do, as it is surely a preferable end for one's woman than to fall into the hands of the enemy, when she would have fewer rights than an eta. But it is not part of the law of bushido."

"So it is up to the individual samurai."

"That is correct," Inouye agreed.

"And now that there are no more eta . . ."

"A woman taken in combat, or in the anger which follows a victory, is still liable to considerable mistreatment," Inouye said, still choosing his words with great care. "Most husbands or fathers would consider them better off dead."

Ralph said nothing, but stared into the darkness. Inouye rested his hand on his arm.

"I thought you had weighed this matter before leaving Kagoshima, Ralph."

"No," Ralph said. "No. I weighed civilized behavior."

"And yet, I have heard that your American pioneers would kill their women rather than let them fall into the hands of the Indians."

"That is . . ."

"Different? Why so? The Indians are men with red skins as opposed to white, and different habits from yours. Nariaka and our Cho-Shu people considered your barbarians as men with white skins as opposed to yellow, and different habits from ours."

"And Saigo? Munetake? They are opposing men with the same color skins and the same habits as their own, excepting possibly Colonel Helsinger and myself."

"To a rebel or the wife of a rebel, all men opposed to him must be terrible," Inouye said.

So haste, galloping onward, without even clearly knowing where he was going, what he was attempting. To Osaka, where, as promised, a fleet of junks was awaiting them. And then down the calm waters of the Inland Sea. Onward to Kyushu. And then? The journey

seemed to take forever, although it was only two days.
But at least Ralph was able to spend them discussing
with Helsinger the training of the guard. And learning,
much to his relief, that it had actually been considerable, especially in marksmanship and volley fire while
advancing. Helsinger had no fears for their tactical
ability, only for their reaction when opposed to samurai.
They would be better on the defensive, he felt. But
merely to stand on the defensive would yield the advantage to the Satsuma and set the stage for a long-drawn-
out conflict and a siege of Kumamoto, with all the
horrors that the end of it suggested. Horrors which
would involve Alison and Jeremy, as well as Suiko and
her children.

No, if Saigo could not be made to see sense, to call
off his rebellion, to make his peace with the emperor
and let his people live, then he had to be utterly defeated in one short, sharp encounter, and Kagoshima
taken before it could be prepared for a siege.

With a brigade of honin? Yet he knew it could be
done, if Saigo fought as he was sure he would fight,
like a samurai.

But nothing would be possible if Kumamoto had
already fallen. So haste, dropping anchor at Shimonoseki
for an hour, less than three weeks after his departure,
to set Inouye ashore, and find all quiet, although the
place was full of rumors coming up from the south.
Satsuma agents had been in the town, recruiting samurai,
and many had crossed to Kyushu, they were told. But
as yet no one knew of any fighting down there, and the
imperial banners still flew over Kumamoto.

But yet haste, to disembark on the north shore of
Kyushu and drive his men onward. The honin no longer
laughed over their evening sake; few of them had ever
spent two days at sea in their lives before, and after the
earlier forced marches they were exhausted; besides,
they had to leave their horses behind in Osaka. Now
they looked at Ralph from scowling faces, and muttered behind his back, and now too they no longer
polished their rifles and bayonets. But there would be
time enough for that when they reached Kumamoto.

And on the fourteenth day after leaving Tokyo, they marched over the hills and looked down on the fortress, from which the Rising Sun of Japan still waved, and then looked at the hills beyond, and the cross and ring of the Satsuma.

—15—
THE TRIUMPH

General Kodama himself rode out of the fortress to meet them, and look past Ralph and Helsinger as the column of honin approached, followed by the sweating artillerymen. "This is what you bring to my relief?" he asked.

"This is the advance guard," Ralph told him. "The emperor follows, with the main body." He pointed. "How long have they been there?"

Kodama shrugged. "They assembled about a week after your departure."

"And they have made no move to attack you?"

"We parleyed, General Freeman. They explained that pending instructions from the emperor, they wished to regain possession of Kumamoto. I informed them that the fortress must be defended. General Saigo then told me that my cause was hopeless, that he disposed of fifteen thousand men, to my two. I acknowledged this, and he offered me seppuku. I agreed, if no word came from the emperor within a fortnight. I asked for a month, but he would allow me only a fortnight."

"Which ends when?" Ralph asked.

"Tomorrow morning," Kodama said, not a twitch of his face indicating the narrowness of his escape. "They did not suppose you, or anyone, could come so soon."

And Saigo was determined to wage this war with all the traditional honor of the samurai. The fool, Ralph thought. The heroic, glorious, magnificent fool.

Or had he just been waiting for Munetake?

"Well," he said, "let us continue to surprise him, if we can."

Now Kodama's face did twitch. "With what, General? He will have seen your force. I do not consider that anything has changed. Tomorrow morning at dawn the fortress will surrender."

"And you will kill yourself," Ralph said.

"All commanding officers present will kill themselves," Kodama pointed out. "Including yourself."

"I do not think that will be necessary, General. I have a letter for you from the emperor."

While Kodama read Mutsuhito's instructions, Ralph studied the Satsuma forces through his binoculars. Their exact dispositions were difficult to decide, for Saigo had not actually occupied the hill overlooking Kuma-moto, no doubt confident that he could do so whenever he wished, but for the time being had kept his men out of sight in the valley beyond. This was strategically sound, but he had made the mistake of leaving all his flags and pennants flying, as was the samurai custom. Munetake's personal banners were missing. In that respect they were still in time.

Kodama folded the letter and placed it in his pocket. His face remained impassive. "Well, General?" he asked.

"We must occupy that ridge if we can. Certainly we must not let the enemy do so. I will parley. But if they do not withdraw, we must attack them immediately."

"Very good," Helsinger said. "Your dispositions?"

"You will attack fifteen thousand samurai with three thousand honin?" Kodama asked.

"It is the only way to gain the initiative, General. If we merely wait for them to come to us, we will be overwhelmed. Now, Colonel, your men will march into that dip beyond the fortress as if to pitch camp. Once they are there, have them unload all their surplus equipment, but instead of pitching their tents, they are to be formed into line, and then they will proceed directly to the top of the rise with loaded rifles. Until they reach the brow they will be hidden from the Satsuma."

"And the artillery?"

"Will also enter the valley, but instead of unlimbering, will be kept in readiness, both batteries together, mind, and the moment the flag of truce is thrown to the ground, they will gain the top of the ridge as rapidly as possible, unlimber, and commence battery firing into the enemy."

Helsinger pulled his nose. "If the riflemen fail to support you, General, the guns will be lost."

"If the riflemen do not support us, Colonel, then everything will be lost, and as General Kodama says, the fortress will be surrendered at dawn. So either way, let us prepare to die like men." He smiled at Kodama. "Like samurai, eh, General?"

Ralph rode across to the nearest company of riflemen, saluted them as they trudged by. They did not look any more cheerful than earlier; they too could see the myriad waving banners on the far side of the hill.

"I need a standard-bearer," he said. "A volunteer."

"I will come with you, my lord." One of the sergeants stepped from the ranks and saluted, and Ralph recognized him in delighted surprise; his name was Fushida, and he was one of the six honin who had left his service in Kagoshima to seek their fortunes in the north.

"You understand that we may not return," he said.

"I understand, my lord."

"Lend this man a horse, Colonel Helsinger," Ralph instructed. "And, Sergeant Fushida, you will address me as sir, or general. You have no lord now, save for the emperor."

The white flag was raised on the end of a lance borne by Fushida, and the pair of them walked their mounts forward, down into the hollow where the main body of the imperial troops were already laying down their surplus equipment and being marshaled into lines by their officers, and then up the slope beyond. Their movements were certainly being overlooked by the Satsuma pickets, and now a body of armored horsemen, their pennons flying in the breeze, moved forward to the ridge itself, to look down on the scene below. But Ralph was relying on the probability that they would be more interested in the flag of truce and the person of the herald himself rather than in the deployment of such a pitifully small body of imperial troops.

"Are you afraid, Sergeant Fushida?" he asked, without turning his head.

"A man can but die, General," Fushida replied.

Spoken like a samurai, Ralph thought, and hoped Fushida's comrades were as spirited. He topped the rise, and now looked down into the valley beyond, where the Satsuma outposts waited, and then the hills beyond that, where the main body of the rebels was grouped, a glittering mass of gleaming armor and sun-reflecting lance heads and waving banners, certainly at least fifteen thousand men, he estimated. A magnificent sight, he thought, reminding him of paintings he had seen of medieval armies awaiting the onset of battle. Because it *was* a medieval army, and thus was doomed to extinction, if not today, then soon enough.

He swung his glasses to the left, made out the three rifle regiments, grouped on the right wing, as he had done outside Tokyo. Saigo was using an identical disposition as on that famous day, unable to grasp that each battle required different tactics. And he had made the same mistake that the Tokugawa had in failing properly to mass his artillery; if he had not placed the guns in complete isolation of each other, he had yet spaced the batteries in an attempt to cover his entire field, and they were incapable of mutual support. Yet did he still possess four batteries to the imperial two, and five men to every guardsman. There was no certain victory in sight as yet.

Now the group of horsemen was close, and Ralph could recognize Saigo himself, and his brother, and his own father-in-law, Saigo Kiyotake, as well as Hayashi and other well-known faces.

"Well, traitor," Saigo Takamori said, "do you suppose that white flag gives you the right to stand before me? Do you suppose it will protect you from my vengeance?"

"I am here on the emperor's business," Ralph said evenly. "You defy me at your peril."

"The emperor's business." Saigo sneered. "Is *that* his army?"

"That is but the advance guard," Ralph said. "The emperor follows with all the strength of the country. Saigo San, old friend, there is no hope of your defeating him. But not a shot has yet been fired. His majesty knows this, and would have it so. He invites you to send your samurai home and to accept his decrees and make your peace."

"That he employs traitors and false samurai is sufficient evidence that his majesty does not speak with his own tongue," Saigo said. "We shall free him from such dishonorable advisers, or die in the attempt. But first we will retake what is rightfully ours. General Kodama has agreed to surrender the fortress of Kumamoto tomorrow morning, unless relieved. He has not been relieved by any force capable of defeating the Satsuma. Therefore tomorrow morning we will take possession of Kumamoto. I have fifteen thousand men back there, barbarian, and five more about to disembark; General Munetake's ships are already in Kagoshima Wan. Your few honin will not stand against us. Flee with them, or remain and for the first time in your miserable life act the honorable part and slit your belly. For be sure that when we take you prisoner, you will die like the dog you are, and they will hear your screams in Tokyo itself."

Ralph gazed at him for several seconds. Then he said, "So be it, General Saigo. What follows is on your own head." He nodded to Fushida, and the pair of them turned their horses and walked them back a few paces. "Now!" Ralph shouted. Fushida threw the white flag to the ground, and from behind him Ralph could clearly hear the call of the bugles and the shouts of Helsinger and his officers commanding the honin infantry to advance.

Saigo also gave a shout and drew his sword, as did his aides, kicking their horses forward. Ralph turned in the saddle, drawing his revolver as he did so, and tumbled the foremost samurai from the saddle with a single shot. Fushida dismounted, unslinging his rifle and bringing down another of his erstwhile masters, while Ralph dropped a third.

It had all happened so suddenly that the remainder dragged on their reins, staring at the deadly revolver and the no less deadly rifle in consternation as Fushida calmly reloaded. Saigo's face was twisted with anger. He was a perfect target, and yet Ralph could not squeeze

the trigger at the man who had so befriended him. He
hesitated, while they stared at each other; then Saigo
wheeled his horse and galloped back down the slope to
his men. And now there came a cheer from behind
them, and the honin infantry started forward, bayonets
flashing in the afternoon sun. They had after all re-
sponded to the command, even if they had as yet no
idea whom or how many they were being called upon
to fight. But certainly the rest of the Satsuma commanders were astonished by the sight. They followed their
general, waving their swords and shouting commands,
while the conch shells started wailing, and the entire
mass of armored warriors rippled, before starting itself
to advance down into the next valley. Ralph turned to
find out where his artillery were, and saw them hurrying up the slope, accompanied by Helsinger himself.
"Sergeant Fushida," Ralph snapped, "ride to the fortress and ask General Kodama to support me with all
his people, forming a right wing. Tell him the battle
will be joined in a few minutes, and his arrival may well
be decisive."

For even as Fushida saluted and rode off, the artillery reached the hilltop, and the guns were unlimbered.
Now the noise from in front of them was deafening, as
the cymbals clashed and the bugles rang out, and the
heavy tread of the samurai thundered down into the
valley. The Satsuma cannon were already firing, sending isolated shot whistling over Ralph's head or into the
earth beneath him, while now too the samurai loosed
an arrow storm, filling the air with sound, but nearly all
the shafts fell short.

"Aim at the center of the Satsuma army," Ralph told
the gunners, riding in front of them and then taking
his place beside them as he saw that all was ready. He
raised his hand, waited for every piece to be set, and
then shouted, "Fire!"

The twelve field pieces exploded together, completely
shrouding themselves in noise and smoke, a noise which
was immediately overtaken by the screams from in front
of them, and as the smoke cleared they could see the
destruction the exploding shells had caused in the Satsuma ranks. The entire rebel army checked, and then

gave a shout of contempt as they saw that they were apparently opposed only by two batteries of artillery. On they came again, urged by the waving swords of their officers; the rifle regiments were also advancing on the imperial left wing, at the double, as he had himself taught them, not firing as yet, again as he had taught them, but waiting to reach the most effective range. They were the principal danger. But now the honin infantry were nearly breasting the hill, still out of sight of the Satsuma.

"Halt!" Ralph shouted, riding along the ridge above them and ignoring the shot whining about him. "Hold, there! Form line. And lie down."

For the Satsuma had raised the trajectory of their guns to fire over the heads of their infantry, and the air on the hilltop was becoming increasingly filled with flying shrapnel—Ralph felt a vague sense of surprise that he had not yet been hit himself.

The honin and their officers gaped at their general in amazement, unable to understand his command. But they obeyed, lying on the grass in orderly lines, their rifles thrust in front af them, while Ralph galloped back to the guns. "Colonel Helsinger, wheel your artillery to the left and fire into those rifle regiments."

Helsinger obeyed without question, although he cast an anxious glance at the main samurai force, now not more than half a mile away, and still advancing, although slowing all the time as they toiled up the slope in their armor. But the riflemen were much closer, and now Ralph watched the first rank drop to their knees and present their weapons. "Fire!" he yelled.

Another storm of shot and shell tore through the riflemen's ranks. It seemed as if at least half had fallen, although some were obviously only taking shelter. And those who could fired in return; even these stray bullets brought down several of the gunners, to reveal what might have happened had the enemy been allowed to develop their full firepower. "Reload," Ralph shouted. "And keep firing. Those men must be dispersed, Colonel Helsinger," and thought how wonderful it would be if he possessed even a company of the United States cavalry to settle them with a charge.

"They will be dispersed, General," the German promised grimly, and Ralph could return along the ridge, and just in time, for the samurai were more than half-way up, shouting and blowing their conch shells, for all their exhaustion clearly discounting their victory as they supposed the honin already fled and penned into the fortress. They were only about four hundred yards off now, point-blank range for a rifle, and their artillery had ceased firing for fear of hitting their own people.

"Now," Ralph bellowed. "The brigade will rise and advance."

With a great shout the honin got to their feet and lined the ridge, and then gasped as they saw the force to which they were being opposed, and more, of *whom* it was composed.

The samurai were no less taken aback by the sudden appearance of this mass of smartly uniformed infantry above them, and they also fell silent as they checked, staring at their foes; for a brief moment the only sound was the continuous roaring of the guns to the east.

"Volley fire," Ralph commanded, dismounting to take his place in the front rank. "Fire!"

For a moment nothing happened, and his heart seemed to stop beating.

"Fire!" he yelled again, and stepped forward.

The first rank moved with him, kneeling, aiming, and firing. He wanted to scream with joy as the second rank followed their example, and then the third, while the first rank reloaded, volley after volley crashing into the mass of samurai, still hesitating halfway up the slope. And definitely wavering, looking to their officers for orders.

Major Yamagata, commanding the infantry, hurried up to Ralph. "I would like to give the order to charge, General," he said.

So would I, Ralph thought. But he dared not let the honin come within reach of the samurai swords, those devastating symbols of a thousand years of supremacy. "Hold your men, Major," he said. "Hold them here, at least until General Kodama arrives." He gazed back at the fortress, saw the group of horsemen approaching, and frowned; the garrison was not marching behind them. "Hold your men, Major," he said again. "Keep firing into the enemy." He remounted and galloped to where Helsinger was still blasting the samurai riflemen with shrapnel, leaving huge mounds of armored men dead and dying on the field. "Keep firing, Colonel," he said, his voice hoarse and his throat burning. "We must not let up for a moment."

He raced back to where Kodama was just breasting the hill, accompanied by his officers. "This was not a battle," Kodama grumbled. "It was a massacre. These bullets—"

"Have gained the day for us, General," Ralph told him. "But now we must secure our victory. Look there." He pointed to where the mass of samurai was beginning to fall back over even the farther hill, as the Satsuma generals realized it would cost them every second man to press their assault, so deadly was the fire of the honin; opposed to ten thousand men in close order before them, even half-trained infantry could hardly miss.

Kodama nodded. "They are retreating. As you say, General Freeman, your *bullets*"—his voice was heavy with contempt—"have gained the day for us."

"So now is the time to charge home with the bayonets, General," Ralph said. "With every man we possess."

Kodama shook his head. "We have gained the day, General, and against a vastly superior force. Let us be content with that."

"Content?" Ralph shouted. "General, these men have been checked, not routed. They are still an army. They will regroup and resume the assault, and we will not catch them napping again. But if we charge them now, as they retreat, we will destroy them as a fighting force. More, we can be in Kagoshima by tomorrow. Before Munetake can disembark his men."

"We will consolidate our hold upon Kumamoto, General Freeman," Kodama insisted. "This was the task we were given by the emperor, and this is the task we have accomplished, most successfully, thanks to you. I congratulate you. Let not hunger for fame lead you astray."

"Lead me . . ." Ralph kept his temper under control with an effort. "General, I believe you have a letter from his majesty, requesting you to take my advice in all matters regarding this campaign."

Kodama's face remained impassive, but his eyes flashed anger. "You are mistaken, General Freeman. The letter requires me to take your advice in all matters concerning the defense of Kumamoto. This I have done, to your great glory. Now we will consolidate. I have not been ordered to assault Kagoshima. That is for the emperor to decide."

Ralph gazed down the hill in impotent rage, as the samurai hurried back out of range of the deadly rifles and the even more deadly cannon. "Cease firing, Major Yamagata," he said.

"But . . . will we not charge, General?"

"No," Ralph said. "Tell your men to dig defensive trenches. We will use this hill as our perimeter." He turned his horse, gazed at the equally dumbfounded Helsinger, and then rode past him, to sit his horse alone and watch the Satsuma banners retiring over the next hill. He had accomplished everything he had set out to do, and had yet failed. Tomorrow Munetake would land at Kagoshima with five thousand fresh troops. And by then, too, Saigo would realize that he had been tactically outmaneuvered but that he had not been decisively defeated, and he would reorganize his men and resume the conflict.

And Alison, and Suiko, and the children, and all the Satsuma, would be forced to prepare for a siege. To the death.

Alison supposed she had to be dreaming, a long, slow, suffering nightmare. It had grown all the way up Kagoshima Wan, as she had realized this was the first time she had been here, that Ralph, and Suiko, were coming closer. And then these personal reflections and uncertainties had been overtaken by the clamor of disaster which surrounded them as they landed, by the horror which filled the city.

And by the anger, too.

She stood at Munetake's shoulder when he encountered General Hayashi. "Beaten?" Munetake shouted.

"How can that be? The Satsuma have never been beaten. How many men did they bring against you?"

Hayashi shrugged. "Perhaps three thousand."

"Three thousand, and you commanded fifteen thousand samurai?"

"They were led by the traitor, Freeman," Hayashi said.

"Freeman?" Munetake whispered, while Alison thought her heart would stop beating. "Freeman led the imperial troops?"

"He is a devil," Hayashi said. "A devil from the seventh pit of hell. Wherever he goes, he spreads death and destruction. There is no man can stand against him. Yes, he led the Imperial Guard. He deserted us the moment Saigo Takamori gave the command to mobilize. He fled north to Tokyo and took command of the guard, and brought it down here, and yesterday, with his cannon shells and his rifle bullets, he blasted our people away. Look there . . ." He flung out his hand to point at the hills behind the city. "He is there, coming, now, with his rifles and his cannon. The man knows no honor, nor is he sated by the spilling of blood. Soon he will be there, and the Satsuma will surrender or be destroyed."

"Surrender?" Munetake shrieked. "Be destroyed? The Satsuma? By three thousand honin and a few guns? Where is General Saigo? I must speak with him."

"General Saigo has retired to his house and does not wish to be disturbed," Hayashi said.

"He will see *me*," Munetake declared. He pointed in turn at the men disembarking from the ships. "Here are five thousand men. Five thousand *samurai*, who will not run away from a few bullets, Hayashi San. Surrender! That is not a word I understand." He stared at Alison. "Freeman," he said. "Now he has betrayed us all, my Alison. Now, when I strike his head from his body, I will receive the praise of every right-thinking Japanese. Now he is your enemy as well, Alison. You will spit on his corpse."

The woman bowed almost to the floor. "You are welcome," she said. And straightened again, to stare at Alison, and then at the two boys.

A sister, Alison thought. She was too young to be a mother. Desperately she tried to stop herself from looking left and right, at the room, the paintings, the flowers. Ralph's house. Here he had lived for eleven years. He could not have been miserable all of that time.

As she had not been miserable all of that time, in Hokkaido. Yet now . . . "Is it possible for me to see Mrs. Freeman?" she asked.

Saigo Shikibu hesitated. "You understand that my sister has been deeply grieved by her husband's act of treachery," she said. "She sought nothing more than death when she realized what he had done, how he had betrayed her people and her family. And herself. She was persuaded not to do this, because she personally was not dishonored by his crimes."

"I will say nothing to upset her," Alison said. "Does she know of me?"

"All Japan knows of you, Munetake's woman," Shikibu said. "Now tell me why you wish to speak with my sister."

Alison bit her lip. "I . . . I wish to try to understand."

Shikibu's caked makeup all but cracked as her face wrinkled with contempt. "How may one understand the mind of a traitor?" she asked, and stepped aside. "My sister is inside."

Alison hesitated, then stepped through the door, gesturing the two boys to follow her. She gazed at Suiko, who knelt on the far side of the room, her face unmade, her hair loose and trailing past her shoulders. Beside her knelt two little girls.

She returned Alison's gaze for several seconds. Then she asked, "Do you hate him too?"

"I . . ." I love him, she thought. More than ever now, for doing what he has done. But she could not say it. "I would understand."

"You shared his bed," Suiko said, her voice harsh.

"We were married," Alison said. "As Christians are," she added hastily, as Suiko's nostrils dilated. She reached behind her, found Jeremy's hand, and drew him forward. "This is Freeman's son."

Jeremy gasped; it was the first time he had heard

that, and Alison realized she had been concentrating so hard on the woman she had forgotten the boy.

"I also have a son," Suiko said. "He is preparing to fight, and die, like a samurai. That boy should do the same if he would atone for his father's crime. You see me, Munetake's woman, sitting here, wearing mourning rags. I mourn for the husband that I had, who is now dead. I wait only for the news of his death to be brought to me, or preferably his head, that I may kick it, and watch it roll across the floor."

There could be no doubt that she meant what she said.

"Can you not believe," Alison said, "that he might have acted out of love for you, for the Satsuma, and more than anything, for Japan, that he is trying to save the Satsuma rather than destroy them?"

Suiko's eyes were like deep pits. "You are a barbarian," she said. "You have no concept of honor. But you will spit on his head, Munetake's woman, or, like us, you will die from the cut on your belly." Almost she smiled. "You will not have long to wait."

Regiment after regiment marched over the hills next to Kumamoto, banners waving in the breeze behind officers proudly mounted, bayonets gleaming in the afternoon sunlight. Hardly fewer than seventy thousand men, Ralph estimated, all clad in Western-style uniforms, all marching with Western precision. The imperial army, come to settle the matter once and for all.

He saluted the emperor, who had Inouye at his side, and behind him a cluster of German and Japanese staff officers. Ralph himself sat his horse to General Kodama's right; Colonel Helsinger and Major Yamagata were immediately behind him. Close by was Lieutenant Fushida, whom Ralph had promoted on the field, and at the same time, to the honin's delight, had taken him as a personal aide.

"Kodama San," Mutsuhito said. "A famous field. A famous fortress. A famous victory."

General Kodama bowed. "The victory was General Freeman's, your Majesty."

"The victory belongs to all of you," the emperor told him. "To all of us. To all Japan." He looked at Ralph. "My congratulations, Freeman San. But I hear you are not satisfied."

"I am satisfied now, your Majesty, that you are here. Yet I must warn you that the Satsuma have had two months to prepare themselves."

"Two months," Mutsuhito mused. "And in all that time they have made no further attempt to capture Kumamoto?"

"No, your Majesty."

"Then is our victory not already gained?"

"That remains to be seen, your Majesty." He had stopped seething now, and nothing was to be gained by recriminations. Useless to tell Mutsuhito how he and Helsinger and Fushida had ridden over the hills to look at the city, the German in total mystification as to why a vastly superior army should so allow itself to be bottled up, while Ralph's heart had sunk as he had inspected the fortifications, and equally wondered. That Saigo had not resumed the assault on Kumamoto, despite the arrival of Munetake's army, must mean that he was determined to stake all on holding the imperial army from a defensive position. Ralph's fear, then, indeed, had been that Munetake might decide to abandon so hopeless a cause and sail away again with his people—and Alison and Jeremy. That at the least had soon become impossible, as Admiral Prince Ito and units of the imperial fleet had stationed themselves at the seaward end of Kagoshima Wan. Then Ralph had even attempted to parley once again, on his own initiative, but his white flag had been fired upon before he could approach within half a mile of the town.

"Well, gentlemen," Mutsuhito said. "Shall we not visit Kagoshima and see if General Saigo is willing to surrender to the inevitable?"

Kagoshima basked in the morning sunlight as the huge glowing ball rose out of the immensity of the Pacific to the east. How often had he watched that sunrise, Ralph thought. How had everyone in the Satsuma city watched it. And how many of them would see it set tonight?

For as far as the eye could see were nothing but the imperial banners. With ponderous efficiency the army had surrounded the town, each unit taking up its allotted position, while the fleet had sailed farther up the bay to complete the coil that lay around the rebels. And all without a shot being fired. The cross and the ring of the Satsuma still flew above the citadel, and last night they had seen lights gleaming there, but the houses outside the wall might have been deserted. His own house was in there, with his wife and children. How he ached to regain possession of them. How he wished to ride ahead of the army, and indeed, how nearly had he deserted last night to do just that. But Inouye, suspecting his emotions, had stayed by his side. "It is in the hands of the gods now, Ralph," he had said. "A man can but do his duty, in the certainty that whatever happens will happen whether he would or no."

It was not a philosophy to which Ralph could subscribe, but he supposed it was a comforting one on the eve of a battle. His problem was a lack of certainty as to where his duty lay. If his mind summoned it to the city itself, and his home, his heart too often summoned it to the battlements of the citadel, and the many verandas of the palace beyond, where Alison would surely be standing this morning, along with all the other Satsuma women, to look at the immense army which was assembled for their destruction.

And still Saigo made no move. Yet he would have to, soon enough. The bugles rang out, and the emperor himself was approaching; he had spent the night at Kumamoto. Now he drew rein beside his generals and gazed at the city. "Well, General Freeman," he said. "The end of the affair, eh? But you at the least need take no part in it. As the Imperial Guard so covered itself with glory in the relief of Kumamoto, I have decided it shall be held in reserve on this occasion. Your place is with them."

"If you will pardon me, your Majesty," Ralph said, "I would beg of you the favor of leading the assault."

Mutsuhito frowned at him. "Are you really in such a hurry to die, General?"

"My family is in that city, your Majesty."

"Of course. I had forgotten. I have already given command of the assault force to General Kuroda, but I grant you permission to ride with him as a volunteer, if you wish."

"My thanks, your Majesty." Ralph saluted. "You have my permission to rejoin your regiment, Lieutenant," he told Fushida.

"I would rather remain with you, General, if you will permit me that," Fushida replied.

They gazed at each other, and then Ralph held out his hand, and after a moment's surprised hesitation, Fushida took it.

"Then let's go," Ralph said, and they rode to where Kuroda waited. He was about the youngest of this new breed of Japanese generals, restless as Saigo had always been, walking his horse to and fro in front of the five picked regiments of foot he was to lead. He shook Ralph's hand warmly. "With you at my side, Freeman San," he said, "we cannot fail. Not that I supposed we would anyway. Are you acquainted with the assault plan?"

Ralph shook his head.

"Why, it is simply this. Should the garrison refuse to surrender when the summons is made, my orders are first of all to secure the town, which is a conventional tactic, but then to pause no longer than is necessary to regroup." He pointed at another ten regiments waiting just behind the first five, and equipped with scaling ladders. "Those will then take over the assault and will carry the citadel itself. A coup de main, is it not?"

"A coup de main," Ralph agreed, his mind teeming with despair. But certainly it was a practical concept—unlike Shimonoseki or even Tokyo, the citadel of Kagoshima was not surrounded by a moat, but rested, like Kumamoto, on a low hill. It could be taken by sufficiently determined men. And then? Mutsuhito obviously sought the total destruction of his enemies. And why should he not?

But also of their women and children?

He watched the herald riding up the road to the outer gate of the castle; this skirted the city, and was singularly exposed. The assault force was grouped to the north and east of it, opposite the houses; the troops to the west and south were defensively positioned, but with them was the main part of the imperial artillery. Mutsuhito and his generals had been well taught by their French and German mentors—and on this first occasion that they had to use their knowledge, they had been allowed to position themselves as if on a parade ground.

White flag fluttering, the horseman stood before the closed gate; through his glasses Ralph could make out the heads of several men standing on the battlements above him, looking down. He could not hear what was being said, but undoubtedly the herald was demanding that the gates of the citadel be thrown open, in the name of the emperor, and for his admittance. Ralph continued to watch the men on the battlements, while a peculiar feeling began to spread through his system. He was sure he recognized Munetake's great bulk, even at this distance. But he could not make out Saigo or Hayashi. He frowned, and then his head jerked at a sudden movement among the Satsuma men, above whom there now rose a puff of smoke. The herald reeled in the saddle and then hit the ground as lifelessly as a sack of grain.

A great shout of anger arose from the throats of the watching soldiers, and Kuroda snapped his fingers. "Now have the Satsuma signed their own death warrants," he said. "Saigo Takamori has revealed his true nature."

"I do not think Saigo is there," Ralph said, half to himself.

Kuroda glanced at him, but had no time to speak, as from the hillock on which the emperor stood with his staff there was fired a signal gun. Immediately the entire morning exploded, as the massed batteries to the west, as well as the ships' batteries to the south, all opened fire at the same moment, concentrating their aims upon the citadel, which was momentarily enveloped in clouds of smoke and dust, soon punctuated by flame. Now indeed there was reason for haste. Ralph glanced at Kuroda, who nodded, and raised his arm, before himself walking his horse down the slope. Ralph and Fushida followed, and with a huge roar the honin infantry of the regular army, every man a conscript and a soldier of scarce two years' experience, hurried behind their officers. Now at last the guns of the fortress replied, sending solid shot as well as explosive shells amid the houses. Those flimsy matchboxes immediately burst into flames; whoever was in command in the fortress was using red-hot shot on his own town.

But of course, it was not *his* town. Because Ralph no longer had any doubts as to who was in command of the Satsuma forces this day. And his tactics were to some extent proving effective, as the assault troops checked before the wall of smoke and flame suddenly erected before them. Ralph himself had to gallop into the inferno, followed immediately by Kuroda and Fushida, before the infantry realized that at least they would be hidden from the bullets of their enemies, and followed by their generals.

The town had been completely evacuated but for terrified stray dogs; no doubt, Ralph thought, most of the inhabitants had just melted away into the surrounding country to await the outcome of this struggle between their betters. The imperial soldiers charged through the streets, smashing down doors, hurling whole buildings to the ground, trampling through gardens on which days and weeks and years of labor had been devoted. Ralph left Kuroda and rode for his own home, but that was no more. But this house, he realized as he drew rein and gazed at the scorched ground, had not happened this morning; even the garden had been dug up and every shrub burned. The Satsuma had resolved the name of Freeman should be expunged altogether from their lives.

Then what of Freeman's family?

Smoke clouded his nostrils, hurt his eyes, but it was not the smoke that induced the tears or the feeling of breathlessness as he galloped through the burning streets to gain Kuroda once again, on the far side of town and looking up at the fortress. "Well, Freeman San," the little general cried, "we have lost scarce a man. And do you know why? We have taken a prisoner. Bring that fellow here," he commanded.

A man was dragged forward, his kimono stained with smoke and with dust from where he had been rolled on the ground. He was old, with white hair and mustaches, and trembled as he was forced to kneel before the generals. "Mercy," he begged. "Have mercy."

Clearly he was not a samurai, but a well-to-do merchant, Ralph estimated—his kimono was of the best silk. No doubt he had been unable to make himself leave all of his warehouses and join the general exodus.

"There will be mercy," Kuroda promised, "if you answer my questions as before, and truthfully, mind. Tell General Freeman where General Saigo is."

"Saigo Takamori is dead," the man gasped.

"Dead?" Ralph snapped.

"He has been dead these two months, great lord," the man said. "He committed seppuku the night following his defeat before Kumamoto. He could not live, after being defeated by a honin army."

"By God," Ralph said. Saigo had not been defeated, merely repulsed. But he had fallen into the final trap forced by the samurai code, an inability to look to the future, no matter what the past. "And we did not know of it?"

"It was kept secret by the lords, great lord, until only a few days ago. There were those wished to do as Lord Saigo had done. Hayashi San was one such, and he would not be denied. But the others obeyed Munetake."

"Munetake," Ralph muttered.

"Lord Munetake has taken command of the citadel. Where others would have surrendered, he has refused to allow it. He has said we will neither surrender nor commit seppuku until the very end; he will take as many of the imperial troops as we can, before we go, so that for all the rest of eternity men will remember the last stand of the Satsuma. We will take the emperor himself, if he comes. And he said, my lord, we will take the barbarian traitor, because *he* will certainly come for his woman."

"And the hatamotos agreed to this?" Ralph cried. "To dooming their women and children to the horrors of a sack?"

"Lord Munetake would have it so, great lord," the man said. "He challenged any lord who would question his decision to meet him, sword in hand, to decide the issue. But none dared face him. Lord Munetake is the greatest swordsman in Japan. So they will follow him, great lord. To the death. He has fifteen thousand samurai at his back. They will fight to the death."

Ralph's jaw was clamped so tightly together his teeth began to hurt.

"Do you believe this fellow?" Kuroda asked.

"Yes," Ralph said. "I believe him, Kuroda San. It will be a bloody battle."

Kuroda smiled. "We have come for a bloody battle, Freeman San." He turned to one of his aides. "Ride back and summon the second wave. We are ready to begin the assault."

Although the morning outside was an immense rumble of sound, punctuated with yells and screams, the audience chamber of Lord Shimadzu was quiet. Only breathing could be heard. Among all the noble Satsuma women gathered here, and even their children, who surely could not understand, there was not a sob. They knew their duty, and that the moment for the performance of that duty was rapidly approaching.

And I kneel among them, Alison thought. Am I demented? Or so hypnotized by what they accept as inevitable, and *how* they accept it, that I will plunge a dagger into my own heart when the signal is given?

"Mother?" Harunari crouched against her. "Why cannot I go outside, like Jeremy?"

"Because you are not old enough," she told him, amazed at the calmness in her voice, when she wanted only to scream, and scream, and scream.

Perhaps the boy was dead. She had a notion that he had sought death ever since he had learned the name of his father. And yet she had thought there had been a certain pride also at the terror Freeman's name seemed to inspire. He wanted to look upon the devil-barbarian's face once before he died.

Before he died, she thought. Oh, God, before he died. Before they all died. It was incredible, it was horrifying, it was impossible for her to kneel here and prepare to die, when Ralph was coming for her—or was he really coming for Saigo Suiko, kneeling in the far corner of the room, her little girls held in her arms; her son was also on the battlements with his Satsuma playmates.

It did not matter whom Ralph was actually coming for, because he would find nothing but reeking bodies; she remembered the end of Nariaka and his women and shuddered. And there was nothing she could do about it. There had been nothing any of them could do about it since the death of Saigo Takamori, when Munetake, huge and brooding and angry, had taken control of all their lives. Even hers. But had he not always had control of her life? For eleven years she had sought to preserve her individuality, had supposed she was proving herself, to him, a person in her own right— but of course for all those eleven years she had been deluding herself. Just as she had been deluding herself as to Munetake himself. She had interpreted the various facets of his character through European eyes, through logical eyes, through Christian eyes. Even after eleven years, she had not understood until these last two months. A man so ambitious, so forceful, so energetic, had to be thinking of power, and empire, and glory. But Munetake had been thinking only of glory and immortality. Even when he had spoken of Hideyoshi, the possibility of carving a fief for himself had ranked a poor second to the determination to remain on every samurai's lips for the rest of time because of the splendor of his death. So he would take an entire city, an entire people, with him, that men might remember, and tremble at his name.

She had even attempted to reason with him, to beg him to show some mercy, at least to the ordinary people of Kagoshima, who had no part in the quarrel. And he had laughed at her. "They have no part because they do not matter," he had shouted. "Only the great matter. I am the greatest warrior in Japan. They will talk of my death forever. Only Freeman seeks to equal me. But I shall take him with me into the shades, my Alison. He, and you, and I will tread that dark road together, but I will be the one remembered, because I will have his head."

He sought no more. And she ... she had contemplated escape, and been surrounded by guards. There were guards on the door now, to prevent any of the women preferring dishonor to death. But even if she could leave this room, where could she go, and what could she do? Jeremy was out there, if he still lived. She could not desert him any more than she could desert Harunari.

Besides, she was falling into the trap of accepting fate, as the Japanese did. It had been her advice that they use ships, because she had wanted only to gain Kagoshima and see Ralph again before the end. And no doubt they had sailed right past him, waiting there on the shore. So that she could die, and he could live ... unless he did come looking for her, and encountered Munetake instead.

Her head jerked, because there he was standing in the doorway, huge and smoke-stained, sheathing his long sword as he looked around him. Jeremy stood at his side, panting.

Munetake found her. "Come," he said. "And bring Harunari with you."

Alison's head jerked. She could not believe her ears. Was he, after all, human enough to be generous? She dared not look at the other women as she held Harunari's hand and hurried to the doorway and into the corridor beyond. "Where are we going?" she gasped. "Are we ... ?" She bit her lip. She dared not ask if he would let them go, to live. Besides, he had seized her other hand and was leading her, not to the stairs going down, but to those leading up.

"They are about to start the final assault," he said. "It will not be long now. And then Freeman will come for you. Will you not wait for him, Alison, my Alison?"

The signals went up, and the artillery ceased firing. The citadel was still clouded in smoke and dust, through which now could be seen leaping flames, from the barracks and stables and storehouses mainly, but also from the palace as well, Ralph was sure. He remembered the blazing holocaust Nariaka's palace had become the moment it started properly to burn, and felt his blood almost run cold.

But now was a time for heat. Covered by rapid rifle fire from the five original regiments of the assault force, every man aiming at the battlements and shooting as quickly as he could squeeze the trigger and reload, then ten regiments of the second wave ran forward carrying their scaling ladders, a quaint mixture of the old and the new, Ralph thought, for on every man's back there was slung a loaded rifle with its bayonet already fixed. His place was there, with them, and not only to lead them—he had to be the first man to reach the palace.

He leaped from his horse, and Kuroda attempted to stop him. "No, no, Freeman San," he shouted. "Scaling a wall is not for a general."

"Then as of now I am a private soldier," Ralph cried, and ran down the slope, Fushida faithfully at his shoulder, into the hail of shot and smoke. But few men actually fell; the defenders' fire, distracted by the shooting from below them, and by the fact that the assault was being carried out all around the circumference of the wall, was mostly wild. But they were not yet defeated. The first ladders were thrown down, only immediately to be replaced, while the honin swarmed up them like the most experienced of seamen going aloft in a gale. Ralph, plunging through the middle of several men, found the ladder in front of him already occupied by another half-dozen eager infantrymen. They climbed over the rock base of the fortress to begin with, and thus gained the hill on which the walls were planted; here they paused, waiting for the ladders to be passed up to them and reset against the walls themselves. Ralph looked up and saw the angry, distorted faces staring down at him, leaning forward to aim their rifles. Then the ladder was in place, and the honin were clambering up once more, leaving several of their number dead and dying at the foot. Now Ralph was at their head, sweat pouring from his hair and dribbling down his face, heart pounding, aware of nothing save his determination to reach the embrasure before he was himself hit.

A samurai leaned out, swinging with his sword, and then kept on coming, shot through the head by one of the infantry still waiting his turn on the ledge. Ralph had to cling to the rungs with both arms as the heavy, armored body struck him on the shoulder on its way down, and blood splashed across his face. He looked up again, drawing his revolver as he did so, and shot at the next face to appear, sending it dissolving into blood and bone. Then he was at the top and bounding into the embrasure, firing left and right at the men who came at him, before holstering the pistol and stooping to pick up one of the discarded samurai long swords. He wrapped both hands around the hilt and swung left and right as he had so often practiced with Togo Heihachiro or Saigo Takamori—or with Munetake himself in the old days of Shimonoseki. Men tumbled away from him, and he realized that he was no longer alone; several honin infantry stood beside him, and others were climbing through the embrasures all the time, while from the far side of the castle there came the shouts of "Banzai!" to indicate that there too the attackers had gained a foothold.

There were officers on the battlements as well. The conduct of the battle could be left to them. Ralph ran forward through the smoke and the noise, leaped down the stone ladder into the courtyard, was approached by a mounted samurai armed with a lance, jumped to one side and swung his sword in an upward arc which tumbled the man from the saddle, blood spouting from the gaping wound in his thigh, and then found himself at the inner gate. But this was open and abandoned, the samurai guards running this way and that as the riflemen began volley-firing from the captured outer walls. Ralph pounded through the opening, thrusting the sword through his belt in order to reload his revolver as he ran, encountering a group of men hurrying to attempt to close the gate and scattering them with three shots. One of the remainder came at him, sword waving, and was sent reeling by a bullet from Fushida, following him through the opening. Ralph could leave the gate and run for the palace itself.

*   *   *

Here too the doors sagged open, unprotected; to his relief he discovered that there was less smoke than he had feared. He dashed inside, and was challenged by a diminutive figure hissing and stamping and waving his sword. "Traitor," the boy yelled. "Traitor."

Ralph sidestepped the blow with difficulty, seized the boy around the waist, and took the sword from his hand. "I am not the traitor, William," he said. "The Satsuma are the traitors. I serve the emperor."

"Mother says you are a traitor, and a devil from hell," William cried, bursting into tears.

"Aye, well, she is mistaken." He looked over his shoulder, discovered the faithful Fushida behind him. "Take the boy, Fushida," he said. "Take him to safety. Take him to the emperor and say I have sent him, to be cared for." He rumpled William's hair. "His majesty will explain it to you, boy. And to your mother too, if I can but find her."

He ran up the stairs to the second floor, paused there, looking left and right at the various corridors, uncertain which way to take, and heard his name called. "Freeman. Freeman San!"

He turned to his left, nearly tripped over a body, stooped to stare at it in horror. It was Saigo Kiyotake, and he had just cut his belly open. Now he vainly tried to hold his intestines from spilling with his blood onto the floor. "I have been deserted," he gasped. "He ran away. Freeman . . ."

"Where are Suiko and my children?" Ralph snapped.

Kiyotake panted, "Up there," and pointed at the next floor.

"And Munetake?"

"He too. At the top. He brought us to this. He . . ."

Ralph ran for the stairs.

"Freeman," Kiyotake screamed. "Help me, Freeman. I cannot stand the pain."

Ralph checked, biting his lip, gazed at several soldiers just reaching the top of the stairs, their bayonets already dull with blood. Then he stepped toward the dying man, long sword in both hands, and swung it with all his strength, to slice through the tendons of Kiyotake's neck and send the head rolling across the floor. The honin roared their approval, but Ralph was already mounting the next flight of stairs, hurling his shoulder against the closed door he found there, and stumbling into Shimadzu's audience chamber. But today it was to be used for a vastly different purpose.

For here were gathered the Saigo women with their children. He estimated there were some forty of them sitting on the floors, now mostly rising as they saw the big American standing there, took in the blood on his sword and on his clothes, and saw, too, the gasping, eager honin at his back. Then Saigo Kiyotake's wife stepped in front of them, her dagger gleaming in her hands, and with a single movement drove the blade into her own breast.

For a moment no one moved, not even the dying woman. Then her knees gave way as her mouth flopped open in pain, and she struck the floor with a dull thud. As if that had been the signal, the woman nearest her stabbed the baby she carried in her arms, and the self-massacre became general.

"Stop them," Ralph shouted, but he had no time for even his mother-in-law as he charged into their midst, seeking only Suiko. Behind him the infantry gave a roar and surged into the room, but they had rape on their minds, and a quality of bestial sexuality was added to the obscene horror of death itself.

Ralph gained the far side of the room, and stared at Suiko. Her daughters were beside her, and she too held a long-bladed knife. "Suiko," he cried, "don't do it."

She held Maureen by the arm. The girl was eleven years old, and utterly bewildered by what had happened, making no resistance to her mother, and no move toward her father, either. Suiko gazed at Ralph, her eyes gleaming, her black-painted teeth showing through her parted lips. "You are a traitor to the Satsuma," she hissed, and turned to murder her child.

Ralph reached her in a single bound, dug his fingers into the shoulder of her kimono, and sent her stumbling backward, pushed Maureen into the arms of her terrified sister, and turned to face his wife. "Suiko," he said, half-commanding and half-imploring.

"You are dishonored," Suiko hissed, looking at Maureen, realized that she could no longer reach her, and before Ralph could truly understand what she intended, drove the knife into her own belly.

He released the girls and hurled himself forward, seizing the already bloodstained fingers, pulling them from the haft of the dagger, pulling the weapon as well from the blood-wet kimono, gazing in horror at the gush which flowed over his own hand, at the tiny features suddenly robbed of all passion and as peaceful as ever he had known them, at the silky black hair uncoiling itself down her back.

He knelt, the dead woman in his arms, oblivious of the tumult about him, gazing into her face. His wife of eleven years.

"She was a Saigo," Kuroda said.

Ralph's head jerked, and he laid Suiko on the floor. "My daughters are in your care, General," he said.

Kuroda nodded, and stared at him. "And you?" But he knew Ralph would never contemplate seppuku. "Munetake? Freeman San . . ."

"I know," Ralph said. "He is the finest swordsman in Japan." He looked down on Suiko for the last time, then ran from the room.

The hallway was crowded with honin soldiers, but they were mainly intent upon gaining access to the audience chamber and the women. Ralph shouldered them aside and took the stairs three at a time, only remembering to stop at the top and get his breathing under control.

From the veranda he looked down on the last pocket of Satsuma resistance, a few samurai waving their swords in the palace gardens as they were ruthlessly shot down by the cheering honin.

He had first seen Suiko in that garden.

"Ralph!" Alison screamed, and he swung around, revolver in hand, gazed through the open door behind him into one of Shimadzu's private apartments—and at Alison, lying on the floor, her wrists bound behind her, and at a young boy, aged about thirteen, he estimated, also bound, staring at him with eyes whose expression was a mixture of admiration and terror. Alison's face was flushed, and her cheeks were stained with tears as she gasped for breath.

He took a step toward her, and checked as a movement came from inside the room.

"I knew you would come, barbarian," Munetake said. "I have waited for this moment. I have driven the entire Satsuma to destruction, for the peasure of meeting you again."

He was hidden behind the door. Ralph took another cautious step forward, cursing silently as the floor creaked, gazing at Alison, taking in all of her, unable fully to grasp that after all these years she was only twelve feet away from him—and yet desperately trying to stop himself from thinking of her, until this business was settled.

"Throw down the gun, barbarian," Munetake said. "Face me like a man, if you *are* a man. Drop the gun before you enter the room, or the woman will die."

Ralph hesitated.

"He'll kill you," Alison shouted. "He'll kill you, Ralph."

Munetake chuckled. "See how she cares for you, barbarian? Oh, yes, she cares for you. When I love her, she thinks of you. She supposes I do not know these things, but I have always known them. I give her ecstasy, Freeman, and she still dreams of you. Twelve years, Freeman, that she has dreamed of you while lying in my arms. But now you will watch my arrow protruding from her belly, if you do not drop the gun."

"He'll kill us anyway, Ralph," Alison cried. "Keep the gun, and avenge us."

"Drop the gun, barbarian," Munetake said. "I will count to five."

Ralph dropped the revolver, drew his sword, and leaped through the door, turning as he did so, seeing Munetake and the drawn bow, but also checking in dismay as he saw the headless body of a boy, younger even than Jeremy or William, lying against the far wall.

Munetake's teeth gleamed. "I killed my son, barbarian, as a father should. As I shall kill my wife and other son before they can be taken prisoner. As I shall kill myself.

But first, they will watch you die. They will realize that no one can stand against Munetake, sword in hand." He threw the bow to the floor, drew his sword. "Prepare to die, barbarian."

Ralph drew a long breath and took several rapid steps backward. He made himself think of what was about to happen as a tactical problem. The room was not very large, not more than six tatami mats—there was hardly room for Munetake to make his tremendous leaps. But by the same reasoning, there was less room for him to avoid the enormous sweeps which he knew were coming. Therefore Munetake had to be surprised, as Saigo had been surprised outside Kumamoto, and even before him, the Tokugawa generals outside Tokyo, by speed and unorthodoxy.

Munetake was placing his feet slowly and carefully, his sword thrust in front of his belly as usual, almost motionless. Ralph also tested the tatami with his toes, and then leaped forward, but instead of swinging, he thrust, releasing the hilt of the sword with his left hand to gain a maximum stretch, knowing that he was utterly exposing himself to a counterthrust, but certain that Munetake, from his stance, would be unable to take advantage of it.

Indeed, caught unawares, Munetake could only think of avoiding such an unorthodox assault. He gave a hiss of outrage and pivoted to his left. Even so, Ralph's sword point caught the skirt of his armor and was deflected away. Off balance, Ralph fell to one knee, but regained the sword hilt with his left hand, and still kneeling, swung a two-handed blow with all his force to his right. The blade sang in the air, and again Munetake, still trying to regain his balance, had to throw himself to one side to avoid having his right leg severed at the knee. He too fell, and for a moment they faced each other, from the floor, both gasping for breath, Munetake's lips drawn back in a snarl. "Barbarian," he growled, and scrambled up.

But Ralph was also on his feet and closing. He had gained the initiative and had no intention of letting it slip. Their swords clashed as Munetake desperately parried the shorter swing of the American, and the steel sent sparks flying upward as the two blades slithered against each other, while the two men's bodies thumped together with a force which left them breathless. But Ralph was the bigger man, and once more Munetake had to give ground, staggering backward and finding himself against the wall, while Ralph again moved forward, already so close there was no room to use his sword at all, releasing the hilt with his right hand, and swinging the fist to catch Munetake a roundhouse blow on the jaw which sent him tumbling to the floor, dropping his own sword in his confusion. Ralph immediately kicked it across the room, jumped over the writhing Japanese, and reached Alison's side, jerking her body forward to slit her bonds in a quick movement.

"Ralph!" she said. "Oh, Ralph ... *Ralph!*" she screamed.

He turned and saw Munetake rolling across the floor to gain the doorway, and the revolver. Ralph stood up and ran at him. Munetake turned, the gun in his hand, lips drawn back in a grin. "As it should be, barbarian," he said. But he had always refused to practice with the pistol. Its kick surprised him, and the bullet smashed into the roof. Before he could recover, Ralph was up to him, cutting with the sword. Munetake threw up his left arm, and gazed in horror as the hand went spinning against the wall. Ralph stepped back, drawing huge breaths. "Surrender," he commanded.

Munetake gazed at him, then at Alison, who was untying Jeremy, then down at the bleeding stump of his arm. Then he gave a great shout, ran to the veranda, and hurled himself over the rail.

"You are regarded as our greatest soldier, and now, by killing Munetake, as our greatest swordsman as well," said the Emperor Mutsuhito. "And you would leave Japan?"

"I did not kill Munetake as a samurai should, your Majesty," Ralph reminded him.

"But samurai are creatures of history now," Mutsuhito said. The two men stood on the hill overlooking Kagoshima, the burned-out ruin of the Satsuma fortress—the end of more than a thousand years of history.

"I have rewarded you, Freeman San, but what you now have is nothing to what you would have, were you to remain here with me." He pointed at the ruin. "That is the end of an era, far more than the abdication of the shogun. A new era, in which Japan must walk with the greatest nations on earth, is about to begin."

Ralph looked at Inouye, and at Ito, who had come ashore from his fleet to celebrate the victory, and now waited their turn to say good-bye. He thought too of Togo, hastening home to discover the ruination of his clan—but Togo, being sensible, would make his peace with the emperor, and undoubtedly rise to high command in the infant Japanese navy. A navy, and an army, which he did not doubt *would* be used as Saigo would have wished, to end the barbarian domination of Japan, even if that had to be accomplished by force, and which might well be used for even greater purposes than that—there could be no doubt that the Japanese people, even if they did not already worship this young man as a god, would follow him anywhere, and for any purpose.

"You have sufficient generals and admirals to accomplish all you desire, your Majesty," he said. "I have been away from my home for seventeen years. And thanks to your rewards, I can return there a wealthy man, must as, thanks to your representations on my behalf, I can return there a free man."

Mutsuhito smiled at the pun, but his eyes remained serious. "And you have regained your woman. You are a strange man, Freeman San. She has been another's for twelve years, and suffered much mistreatment in that time. Yet you would have her still?"

Ralph turned to look at Alison, waiting some distance away with the children. The breeze fluttered her hair and the skirt of her kimono, and twelve years might never have been. Yet they had been, as the emperor had just reminded him. His future was as clouded as ever his past.

Save that there would be no doubts, on his side, at least. "I wish her still, your Majesty," he said.

Mutsuhito also looked at the children. "They saw

their mother die," he observed. "The girls, anyway. And the boy . . ."

"Will know of it, in time, your Majesty. I do not imagine it will be easy. Yet is he my son more than a Satsuma. At least, it must be my duty to educate him to that."

"To educate him to be an American, you mean."

"To educate him to be a man, your Majesty. He will choose for himself whether he wishes to be an American or a Japanese. But, your Majesty, if I have accomplished anything which has aided you or pleased you, I would beg one last favor of you. Do not dismiss the Satsuma as rebels, or Saigo as a villain. He sought only to preserve what he thought was the best of his country and its history."

Mutsuhito gazed at him for several seconds; then he nodded. "Saigo Takamori is now a part of that history, Freeman San. And as you say, by his own lights, an honorable part. You have been privileged, as have we all, to have lived through the most tremendous years in Japan's history. Think well of us, and come back to see us again." He held out his hand. "And live your future years as you have lived your past, that all men may know, when they speak with you, that they are in the presence of greatness."

It was necessary to pose on the Tokyo dockside, a family group, for a photograph, while Mr. Coates fussed about them like a mother hen. "A great day, Mr. Freeman," he said. "Oh, a great day. You are famous, sir, in the States."

Ralph gazed at the shutter and the sudden cloud of smoke. He was conscious of the two girls, Maureen and Shikibu, holding hands and totally confounded by what was happening; they had seen their mother die—but that was an understanding which would come to them only as they grew older, and could be alleviated by their other mother, if she chose, and would. Just as he was conscious of Jeremy, standing very straight beside him—no problem there, he thought, as he was Alison's son—and William, glaring at the camera as if it were an enemy cannon. *There* was the problem. But not insoluble, with Alison at his side.

And she was at his side, at least physically. Yet they had not been allowed a waking moment alone, for a week, and he would not force himself upon her. Twelve years, and her personal tragedy, was too long a time. He had to wait, for her.

They strolled the deck together, the children dismissed to run screaming their excitement into the interior of the ship, chased by stewards and pursers. The gangplanks were being taken up, and their last link with Japan was being severed.

"Seventeen years," he said. "I never truly thought to see this moment."

"Nor I," she said. "Not in Kagoshima." She gave a little shiver.

He hesitated, biting his lip. But now was no time for cowardice. "I loved Suiko," he said. "And she was a good wife to me. But I could never be her husband."

Alison gazed at the slowly widening moat of water between ship and shore. "There were moments when I almost wanted to love Munetake," she said. "But I never could. And when he murdered Harunari, I wanted only his death."

They had each known personal tragedy, the Japanese way. Now she must decide whether she would look back or only forward.

"Ralph . . ." She turned to face him, and found him gazing at her, cheeks equally pink. "When I was with Munetake, until that day, I did not care what happened, what he did to me, as I was *your* wife. I want you to know that. And that, if you still want me, I will be a mother to your children. All of your children. And . . ." Her turn to bite her lip. "A wife to you."

They had not even honeymooned. "Want you?" he asked. "My darling girl, I think I wanted you before I knew Japan existed."

She was in his arms, her magnificent sweet-smelling hair resting against his mouth, while he looked past her at the early-morning sun still climbing out of the ocean beyond Tokyo Wan. Japan was the land of eternal sunrise. But they were bound beyond even the dawn, into the land of dreams come true.

Romantic Reading from SIGNET

(0451)

- [ ] **THE VISION IS FULFILLED** by Kay L. McDonald.   (129016—$3.50)*
- [ ] **DOMINA** by Barbara Wood.   (128567—$3.95)*
- [ ] **JUDITH: A LOVE STORY OF NEWPORT** by Sol Stember. (125045—$3.25)*
- [ ] **MOLLY** by Teresa Crane.   (124707—$3.50)*
- [ ] **GILDED SPLENDOUR** by Rosalind Laker.   (124367—$3.50)*
- [ ] **BANNERS OF SILK** by Rosalind Laker.   (115457—$3.50)*
- [ ] **CLAUDINE'S DAUGHTER** by Rosalind Laker.   (091590—$2.25)*
- [ ] **WARWYCK'S WOMAN** by Rosalind Laker.   (088131—$2.25)*
- [ ] **THE IMMORTAL DRAGON** by Michael Peterson.   (122453—$3.50)*
- [ ] **THE CRIMSON PAGODA** by Christopher Nicole.   (126025—$3.50)*
- [ ] **WILD HARVEST** by Allison Mitchell.   (122720—$3.50)*
- [ ] **EMERALD'S HOPE** by Joyce Carlow.   (123263—$3.50)*

*Prices slightly higher in Canada

Buy them at your local bookstore or use this convenient coupon for ordering.

NEW AMERICAN LIBRARY,
P.O. Box 999, Bergenfield, New Jersey 07621

Please send me the books I have checked above. I am enclosing $_____
(please add $1.00 to this order to cover postage and handling). Send check
or money order—no cash or C.O.D.'s. Prices and numbers are subject to change
without notice.

Name _____

Address_____

City_____ State_____ Zip Code_____

Allow 4-6 weeks for delivery.
This offer is subject to withdrawal without notice.